DRAVEN'S
RUN

IN THE YEAR 2050

BY
GLENN SOMODI

ALSO BY GLENN SOMODI

Olly & the Spores of Oak Hill

Olly & the Spores of Sapphire Creek

FIRST EDITION / FIRST PRINTING 04-2025

ISBN: 979-8-9872909-9-6

3-D creature renderings, cover art, and chapter icons by Glenn Somodi. Cover photo credits—Blood Splatter: Photo by Racool_studio on Freepik; Cacti/Isla Incahuasi, Bolivia: Photo by Mark Kuiper on Unsplash (mark-kuiper-O3q0rOO8hqI-unsplash); Red-and-blue wallpaper photo: Photo by Pawel Czerwinski on Unsplash (pawel-czerwinski-6lQDFGOB1iw-unsplash); A close-up of a white wall with cracks in it: Photo by Vincent Burkhead on Unsplash (vincent-burkhead-LhlxYMfnTF0-unsplash); Statue of Liberty by Tom Coe on Unsplash (tom-coe-A7KD1kdXD-o-unsplash).

Glenn Somodi
Three Bobcats Publishing LLC
3528 Abington Court
Brunswick, OH 44212
info@ThreeBobcats.com

DEDICATION

To my wife, Merri-jo, for dealing with the hours I spend in my writing nook while making up stories, designing, and painting. She supplies patience and praise during my creative bouts, plus a celebration with each project I complete.

To my parents, who always show their pride in my work.

And to my great-grandparents, who took a chance on coming to America for a better life.

CONTENTS

52 PERCENT BELIEVE ...

"Without sovereignty, a nation cannot exist. Without borders, it can't be defined or protected."

— Geert Wilders

48 PERCENT BELIEVE ...

"Give me your tired, your poor, your huddled masses yearning to breathe free, the wretched refuse of your teeming shore."

— Emma Lazarus

CIVIL WATCH

IMMERSIVE VIDEO GAME

PROTECT THE NATION.
CATCH THE HOPPERS.
EARN MONEY.

JOIN THE MISSION:

Place advanced traps to outsmart the Hoppers. Deploy surveillance drones to spot threats from above. Command mechanical creatures to intercept Hoppers before they breach our border. Earn money and rank as you play.

Eligibility: Available to US citizens aged 18+ who pass a quick, online background check. State-issued ID or license required for sign-up.

TEAM UP:

Join forces with up to three friends to form your squad. Together, you'll dominate the leaderboards and earn rewards faster.

GO VIRAL AND WIN BIG!

Post your best gameplay moments on DravenTV for a chance to earn exclusive rewards, cash prizes, and elite promotions.

THE RED ZONE IS UNDER ATTACK. ARE YOU READY TO STEP UP?

Become a subscriber today: www.DravensRun.com

I: CROSSING RED

The large, red sign stood like a tombstone jutting out of the dirt. Aside from English, the message was translated into four other languages: Spanish, Chinese, Arabic, and Russian.

RED ZONE
RESTRICTED AREA—DO NOT ENTER.
US GOVERNMENT PROPERTY.
WARNING: UNMANNED DETERRENTS
IN USE. INJURY OR DEATH MAY OCCUR.
UNDER CONTRACT BY DRAVEN LABS.

With their last glimpse of civilization more than twelve hours behind them, Gabriella, her mom, and the eight other border crossers stood before the Rio Grande River … the start of the Red Zone. Their goal was to successfully complete a journey across the Red Zone and into America, a journey that came to be known as Draven's Run. The nickname mocked the creator and owner of Draven Labs, Red Draven. Most of them were making the journey to obtain a better life. For at least two in the group, it was a task ordered by the Mexican cartel—they were forced to carry drugs across the border.

Gabriella turned from the setting sun and brushed off her arms, watching as small particles swirled away into the hot breeze. She wasn't sure if they were flakes of her baked skin or remnants of the dust and brush that had stowed away during their journey to this point.

"I've got a bad burn," Gabriella whispered to her mom. "I thought all of those years working in the sun would have prepared me for this."

"It's a different kind of sun out here, Mijita," replied Rosario.

Gabriella's friends had warned her of rumors that this area was like a blast furnace, but she hadn't believed them. She thought she could handle the heat. After all, she had spent much of her childhood under this same sun while harvesting agave plants for tequila in the Jaliscan Highlands. It was just one of the jobs she did to help her family make ends meet.

She tried to find a reason why the sun felt hotter here, especially because it was much farther north of the equator than her home. Gabriella thought that maybe it was because the leaves from the agave plants back on the farm provided her some small respite of shade, or that the farm's highlands were awarded a slight breeze from the valley below. She decided the heat was worse here because this place was flat, barren, and dry, and there was no place to escape from it all. She said a short prayer under her breath that the terrain would change. At least this river crossing would temporarily cool her and her mom.

Gabriella, her mom, and the others trying to cross into America were called "Hoppers" or "invaders" by some Americans. But Gabriella didn't feel like an invader. She was only sixteen years old and not old enough to invade anything. Her love of computers and programming made her want to move to a place where she could grow these skills and give something back to society. Her town in Mexico didn't offer any opportunities, unless you were okay with working on a farm or, worse yet, as a drug mule or sex worker for the drug cartels.

Thanks to free internet access in the back office at her best friend Emily Garcia's family market, Gabriella had signed up for free online classes about computers, programming, and networking. Emily's dad was happy to let her use the computer and internet connection because, in turn, she helped keep his computer running and free of viruses. It was the perfect trade in both of their minds.

Gabriella was different from other girls in the neighborhood. She was inquisitive and devoured books like no one she had ever met. While the other girls hung out and flirted with the boys at the small park in the center of town, Gabriella spent her time on the computer or reading at the library. Her mom knew she needed to get her smart girl to a better life.

Gabriella's dad also believed this and had tried to gain entry into America ahead of them to plant new roots for the family and secure a way for Rosario and her to join him. An activist group had promised a way he could make it across, but it didn't work. He left for the last crossing with two "marks," and she and her mom had never heard from him again.

Marks were digital tattoos engraved into the skin and bone of a Hopper's forearm. These marks branded the person with a unique identification number, coordinates of their capture, and the court's ruling of a reason for return to their home country. Aside from cutting off one's arm, there was no hiding this information. Each time a Hopper was caught while crossing, they'd be branded with one of these marks. It was an unspoken truth that if a Hopper was picked up again with two marks, they simply disappeared.

The US government was under increased pressure to look into these third-mark disappearances. Still, the politicians brushed off any investigations by claiming these Hoppers must have died on the Mexican side of the border. They declared that these people had decided to break the law multiple times, and it was their fault for putting themselves in a dangerous situation. They could also direct attention to the private company that managed the border, Draven Labs.

Gabriella still wrestled with her father's fate as it had been a year, and he should have contacted them by now.

They were both thirsty from the trek, but the murky, green water in front of them didn't offer relief. Gabriella had stepped up to refill an empty water bottle but backed away when the muddy water carried a piece of trash and a rotting armadillo carcass on its way to the Gulf Coast. She realized they would need to rely on their two remaining water bottles, which probably wouldn't be enough.

Emilio, their hired guide, had detached from the group about ten minutes earlier when they were about to enter the Red Zone. That was the plan all along. He would lead everyone up to the Red

Zone and offer his best advice, but nothing more.

Gabriella felt that Emilio, although a coyote by trade, was a kind man. After all, he had secretly handed her and her mom two full water bottles a mile back. Emilio saw someone in the group steal their water earlier when they weren't paying attention, and he knew the thief was another crosser, Cisco, who wouldn't respond well to accusations.

Cisco was a young cartel member, and the purpose of his trip was to carry a big duffel bag of cocaine across the border. Cisco had let the other Hoppers know he wasn't one to be trifled with. It didn't need to be said because the two teardrop tattoos under his right eye had already informed everyone. Gabriella, and everyone else, understood that each teardrop represented a murder, and from his demeanor, she was convinced he should have more than two. She and her mom had done a good job of avoiding him so far, but the trip was far from over.

Before parting from the group, Emilio stopped to give the group some advice from his years of starting Hoppers on their journey.

"When you hear anything out of the ordinary, seek cover," he had instructed them.

"What do you mean by out of the ordinary?" Gabriella bravely asked on behalf of the group.

"If you hear something moving and it's getting closer to your group, know that it's on the hunt and you are its prey," Emilio said in a hushed voice, as if the creatures were already listening for them. "I've been told many stories about metal creatures that hunt like animals, circle like birds, or just set traps and wait."

Everyone went silent with a new fear of what was to come. Emilio reached into his bag and pulled out his last parting gift, handing each of them a silver, Mylar blanket.

"Use these to mask your body heat from detection," he said.

Emilio gave Gabriella and her mom an extra blanket when the others weren't looking. "You two remind me of my wife and daughter back home. Please be careful," he urged as he discreetly handed them over. He knew Cisco would steal them when he had the chance if he noticed them receiving the extras. Gabriella and her mom quickly stuffed them into the front of their pants, the only place they could store anything since they wanted to travel lightly and make the journey without backpacks.

Gabriella had grown up around the cartel and knew better than to make enemies with any of its members. She felt dirty, her dark-brown hair was greasy and disheveled, and she wore old, tattered pants and a very loose, sweat-drenched T-shirt. She knew that, even with her disgusting condition and young age, she was still a prime target for any creep who wanted to have his way with her—especially out here, where they were crossing a lawless area. And Cisco seemed like just the type to take advantage of their situation. For this reason, Gabriella's mom, and an empathetic, twenty-five-year-old man in the group, Manuel, took on the unspoken responsibility of forming a protective circle around her.

Earlier, Manuel told Gabriella and her mom that he didn't care for Cisco, even though they were in the same cartel. He had joined Cisco on this trip as his partner, although not a willing one.

Manuel had explained how he was forced into the cartel as a boy when there was no other option for kids from the orphanage. The cartel offered him protection, food, friendship, and an odd semblance of family.

"These were things an orphan boy like me wished for and needed to survive," he explained.

Gabriella could tell Manuel was not a bad person. He had confided in them that this trip was supposed to be a test to earn his rank in the cartel, which is why he carried a large bag stuffed with cocaine. They deduced, from some of the things he'd said, that the real purpose of his trip was not to deliver those drugs or earn rank, but rather, to get across the border to start a new life and escape the grasp of the cartel.

The sun had almost set, and crossing the river in the dark didn't seem like the best idea to Gabriella, her mom, or Manuel. But Cisco jumped right in to prove he had no fear, pushing his black, plastic-wrapped duffel of cocaine out in front of him to use as a float. The rest of the group reluctantly followed behind him. It was apparent to Gabriella that a few in the group couldn't swim, and she worried about them making it across. There was nothing she could do to help them, and that pulled at her heartstrings. She felt a little better when she noticed that the group of non-swimmers held arms and collectively tried to navigate toward what looked like the lowest points of the river.

As usual, Manuel stayed back with Gabriella and her mom. All three looked at each other, nodded in silent agreement, and then slowly waded into the water to join the group. She and her mom knew they needed to cross now and stick with Manuel if the three of them were going to make it across the Red Zone.

The river's current wasn't strong, but the sticky muck of the riverbed grabbed at their feet as they slogged along, slowing their progress. Cisco had made it halfway across the water when one of the other Hoppers screamed out in fear, startling everyone to a stop.

"El Diablo. El Diablo!" the man screamed repeatedly, aggressively directing everyone to look out toward the middle of the river. He pointed at a spot only twenty feet away from where Cisco halted.

The group stopped and stared, wondering why the man continued screaming about the devil. Then Gabriella and the rest of the group spotted what had frightened him.

A semi-transparent, bulbous, red shape popped up from the water, bobbing up and down in the ripples it caused. Its single, glowing, red eye peeked over the surface of the dark water and appeared to home in on the closest members of the group. Metal tentacles extended out from the creature's body and started moving in sync. It was as if the thing were crawling its way through the water and on a direct path toward Cisco.

Gabriella whispered to her mom, "Is that a Jellyfish?"

Before her mom could answer, the creature gained speed, causing a small surge of water ahead of itself. Cisco noticed he was being targeted, and he no longer looked to be the brave man who had entered the water. He panicked, swung his duffel between his body and the advancing, red-eyed devil, and splashed backward quickly. He grabbed the nearest man—Caesar—the one who had screamed, "El Diablo!" The man struggled to escape his grasp, but Cisco was much stronger, younger, and more agile than the sixty-five-year-old man. Cisco pushed Caesar out in front, making the poor, old man the closest person to the advancing creature.

The red eye blinked once and went dark, and the creature's

bobbing head sunk under the water only ten feet from Caesar. Caesar and Cisco stood frozen in a ripple of the creature's wake. Everything went still, and the whole group watched silently, unsure what the purpose of this creature's little show was all about.

After a minute of silence, Cisco appeared to relax, laughed loudly, and yelled, "That's right! Screw you, El Diablo!" With the creature's disappearance, his bravado returned.

He turned to continue his journey across the river when El Diablo's head bobbed above the water once again, now three feet behind Caesar.

Two metal tentacles shot up from the water, whipping around Caesar's upper body and neck. An odd gurgling sound stirred in his throat, his body shook violently, and the splashing, murky water began pulsing with the luminous, red light. A grating, squeaking, metal sound grew louder as tentacles tightened around his body.

A crackling noise echoed with each small, white, electrical flash that appeared wherever the tentacles touched Caesar's body. With each *CRACK*, his body jerked violently. His eyes expressed severe pain, and he was so tightly wrapped that sound could not escape his throat. His eyes met Gabriella's, and she could sense his fear and silent plea for help.

One more *CRACK* and Caesar's entire body slumped. He floated on his back as the creature's tentacles cradled his motionless body. The red light from the creature's eye made the water look like blood.

Just feet from Caesar, Cisco finally broke his silence and let out an impish shriek. He waded frantically toward safety on the other side of the river, pushing everyone out of his way as he trudged through the thick mud of the river. The group panicked and followed behind him as quickly as they could. Somehow, even the non-swimmers seemed to learn how to swim, motivated by sheer fright.

As Gabriella pushed through the water, she nervously glanced back and noticed that the red light stayed near Caesar's body and was not advancing on the group. It was as if the creature was protecting its prey, satisfied with its catch for the day. That didn't slow her down, though, as she and her mom made it to shore in what seemed like record time. She helped pull her mom out of the water and urged her to calm down and catch her breath, all while keeping a close eye on the creature.

The group didn't trust that the thing couldn't come on land, so they all scurried up the muddy embankment.

Gabriella reached the top after helping to push some of the group's older members up the slope. "Hide and wrap yourselves in your blankets," she urged the group. Somehow, she had just become the group's leader. When she glanced over at Cisco, she realized he didn't like that she had taken control of the situation. He gave her an uncomfortable grin. That small facial movement made her understand she had just put herself in his crosshairs.

They all settled in some long grass on the bank, wrapped themselves in their Mylar blankets, and peered down into the river where they had just been. It had gotten dark quickly, and it was difficult to assess Caesar's condition. The red light remained, illuminating the outline of his body in the water. Slowly, the red light changed to a bright-blue light and started flashing. It reminded Gabriella of police lights. She thought she saw Caesar's body twitch but couldn't be sure if it was her mind playing tricks or just her hoping he was still alive.

After five minutes of watching him float in the red soup, she heard a faint humming sound approaching from a distance.

She remembered Emilio's warning: "If you hear something moving and it's getting closer to your group, know that it's on the hunt and you are its prey."

"Get low! Make sure your blankets are covering your bodies!" she whispered to the group. "Something's coming!"

Ten seconds after she warned them, the sound of propellers became deafening, and it flew directly overhead. As it passed over, it blew their brushy hiding place like a tornado, exposing the group of silver-wrapped, bundled Hoppers. It seemed to ignore them and go for Caesar instead.

Gabriella peeked from her blanket to get a closer look at what it was. It was a large, silver drone, about the size of a pickup truck, trimmed in matte black with four huge propellers extending from its hull. She could make out white lettering on the side of the drone—DRAVEN LABS.

Yellow lights flashed on top of the drone as it started to position itself directly over Caesar's body. A bright, downward spotlight snapped on as soon as it had steadied. The tentacled creature seemed to sense the drone's presence and loosened its grip, letting Caesar free. The red eye disappeared as the creature sank back into the water, as if its job was done.

The drone's belly opened like a trapdoor, and a metal basket dropped. The bottom of the basket expanded and contracted slowly, as if it were precisely measuring Caesar's body. Once they had aligned, the basket lowered into the water to surgically envelop the body, closing just enough to secure Caesar's body. In one quick movement, Caesar was yanked into the basket, and the basket constricted around his body. The drone turned 180 degrees and flew off, leaving the group in silence.

"Cisco, you asshole," Gabriella seethed under her breath. Rosario was crying, replaying the pain that man had experienced in his fight.

Manuel rested a hand on their shoulders to let them know he shared their sadness for Caesar and hatred toward Cisco.

Their grief was interrupted by Cisco's loud voice, "Oh, poor fucking Caesar! Better him than us!"

Everyone in the group stared in disbelief, sickened by his audacity.

Cisco had to feel the resentment pouring from the group, but he sloughed off their looks, stuffed his silver blanket into his backpack, and slipped down to the riverbank to retrieve his bundle of cocaine. He grabbed Manuel's bag and dragged it back up the slope.

"Don't want to forget this, do you, Manny?" Cisco asked, pushing the bag toward Manuel's feet.

Cisco reached into his backpack and pulled out a small flashlight as it was already dark.

"Don't turn that on, Cisco," Manuel warned him. "I don't think it's safe yet."

Cisco ignored him and clicked on the flashlight. "You worry about you, Manny!"

He panned the group with his flashlight and laughed at the look of fear on their faces.

"Oooooh, the water devil's going to get me now!" he said sarcastically. But the faces he splashed with light didn't appear to be looking at him, but rather, past him.

Something made Cisco's hair stand on the back of his neck. It was the sound of dry grass being crushed behind him, right where the group was staring. He turned, directing the flashlight toward whatever was making the sound.

The creature that parted the tall grass in front of him could only be described as an abomination of an animal. Its skin was a bronze-colored metal with a dimpled pattern. The rounded body parts, riveted together, created the shape of a huge, silver porcupine with wheels for feet. Sections of its body twisted independently, and the movement stopped when the creature was only feet from where Cisco stood.

Aside from its glowing, red eyes, this creature was much different from the water creature they had just met. Cisco's flashlight reflected off the silver, metal needles extending from the animal's body sections, each five-inch needle pointing in a different direction. The tips of the needles were painted in black-and-white stripes, almost camouflaging the animal in the strands of grass. They were quills, designed to look much like a porcupine's. The creature's eyes focused on Cisco, whose light beam was now shaking.

Cisco opened his mouth to seek help from the group, but there were several successive noises before he could get a word out.

HISS. HISS. HISS ... HISS. HISS. HISS.

Everyone in the group gasped in unison.

Cisco's eyes grew in size, and he slowly looked down. Three metal darts stuck out of his body from his chest down to his thighs. He moved his lips as if to speak, but a white foam dripped from the corner of his lip, replacing any words. Real tears rolled over his facial tattoos. His body went limp, and he fell to his knees. Two other men—the ones nearest Cisco—also fell over as if on cue. The porcupine's quills had reached all three of them, injecting a paralyzing toxin.

Gabriella noticed the porcupine's body sections started to realign, and the wheels began spinning and kicking up the loose dirt.

It's repositioning itself to attack the rest of the group.

"Get down!" she yelled, shoving Manuel and her mom to the ground. She pushed Manuel's large duffel of cocaine between them and the porcupine to act as a shield.

A few more hisses, and there was a *THWACK*. The quills intended for them stuck into the cocaine bundle instead.

Gabriella could hear two group members groan and fall to the ground. The porcupine's spinning wheels sounded louder now, and she realized it was moving toward her, her mom, and Manuel. It was as if the metal creature had intelligence as it made its way around the cocaine bundle and was beginning to turn its body to redirect its remaining quills at them.

She kicked the large cocaine bundle in front of the creature, temporarily blocking its intended course once again. The wheels started spinning faster this time.

"RUN!" she screamed.

Gabriella yanked her mom from the ground, and Manuel followed. As they ran, they could hear the hisses of the porcupine's needles firing. Her quick thinking had paid off, and they created enough distance to avoid the onslaught of paralyzing quills. Gabriella could hear the creature's wheels spinning again, and it made her realize just how motivated these creatures were.

2: YARDS FROM FREEDOM

Gabriella, her mom, and Manuel ran hard for as long as they could. Gabriella was surprised at her mom's ability to keep up. After about fifty yards, Manuel noticed an outcropping of rocks in the distance, just barely outlined by the last bit of the sun as it disappeared.

"Get to those rocks. I'm hoping that thing can't climb!" Manuel shouted.

All three sprinted toward the outcropping, scaled the huge boulders quickly, and helped each other get to the top. Conveniently, there was an area in the center of the outcropping that fit all three of them and was surrounded by large boulders. Gabriella claimed it as their castle … a place where they could escape the metal devil and take a quick break.

It took a few minutes for them to catch their breath and slow their hearts enough to pay attention to any noise around the exterior of their castle.

"Gabriella, we should all get under the Mylar blankets, just in case any flying creatures appear," Manuel suggested.

"You can call me Gabby. That's what my friends call me. Only my mom calls me by my full name." She smiled at him.

Gabby kept staring above the big boulders surrounding them, fully expecting those evil, red eyes to peer down at any moment. She calmed once she convinced herself that Manuel was right—there was no way that thing could climb to where they were hiding. It was hard enough for the three of them to get up there.

After an hour of waiting, their minds started playing tricks on them. At times, Gabby could swear she heard the wheels of the porcupine spinning, crushing the dry, crisp brush surrounding their castle. Each time, Manuel bravely volunteered to peer over the big boulders and returned to assure her and her mom that it was just the wind. He could see no movement and no red eyes, only the hot wind blowing the tumbleweeds around the sandy moat surrounding their castle.

After a couple of hours of waiting, they decided to plan their next move. According to their expert guide, Emilio, the night was the best time to proceed, albeit wrapped in their silver blankets.

Manuel noted that, in the last bit of light, he had seen several rock outcroppings to the north.

"Our best chance is to run between rock outcroppings and take short breaks. We can avoid detection with the silver blankets. Hopefully, they won't have any creatures that know how to climb," Manuel said.

This strategy might allow them to make it the rest of the way, but they all knew it was going to be a long and dangerous night.

After one more scouting mission from Manuel, he assured them the coast was clear of the metal creature, so they decided to climb down and head toward the next outcropping.

They made good progress running between outcroppings, only stopping once for an extended period.

Manuel heard the propellers of another drone coming. "Duck under that boulder!"

All three rushed for shelter.

They weren't sure if it was the boulder that hid their warm bodies or the silver blankets, but the drone sped directly overhead and far off into the distance, ignoring their presence. They could hear another faraway drone a few times, seeming to circle their location, but it never got close enough to force them to take cover again.

In the short time they'd been running, all three had fine-tuned their hearing to pay attention to the telltale sound of threats. They listened for whirring propellers that signaled a drone was nearby and also the squeak of moving wheels warning of metal creatures.

The concentration level was intense, from trying to listen to their environment to guessing the correct direction in the dark through a maze of cacti, deep swales, and natural obstacles. It created a kind of fatigue that none of them had ever experienced before. At the risk of losing the advantage of the darkness, they decided to rest for an extended period. The group needed to calm their minds and regain their sanity. They also agreed that without rest, they would surely make a costly mistake.

Manuel scouted a rock outcropping that offered the height and cover they desperately needed, affording them an opportunity to take a break from their current mental state.

None of them expected to fall asleep in their silver blankets. It just happened. The crease of the sunrise hitting her face jolted Gabby awake, alerting her to the fact they had slept away any advantage offered by the darkness. They were now three large, silver, curled-up balls exposed to a world of surveillance that was surely hunting them. Her only solace was that they were still alive and had avoided detection all night. But the sound of a drone humming ever closer catapulted her back into survival mode.

"Take off your blankets, quickly!" Gabby urged, startling the others awake. "We look like little mirrors out here in the sunlight."

Manuel and Rosario promptly stowed away their blankets, hoping they hadn't already given away their position.

The drone seemed to miss them and moved far enough away that Manuel took a chance and peeked over the boulders they used for cover. Knowing the sun was to his east, he stared due north and toward the distant humming sound. Gabby saw his look of panic turn into happiness.

"What is it, Manuel?" she asked, pulling him back into their hiding place. "What do you see?"

"Freedom," Manuel announced. "I can see a large city off in the distance. Lines of cars moving. It looks like it might be one of the border-crossing towns. El Paso, Texas?"

This news made her and Rosario hug. They realized they were close to the end of the Red Zone and the future that Gabby's dad had wanted for both of them.

She released the hug with her mom and climbed to see for herself.

Gabby observed the town in the distance, which fit Manuel's description perfectly. But she noticed something else … something Manuel hadn't noticed or maybe just didn't want to mention. It was closer to their position than the town—something she had only read about—instantly causing her to panic.

On either side of the town were two massive, metal towers reflecting the morning's already-hot sun. Each tower stood about eighty feet tall, with watchtowers surrounded by mirrored glass windows. As she watched, the closest tower showed some movement. A door in front of the tower opened, and something perfectly round and shiny rolled out and down a huge, metal slide extending to the ground. As soon as the object spun out of sight, the turret door closed quickly and Gabby ducked back down.

"There are two towers out there, and I think I know where those creatures are coming from," she said. "I saw the closest tower open and send something shiny down its slide."

They all agreed it would be suicide to leave their protective nest in broad daylight, especially with the towers watching over their position.

"We could try to make a run for it and mask our body heat with the blankets, but we would look like aluminum foil balls scurrying around in the flats. They would surely see us," Gabby said.

"Yeah. We seem to have found decent cover here. I think we need to wait for dark again," Manuel suggested.

Rosario nervously held out her water bottle and shook it, showing it was bone dry.

Gabby held up her water bottle and realized she had, at best, enough for two small sips between the three of them. "I'm not sure we can last the entire day in this sun with this little water," she said.

"We're going to have to make it work. We don't have a choice," Manuel advised.

They sat for a few hours in the heat and tried to find whatever bit of shade they could as the sun moved overhead. The massive boulders surrounding them were heating up as the minutes passed, and Gabby realized it was like being in a tiny brick oven and they were the food being cooked alive. To make matters worse, their water was now gone.

"I don't think we can last much longer up here. My lips are starting to crack from the heat," Gabby said.

"If we go out there, we're sure to be captured. We just need to wait until dusk, and we'll be free," Manuel urged.

Just as he'd said it, a shadow quickly moved over them. At first, all three were startled, assuming a drone had discovered them. But when they looked up, they realized it was just a very dark storm cloud rolling overhead, blocking the sun entirely.

It was one of the darkest storms Gabby had ever seen. She and her mom stared at each other, and her mom was the first to say what they were both thinking.

"Your papá is watching over us," she said with a big smile.

As soon as Rosario said it, large raindrops fell, drenching their hiding place and cooling their skin. Gabby could feel the dirt and sweat dripping off her body, and she suddenly felt a sense of hope again. They all quietly cheered and hugged. Manuel held up his Mylar blanket to catch the rain and funnel it into their empty water bottles. They each drank a bottle of the rainwater, and Manuel refilled them again for the rest of the journey.

"That storm is a godsend. It created the darkness we need, and it doesn't look like it's going to end anytime soon. Now's the time to make our move," Manuel said.

Gabby and Rosario agreed, and the three wrapped themselves in their blankets and climbed over the boulders and down to the ground. It was too dark for any person to see their Mylar blankets. Lightning struck in the distance, outlining the city and the looming tower five hundred yards before them. Manuel pointed in a direction far left of the tower.

"We should avoid crossing near the city because it'll be heavily policed. Let's steer far left of that tower, and we'll cross the border over there," he said, pointing to an imaginary destination they could run toward. "I saw some more rock outcroppings and a couple of deserted buildings in that direction that might give us a place to rest, too."

A few steps into their new route, they found themselves sliding down into a six-foot swale, which the rain had turned into a small creek. It was another stroke of luck, as the swale would conceal them as they crossed parallel to the border until they were far enough past the tower to head north again. Even though they couldn't see the tower from the bottom of the swale, they still hunched over to make doubly sure they wouldn't be spotted. They shuffled as quickly as they could in the mud and water.

Gabby noticed the drones were no longer flying around the area and wondered if they had discovered a weakness of the border defenses—rain and lightning.

It was smooth sailing, and their hopes were high because they could see no end to the storm clouds. It was evident in their strides and sense of excitement that they felt as though they just might make it.

They reached a turn in the swale, and Manuel stopped them. He climbed to the top of the ridge and peered over, waiting for the next flash of lightning to give him an idea of where the turret was and how close they were to their destination. It only took a few seconds for a flash to appear, followed instantly by a deafening clap of thunder. The lightning exposed the turret far off in the distance and also an abandoned building only one hundred yards in front of them.

Somehow, he had perfectly aligned the group just south of the abandoned building and far from what he guessed would be the reach of the turret's view.

Manuel motioned to Gabby and her mom to be ready.

"Next flash of lightning, we make a run for it," he whispered.

It didn't take long for the lightning to strike, as the storm had now moved almost directly over them, and they were in the thick of it. Gabby weighed in her mind the risk of wearing a silver blanket and getting hit by lightning over the chance of her body heat being detected by some creature. She decided to keep the silver blanket wrapped tightly around her body. Her mom followed her lead. Manuel had already decided to leave his blanket on as well.

They climbed up and out of the swale and sprinted toward the building with Manuel leading the way. Gabby positioned her mom between her and Manuel to ensure their pace wasn't too fast for her.

Even though the sound of the thunder and the beating of her heart numbed her hearing, Gabby still heard the noise she had grown to fear. It was the sound of a drone's propellers, and it was getting closer. She turned to see flashing, blue lights off in the distance, heading on a path that would intercept them on their way to the building.

"Manuel!" she screamed over the rain and thunder. "DRONE!" she yelled, pointing in its direction. Manuel swung his head but kept running. They were a quarter of the way to the building, and he made a quick calculation in his head.

He abruptly stopped running, and Rosario and Gabby almost crashed into him in the dark. "The drone's going to beat us there," he yelled. "You two stay here and don't move a muscle. I'll lead it away and find another rock outcropping. Get to the building, and I'll catch up with you when it's clear."

"No, Manuel! You can't outrun it. Please just keep moving. We can make it," Gabby pleaded.

But Manuel's plan was already in motion. He threw his silver blanket over Gabby and started sprinting parallel to the border and off into the dark. He didn't give Gabby a chance to argue.

Why did he ditch his blanket? He's exposing himself on purpose to lead the drone away, Gabby realized.

Not a minute later, the drone, with all propellers whipping at full strength, flew right over where Gabby and her mom were huddled under their silver blankets. They didn't dare move. It followed the path Manuel had just taken.

Gabby was stunned that Manuel, a stranger just a day ago, had risked his freedom for them. She decided they couldn't waste the golden opportunity he had afforded them.

"Move," she yelled to her mom, and they started running again.

Whenever she had the chance, she looked to her left to see where the drone was and what it was doing. The drone appeared to be circling an area in the distance, and she could only assume it was trying to find Manuel. Her heart sank.

They finally made it to the building and flattened their bodies against the wall facing away from the turret. Gabby and her mom could now see that the drone had stopped circling. A bright spotlight appeared under the drone, and they saw the now-familiar basket dropping.

"No! Manuel!" Gabby screamed, starting to run in his direction. Rosario grabbed her arm and pulled her back toward the wall and into a tight, comforting hug.

"You can't do anything now. Manuel sacrificed himself for

us," she whispered in Gabby's ear. Gabby started to cry.

She wiped her eyes, then got a furious, focused look on her face.

"If we make it across the border, I am going to find a way to stop these bastards," she vowed.

Her mom put a hand on each of Gabby's cheeks. "I believe you are the one who can do it, Mija!"

Gabby peeked around the north side of the building, and with the next lightning flash, she could make out two windows and a large doorway.

"I'm going inside to check it out. I'll let you know if it's safe in there," Gabby said, not giving her mom a chance to argue about who would enter first.

She crouched, shuffled around the front, and climbed in through the nearest window opening. The building must have previously been used as a border patrol station as she discovered some maps of the former border still hanging on the wall. There was some wiring connected to an old, destroyed radio dangling from a metal shelf. It looked as though the border patrol left in a hurry and wanted to ensure nobody could use any of the equipment they had left behind.

There was a tiny bathroom in one corner with a sink and a toilet. Gabby noticed a small storage room with an old water heater and a floor littered with cardboard. The metal roof was rusted entirely away at the front of the building, and only the bathroom and storage area received any protection from it. It would hide them from the storm and the drones, allowing them to wait until nighttime to cross into America.

Gabby stared out the front door and saw lights from buildings on the other side of the border. She felt as if she could reach out and touch them. That's how close freedom was.

"It's clear! Come in," Gabby yelled to her mom.

She watched her mom's silhouette in a flash of lightning as it passed by the window opening. But then her mom unexpectedly stopped at the entrance to the building for some reason.

"In here!" Gabby said, waving her hands vigorously so her mom could see where she was hiding near the back of the building.

But her mom didn't turn to enter the building. She just

remained perfectly still, staring off toward the turret.

"What's wrong?" Gabby asked as she started toward her.

Small flashes of white light pulsed all around her mom's body. Another flash of lightning revealed that a fine, silver net had wound around her mom's body, from her feet to her chest. The net was attached to a silver mat at the doorway of the building, something that Gabby hadn't perceived earlier.

It wasn't that her mom didn't want to move—she couldn't. Gabby realized the tight, metal net had entrapped her mom.

Gabby stepped toward her, but her mom shook her head NO as well as she could. Her mom's eyes grew wide with fear, and a quick, crackling noise broke the silence. The crackling noise reminded Gabby of the devil creature that had taken Caesar. The pulsing flashes of light reappeared around her mom's lower body, causing her to shake from head to toe.

She's being killed with electricity.

Gabby panicked, noticing her mom had stepped onto some kind of electrical snare strategically placed at the entrance to the building.

You fucking, sick bastards.

Gabby ran through scenarios of how she could safely set her mom free. There was nothing like a wooden pole or a plastic chair she could use to try and free her mom without getting electrocuted herself. She looked back at the storage area and saw something that might work—the dry cardboard lying on the ground. She could use it as an insulator on her hands and try to wrestle her mom loose from the net.

She grabbed a large piece of cardboard from the floor and froze when she heard something. She realized that, in the chaos of the situation, she had missed the sound of propellers approaching. The thunder and the rain against the metal roof had masked the sound until it was too late.

Gabby turned back toward her mom to see her surrounded by a flood of light, her body already rising from the ground, a silver mat dangling from her feet. The recognizable basket of a drone Gabby knew all too well encircled her mother, and she was lifted into the air.

Her mom was gone, and the drone shot off before Gabby could

sprint back across the room.

Defeated, Gabby stumbled back to the protection of the storage room, fell to her knees, and cried more than she ever had in her life.

We were so close.

Time passed slowly, and the morning sun finally scared away the storm. The sunshine streaming through the holes in the roof offered little comfort to Gabby. Losing her mom and Manuel so close to freedom wrecked her soul. The sounds of the electricity crackling through her mom's body played over and over in her head, causing a severe headache. She sat in the dark corner, rubbed her temples, and stared at the ground, and that's when she noticed it in a ray of sunlight.

Someone had etched something into the floor— WALLFLOWERS.

Wallflowers? That's the name of the activist group my dad said would help him across the border.

It was right there where she had removed the big piece of cardboard earlier. She quickly peeled the other sections of cardboard away to see if there was more to the message. She stood back in disbelief. In the center of the storage room was a two-foot-square trapdoor with a round, metal, ring-pull handle. The word WALLFLOWERS had been etched directly in the center of the door.

Gabby heard a noise outside the building on the side nearest the turret. It was the all too familiar squeaking sound of the porcupine's metal wheels spinning.

Her heart jumped and her spine tingled.

She yanked hard on the ring pull to the trapdoor, exposing a large hole and metal rungs of a ladder. A small flashlight hung from an S-shaped hook on the first rung. She grabbed the flashlight and descended the ladder into the dark, quietly closing the trapdoor behind her.

Just as she touched the bottom rung, she heard the metallic squeaking and the sound of wheels rolling overhead on the trapdoor, confirming her assumption was correct. The metal creature was above, and it was hunting her.

"Those things can't open doors, can they?" she asked herself.

The door above rattled, startling her. She remained completely still, hoping it didn't have the dexterity to enter her hideout.

She waited until the creature rolled away and she could no longer hear any noise above.

Gabby panned the space with her flashlight. On the wall opposite the ladder, there was a hook from which hung a cell phone and a lanyard containing a laminated set of instructions.

Repeated in English, Spanish, Chinese, Arabic, and Russian, the card read:

1. CALL WAL-LFL-OWER (925-535-6937).
2. STATE YOUR FIRST NAME, COUNTRY, AGE, AND LANGUAGE.
3. AWAIT INSTRUCTIONS.

Gabby fumbled the phone, hands shaking, realizing the last few minutes had completely drained her of all her energy. Or maybe it was the fear-induced adrenaline shooting through her body. It made an easy task, such as holding and dialing a phone, a colossal task. She slowly managed to dial the number.

RING.

RING.

RING.

The ringing stopped.

Someone on the other end picked up, and there was an odd silence as if they were awaiting her information.

"Gabby, Mexico, fifteen, English or Spanish," she stated as slowly and clearly as she could, her voice shaking.

There was a long pause on the other end of the line, followed by a repetitive clicking sound. Gabby wondered if she had dialed the wrong number, so she looked at the card to compare numbers.

A voice interrupted her examination, "Welcome to America, Gabby. Leave the phone and instruction card where you found them. Crawl to the other end of the tunnel. Exit the tunnel and cross the street to the flower shop. Someone will be there to greet you. Please confirm that you understand these instructions," said the robotic-sounding voice on the other end.

"I understand," Gabby replied. The call ended, leaving her listening to the dial tone. Fresh tears dripped halfway down her cheek, trapped by the dust that had caked on her skin.

I made it.

She put everything back where she found it and began crawling through the tunnel as quickly as possible, even though her knees screamed in pain. Every part of her body ached, and her mouth was as dry as the dust kicking up from the tunnel floor. Each breath became more difficult the farther she got into the tunnel.

There has to be an end to this thing.

Just as she thought it, her flashlight illuminated a dead end in the tunnel and another ladder. Slumped at the bottom of the ladder, Gabby wondered if she had the energy to climb the ten rungs that would lead her to freedom.

She thought about the loss of both of her parents. Her anger inspired a second wind. Her attitude changed from desperation to one of determination, and she started to climb.

This is for you, Mamá and Papá.

Reaching the top, Gabby pushed on a heavy, metal trapdoor without fear of anyone on the surface seeing or hearing her. She popped her head out of the hole and scrutinized her surroundings.

The exit had been strategically constructed under the first platform of a metal fire escape in the dead end of an alley lined with dumpsters.

A warm breeze brought the odor of the alley to her nose, and she didn't care that it smelled like garbage. She knew she was breathing American air, and that made her smile.

Gabby hoisted herself out of the hole and crawled from under the fire escape. Stretching her arms high above her head, she arched her body to force her back to crack and straighten to regain its normal shape. She could only imagine how dirty she looked and tried to brush off as much dirt and debris as possible. It seemed to make no difference as the rain had caked and hardened the dirt covering every inch of her body.

She was startled when she saw something move past the entrance to the alley, and then a second dark shape ran in the opposite direction. Gabby realized they were people running with umbrellas. The black cloud of the storm had reappeared overhead, and she guessed they were all attempting to reach their destinations before the storm dumped another load of rain on them. She figured the tunnel must have placed her right into the bluster of the city during the morning rush hour.

Gabby slowly advanced through the alley, staying prone behind the dumpsters as she neared the street activity. Her heart raced when she noticed the shop directly across the street from the alley. Above a huge window hung a sign adorned with a large daisy and the words El Paso Flower Shop.

She laughed when she thought about the meaning behind the flower shop's name. Gabby had read about the history of the town of El Paso in one of her books. El Paso, Texas, actually got its name from Spanish and translates to "The Pass" or "The Crossing" in English. The city's location made it an important crossing point between Texas and Mexico.

How fitting.

She inched along the brick wall to the end of the alley, poking her head around the corner to glance down the street in both directions. She realized everyone was tucked under their umbrellas, staring down at their feet as they walked. They were too busy to notice her.

CRACK!

The thunder startled Gabby, causing her to jump, clearing her body of any remaining tightness imposed by crawling through the small tunnel.

Everyone on the street appeared equally startled as they began running faster for cover. The rain started to pour down.

Gabby darted for the flower shop, hoping everyone would think she was another soul attempting to avoid the storm. She didn't hesitate when she reached the front door, passing through and slamming the door quickly behind her. She rested her back against the door, trying to regain her breath and overcome the adrenaline rush caused by her dash to freedom.

"Welcome to America, Gabby," came a soft voice from behind the counter, catching her off guard. "We've been waiting for you."

Gabby turned to find an older woman with short, gray hair smiling at her. She had a motherly look to her and wore a tan apron bearing the flower shop's logo. It was stained with shades of green, red, and pink from the fresh bouquet she had just arranged.

Gabby didn't know how to respond, and there was an awkward

silence.

The woman sensed her fear and broke the silence. "Awe, don't worry, hon … you're completely safe here. You made it to America, and we're here to assist you on the rest of your journey. I'm Rose."

Gabby slumped to the floor, exhausted and relieved. The lady's name had to be a sign from her dad. He used to call her mom Rose all the time.

Rose came around the counter and helped Gabby up from the floor.

"What do you say we get you cleaned up, fed, and rested?"

Gabby nodded.

Rose led her to a back hallway with several doors, unlocking the last door. She walked through the door and welcomed Gabby in.

"There's a shower, soap, and fresh towels for you. Go ahead and take a hot shower and get that dirt off you. Just throw those old clothes in the trash can over there. There are new clothes in the wardrobe. You should be able to find something that fits you. Feel free to take whatever you need. That red bag has makeup, a toothbrush, and other items. By the way, the El Paso Flower Shop T-shirts seem to be a favorite with my guests." She smiled.

Rose grabbed two of four water bottles from a shelf and handed them to Gabby.

"You must be thirsty and hungry. I'll drop off a food tray in a minute. You're safe, and nobody will bother you here. We can talk once you're fed and rested. Get yourself some real sleep."

"Thank you," Gabby said, hugging the woman. Gabby was embarrassed when she realized she left some dirt on the front of Rose's apron. They both laughed at that.

3: CIVIL WATCH

Lucas glared at his seventy-five-inch screen, whipped his controller to the floor, and yelled into his microphone.

"Dammit! I lost her. That would have been a record for me. Almost eight Hoppers in one session!"

He threw his head back into the padded, leather headrest of his gaming chair.

Through the headphones, his three friends laughed and razzed him.

"It took you long enough to catch the other seven," a female voice chided.

"And you lost the smallest one of the pack. How do you do that?" a male voice added.

The four were in a squad playing *Civil Watch*, a wildly popular video game among American citizens, young and old. The video game allowed anyone over eighteen to help guard the American borders from Hoppers. Players controlled an arsenal of terrifying, semi-autonomous, mechanical creatures and drone surveillance technology to spot and capture their targets. It was the brainchild of Red Draven, owner of Draven Labs, bringing hundreds of millions of dollars to his company's coffers annually.

Each squad was assigned a section of the Red Zone to guard, virtually, through the game's interface. Players were required to be active during their entire shift or risk losing rank, any money earned, and their subscription could even be terminated. Although the subscription cost was steep for an eighteen-year-old, starting at eighty dollars monthly, they could easily earn that back after only a few nights of play. The most active sections of the Red Zone cost more than the others but also offered a more significant opportunity to earn money.

Players selected different tracking technologies and non-lethal deterrents from their on-screen arsenal to capture Hoppers trying to get across the American borders illegally. Improved technologies were continually being developed, and as players increased in rank, they could earn better equipment as a reward. It was also possible to purchase the newer equipment at a price most players couldn't afford.

A player would be credited ten dollars for each Hopper caught, and earnings could grow quickly. Some high school students were making as much as a thousand dollars a month playing the game, equivalent to a college scholarship.

Aside from the monetary reward, one's *Civil Watch* rank was a status symbol within Generation Beta. Special chrome badges were awarded for each rank, and achievement patches were given to praise a player's unique abilities. Players waited anxiously for their new badges of honor to arrive in the mail. Wearing them to school was better than wearing a new pair of brand-name sneakers or even driving a new car into the parking lot.

The game notification system advertised the ranks and achievements one could earn, the names of the highest-ranking players in their area, and the newest achievements awarded. These announcements were made with great fanfare whenever a player started a new game session.

Gameplay could be recorded and shared as video clips on DravenTV, a popular streaming service that is free for anyone to watch. DravenTV was just one more way the marketing team at Draven Labs could publicize the *Civil Watch* game and recruit new players to the platform.

If a player's capture clip was shared on DravenTV and received more than one hundred thousand views, they were awarded the rare "Freedom Fighter" rank. Just having a clip selected earns players recognition and bragging rights among their peers. Every clip also bolstered the optics of the president of the United States and supported his message that his plan to stop illegal immigration was working.

Civil Watch allowed friends to form four-player squads and share their screens as they played.

Lucas, Ariel, Mason, and Eric were on a team together and played almost every night. They worked together to catch Hoppers, earn money, rank up, and, most importantly, have bragging rights at school.

Lucas's friends had celebrated with him earlier when he snared a Hopper with the new Jellyfish 2.0. The water-based deterrent moved quickly and wrapped its prey in metal tentacles, paralyzing them with an electric charge. They also watched when his Porcupine narrowly missed spiking the female Hopper, who seemed to disappear and escape somewhere inside an abandoned building.

"I only lost her because the early model of these damn Porcupines is freaking slow as hell," Lucas complained. "They have the turning speed of a turtle. That's what they should call these things—turtles! I'm sending a ticket to the support team to either fix these deterrents or replace them."

"Sure, blame it on the tech. Maybe one day, you'll rank up and get some new stuff. My Tarantula moves twice as fast as that Porcupine, even with a damaged leg," Mason joked.

"Well, Mason, some of us don't have the money to buy the expensive gear like you because some of us don't have a senator for a dad!" Lucas snapped angrily, instantly feeling bad about saying this to his best friend and in front of the whole squad.

Mason blurted back, "I don't buy my gear, asshole, I EARN it. I have close to four hundred captures this year alone. I just caught ten today."

The tension was broken by a loud notification that blared over everyone's headsets.

Mason yelled out, "No way! Guess what? I just ranked up to silver. You have to see some of the new deterrents they're awarding me."

Lucas dropped his head and groaned audibly. He had worked hard to catch up to Mason's level but realized his best friend and gaming nemesis had jumped way ahead again. Earning silver was rare, so Lucas's envy quickly turned to pride when he realized they all shared glory being in the same squadron as Mason.

"That's pretty cool, Mason," Lucas conceded. "Sorry I said that stuff. I'm just pissed that I lost one."

"Don't worry about it, bud. It takes more than that to hurt my feelings. And I get it … it sucks losing any Hoppers. I'll gift you something to make you feel better. It'll keep you from letting any more of those strays get away!" Mason offered.

DING!

Lucas's screen flashed, displaying a rendering of a terrifying, large, Black Widow Spider with circular, red shapes on its back. Under the picture was the headline, "You've been gifted the BLACK WIDOW."

"Now that's fucking cool! Thanks, Mason!" Lucas smiled. Any remaining envy he had toward his friend Mason disappeared.

"And that's the newest model. Enjoy!" Mason announced proudly.

"This is awesome. I can't wait to try it out," Lucas said, clicking the ACCEPT GIFT button.

A fast-paced animation showed a rendering of a Black Widow climbing over a large rock and advancing quickly on its prey—a CGI-generated outline of a Hopper running. Reeling back on its hind legs, it exposed its abdomen and shot out a huge, metal web, encasing the Hopper. The animation faded away, and a small icon representing the Black Widow Spider dropped into the sidebar menu of Lucas's game interface. It joined icons of a Porcupine, Zombie Ant, Centipede, Beetle, Scorpion, Dragonfly, Jellyfish, and Piranha.

4: A NEW LIFE

Gabby jerked from a sound sleep. Muffled voices came from the hall. She recognized Rose's voice but not the new male voice. She sat up and rubbed away the sleep and a small remnant of dust that had collected in the corner of her eye.

There was a soft knock at the door.

"Gabby, are you awake?" Rose asked.

"Yes!" Gabby said, straightening up.

The door opened, and Rose entered, followed by a bearded man.

"Hello, Gabby. I want to introduce you to Noah. He's with the Wallflowers, the people who helped you escape over the border." She smiled.

The Wallflowers? That's the group fighting for immigration rights.

Gabby took in how good-looking this man was. She guessed him to be in his early thirties, and his skin was tan, his eyes brown, and his black hair was pulled back into a short ponytail. His white smile glowed against his darkened skin. His features led her to believe they shared Mexican heritage. His beard was well-kept, and he wore khaki cargo pants and a white, cotton shirt that partially exposed a muscular chest. Gabby's eyes went directly to his left hand, where she noticed a silver wedding band.

The band calmed Gabby as her initial fear was that she had

been fooled and he might be a sex trade worker coming to take her away. Surely, a sex trade worker wouldn't be wearing a wedding ring. To this point, Gabby had only heard rumors of the Wallflowers, and they seemed to be a faceless, imaginary thing. Seeing Noah changed that.

"Hi, Gabby! I'm sure you have many questions. I'm here to answer them and get you into your new life here in the States," Noah assured her.

"Do I know you?" Gabby asked.

"Emilio, the man who guided you and your mom up to the Red Zone, always sends us a list of the names and backgrounds of the people he is sending through. It's one way we can be sure you aren't a drug smuggler, sex trade worker, or a spy sent by the government or Draven Labs. They've been trying to catch me and stop the Wallflowers any way they can. Emilio listed you as the only sixteen-year-old female with the last group crossing," he said.

Gabby realized the conversations she and her mom had with Emilio before entering the Red Zone were NOT totally out of kindness or personal curiosity. She wondered if she truly had reminded Emilio of his daughter as he had claimed. She now realized Emilio was just doing his job and gathering background information on her and her mom.

She ran through her memory and some of the questions Emilio had asked. How old are you? Do you have any hobbies? What do you want to do when you get to the United States?
Have you ever heard rumors of a group that helps Hoppers get across the border? Where do you and your mom come from?

Gabby snapped out of the memories and back to the present. "My mom? Do you know what they did to her?"

"Yes, Gabby. Don't worry. She was taken to the processing center and is doing okay. Aside from some bruising and a few minor burns, she's good. We have a few people inside Draven Labs who update us on the Hoppers who get picked up.

Unfortunately, Draven Labs has already added a first mark to your mom's arm, and she'll be taken back to your hometown on the next transport," he advised.

"What about the young man named Manuel? He sacrificed himself so my mom and I could get away. He said the cartel made him cross, but he was a good person and didn't want to do it. He was forced. And that poor, older man, Caesar? Some type of Jellyfish creature grabbed him in the river, and we all watched him struggle in the water. Is he okay?"

"I'll check on Manuel. Unfortunately, the older man, Caesar, didn't make it. And that will be a problem for Draven Labs," Noah said seriously.

"And my dad, Felix Alvarez of La Coronilla, Mexico? He tried to cross over a year ago with two marks, but we never heard from him again. Do you know what happened to him?" Gabby asked, sure that Noah's intelligence network must have some information for her.

"I'm so sorry, Gabby. If he crossed more than a year ago, we wouldn't know. We didn't have the right people inside Draven Labs until January of 2049," Noah said. "I'll ask my people to research and see if they can learn anything about what happened to him."

Gabby's shoulders slumped.

"Look, I'm not going to lie or sugarcoat anything, Gabby. If your dad had two marks entering the Red Zone and was caught, you may never hear from him again."

Gabby seemed to know this already, but she held out hope anyway.

Noah reached into a satchel, removed a small box containing a new cell phone, and handed it to Gabby.

"Let's worry about your mom for now, okay? She probably wants to know that you're safe. You should be able to reach her at home in a day or two. This phone is active and charged, and it's

35

yours to keep. The phone number is on the back of the box. I already added my contact info under the name Noah."

He stepped toward Gabby, rested a hand on her shoulder, and looked into her eyes.

"Feel free to call me or whoever you need to. I only ask that, from this point on, please never mention anything to anyone about me, the Wallflowers, or how we got you out of the Red Zone. You'll see some things you can't discuss with anyone outside our group in the coming days. Your future, your mom's future, and the future of our group and other crossers like you depend on it. Deal?"

Gabby was smart enough to know that what he and the Wallflowers were doing was illegal in the United States, and any secrets she might reveal could put many people at risk, including Rose, who stood behind Noah with a compassionate smile. She also understood that these Wallflowers were probably the only way to get her mom over the border to join her.

"I promise! I also want to help you in any way I can," Gabby replied, making sure Noah and Rose heard her promise. "Did Emilio also tell you that I'm good with computers?"

"Yes, he did, and we also had someone call and talk to some of your friends in La Coronilla. From what we hear, you're a bit of a computer phenom." Noah smiled.

Gabby was impressed that the Wallflower network could do a background check on her in such a short amount of time. Noah could tell what she was thinking.

"Yes, Gabby, we make sure we know everything we can about the people we assist. It allows me to sleep at night. But I don't want you worrying about how you can help us now. Let's get you into your new life here first, and then we can talk about your role in the Wallflowers, okay?" Noah suggested.

With that, Rose and Noah led Gabby through a utility room and out the back door of the flower shop, where a white SUV was sitting, engine running. The large vehicle had tinted windows, but she saw the outline of a driver waiting for her and Noah to arrive. As they approached the car, Noah opened the door for Gabby. She turned to Rose and gave her another hug.

"Well, that was a much cleaner hug than last time," Rose joked. She handed Gabby a red rose, which she had been hiding behind her back. The flower was a tradition that Rose started doing ever since she opened the flower shop.

"A little something to make your day brighter, Gabby," Rose whispered.

"Thank you for everything," Gabby whispered back.

Rose beamed like a proud mother and nodded. Even though Rose had only briefly been in Gabby's life, she acted like a new mom and seemed delighted to be part of Gabby's newfound freedom.

"This is why I help the Wallflowers by giving sanctuary to Hoppers. It brings me more happiness than selling any bouquet ever could." Rose smiled.

Gabby slid into the leather seat of the SUV and felt the chill of the air conditioning that filled the car. It reminded her how hot the Red Zone had been during her journey.

Noah slipped into the passenger seat. "This is Peter, a good friend. Peter, meet Gabby."

"Welcome to America!" Peter looked back in the rearview mirror and gave her a big smile.

"Nice to meet you, Peter."

As Peter pulled away, Noah explained how she would get a new life in the United States.

"The next few days will be a whirlwind for you, and you'll probably get a little homesick. That's completely normal, and we have people who will help sort that out if you need assistance. We'll get you a US birth certificate and enough info to allow you to get a driver's license. We've found a host family that will provide you with a place to call home, and they'll be known as your aunt and uncle for as long as you decide to stay with them. The family lives near a local school where you can finish high school. The school has one of the best STEM programs—STEM stands for science, technology, engineering, and math. They have an excellent computer teacher, too. I know him personally, and he is one of the best."

Gabby smiled. She knew what STEM was but didn't want to tell Noah and embarrass him.

"So you can get right back into what you enjoy studying," Noah said proudly.

"Yes, I'm a bit of a nerd, some say. It's a hobby I hope to turn into a career," Gabby replied.

"We could use some good technology people helping the Wallflowers. It's all volunteer, though, so I'll leave that up to you when the time comes. We do provide friendship, great pizza, free pop, and some of the best buñuelos in the neighborhood."

"Damn straight," Peter jumped in. "That's why I volunteer—for the buñuelos."

Noah continued, "In a few days, you'll be considered an American citizen with all the proper paperwork. Aside from you admitting otherwise, there will be no way for anyone to question it."

"Why are you doing all of this for me?"

"We share a similar story, Gabby. I'm a Mexican immigrant, and I lost people I love to the Red Zone, too. My parents sent me over with a coyote before the Red Zone construction was finished. They could only afford to send me at the time, and they stayed behind until they could raise the funds to make the journey themselves. By the time they had saved enough to cross, the Red Zone had been completed. They were with one of the first groups to try to cross, but nobody realized how effective Draven's creatures would be. The last time we talked, they told me they'd found a safe passage through the Red Zone and would be joining me for Christmas. They were captured making the journey, and both already had two marks. That was the last time I heard from either of them."

"So you think Draven Labs killed them because they had two marks? Is that what happened to my father?"

Noah felt terrible about telling his story, as it implied Gabby should let go of hope about her father being alive.

"We aren't sure. We're trying to figure out what's happening to the two marks. We have some volunteers with legal backgrounds who have filed Freedom of Information requests for any Draven Labs data about two-marked Hoppers. To date, the government claims they can't force that information out of Draven Labs because it's a private company. And without any proof or bodies to show, there's no way to claim a crime has occurred or tie Draven Labs to the disappearances.

"The Red Zone has an unmarked area that neither the United States nor Mexico claim. Both governments maintain that these two-mark Hoppers must have died in that area during the journey. And neither government wants to do an investigation as it wouldn't benefit either to discover the truth. Because the *Civil Watch* players guard the Red Zone, we have a hard time finding anyone who wants to walk around looking for bodies or evidence out there."

Gabby started to tear up.

"Sorry, Gabby. I honor my parents' memory by keeping the Wallflowers working toward taking down Draven Labs and its entire network of creatures and surveillance drones. We want to reopen the Red Zone to let other families come through. We're going to expose Red Draven for what he is—a murderer sponsored by the American government."

"I want to help," Gabby said. A look of anger took over, and she wiped the tears from her eyes.

"We'd love for you to help, but let's get you settled into your new life here in America first, okay?" Noah suggested as they turned the corner and entered a cute neighborhood.

Gabby noticed the street name. "Orchid Street. That's a pretty name."

They passed a small park filled with kids playing on swings. She could hear them laughing, and it made her smile again.

They pulled into a driveway across from the park, which led to an average, white, ranch-style house. It was larger than her home in Mexico but modest compared to some of the mansions she had passed by on her ride here. On the porch sat a couple who appeared to be the same age as her parents, and by their skin tone and dark hair, they looked to share her Mexican heritage, too.

"That's Carlos and Mariana Rivera, your host family until we can reconnect you and your mom and get you two into your own home. You can call them your aunt and uncle if anyone asks." Noah smiled.

Peter jumped out and grabbed the little bag that held everything Gabby now owned. She slid out of the SUV and onto the freshly manicured lawn. The couple on the porch stood, smiled, and waved at her, motioning for her to come inside.

"Thank you, Noah, and you, too, Peter," Gabby said nervously. "I hope I'll get to see you again soon. I do want to help!"

"Yes, Gabby, very soon. I promise!" Noah responded. He and Peter both hugged her.

Gabby walked up to the couple, and they both surrounded her with a hug and led her inside.

"Hello, Aunt and Uncle," Gabby said.

"Bienvenida, mi sobrina," the woman replied.

"Yes, welcome to your home, Gabby," said the man. "Anything we can do to make you comfortable here, just say the word."

They entered the house, and Gabby waved goodbye to Noah

and Peter, who were watching like two parents, ensuring Gabby made it inside safely.

5: WALLFLOWER HEADQUARTERS

Noah Torres rode in the passenger seat of the white SUV as it pulled away from Gabby's new home. His driver, Peter Vieja, had become a trusted friend and coworker over the years. Noah helped Peter's mother cross the border, earning him Peter's loyalty forever. Since then, Peter pledged to do just about anything—as long as it was legal—to assist Noah and the Wallflowers with their mission.

With the flurry of activity lately, the drive back to Wallflower headquarters was Peter's first chance to talk with Noah about anything other than Wallflower missions and strategy.

"Seeing them into good homes is my favorite part of this job," Peter said with a toothy grin.

"Mine, too, Peter. Even though I don't have kids yet, I envision this is the closest thing to having a kid and releasing them into the world," Noah responded.

"Well, with all of the young Hoppers I've seen you help in just the last six months, you're like the modern-day version of Noah's Ark, rescuing immigrants and delivering them safely to a new home."

Noah shook his head, a bit embarrassed by the biblical reference. He couldn't take credit for everything the group did, and hearing himself compared to a biblical character made him uneasy. Some of the things he had to do in order to achieve his mission wouldn't sit well with Saint Peter at the gates of heaven.

"We all do the good work, Peter, every one of us. It's a group effort," Noah replied, patting Peter on the back.

"I know. You've never told me your whole life story. You've

42

mentioned parts of it, but not enough to fill in the holes about how you came to start the Wallflowers," Peter said.

"Oh boy, that might take more time than we have. I can give you the condensed version now. When we have time to finish a bottle of good rum together, I'll tell you the rest," Noah replied.

"I was a fifteen-year-old, illegal Mexican immigrant—or 'Hopper' as they call us now. I was lucky enough to be helped by a very kind American man who took me in and became like a second father to me. He sent me to a good high school and paid my way through Texas A&M for four years."

"Gig 'em, Aggies," Peter said, sticking up his thumb. "My son is now a proud Texas A&M student."

"Good bull!" Noah responded with the typical Aggie response, surprised and delighted to hear they had another thing in common.

"So I spent my time studying electrical engineering and toying around with software development. Just out of school, I started a job with a company that subcontracted to a larger robotics company that needed an extra workforce. That company was doing some impressive things with autonomous robots that worked from an early version of AI software—robots that could perform tasks and make basic decisions, all within a set of rules hard-coded into their programming. I helped test the programming under different scenarios, making sure the robots couldn't find a way around their ruleset. It wasn't until later that I realized how that company was also building the robots for military use, presumably for deadly purposes," Noah explained.

"Wait, Draven Labs? You worked for the enemy?" Peter put the pieces together.

"Trust me, I wasn't too happy with it, either. There I was, blindly working on the programming for the same creatures that probably killed my parents," Noah said.

"So you quit?" Peter asked.

"Almost. I was just working up the courage to walk into the boss's office to quit when one of my coworkers said something to me over my cubicle wall. 'Another day, another killing machine,' he had joked. That made me even more upset, but it opened my eyes to the fact that I was in a unique position. I could use my time in that company to learn everything I could about those machines.

If I had quit, I would no longer have insider access to the programming in those creatures."

"So what happened? Did they discover you?" Peter probed.

"No. Draven Labs got the government contract to manage the borders, and they grew exponentially almost overnight. They started hiring everyone away from our company—even my boss—and poached people from every other Texas robotics, engineering, and software development company, too. Ironically, I didn't receive an offer to join Draven Labs. I guess hiring someone with a Mexican name of Torres and my heritage was a red flag in their hiring process."

"Damn, I had no idea you were in the belly of the beast," Peter said. "So by not offering you a job, they unknowingly birthed the Wallflowers?" Peter asked.

"I would have created the group, regardless. I just wasn't able to get insider information anymore. So we started to develop a network of our own coders, engineers, utility workers, and other roles to obtain jobs inside Draven Labs. We even got an HR manager in there, which made hiring our people into the company much easier. We rely on these people to get us what we need now. To date, we haven't been caught. Draven Labs has been so busy making money and rubbing palms with politicians, they've been blind to the enemy gathering within. And I want to keep it that way for as long as possible."

"Brilliant!" Peter exclaimed. "So I notice you wear a silver ring on your hand. You said you had no kids yet but never mentioned you're married," Peter observed.

Noah rolled the ring around on his finger. "Oh, this is just a promise ring. I'm not married yet. It's complicated. I'll tell you that part of the story another day." Noah grinned, wanting to tell Peter about his love for Izzy but not wanting to risk compromising her position at Draven Labs.

They were pulling up to Wallflower headquarters, which gave Noah an easy out of the conversation. "I'll tell you more over that bottle of rum. Thanks for driving, Peter. I appreciate you," Noah said, patting Peter's arm as he exited the car.

"¡Viva la resistencia!" Peter responded with a fist bump. The call to battle made Noah laugh. He returned the fist bump, closed the door, and watched Peter pull away.

Wallflower headquarters was unassuming. It was an old, brick storefront with two large windows and a screen door that opened into a fully operational Mexican bakery. The name on the sign above the bakery was Pared de Harina, which translated to Wall of Flour. It made everything from bread to pastries and donuts. It was part of the Wallflowers' strategy of hiding in plain sight, but Noah often wondered if the bakery's name might have gone too far and been too obvious a clue to anyone searching for the Wallflower group. The smell of the fresh-baked churros escaping the bakery took his mind off any perceived risk.

This is not a bad place to come to work!

Noah walked through the door, ensured no customers were lurking, and proceeded past the front counter and into the kitchen. He hugged the two female bakers who had stopped kneading fresh dough on the steel counter. They blushed, happy to return a hug from Noah. To them, and many others, Noah was a hero of sorts. Melania, the larger of the two bakers, handed him a wrapped buñuelo just pulled from the fryer and sprinkled with cinnamon.

"¡Buenos dias, Senor Torres!" greeted the shorter baker, giggling, trying to hide her obvious crush on him. Noah flirted back, mostly so he wouldn't lose the free, hot buñuelos whenever he walked through their kitchen.

These two bakers were also Wallflower volunteers. They were the first wall of defense to anyone trying to find Wallflower headquarters. If anyone was dressed as if they were from a three-letter agency and had entered the bakery, the workers could simply press one of several buttons hidden around the bakery. The ladies could alert everyone in the offices underneath the bakery to get ready to abandon their posts and destroy everything, if they had to. The Wallflower volunteers in the underground headquarters could use several entrances and exits to escape the authorities if it ever came to that. The volunteers also used those tunnels to come and go from work unnoticed without having to flood the bakery entrance with daily foot traffic.

As the bakery had become a favorite of the local police department, it made it a little tricky for the women to determine who might be there to investigate the Wallflowers versus a cop who just wanted to buy a box of Mexican pastries.

Noah made small talk with the ladies, then walked into the freezer and latched the door behind him. He pulled on a shelf lined with freshly canned fruit, revealing a security door with a digital keypad lock. Two flights of steps led to a tall room that looked like a defense department control center. Ten large, digital screens covered the longest wall of the brick room, displaying live-action feeds of gamers playing the *Civil Watch* game. Five volunteer watchers sat in comfortable, Aeron chairs in front of the screens. They all turned and welcomed Noah with a smile.

Noah's team had found a way to hack into any *Civil Watch* gamer's feed anywhere in the country. Since they couldn't watch every feed, a gamer's feed only appeared on their screens when a gamer activated a creature deterrent and the Hopper being targeted was near a Wallflower escape tunnel. They could listen to the audio, although usually the audio was muted. This was because the loud music playing through the speakers surrounding the control room would make it difficult to hear anything the gamers said.

Noah didn't mind the music because these weren't employees. They were all volunteers, and as long as it didn't interfere with their mission, he allowed them little luxuries like their weird selection of new wave and rock music from way back in the '90s. It seemed to keep them more alert while doing their job anyway.

The volunteer watch team was staring at the scenes in front of them. It was like watching the worst kind of reality game show.

Their job was to look for any Hoppers who might make it near a Wallflower tunnel. If a Hopper got close enough, the watch team would be ready to temporarily black out the gamer's video feed and direct the Hopper toward an escape route. This was all made very simple. The volunteer pressed a single, red button mounted under the appropriate feed's display. That, in turn, caused a preprogrammed computer process to turn off the gamer's video and audio feed for five minutes, at which time small speakers hidden in the brush near the tunnel offered escape instructions to the Hopper. The gamer's feed would turn back on once the Hopper was out of sight. When the Hopper was in the tunnel, Noah, or another welcome party volunteer, would pick up the Hopper at the other end.

Draven Labs hadn't noticed this ingenious breach yet, but Noah was sure they would catch on to it eventually. The Wallflower team had to limit how often they cut gamers' feeds. He was sure that multiple support tickets about gamers' screens going black would eventually raise concerns at Draven Labs, especially if it were a pattern of activity happening repeatedly in the same locations in the Red Zone. It was decided that the watch team had to shake things up and could only save half of the Hoppers they wanted to because of this risk.

There were currently fifty Wallflower tunnels strategically located in the most-crossed parts of the southern Red Zone, and more were being worked on every day. A gift from a very wealthy donor, an immigrant herself, allowed the Wallflowers to purchase two tunneling machines that could rip through the ground at almost fifty feet a day.

Only Noah knew the locations of all of the tunnels, and that was to protect the entire Wallflower volunteer force. Each tunnel was assigned to a different Wallflower welcome party team as a safeguard. If a tunnel was ever discovered, and a member of that tunnel's welcome party was caught and questioned, they would never be able to divulge any of the other tunnel locations or where Wallflower headquarters was.

Noah spent today pacing across the room as he studied the screens, imagining each one of the Hoppers was one of his parents making their way through Draven's Run. Watching everything unfold in real time hurt his heart, but he knew that he was saving many from harm, which eased the pain.

At one point, his attention moved to a screen where a rather vicious scene, showing a Black Widow Spider deterrent wrapping a Hopper in its web, was revealed. The fear on the Hopper's face would probably keep Noah awake that night.

Unfortunately, his team could do nothing for this Hopper, as he had turned left at a fork in the path away from the Wallflower escape tunnel. If he had turned right, they would have been able to help. Noah made a mental note to find a way to block the path to the left for future Hoppers.

His wristwatch vibrated, startling him and allowing him to remove his eyes from the poor man's destiny. A message appeared.

"Need items from the grocery store if you don't mind—a bottle of red wine and chocolate. I should be home by six. It's been a tough day. Thanks, Roomie!"

Roomie meant this was a message from Izzy, even though he wasn't her roomie. They didn't even share a place and were never seen together in public for safety reasons. The bit about the groceries and her arrival time was their secret code to tell him to meet behind their favorite grocery store at six that evening. The red wine and chocolate were just her way of showing affection toward Noah, a way to say, "I love you." To anyone else possibly spying on Izzy's messages, they would think she was just talking to her actual roommate.

It was already 5:30, so he knew he had to get going if he was to meet her at 6 p.m. Traffic could be rough around this time.

"Wine and chocolate? Have boyfriend troubles? Just ditch him," Noah texted back.

"LOL. Yeah, I've got no time for immature boys," she responded. Noah chuckled to himself and got ready to leave.

"Keep up the good work, everyone," Noah yelled over the loud music, and they all turned to wave goodbye. Ironically, The Who's "Boris the Spider" was playing on the radio as the Hopper continued struggling with the Black Widow creature on the screen.

Sick coincidence.

Noah exited through the main tunnel, which let him out through a rusty locker door inside a dirty garage. His car, an inconspicuous, five-year-old, black Honda, sat in the darkest corner. As he drove into the alley, he wondered if the warmth he felt was out of excitement to see Izzy again or if it was just the Texas heat pushing through his air vents.

He and Izzy tried to see each other in these little meetups weekly to keep the flame alive. Every once in a while, they booked a nice hotel room far outside town to spend quality time together. They were always careful not to be followed and often tried switching meeting places. Each meeting place had its secret code.

"Grocery store" was obvious. "Going to work out" meant meeting in the parking lot near Izzy's favorite fitness facility. "Want pizza tonight?" meant to meet in the lot near Grimaldi's Pizza place. "Feed the cat" was code for running into each other in the pet food aisle at the local pet store, usually a sign of a need for a quick meeting. "Catch a movie" was Noah's favorite, as they would meet in adjacent seats in a dark movie theater at the mall. Izzy never specified what movie, but Noah had learned that he should always buy a ticket to whatever rom-com was playing. He tried to convince her that an action movie would be a better pick as the sound would conceal their conversations better, but Izzy would never agree.

They were both ready to be done with all of these secretive meetings and get on with their love life, but they had one common mission to finish before they could do that. In a few weeks, this would all be behind them, and they could see each other publicly and maybe even talk more seriously about getting married. Noah also looked forward to fighting over which movie to see together as a married couple. He was tired of rom-coms.

Noah pulled up to the grocery store, parked his car in the front lot, and turned off the engine. He spent five minutes watching all of the vehicles that had come in behind him to see where they parked. He verified that each driver exited their car and entered the store before he turned his car on again and drove around the back of the store. This routine was all just a way to ensure he wasn't being followed.

Izzy's car was already sitting in the row of parking spots behind the grocery store, and there was an open spot next to her. Noah pulled up so his window was facing hers. He rolled his window down and stared at Izzy's smiling face.

"What's this about immature boys?" he asked through the window.

"Oh, they're the best," Izzy said, smiling. They both exited their vehicles and walked to the back of their cars, where the parking lot lights couldn't reach. After a long embrace and kiss, Noah pulled back and stared Izzy in the eye.

"Getting a little sick of all this covert shit yet?" he asked.

"I'm getting tired of pretending to be so great at my job at the lab. But I can't wait to see Brock Murphy's face when his world falls apart, and there's nothing his little security team can do to stop it. How much longer before we can put our plan into action?" Izzy asked.

"We just need access to the *Civil Watch* command and control center. Once we know we can control all of the creatures along the Red Zone, the attack can happen," Noah explained.

"Well, that will take some serious computer skills, Noah. Brock Murphy has hired some of the best developers and network engineers to lock the place down," Izzy replied.

"Yes, he's hired some of MY best developers and network engineers," Noah said with an evil grin. "They even hired one of my guys to be on his security team."

"You're amazing. Remind me not to play you in a chess game." Izzy smirked.

"That might be the only game I can beat you at! I almost forgot. Do you remember that young hacker, Aiden, the boy at the local high school? The one Jack Dempsey's been training? He said the kid is a computer whiz, has a distaste for Draven Labs and the *Civil Watch* game, and has been helping him with our final phase. I'm also placing someone new into the school. It's a young girl we just helped escape over the border. Her name is Gabby, and she'll be starting school soon. I've told Jack to take her under his wing. She's also really into computers and wants to help."

"Just be careful and don't take too many risks. I don't need you getting caught this close to the finish line," Izzy cautioned.

"Don't worry. I'm not going to risk getting caught. I have some very immature things I want to do with you when we're done with all of this secret spy shit," Noah said, giggling.

"UGH! Boys. I've got no time for them." Izzy laughed. She planted a kiss on him, jumped back into her car, and sped off.

6: ROJA MEANS RED

Located between El Paso, Texas, and Las Cruces, New Mexico, the new town of Solace became the headquarters for Draven Labs and also Red Draven's home. Over four years, the city had grown from a single manufacturing warehouse to a well-fortified campus of administrative, research, and production facilities. It also boasted high-end residential housing and a town center built for its large team of employees.

Like any small town, Red designed it to have everything a resident would need to live comfortably. Retail stores, beauty salons, a medical facility, a movie theater, a grocery store, and fine restaurants lined the town's Main Street. There was even an elected town mayor, Dan Hawkins, although any power the mayor had was usurped by anything Red Draven deemed necessary for the best interest of Draven Labs. Most residents understood that Red usually hand-picked the candidates for mayor. Nobody was brave enough to risk their livelihoods and ask questions about this slight on democracy.

Having everything available on campus was one way Red kept tabs on his employees. It made it easier to spy on them and keep secrets from escaping the walls. The remote location, a single entrance and exit, and the defensive systems around town also made it simpler to protect against the hacktivists—the ones who called themselves "The Wallflowers."

Red knew the Wallflowers were solely focused on destroying Draven Labs and were against the company's mission to stop illegal immigration altogether. The group was known to recruit a mix of computer hackers and organized protesters who were sympathetic to "those damn Hoppers trying to invade our country," as Red would often repeat in his press events.

Originally born on American soil as Roja Diaz, he legally changed his name to Red Draven when he had turned eighteen. His new last name, Draven, was a modernization of the name Dræfend, which means "hunter," and was a common surname in Scotland. The name sounded less Latino and would allow him to avoid any uncomfortable questions about his parents and his family's cultural ties to Mexico.

One would think that his family's migration across the border forty-five years ago would foster empathy for the Hoppers, but instead, Red despised them. He had a hatred toward them.

In his mind, these Hoppers were nothing like his parents, refugees looking for a better life, trying to become good American citizens. He saw them as a mix of terrorists, drug runners, and sex trade smugglers intent on ruining the perfect world he'd built for himself inside this new America.

His parents had done everything the right way. They assimilated into American life and learned English and all they could about America's history and culture. After years of living in Texas, they passed the US Citizenship test and became naturalized citizens. It was a proud day for Red, the day he could call his parents fellow Americans.

Five years into their new lives as American citizens, an illegal immigrant smuggling drugs over the border had killed them.

He remembered the day as if it were yesterday. He was a high school senior studying at the kitchen table. The yellow Post-it Note on the refrigerator let him know his parents would be home soon.

Stopping at the market for groceries. Getting your favorite from Rosita's Taqueria. Los quiero. Mamá y Papá.

Rosita's made the best Enchiladas Verdes, his favorite meal. Rosita was a family friend who owned a small food stand selling homemade takeout meals in the market. Anytime they wanted authentic Mexican takeout, it had to be from Rosita's.

When there was a knock at the door, he assumed it was his parents. He opened the door to find two El Paso police officers holding their hats, staring at the ground somberly.

"Is this the home of Maria and Carmen Diaz?" one of them

asked.

"Yes. What can I do for you?"

"Well, we regret to inform you that there was an accident—or rather an incident—outside the Mexican food market. It appears to have been a carjacking. Your parents were both shot and are deceased. We need someone from the family to come with us to the morgue to identify the bodies."

Red remembered how matter-of-fact they were when they said it as if it were an everyday occurrence in the area. The request made him realize no one else was left in his world. And there was no one to perform the task of identifying the bodies other than him. Without a car, he had to endure the long, silent ride in the back of their squad car to get to the morgue. It was the longest ride of his life.

The scene at the morgue, seeing both parents shot in the head, forever changed his life. One week later, the police had captured a suspect who confessed to the killings and blamed it on the cartel, claiming they had forced him to steal cars for drug runs across the border.

Red sat through every court hearing, just sitting in a corner, staring at the man and thinking of ways he could get revenge. At eighteen years old, Red had neither the money to hire a hit man nor the means to do the killing himself. The convicted felon was eventually sentenced to life in prison and placed in the El Paso Federal Penitentiary, well out of Red's reach. To Red's surprise, and only two weeks into the man's sentence, he learned the cartel had the man killed in his sleep, saving Red the trouble and taking away the pleasure of doing it himself.

Red crossed his arms and fell back into the soft, leather chair facing the window, enjoying a panoramic view of Solace. It was his throne, and he enjoyed peering out over the empire he had built since his parents left this world.

His mind retraced his successes over the last few years.

Draven Labs had become the sole supplier of many of the government's defensive systems protecting the homeland through a strategic partnership with Senator Stanwell, two other longtime senators, and some backroom deals.

It was well known that President Ferris was elected because

Red had backed his campaign with a significant contribution from Draven Labs, as well as his very vocal public support. Once elected, President Ferris was more than happy to return the favor by giving Red the contract to guard the border and whatever he needed both financially and politically to keep the country safe. No other company in the States could do what Draven Labs could, so the competition for the contract was non-existent.

The three senators endorsing Draven Labs had often bragged about the amount of money saved by using its technology instead of traditional border patrol agents. It had been a central talking point at each of their reelection rallies. When they'd added up the cost of salaries, benefits, pensions, and healthcare for the 25,000 border patrol agents who used to be employed, they claimed to have saved the US taxpayers over four billion dollars a year by using Draven Labs. It always won them the votes they needed.

Red's relationship with the president had been symbiotic as the public optics and cost savings made President Ferris look strong as a protector and fiscally responsible. Government deficits had started to recede for the first time in almost thirty years. The savings meant more money was freed up for the senators and the president to spend on their other political endeavors and policy changes.

With Draven Labs having garnered many successes to date, Red knew it would be tough for any future president to be elected without his company's support. His only threat was from the press and a small group of liberal senators who thought he had been given too much power and influence in the national defense realm. There was talk among those senators about pulling Draven Labs into the fold of the US government so they could have some insight into the company's operations.

Thinking about that scenario made Red laugh out loud. There was no way he would allow himself, or his company, to be controlled by a bunch of power-hungry, spineless senators. He would move his company to another country if it ever came to that.

This country would slip back to its old ways quickly. *Fucking liberals.*

Money was only half of his mission. He was equally interested in stopping all illegal immigration into the United States.

The yearly subsidies Draven Labs received from the government to run the defensive systems were quickly being rivaled by another successful product Draven Labs had introduced—a video game he had named *Civil Watch*. It was a game intended to stop illegal immigration.

The idea for that software and gamification of the border defenses was conceived over a bottle of ten-year-old, Basil Hayden Bourbon he was sharing with his friend and business partner, Brock Murphy.

Red had met Brock at a robotics camp for kids. Brock had stepped in to protect Red from some rich, white kids who noticed Red's skin color was just a bit darker than theirs. Red remembered thinking how ironic it was that a red-headed, Irish American, the whitest kid there, stood up for the darker-skinned kid with Mexican parents.

Brock knew Red back when he was named Roja, and he was the only person who could get away with calling Red by that birth name today. Anyone else would be fired or defriended on the spot.

However, Brock was careful not to call Red by his real name whenever he was around other people, as he knew Red didn't want anyone to know his parents were immigrants.

Brock became Red's best friend and was now a partner, adviser, and head of security for Draven Labs. They shared the same viewpoints. They considered themselves true patriots and nationalists, protecting their country from invaders. Red trusted Brock with his life and all of his secrets, and Brock was as loyal a friend and partner as they came. Brock's loyalty was emboldened by a hefty fortune he'd earned when Draven Labs won the border patrol contract after the election.

The idea for the *Civil Watch* game started when Red and Brock were reminiscing about how they used to play video games together as kids, sometimes until the sun came up. First-person shooter and warfare simulation games were their staples, and their friends spent endless nights laughing while playing them.

Politics entered a liquor-fueled jaunt down memory lane, and Brock brought up the memory of how he had lost his warehouse job to illegal immigrants twenty-five years earlier. He ranted about how mentally damaging it was to learn that the company he had been loyal to for over two years decided to save some money by hiring "illegals." Although there were systems in place to verify employment status and citizenship, the company ignored them, and the local authorities were "spineless turds who wouldn't enforce the laws."

Red and Brock had thought about ways to stop that practice and return the jobs to the American citizens. Aside from some rather dark ideas, Red had offered an idea that made him and Brock put down their drinks and start more serious conversations.

"We should create a video game where players can watch the border through cameras and collect bounties by spotting illegal immigrants as they try to cross. It would make it easier and cheaper than hiring more border patrol agents," Red said.

Brock had always been quite creative but a bit more aggressive and offered his spin on the idea. "Just spot them? How about we create machines with weapons so they can permanently stop them? Do you know what I mean? Players can pay us to add better weapons to their arsenal. For every immigrant they kill, they earn money. I'd pay big money to play that version!"

Red calmed Brock down and pulled him back to reality. "We can't just go around killing people, Brock. That would never fly with the softies out there. We'd have to find a way to be 'ethical' about this. Maybe we make machines that stun the crossers long enough for the border patrol agents to catch them?"

That idea, and several nights of brainstorming, had spawned the idea behind the *Civil Watch* online game. Once Red and Brock had calculated the monetary returns that could be generated from the idea, Red decided to start a new software development division within Draven Labs to build the prototype. It didn't take long for the idea to take hold. This new software division was integrated with the manufacturing and electronics divisions to connect the game to the mechanical creature deterrents.

Many of the deterrents had already been designed to be remotely controlled by a person. It was just a matter of rerouting those connections through a secure network and adding the permission levels to allow the *Civil Watch* game subscribers around the country to control the creatures.

The first creature was pretty basic and didn't have anywhere near the state-of-the-art robotics Draven Labs had now, but the prototype had worked well enough to prove to a few senators that the idea could work. The senators had provided some private financial backing and support to get the idea moving.

The game concept was a huge success, and Red and Brock continued improving it ever since.

Red's thoughts snapped back to what Draven Labs was today.

Even with all his success, he couldn't get his mind past the one big thorn in his side—the Wallflowers. The activist group had tried to ruin his success ever since his company was awarded the government contract. They had evaded the authorities at every turn and seemed to be backed by bright, technical, motivated people. They'd hacked into his security systems more than once, destroyed at least five turrets, and had even dug tunnels to help the Hoppers avoid capture.

The closest the authorities ever got to the group was when they had captured two men digging one of the tunnels for the Wallflowers. Both men got misdirected and just happened to pop up in the middle of a parking lot across from a police cruiser, watching for speeders on the road closest to the border.

The two men were captured and interrogated but could only identify their employer as a "Latino man who spoke with them on the phone and offered them the job." They couldn't provide a name and had never met with the man in person. They said they had each been paid three thousand dollars in cash and would receive an additional three thousand dollars once the tunnel was completed. The first payment had been delivered to them under a bench in a community park, and the final payment would be dropped off at a location that would be texted to them upon completion of the job. The police could never identify their employer, and the phone number was not traceable.

Because the two men had never made it across the border with the tunnel, they could only be booked with destruction of property and in violation of building zoning laws. They were released on bond against Red's demand to punish them with jail time.

Red's watch alerted him to someone at the door. With a tap on his watch, the door to the office slid open with a soft hiss of air.

He didn't turn around as he knew who was coming to visit. It was a morning ritual.

"Roja, it looks like a nice, hot summer day out there, eh?" Brock Murphy said sarcastically in a slight Irish accent.

A smile creased Red's face. "Oh yeah, it's another hot one … but it's a dry heat," he said, chuckling as the air conditioning vent sent a blast of cold air across his face. Solace was always hot and humid, and air conditioners were constantly installed or replaced across town to keep its residents happy and comfortable.

"Numbers are in. The new *Civil Watch* upgrade is killing it," Brock announced proudly. "The analytics department said subscriptions have increased by 20 percent. Subscribers are jumping at the chance to be a part of the new release, and we have a queue of prospective gamers waiting for spots to fill."

"Have the strategy team look into areas along the Red Zone that are getting more active, and have them build some more turrets there," Red directed. "Let's create spots for these new subscribers to get involved. Each is worth at least $480 annually, plus any upgrade costs and merch they buy. Our little army needs as many participants as possible."

Brock typed a short message on a handheld device and hit the send button hard enough for Red to hear the tap. "Done! They'll get started on it this morning."

Red noticed Brock was being hesitant about something else.

"What is it, Brock? Spit it out," Red ordered.

"Well, we had another casualty with the Jellyfish, and someone may have leaked it to the press. It appears there's a rumor circulating that we had a Hopper drown after an electrical shock," Brock said nervously.

"A rumor? That's all? Then we must be ready if this rumor becomes more than that. What the hell, Brock? I thought research and development had worked out the kinks on that machine. They were supposed to add flotation devices to prevent that, right?"

"They did, but watching the playback video we retrieved from the Jellyfish, it looks as though the Hopper was struggling so much, he tore one of the flotation balloons while trying to get free."

"Well, that seems like an easy fix, doesn't it? We pay these designers and engineers good money to think through and correct these problems before they become an issue. Didn't they do any testing before releasing it into the field?" Red asked, closing his eyes and rubbing his temples.

"They claim to have tested it on a willing intern, but I guess the intern was a good swimmer and didn't struggle as much as the Hopper did."

"Get Izzy involved in the fix, and I'll have our PR team prepare press releases to blame it on the Hopper and Mexico's lack of border enforcement if it becomes more than just a rumor. Did you delete any video evidence? I assume a DLED drone retrieved the body and returned it to central processing?"

"I'll delete the video now. I thought you'd want to see it first," Brock offered.

"Not today," Red replied. "I have enough excitement planned already."

Brock clicked on the keyboard of his handheld device again. "All video evidence is gone. The other Hoppers crossing with him just think he was unconscious when he got picked up, so they don't know he died. Someone from processing reported the death to the media, but HR has already fired them, reminding them of the hefty cost of breaking their non-disclosure agreement with us. Our security team also learned this Hopper was a drinker and couldn't swim, so we can always say his death was a result of the alcohol in his system."

"Let's run with that. We can't afford any more issues like this. We have prospective clients coming in from around the world today to get a preview of our new line of deterrents and drones. I had to extend an invite to Senator Stanwell, too. If he gets a whiff of any of this, we'll have to deal with him and his lackeys and possibly added government oversight," Red stressed.

"I'll personally talk with R&D to ensure they do more elaborate testing on new deterrents before they're put into production."

Brock turned and headed for the door.

"Oh, I have a new bottle of bourbon waiting to be shared later tonight if you're interested. And Chef Lamond is cooking up his chipotle-crusted, barbeque rib dish again," Red yelled as he neared the exit.

"Sounds like I'll be enjoying some great food and drink tonight. Usual time?"

"Be here at 7 p.m., and don't be a minute late or I'll eat your share of the ribs," Red threatened.

The door hissed shut, and Red slumped back into his comfortable chair.

I HATE this part of the job, having to answer to people.

He touched his watch, and someone responded right away.

"Mr. Draven, good morning!" said a soft, female voice on the other end.

"Good morning, Maeve. Can you get the PR team up to my office right away?"

"Yes, sir," Maeve replied. A few electronic beeps after her reply revealed that Maeve was an artificial intelligence assistant and not a human being on the other end.

Red moved across the room to a closet door almost invisible to the naked eye. You would never notice it if you didn't know it was there. A firm push against the door caused it to pop open, exposing a small wardrobe room. The lights clicked on automatically, revealing a row of different-colored suits, pressed dress shirts, ties of every color, polished shoes, expensive watches, and more. Red grabbed his blue suit and a simple, white dress shirt. He decided today was just too hot for a tie.

Just as he finished dressing, his watch alerted him to visitors at the office door. He stepped out of the closet and closed the door.

"Get in here," he said to his watch, and the door to the office opened.

The small team of public relations people marched in and knew to sit in their spots at a large conference table, each of them silent, not wanting to draw any attention to themselves.

"Who's lead on this recent fiasco with the Jellyfish?" Red asked the sharply dressed blonde woman in the seat next to him.

She shifted in her seat and started to speak. Her voice cracked.

"Ahem. Sorry about that. It's a bit dusty outside today," she said, clearing her throat with a slight cough. "I'm taking the lead. This one should be easy. Brock explained the situation to us earlier, and it seems this Hopper drowned while entering the Rio Grande near the Mexican side of the river. We can just tell the press the truth. We explain that the Hopper ignored the signs and tried crossing a river without knowing how to swim."

"And do we know that for a fact? He couldn't swim?"

"I had our contact in Mexico anonymously question some of the Hopper's close friends, and they confirmed he was deathly afraid of water. The closest thing to water he'd ever seen was alcohol at the bottom of a bottle."

"So we can stick with the story that he was drunk and couldn't swim. And there are only rumors of his death? No evidence?" Red queried.

"The other crossers we had caught and questioned thought he was unconscious, not dead. But our insider in the press caught wind that a reporter was going to try and investigate for a story."

"Have all the press materials with that information ready to go, just in case we have to react quickly. Hopefully, it just stays a rumor. Check with HR to ensure ALL of our employees have signed non-disclosure and confidentiality agreements, from the top to the bottom. Even that guy I saw outside cleaning the windows should have one on file," Red directed.

"Understood, sir," she replied, gathering her papers. "We're on it."

7: THE FIXER

Izzy Davis swiped through some of the marketing department's newest creature designs on her screen. The graphics team modeled half of the creature in the traditional, white-line drawing on a dark-blue background. They rendered the other half to look like the actual creature, complete with colors and skin texture. Each one showcased some of the mechanical features conceived by the engineers, along with the colors and textures applied by the design team. The colors and material renderings gave the creatures realistic-looking characteristics. Any one of the drawings could have been framed and hung in some cool art exhibit in any big city.

Each sketch listed some of the creature's proposed features. Izzy chuckled at a few of them, knowing Mr. Draven would throw them into a trash can without hesitation. When she landed on the ladybug sketch, she stopped scrolling and turned away from the screen, laughing.

Yeah, here comes the scary ladybug. Run for your life.

She didn't hold it against the designers or the engineers. When Mr. Draven thought up a theme for the next set of creatures he wanted, it became quite challenging to develop new creatures that fit into that theme and yet still instilled the terror he desired. With the latest insect theme, the engineers and designers had already gone through the scariest of the creatures. They had started diving into the remainder of the species—the lovable group of insects.

But a ladybug? What a waste of everyone's time.

Izzy instantly felt a twinge of hypocrisy and sadness, almost forgetting that she shouldn't be sad about their bad ideas. She should be celebrating them, as she was secretly working for the

Wallflowers. A lousy idea meant one less creature to put into the Red Zone, and one less Hopper would suffer the same fate as many others trying to get into the United States. She was careful never to give anyone at Draven Labs a reason to suspect her of being a mole for the organization.

Every so often, Izzy had to remind herself of her true mission during her day-to-day routine. She had worked her way into Draven Labs to help take it down. The most challenging part of the job was offering ideas that would gain her credibility and more access to Draven's plans while secretly finding ways the Wallflowers could sabotage the development of the same technologies across the Red Zone.

Izzy had joined the Wallflowers after literally bumping into its founder, Noah, at a coffee shop. When she looked at the coffee dripping down the front of his stark-white, dress shirt and followed the stain up to his hazel eyes, she instantly fell in love with him. His fashionable bohemian wardrobe, ultra-white teeth, well-shaped beard, and long ponytail convinced her he must be one of those models from a *GQ* magazine.

Noah was equally impressed with Izzy. He could tell she was smart and had a soft side as she tried to wipe off his shirt and then offered to get it dry-cleaned. Noah had turned down her offer in exchange for agreeing to a dinner date.

After six months of dating, Noah revealed his secret to Izzy— he was the founder of the Wallflowers. He explained that his work was focused solely on taking down Red Draven and his company's virtual wall guarding the Red Zone and stopping illegal immigration at the borders.

From day one, Izzy had been very open about her political views with Noah, and they shared the same views on immigration. Her soft spot for immigrants came from being the daughter of immigrants from Hungary. She announced her feelings about the border and immigration policies on her first date with Noah. The six months Noah waited to tell Izzy about his involvement in that fight wasn't necessary, at least not in Izzy's mind. But she understood his caution because the media was flooding the nightly news with false stories about the things the Wallflowers had supposedly done … all untrue.

Once she'd joined the Wallflowers, Izzy realized just how "in the pocket" of Draven Labs the media had become. She knew the press spread false stories about the Wallflowers to increase viewership and make the news anchors look more exciting and pertinent. Izzy was sure the news channels were also getting monetary kickbacks to portray Draven Labs in a good light.

The media's involvement made Izzy furious and was one of the reasons she had volunteered to join the Wallflowers and work her way into the Draven Labs organization. She'd graduated from Texas A&M and worked two internships, then worked full-time as an electrical and mechanical engineer for a robotics company. That combination of skills assured she would be a shoo-in for any job inside Draven Labs.

Noah knew Izzy had the smarts and experience to get into the company and the will to take it down. The only downside was that she would have to sacrifice a public relationship with him for as long as necessary just to avoid any chance of anyone connecting her to him and the Wallflower organization. They couldn't risk Izzy being seen publicly with Noah or any of the others in the secretive group, just in case one of Red Draven's many spies happened to discover their identity.

Izzy was staring at the floor, thinking about all the lame insects that might be coming from the design team soon. Aphids, inchworms, and potato bugs ran through her mind as possibilities.

"Izzy, did you hear me?" a voice boomed from the doorway. Izzy jumped a bit, not realizing her coworker had been standing there, talking to her for the last minute. He laughed when he realized he had scared her out of deep thought.

"What, did that ladybug put the fear of God in you?" Scott asked, pointing at her screen.

"Yeah, that's how I envision dying. A swarm of cute ladybugs chewing away at me," Izzy responded sarcastically. "These sketches from the design team are getting worse!"

Scott leaned farther into the doorway. "Maybe that's why Draven called a meeting of all of R&D. We need to get to the conference hall, PRONTO. He probably wants to tell us he is switching the theme to plants next."

Izzy shook her head. "Great! So it's going to be deadly

dandelions and killer kale to go with these lethal ladybugs."

"I'd ROOT for any plant ideas over the latest designs," Scott said as he raised his coffee and exited the doorway. His pun wasn't lost on Izzy. Scott's humor made Izzy think about how much she liked the people she worked with. She would miss them when she finished her part in taking down the company.

Izzy grabbed her clipboard, which contained a list of the latest broken deterrents, drones, and equipment, along with a long checklist of malfunctions. It was her job to try and figure out how to fix the issues that popped up once the creatures were tested in the field. She was good at her job but didn't do it to impress Draven. If she could prevent Hoppers from getting hurt by some creature's malfunction or a faulty piece of equipment, she was making her small contribution in this war.

She walked down to the large auditorium, which was packed and buzzing with many different conversations. Everyone discussed why they thought this impromptu meeting was taking place. After all, Draven Labs was losing a fortune in salaries for these expensive employees for each minute that passed.

As Izzy panned the room, she mentally noted how funny it was that the designers sat on one side of the room and the engineers on the other. It was common knowledge that the left and right brains didn't mingle, or at least that was the line they seemed to toe. Izzy decided to sit on a step in the aisle between the two groups, opting not to side with one group or the other. This diplomatic nature helped her rise quickly in the ranks since she had joined the company.

Draven always entered the room five minutes after everyone had settled, and Brock ensured there was silence ahead of his onstage appearance. Draven wasn't one for niceties and always just got right to the point. He showed no emotion when he spoke and never offered praise toward any individual in the R&D group, even with their many successes.

"Okay, people. We have a new problem we need to figure out. I'm bringing you all here to confirm that you understand what is happening and hope your future designs don't exhibit the same stupidity. Our government sponsors are watching us closely, and we can't afford any slipups with our tech. Jellyfish team, stand up," Draven commanded sternly.

It took a few scared glances between them, but anyone who worked even tangentially on the Jellyfish project eventually stood up. Most of the core team congregated in the back corner of the room. A spotlight swung to illuminate the entire group, almost on cue. It was evident to everyone that this team had heard of a problem and anticipated being called out.

Izzy thought it was funny that they believed it safer to sit as a significant group versus dispersing as individuals around the room. That was a stupid move. *Now all eyes can focus on your entire group, you idiots.*

"Who's the project lead on this creature?" Draven yelled to the back of the room while walking to the front of the stage to get out from under the bright stage lights. He lifted his chin, awaiting an answer.

"I am, sir," came a mousy, female voice from a small woman standing in the middle of the group. Izzy could tell by the voice that it was the department engineering lead, Dr. Linnea Sorensen, someone she had worked with quite closely over the last few months. Anyone standing near her took a visible step away from her.

Poor Linnea. They pushed the injured animal right into the lion's path. That's loyalty for you.

"What on God's damned earth did you think would happen when you shock a man into unconsciousness in the middle of the water with a one-hundred-fifty-pound metal creature clinging to his body? Have you ever heard of the term 'dead weight'?" Draven challenged, not expecting an answer.

The woman shot her head down in shame, now realizing she may have someone's death squarely on her shoulders.

Draven kept berating her. "We're going to get a lot of flak for this mistake. I expect you to do your job. Ms. Sorensen, in the future, please think through all possible scenarios and perform every test available in the lab. Heck, test it on one of your coworkers if you have to. That goes for all of you!" he yelled.

Some coworkers took one more step away from a trembling Ms. Sorensen.

"I don't care what it takes. Just get these things working to the point where they are scary but not deadly. Got it?"

Dr. Sorensen nodded and slinked back down into her seat. The others quickly shifted their bodies and got their faces out of the spotlight.

During the entire public scolding, Izzy jotted some notes on her clipboard. She was busy adding the Jellyfish deterrent to what she coined her list of "creature misfeatures."

Draven noticed Izzy sitting dead-center in the aisle, writing away. She was the only one in the room who chose to sit in the aisle and did not appear to pay much attention to him.

"Miss Davis, are you on top of this?" he asked her.

"Yes, sir, Mr. Draven. I already have some ideas," Izzy replied confidently, holding up her clipboard.

Draven winked at her, turned in place, and rushed through a door and offstage.

There was an audible sigh of relief from many sitting in the audience, fearing their work would be scrutinized next.

Izzy looked over and noticed Linnea was now sobbing into her hands. Her coworkers, who had so quickly deserted her earlier, had come to her rescue, offering comforting words and patting her on the back.

She had never been scared of Mr. Draven like the rest of these timid souls. Probably because Izzy did not care much about his approval, the company's mission, or their success. After all, her job was to sink the company eventually, so to her, it didn't matter what happened. Any brown-nosing was a means to an end and nothing more. She was more scared of disappointing Noah and hurting the mission of the Wallflowers, and that's what kept her doing her job so well.

Izzy walked over toward Dr. Sorensen and her team and interrupted the sobbing and consoling. "Linnea, the team working on the new water series deterrents have perfected a flotation system that we could probably retrofit onto the Jellyfish. We should take care of that problem fairly quickly. Come to my office around 4 p.m., and we can review the schematics. We'll get you squared away in no time."

Linnea mouthed a thank you between sobs. Izzy could tell the coworkers liked Linnea, just not enough to sacrifice their careers by standing up to Mr. Draven. Izzy could tell they were mad about how he had called out Linnea—in front of everyone. While watching the angry expressions on some of their faces, Izzy wondered how many of those coworkers she could turn against Draven when the time came. But trying to do so now could risk everything she and Noah had achieved.

"What a dickhead," Scott whispered in Izzy's ear, startling her for the second time today. She turned to find Scott shaking his head.

"You need to stop scaring me like that, Scott. Otherwise, I'll test the Jellyfish on you after we make the next round of improvements."

"You joke, but I hear Draven's using real volunteers to show off our creatures at today's big presentation."

"What big presentation?"

"Come on, seriously? Do you not log into the intranet and read the headlines in the morning?" Scott asked.

"No, Scott. I'm too busy fixing all the broken shit around here. What presentation?"

"Draven's putting on a massive show-and-tell today. Some of the most expensive cars I've ever seen have been pulling into the visitor lot, and I hear some important people are walking around in the main lobby. Security around here has been on edge since yesterday. Kings, ambassadors, and even one of our senators are in attendance."

"Well, I hope they don't go and show off the fuckin' Jellyfish today!" Izzy laughed.

"Mostly the new insect line, I hear."

"Catch you later, Scott. I have to see this firsthand," Izzy said as she started toward the lobby.

"Good luck getting in there. Brock Murphy is being a big dick on campus and turning away all employees."

Izzy held up her badge. "This hall pass gets me anywhere and everywhere, compliments of Mr. Draven himself."

"Must be nice! Grab me some crab legs and caviar from the buffet on your way back up here, then."

8: SHOW-AND-TELL

The gate entering Solace was abnormally busy for ten o'clock in the morning, and the makes of the cars entering were much different from every other day. Anyone not chauffeured in a stretch limo was driving a high-end sports car or a decked-out, top-of-the-line SUV. Red Draven had invited potential clients from almost every corner of the world—Saudi Arabia, Israel, China, Russia, and even North Korea.

Knowing this made Senator Stanwell very nervous as he sat in his generic-looking, government-issued, electric car, watching a line of people pull into the visitor parking lot. He had arrived early and used the time to keep President Ferris updated on his visit to Draven Labs.

"Our friend appears to have invited every country to this shindig. It starts at ten thirty. I feel as though I'm at a red-carpet event in Dubai," Senator Stanwell told the president.

"Well, just take notes of who's there and what Draven's showing them, and get back to me before the end of the day. The last thing I want is for Mr. Draven to begin taking the technology we're paying him to develop and selling it to all of our enemies," President Ferris replied.

"I think it's obvious he's already doing that, judging by the guests I've seen. I don't think these types are flying in to see run-of-the-mill drone technologies they can buy at their local Weapons-R-Us warehouses. They're here for the good stuff, Mr. President," Stanwell said, peering out through his tinted window.

The heat was sweltering, especially for this early in the morning, and his air conditioning was on full blast, making it difficult to hear the conversation over the secure line. The car couldn't keep up with the heat, and Stanwell was sweating through his shirt.

"So what's Draven got planned? Did he tell you?" the president asked.

"No clue, sir. It looks as if he's pulled out all of the stops for this event, though. He invited me but didn't give me any clue as to what he's up to."

"Well, smile and try to talk with him at some point. We must ensure he knows where the American government stands regarding weapons technology deals with other countries. I know he's running a private company, but he needs to understand that his biggest client has teeth that can chew right through the small monopoly he has going on. His contract with our country should be enough to overstuff his wallet," said the president.

"I don't think Draven knows what a wallet is. People like him think in terms of dump trucks full of money. BIG dump trucks." Stanwell laughed.

"Well, we may need to exert a little pressure on him to get him to realize he should be happy with the dump truck he's currently driving," the president remarked. "This could become an issue of national security, allowing me to take control of everything he owns. Call me after eight o'clock tonight. I'm having dinner with the prime minister of Canada."

"What's Prime Minister Bouchard complaining about now?" Stanwell asked.

"Seems he's not too happy about some Canadians missing on our northern border. Hell, I can't help it if his constituents are tired of waiting two years to get an x-ray and want to leave Canada for our country. He knows it's just as illegal for the northern Hoppers to come over as it is for those crossing on our southern border. We can't be held responsible when they fall into a ravine or drown in some river as they try to cross illegally."

"Good luck with that. I'm not sure which of us got the short end of the stick today, sir." Stanwell laughed.

"Want to trade?" the president joked.

"I'd rather stare at Draven's mechanical creatures and watch all these men wearing ghutras and kanduras as they fight over who gets one first. I can't wait to see how quickly they pull out their checkbooks at today's event," Stanwell commented.

"Him selling equipment is what we need to avoid. Fill me in later."

"Yes, Mr. President."

Stanwell stepped out of the car, and sweat started dripping down his back. He opted to carry his suit jacket over his shoulder until he passed the metal detectors and guard detail in front of the air-conditioned building.

Screw formalities, it's fucking hot.

Even though Senator Stanwell had been here many times before, the visitor entrance to Draven Labs still made an impression on him. A huge, stainless-steel frame held green-tinted windows that surrounded an expansive, biophilic lobby, combining nature and an industrial look. The room was large enough to showcase two natural environments. There were tropical plants and palm trees on one side and a desert environment with sand and cacti on the other. With today's heat, he wished Draven had built out an Arctic environment somewhere, but no such luck. Red Draven had once told him the two environments represented the paradise of America on one side and the dangers of the Red Zone on the other.

Today, Draven caused a stir with a Dragonfly drone programmed to fly in and out of the trees on the tropical side, and one of his big, metal, red Zombie Ant creatures foraging around a massive cactus on the desert side.

Stanwell watched as one of the Asian visitors walked up to the edge of the desert exhibit to take a photo of the Zombie Ant creature. Just as the man leaned forward to take a picture, the Zombie Ant raised up onto its hind legs and snapped at him. The man dropped his phone, fell backward, and scooted back to his group, who all laughed at him. Stanwell was so focused on the man's terror that he didn't notice the beautiful lady beside him.

"Senator Stanwell?" she said, startling him.

"Holy fuck!" Stanwell yelled.

"Sorry about that. I'm Melissa Umbridge, Mr. Draven's press liaison. Mr. Draven asked me to personally escort you to your seat."

71

"Oh, thank you. Nice to meet you," Stanwell replied, following her but still watching the Asian men fighting over who was going to risk getting close enough to the Zombie Ant to grab their friend's phone.

She led him into an auditorium surrounded by a 360-degree, floor-to-ceiling, digital screen. An animated Draven Labs' logo flew around the room every so often. Many guests were already seated, and Ms. Umbridge led him to a seat she had reserved in the front row. She handed him a glass of champagne she grabbed from one of the many servers walking by.

"A little early in the morning for champagne, isn't it?" he asked.

"It'll calm your nerves!" She smiled and walked toward a room offstage.

Just as he took his seat, the lights dimmed twice.

Any remaining guests flooded in from the lobby and claimed their assigned seats just as the room went dark.

A red sunrise appeared on the digital screens, rising from the floor and exposing a desert scene of cacti and rock outcroppings surrounding the room. It was as if the crowd were sitting in the expansive desert in the Red Zone. A booming narration filled the room.

"Without sovereignty, a nation cannot exist. Without borders, it cannot be defined or protected. Draven Labs has become the uncontested leader in software and technologies that can help you guard your borders every minute of every hour of every day. Imagine a border guarded by the most terrifying machines, engineered to mimic the animals and insects of the natural world, stalking intruders night and day."

The digital screens transitioned the daytime desert scene into nighttime. The grass in the scene was waving as the surround sound system mimicked the wind blowing around the room. Warm air streamed into the room to add to the effect.

Faint, metallic, clicking sounds echoed, growing louder and sounding as if they were coming from all directions.

The tips of spindly, metal legs suddenly appeared over the rock outcroppings and in between cacti looking so realistic, the crowd leaned in toward the center of the room to escape whatever was attached to them. Draven's terrifying creatures, of all shapes and sizes, crawled over the rocks and toward the crowd, advancing from every direction on the screens around the room.

As soon as they appeared to be close enough to touch the audience, the screens went black, but the sound of the wind, the hot air, and clicking noises continued. Glowing, red eyes were visible around the room, slowly fading in and out. Some looked as though they were blinking. In the middle of the auditorium, where there were aisles between the rows of seats, pairs of gleaming, red eyes materialized as if the creatures had entered the room and were now walking down the aisles.

"Very cool," Stanwell said to himself.

Then the room went completely dark, the hot air stopped blowing, and everything went silent for ten seconds.

Stanwell could hear his heart beating out of his chest, along with the hearts of the two guests sitting next to him.

A bright beam of red light snapped on, causing a few people in the audience to scream. The light illuminated a spot on center stage, and Red Draven stepped into it. He stared at the crowd, smiling. The lights in the room slowly came up, and the red light disappeared. You could hear a mix of relief and what Stanwell only guessed was swearing in many different languages coming from around the room.

He noticed Brock Murphy and another security guard standing on either side of the stage, surveying the room for threats to Mr. Draven. They were dressed in black and occasionally touched their earpieces with one hand, whispering into their invisible microphones.

"Scary stuff, isn't it?" Draven asked as he strolled across the stage, pointing at the screen circling the room.

"Do you think you'd risk coming face-to-face with these horrors to make it across a border? Imagine if you were out in the desert, and this was all real, those creatures hunting you," he said, pointing offstage to his left and right.

On cue, an eight-foot, metal, mechanical Beetle crawled from Draven's left onto the stage. Its legs sounded like scissor blades slicing as the creature performed perfectly choreographed movements.

The crowd clapped when it appeared.

Then, a large, six-foot-tall, Black Widow Spider entered from the right side of the stage. The creatures moved like insects, turning their heads to take in their surroundings as they proceeded toward Draven. They opened and closed their pincers as they advanced.

Draven lowered his arms and pointed at two spots on either side of his body. The Beetle and Black Widow changed position to face the crowd, stopping exactly where he pointed. Both stood up on their hind legs and exposed their abdomens as if in an attack position.

"I'd like to introduce you to some of my friends. Beautiful beasts, aren't they?" he announced, admiring his creatures from head to toe.

"We've brought you all here today to observe what Draven Labs has done with the latest technologies. You'll see new evolutions in artificial intelligence, cutting-edge surveillance systems, and autonomous, robotic creatures like my friends here. These creatures have highly advanced transmission systems engineered to traverse and withstand almost any terrain. They can charge themselves with an electric charge or even while they sit under the sun. These creatures have learned to use a Hive mentality, talking to each other and working together to develop better strategies as a team. Under your chairs, you'll find a packet highlighting these latest inventions."

Everyone appeared excited to pull their packets from beneath their chairs. Each was wrapped in a reflective, lime-green, foil cover resembling the metal skin of the Beetle at the front of the room. The front had an embossed Draven Labs' logo stamped into it. Inside were renderings and specifications of the creatures recently released, along with details about the DLED drones and turret designs.

Stanwell quickly rifled through the papers to see if he could find a price list or order form. He let out a sigh of relief when he found none. But he knew that Draven wasn't spending this kind of money on a show just for his ego. He knew he was doing it to court a few new clients with much larger dump trucks of money than his government could offer.

The Beetle and Black Widow Spider exited as the guests started to review their packets. Draven motioned to Melissa Umbridge, who eagerly awaited her cue.

"Dr. Umbridge, will you please walk them through some demonstrations to reveal some of the other creatures in action?" He turned to the crowd again. "We'll do a Q&A session and then have lunch afterward. I promise there will be no creatures around while we eat," he announced, exiting through a back door.

Everyone laughed, and Melissa Umbridge moved to the center of the stage.

Brock Murphy followed Mr. Draven, leaving the other security guard to watch the room.

Izzy Davis had been listening from the lobby area, and when she heard Draven introduce Dr. Umbridge, she decided she wanted to sit in on the presentation. Izzy walked toward the door, and two security guards stepped before her, blocking her path.

"Come on, you two. Are you new here?" She smiled, pulling a badge out of the front pocket of her lab coat. One of the guards examined it closely, then stepped aside swiftly. Izzy noticed a Russian name, Viktor Rodan, sewn into the patch over the left side of his chest.

"Sorry, Ms. Davis," Viktor said with a smile. Then he nodded at the other guard and said, "She's good!"

They held the doors open for her.

"Thanks, boys. You know I was just teasing you two? I appreciate your dedication to detail," Izzy said with a warm smile and winked at Viktor.

Izzy took a seat in a dark corner in the back. She was supposed to be working, but she wanted to see how Mr. Draven and Dr. Umbridge portrayed the lab to the public and which creatures they had decided to show the attendees.

Dr. Umbridge was confident and very knowledgeable during her presentation. She earned her PhD in engineering from MIT and loved politics, public speaking, and debate. She could also speak several languages. This combination of skills was a rarity, so Draven hired her on the spot after meeting her only once. The company needed a spokesperson who could speak to engineers, buyers, and politicians, and she was the total package.

Dr. Umbridge silenced the room by just holding her hand in the air.

"Mrhbaan. Dobro pozhalovat'. Yōkoso. Huān yíng. Bienvenido. Welcome," she said with a slight bow. The screens illuminated, displaying seven new creatures as they paraded into view on the digital screen from Dr. Umbridge's right and virtually walked around the room to her left side. Each creature appeared lifelike, and their skin even mimicked that of their natural counterparts. The only difference was that they looked to be constructed of metal, gears, servo motors, and actuators. The first creature, the Black Widow Spider, walked off-screen, and the real version of it walked back onto the stage.

"Well, that was a cool effect," Stanwell whispered to the lady beside him. The lady rudely ignored him and seemed perturbed to have to sit through the show.

Tough crowd.

Dr. Umbridge moved to the opposite side of the floor, and a man stepped into the center of the stage, dressed in black from head to toe. His anonymity was purposeful, as Draven Labs did not want to show any indicators of his nationality. They did not want to offend anyone present by making this fake "Hopper" of any specific ethnicity.

As the man approached the Black Widow, its eyes glowed red, then it pushed off its front legs so that its body was upright, exposing its abdomen. The man in black froze and then started backing up.

PSSST.

The crowd gasped as a silver jet of metal webbing sprayed from the Black Widow's abdomen, surrounding the man's body. With a quick SNAP, the string tightened, forcing the man to fall to the floor. The man struggled to move his arms and legs. It was as if he were trapped in a tightly wrapped cocoon.

There were audible gasps around the room.

Dr. Umbridge calmed the crowd. "Now, if we were in the Red Zone, the Black Widow Spider would have already sent electrical shocks to the netting, incapacitating its prey. The man would be knocked out for about two hours, which would be plenty of time for our DLED drones to pick up his body and bring him back to headquarters for a trial.

Just as she talked about a drone, one appeared on-screen on the displays, starting in the back of the room and then flying off-screen near the stage.

The Black Widow lowered to its normal posture and stepped over the man, still struggling in his cocoon. Then it crawled toward the exit on the opposite side of the room, dragging the man behind.

"Don't worry. He's one of our volunteers and won't be harmed."

Just as the Black Widow and its prey were out of sight, the next creature parted from the parade on the digital screen, and the real version flew out of the stage door and hovered above the stage.

"Introducing the Dragonfly, our newest surveillance drone," Dr. Umbridge said as the drone slowly started flying around the room. Its wings flapped quickly, and the wind it produced sent some of the guests' papers flying. "It can reach fifty miles per hour and has motion, heat, and sound sensors. It even has infrared and night vision. During daylight hours, it can use solar power to charge itself, allowing it to stay in the air for twelve hours. A data streaming feature can send our AI system a picture of a face and run it through our facial recognition program almost instantly."

As the drone flew around the room, candid pictures of the attendees sitting in the audience appeared randomly across the digital screen. Each image had the person's name next to it, extracted from a database of faces. Senator Stanwell's photo was visible on the screen to his left, and he nodded in approval of its accuracy.

SENATOR MICHAEL STANWELL, SENATOR, USA

"It can tell us if someone is on a wanted list anywhere in the world from just one picture of their face."

She sensed that some audience members looked uneasy at that statement and tried to hide their faces. "Don't worry, we're not running that program today." She laughed, attempting to ease the tension.

The drone flew back toward the stage and easily maneuvered through the exit door.

Dr. Umbridge pointed at the next creature on the digital screen—the Centipede. As it emerged from the doorway, it moved all of its tiny, metal legs in sync. It looked like a choreographed dance, and the creature slithered back and forth like a snake.

Another volunteer entered the stage, again dressed in black. It was apparent this volunteer was female as her costume was form-fitting and her breasts were enormous. She nervously moved to the center of the stage and glanced at Dr. Umbridge, looking for a sign that she would be safe. Dr. Umbridge just nodded and urged her to continue.

The Centipede circled the floor around the volunteer's body once, then lifted its head and sprang toward her upper body, latching onto her upper arm with its pincers. The speed of the attack caught the volunteer off guard.

"Ouch. That hurts!" the lady screamed, flailing her arm violently to try to loosen the creature's grip. The rest of the Centipede's segments wrapped around her from her chest down to her feet, then appeared to contract, creating a tight grip around her extremities. She could no longer move, and it was evident that she was frightened.

"Get me out of this thing!" the lady wailed. "Get this thing the fuck off me!"

Izzy jumped from her seat and ran down the aisle to the stage to help.

The Centipede shouldn't have acted that way, especially in demo mode.

She made it halfway down the aisle when Dr. Umbridge clicked a remote in her hand, and the Centipede went lifeless, falling to the floor in a heap of body segments covered in little, metal feet that were still kicking. The volunteer grabbed her arm, kicked the Centipede angrily, and ran off the stage in tears.

Izzy stopped, turned, and walked back to her seat.

Goddamn! That's not going to leave a good impression.

"Sorry, folks. The creatures sometimes overreact when their victims try to fight back. If our poor volunteer is injured, we'll take care of her, don't you worry," Dr. Umbridge assured everyone.

The back door of the stage flew open, and Draven and Murphy ran back onto the stage. Draven stepped up to Dr. Umbridge and whispered, "What happened? Is everything okay?"

She moved the microphone away from her mouth. "Yes, sir. Our volunteer got a little spooked when the Centipede latched onto her arm. She's fine. I've got this."

Just then, the lady sitting next to Senator Stanwell and another gentleman to her right stood up. The gentleman pulled out his phone and started recording.

The woman yelled, "Mr. Draven? Emily Faro from World Tribune News. Is this what happened to the Hopper in the river? I heard one of your Jellyfish creatures killed a man in the Rio Grande?" She moved closer to the stage as the man behind her kept recording to a livestream. "We've learned the man's name was Caesar Peñas of Monterrey, Mexico."

Brock Murphy glared at his security guards to tell them to stop the woman, but they were already in motion and on their way to intercept her.

Before the closest security guard could reach her, she turned to the crowd and yelled, "Is Draven Labs covering it up? Why hasn't it been reported to the authorities? How many deaths have there been in the Red Zone that you haven't told us about?"

Izzy sat in the back of the room, trying to hide her joy, watching someone embarrass Draven. It never happened.

Way to go, girl.

Draven's face and body language proved his guilt. He stood there, silent, trying to think of a good answer to her questions. He knew anything he'd say would be plastered all over the papers and repeated on the internet within the hour.

STOP THE CRISIS BEFORE IT HAPPENS.

He remembered the lesson from the crisis management training his public relations firm had required him to take.

Draven grabbed the microphone from the podium. "Yes, I was made aware of the situation. We're trying to gather the details and locate exactly where it happened so we can get the proper American or Mexican authorities to investigate."

Draven turned and walked back out the door with Murphy following. They could hear Dr. Umbridge trying to regain control of the room as they shut the door behind them.

"How the fuck did a reporter get in here, Brock?" Red asked. "I went over that guest list a hundred times. FUCK, FUCK, FUCK! This isn't good. Someone must have talked to her, or else she wouldn't know about that damn Jellyfish incident. She even knew the man's name. We've got a fucking leak, Brock. You need to deal with this shit. Get me a name."

"I'm on it, Red. Go to your office, grab a drink, and relax. You need to look calm and collected for the rest of today's events. The more confident and compassionate you sound about this mess, the better it will be for you and Draven Labs. The cat's already out of the bag, so now we need to make it appear as though the cat is a stray and it's just shitting in our litter box."

Brock returned to the auditorium to ensure security had escorted the uninvited guests out of the building.

Red grunted, tugged at his hair, and walked to the executive elevator to ride up to his office. He hoped Dr. Umbridge was worth the six figures he paid her. It was now in her hands to create ANY success out of today's event.

Just as the elevator door was shutting, a hand pushed through and stopped it. Senator Stanwell appeared. "Going up?" he asked.

"Awe, come on. I can't do this right now!" Draven responded, irked that the door hadn't closed quicker.

"We need to talk, and I need to get the president some information tonight. What the hell was that all about, Draven? Why didn't I hear about the dead Hopper? Was that reporter telling the truth?" Stanwell asked.

"Yes, we had a Hopper drown. We have the situation under control. Look, this is what liability insurance and the full support of the American government is for, isn't it? There will be bumps along the way, just like any company dealing with the cutting edge of technology, and we'll deal with these problems and improve," Draven answered.

"The only problem is, liability insurance doesn't cover the president's image, Draven. He put his full support behind your company, in full view of the American people, and any bad PR will fall back on him. The liberals will destroy him with this."

"Fuck the Left. They were never behind border control, and they're already making up stories to hurt the president. When the American people see the amount of money my company is saving them, and they see the reduction in immigration numbers next month, they'll forget about this little incident and cheer for the president," Draven replied with a smile. "And when you get your next check from me, you'll be smiling, too."

"Draven, you're such a bastard! Don't think that your money can buy my silence. If I observe things veering in the wrong direction, don't think I won't recommend that our president bring back the border patrol and sideline your little project," Stanwell said, sticking a finger in Draven's chest.

Draven didn't hesitate. He grabbed Stanwell's finger and bent it backward, forcing him to a knee.

"Stop it, goddammit!" Stanwell begged. "I'm a fucking US senator."

Draven pushed his hand away and let him get back up. "This little project protects the American people and costs them a tiny fortune. If you pull that shit, you can be assured I will spend every fucking dime I have left to sink your chances in the next election. That also goes for your two senate friends ... the ones feeding off our profits and happily accepting my rather large donations for their reelection campaigns."

"Well, at the very least, I need you to either keep me informed of 'little incidents' like this in the future, or find a way to make them disappear without the media, me, or the president hearing about it. The media can't get any ammunition if you and I are going to keep things friendly."

"This has never been 'friendly,' Stanwell. This is business— the business that I built from nothing."

Stanwell interrupted him, "Speaking of 'friends,' why are you inviting America's enemies to our doorstep and showing off the technology the American people are paying you to develop? Are you planning to sell technology that will end up on the battlefield, facing off against American soldiers?" Stanwell probed.

"This is a private company, and it needs to keep making a profit. I know you politicians are used to getting loads of money handed to you by the American taxpayers, but I have to sell things to make my money. What did you think I was going to do? Don't worry. I'm not selling battlefield weapons. I'm just selling security systems. Other countries are also interested in securing their borders, and there's a lot of money in that auditorium.

"Now, if the president is worried that my creatures and drones can be used for warfare, tell him we've built safety measures into them and can disable them if they're compromised anywhere in the world. If anyone tries accessing the processors or software in my machines, it instantly fries the motherboard and deletes the programming. I'd be more than happy to give the president a demonstration if he'd ever leave the Oval Office and visit us here on the border," Draven said.

"You're walking a fine line and know that the president isn't too happy about it, Draven."

The elevator door opened to Draven's office, and he stepped off the elevator and turned to Stanwell.

"Well, at the very least, me, you, and your two friends in the senate will be fine if you can get him to understand there will be some 'little incidents' along the way, just as the defense department has 'little incidents' with their new weapons. They claim collateral damage all the time. We should be given the same flexibility, and we're not even TRYING to kill anyone—yet!"

The elevator door shut.

Stanwell slunk back to the auditorium to find Dr. Umbridge in complete control of the show again. The reporters had been removed, and some very interested men from Saudi Arabia had stolen the reporters' and his seat in the front row. He found a seat in the very back row.

Stanwell didn't see Draven again until he appeared at the luncheon. Draven acted as if nothing had happened and greeted each guest personally. Stanwell could see that every guest handed Draven a business card or shared contact info from their phone. He could only assume they were expressing interest in Draven's technologies.

I'm not looking forward to explaining all of this to the president.

2050

DETERRENT AND DRONE TECHNOLOGY

DRAVENLABS

ZOMBIE ANT
ANT

The Zombie Ant silently stalks its prey using motion, sound, and heat sensors. Its precision-engineered pincers clamp down on victims, pinning them with an unyielding grip while injecting them with a non-lethal toxin. This toxin creates a zombielike state of confusion in its prey, turning them zombielike. The Zombie Ant can traverse most terrain and climb over large boulders and up forty-five-degree inclines. The Zombie Ant requires charging after eight hours via a powered connection and communicates with other deterrents and drones through near-field communication.

**5.5' TALL
7.5' LONG
405 LBS GW**

INSECT SERIES

STEEP TERRAIN

HUNTER

TOXIN CREATES ZOMBIE-LIKE STATE

GRASPING PINCERS

CLIMBS LARGE OBSTACLES AND STEEP INCLINES

THERMAL SENSORS

MOTION TRACKING

NIGHT VISION

ACOUSTIC TRIANGULATION

Amber Kolojnc
EERING LEAD

Red Draven
PRODUCTION APPROVAL

DRAVENLABS

PORCUPINE

JELLYFISH

PIRANHA

DRAGONFLY

GRASSHOPPER

BEETLE

CHIGGER

CENTIPEDE

ANT

SPIDER

DRAVENLABS

STEEL SCARAB
BEETLE

The Beetle is engineered for never-ending human pursuit. Equipped with infrared vision, motion sensors, and hyper-sensitive acoustic detection, it tracks its prey with eerie precision. When its stainless-steel pincers capture prey, it injects a paralytic neurotoxin that leaves victims temporarily helpless. Powered by a photovoltaic exoskeleton, it operates tirelessly under the sun, hiding in the bush, waiting for its next ambush. It communicates with other deterrents and drones through near-field communication.

5.5' TALL
7.5' LONG
405 LBS GW

INSECT SERIES

STEEP TERRAIN

HUNTER

GRASPING STAINLESS-STEEL PINCERS

CLIMBS LARGE OBSTACLES

FANGS DELIVER PARALYTIC NEUROTOXIN

THERMAL SENSORS

NIGHT VISION

MOTION TRACKING

ACOUSTIC TRIANGULATION

ENGINEERING LEAD

PRODUCTION APPROVAL

DRAVENLABS

PORCUPINE
JELLYFISH
PIRANHA
DRAGONFLY
GRASSHOPPER
BEETLE
CHIGGER
CENTIPEDE
ANT
SPIDER

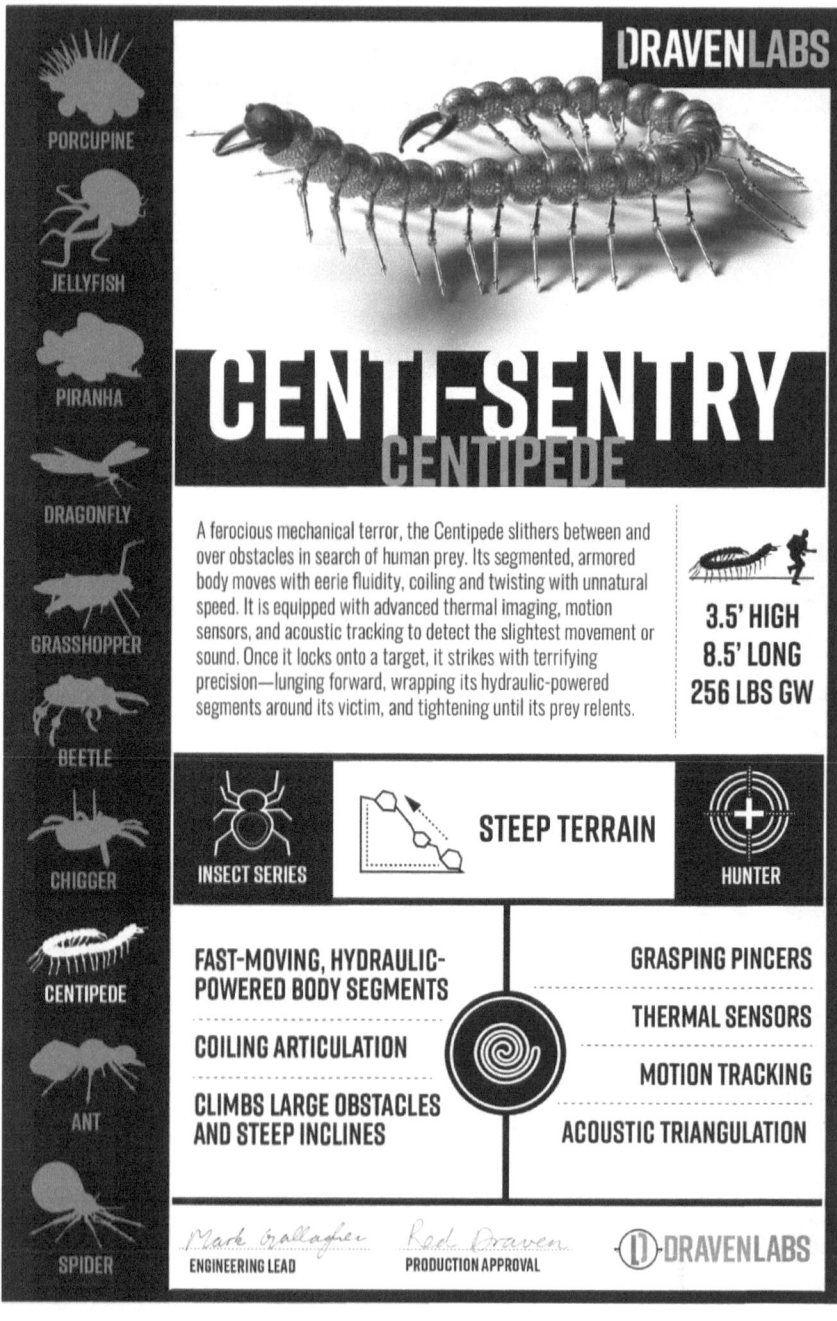

DRAVENLABS

CENTI-SENTRY
CENTIPEDE

A ferocious mechanical terror, the Centipede slithers between and over obstacles in search of human prey. Its segmented, armored body moves with eerie fluidity, coiling and twisting with unnatural speed. It is equipped with advanced thermal imaging, motion sensors, and acoustic tracking to detect the slightest movement or sound. Once it locks onto a target, it strikes with terrifying precision—lunging forward, wrapping its hydraulic-powered segments around its victim, and tightening until its prey relents.

3.5' HIGH
8.5' LONG
256 LBS GW

INSECT SERIES

STEEP TERRAIN

HUNTER

FAST-MOVING, HYDRAULIC-POWERED BODY SEGMENTS

COILING ARTICULATION

CLIMBS LARGE OBSTACLES AND STEEP INCLINES

GRASPING PINCERS

THERMAL SENSORS

MOTION TRACKING

ACOUSTIC TRIANGULATION

Mark Gallagher
ENGINEERING LEAD

Red Draven
PRODUCTION APPROVAL

DRAVENLABS

PORCUPINE

JELLYFISH

PIRANHA

DRAGONFLY

GRASSHOPPER

BEETLE

CHIGGER

CENTIPEDE

ANT

SPIDER

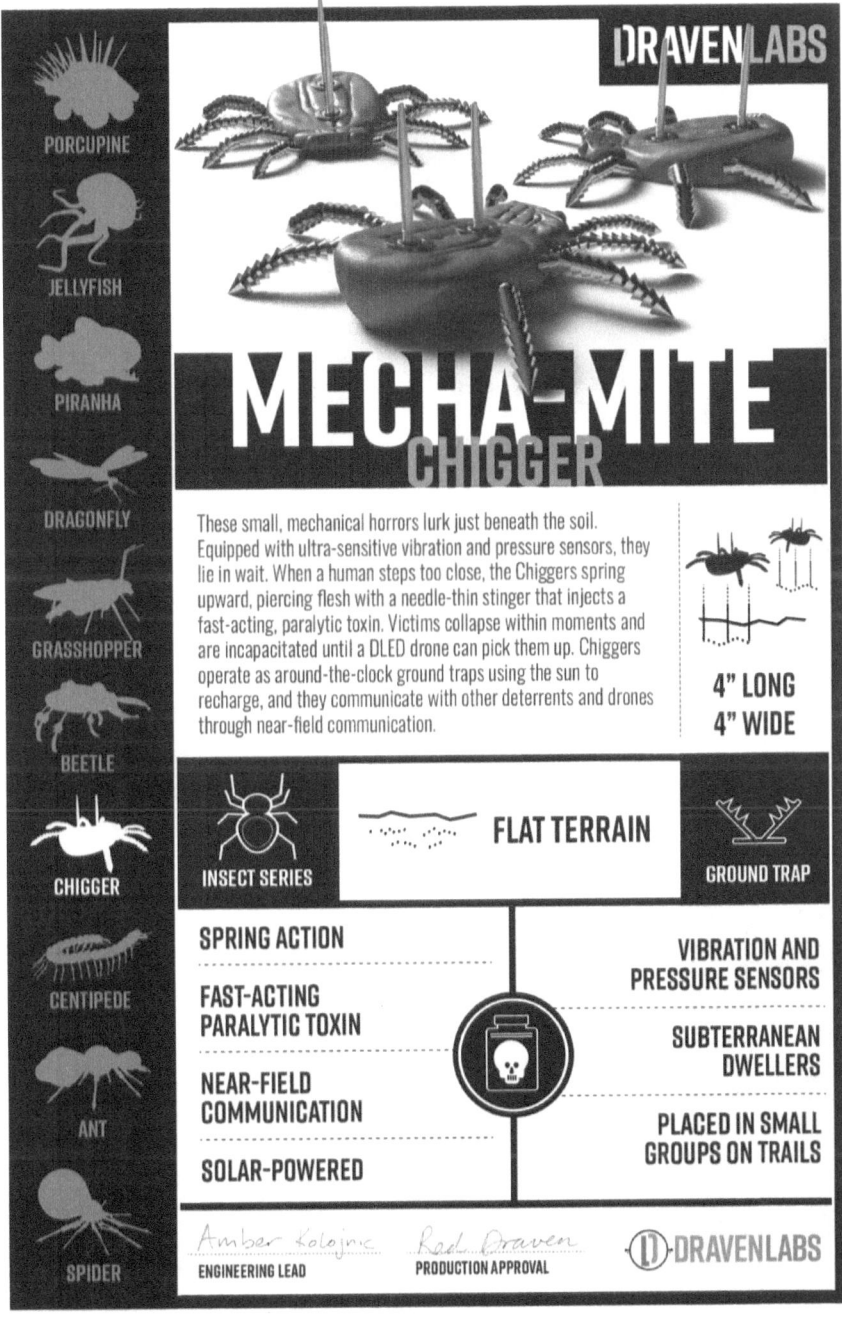

DRAVENLABS

MECHA-MITE
CHIGGER

These small, mechanical horrors lurk just beneath the soil. Equipped with ultra-sensitive vibration and pressure sensors, they lie in wait. When a human steps too close, the Chiggers spring upward, piercing flesh with a needle-thin stinger that injects a fast-acting, paralytic toxin. Victims collapse within moments and are incapacitated until a DLED drone can pick them up. Chiggers operate as around-the-clock ground traps using the sun to recharge, and they communicate with other deterrents and drones through near-field communication.

4" LONG
4" WIDE

INSECT SERIES   **FLAT TERRAIN**   **GROUND TRAP**

SPRING ACTION

FAST-ACTING PARALYTIC TOXIN

NEAR-FIELD COMMUNICATION

SOLAR-POWERED

VIBRATION AND PRESSURE SENSORS

SUBTERRANEAN DWELLERS

PLACED IN SMALL GROUPS ON TRAILS

Amber Kolojnic
ENGINEERING LEAD

Rad Draven
PRODUCTION APPROVAL

DRAVENLABS

PORCUPINE
JELLYFISH
PIRANHA
DRAGONFLY
GRASSHOPPER
BEETLE
CHIGGER
CENTIPEDE
ANT
SPIDER

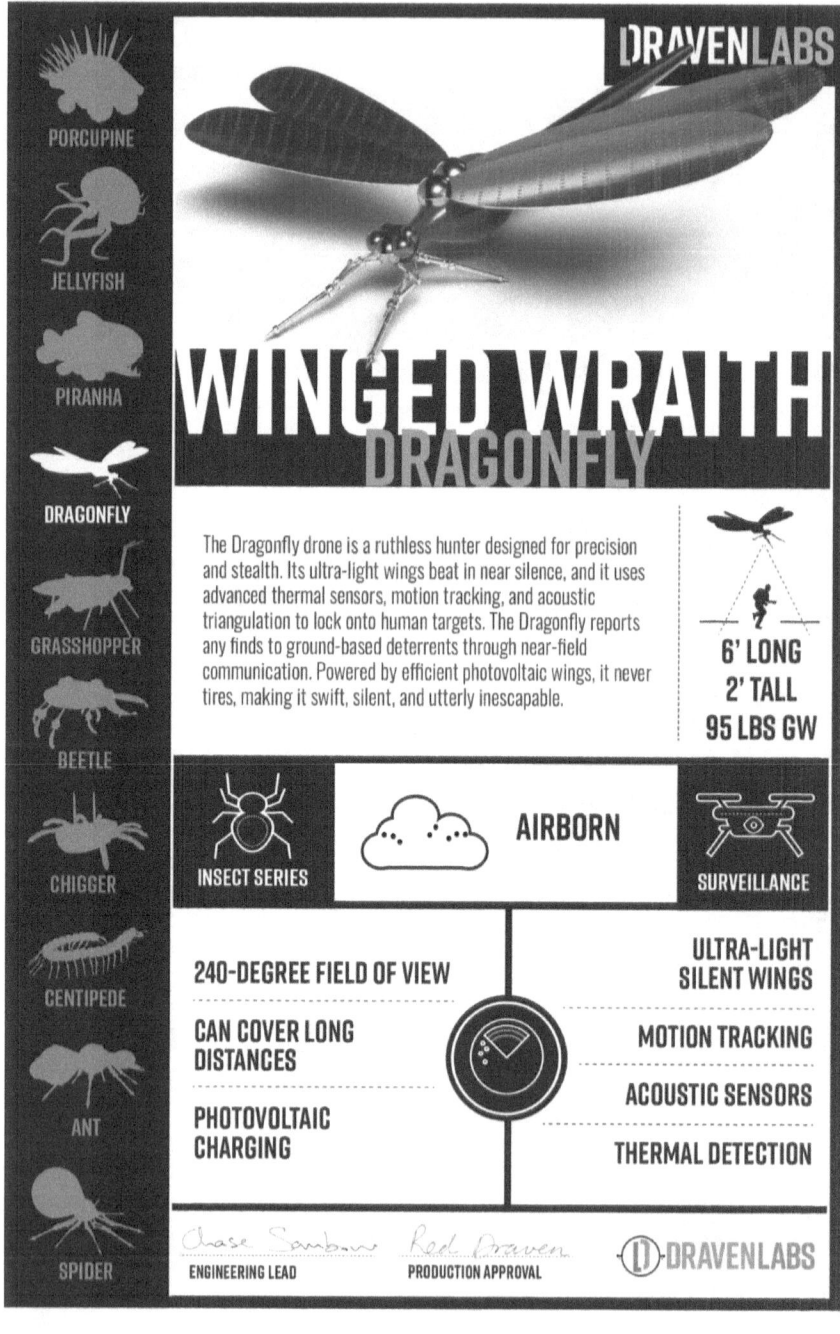

DRAVENLABS

WINGED WRAITH
DRAGONFLY

The Dragonfly drone is a ruthless hunter designed for precision and stealth. Its ultra-light wings beat in near silence, and it uses advanced thermal sensors, motion tracking, and acoustic triangulation to lock onto human targets. The Dragonfly reports any finds to ground-based deterrents through near-field communication. Powered by efficient photovoltaic wings, it never tires, making it swift, silent, and utterly inescapable.

6' LONG
2' TALL
95 LBS GW

PORCUPINE
JELLYFISH
PIRANHA
DRAGONFLY
GRASSHOPPER
BEETLE
CHIGGER
CENTIPEDE
ANT
SPIDER

INSECT SERIES
AIRBORN
SURVEILLANCE

240-DEGREE FIELD OF VIEW

CAN COVER LONG DISTANCES

PHOTOVOLTAIC CHARGING

ULTRA-LIGHT SILENT WINGS

MOTION TRACKING

ACOUSTIC SENSORS

THERMAL DETECTION

Chase Sambaw
ENGINEERING LEAD

Red Draven
PRODUCTION APPROVAL

DRAVENLABS

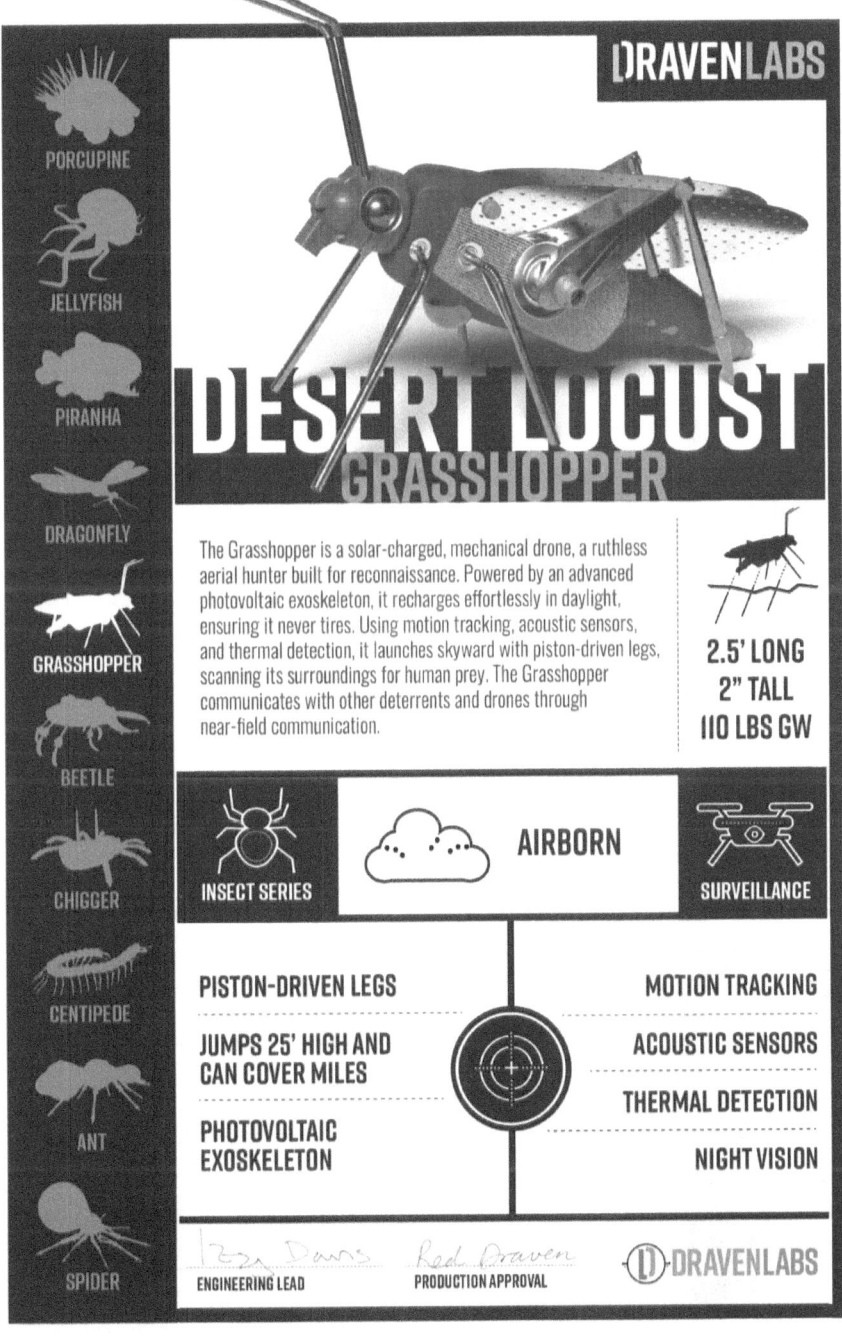

DRAVENLABS

DESERT LOCUST
GRASSHOPPER

The Grasshopper is a solar-charged, mechanical drone, a ruthless aerial hunter built for reconnaissance. Powered by an advanced photovoltaic exoskeleton, it recharges effortlessly in daylight, ensuring it never tires. Using motion tracking, acoustic sensors, and thermal detection, it launches skyward with piston-driven legs, scanning its surroundings for human prey. The Grasshopper communicates with other deterrents and drones through near-field communication.

2.5' LONG
2" TALL
110 LBS GW

INSECT SERIES

AIRBORN

SURVEILLANCE

PISTON-DRIVEN LEGS

JUMPS 25' HIGH AND CAN COVER MILES

PHOTOVOLTAIC EXOSKELETON

MOTION TRACKING

ACOUSTIC SENSORS

THERMAL DETECTION

NIGHT VISION

Izzy Davis
ENGINEERING LEAD

Red Draven
PRODUCTION APPROVAL

DRAVENLABS

Sidebar: PORCUPINE, JELLYFISH, PIRANHA, DRAGONFLY, GRASSHOPPER, BEETLE, CHIGGER, CENTIPEDE, ANT, SPIDER

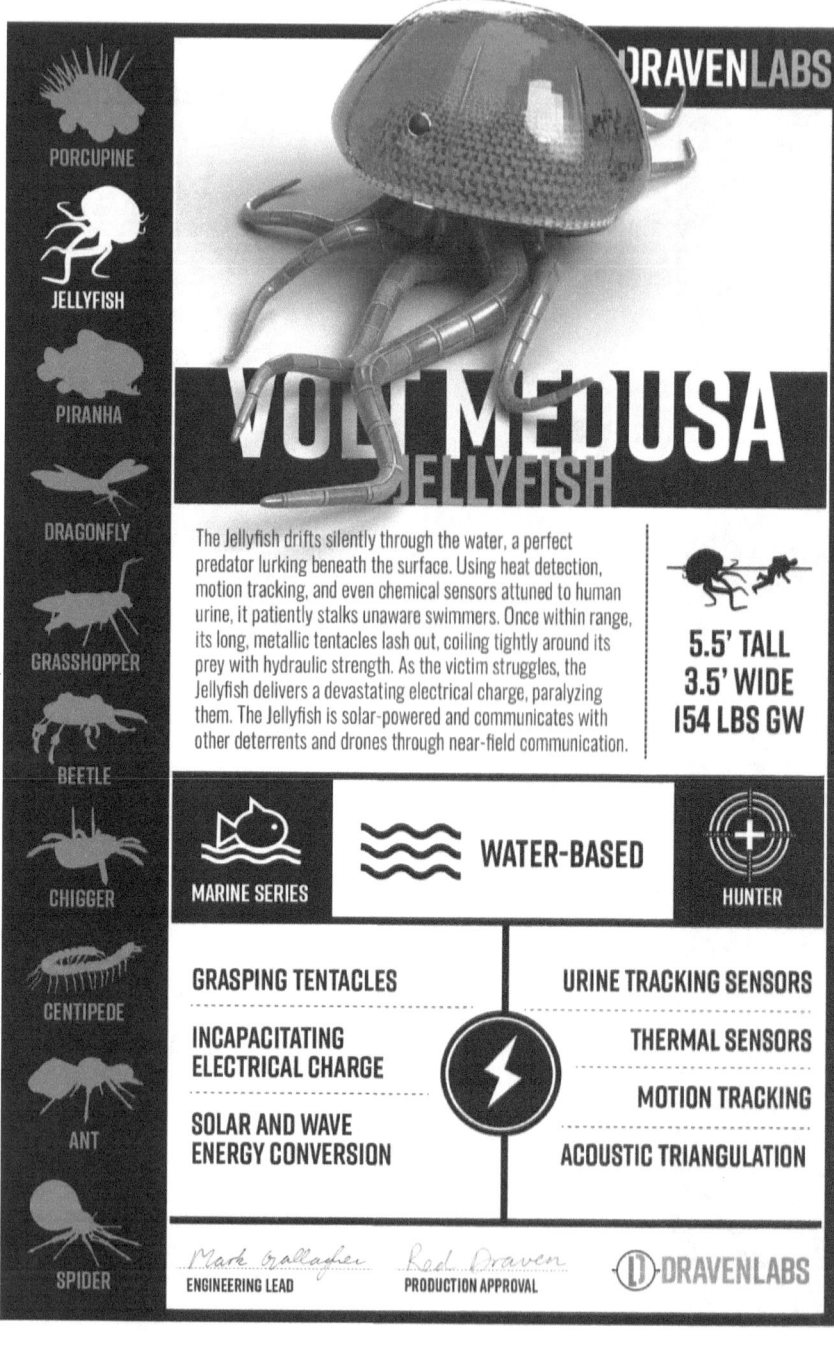

DRAVENLABS

VOLT MEDUSA
JELLYFISH

The Jellyfish drifts silently through the water, a perfect predator lurking beneath the surface. Using heat detection, motion tracking, and even chemical sensors attuned to human urine, it patiently stalks unaware swimmers. Once within range, its long, metallic tentacles lash out, coiling tightly around its prey with hydraulic strength. As the victim struggles, the Jellyfish delivers a devastating electrical charge, paralyzing them. The Jellyfish is solar-powered and communicates with other deterrents and drones through near-field communication.

5.5' TALL
3.5' WIDE
154 LBS GW

MARINE SERIES | **WATER-BASED** | **HUNTER**

GRASPING TENTACLES | URINE TRACKING SENSORS
INCAPACITATING ELECTRICAL CHARGE | THERMAL SENSORS
 | MOTION TRACKING
SOLAR AND WAVE ENERGY CONVERSION | ACOUSTIC TRIANGULATION

Mark Gallagher
ENGINEERING LEAD

Rod Draven
PRODUCTION APPROVAL

DRAVENLABS

Sidebar icons: PORCUPINE, JELLYFISH, PIRANHA, DRAGONFLY, GRASSHOPPER, BEETLE, CHIGGER, CENTIPEDE, ANT, SPIDER

DRAVENLABS

STEELJAW
PIRANHA

The Piranha is a ruthless aquatic predator—silent, swift, and insatiable. Engineered with advanced heat, motion, and urine sensors, it homes in on unsuspecting prey when they enter the water. Moving in coordinated swarms, they strike with lightning speed, their needled jaws delivering deep, precise bites laced with a fast-acting neurotoxin. The swarm of Piranhas pulls the victim to the shore, where they are left temporarily paralyzed, awaiting pickup by a DLED drone.

1' TALL
2' WIDE
45 LBS GW

MARINE SERIES | **WATER-BASED** | **HUNTER**

AQUATIC PREDATOR

MOVES IN SWARMS

SOLAR AND WAVE ENERGY CONVERSION

JAWS DELIVER FAST-ACING NEUROTOXIN

URINE TRACKING SENSORS

THERMAL SENSORS

MOTION TRACKING

ACOUSTIC TRIANGULATION

Mark Gallagher
ENGINEERING LEAD

Red Draven
PRODUCTION APPROVAL

DRAVENLABS

PORCUPINE

JELLYFISH

PIRANHA

DRAGONFLY

GRASSHOPPER

BEETLE

CHIGGER

CENTIPEDE

ANT

SPIDER

DRAVENLABS

QUILLBOT
PORCUPINE

The Porcupine is a semi-autonomous hunting machine designed for relentless pursuit. Covered in sharp quills tipped with fast-acting neurotoxin, it silently stalks its prey through infrared tracking and advanced motion sensors. When it strikes, its metal quills launch with pinpoint accuracy, temporarily paralyzing victims in moments. Its adaptive artificial intelligence makes escape nearly impossible. The Porcupine requires charging after eight hours via a powered connection and communicates with other deterrents and drones through near-field communication.

2' LONG
1.5' TALL
90 LBS GW

PORCUPINE

JELLYFISH

PIRANHA

DRAGONFLY

GRASSHOPPER

BEETLE

CHIGGER

CENTIPEDE

ANT

SPIDER

ANIMAL SERIES

FLAT TERRAIN

HUNTER

GAS-POWERED QUILLS

FAST TURN RADIUS

ADAPTIVE ARTIFICIAL INTELLIGENCE

FAST-ACTING PARALYTIC NEUROTOXIN

MOTION TRACKING

ACOUSTIC SENSORS

THERMAL SENSORS

NIGHT VISION

ENGINEERING LEAD

PRODUCTION APPROVAL

DRAVENLABS

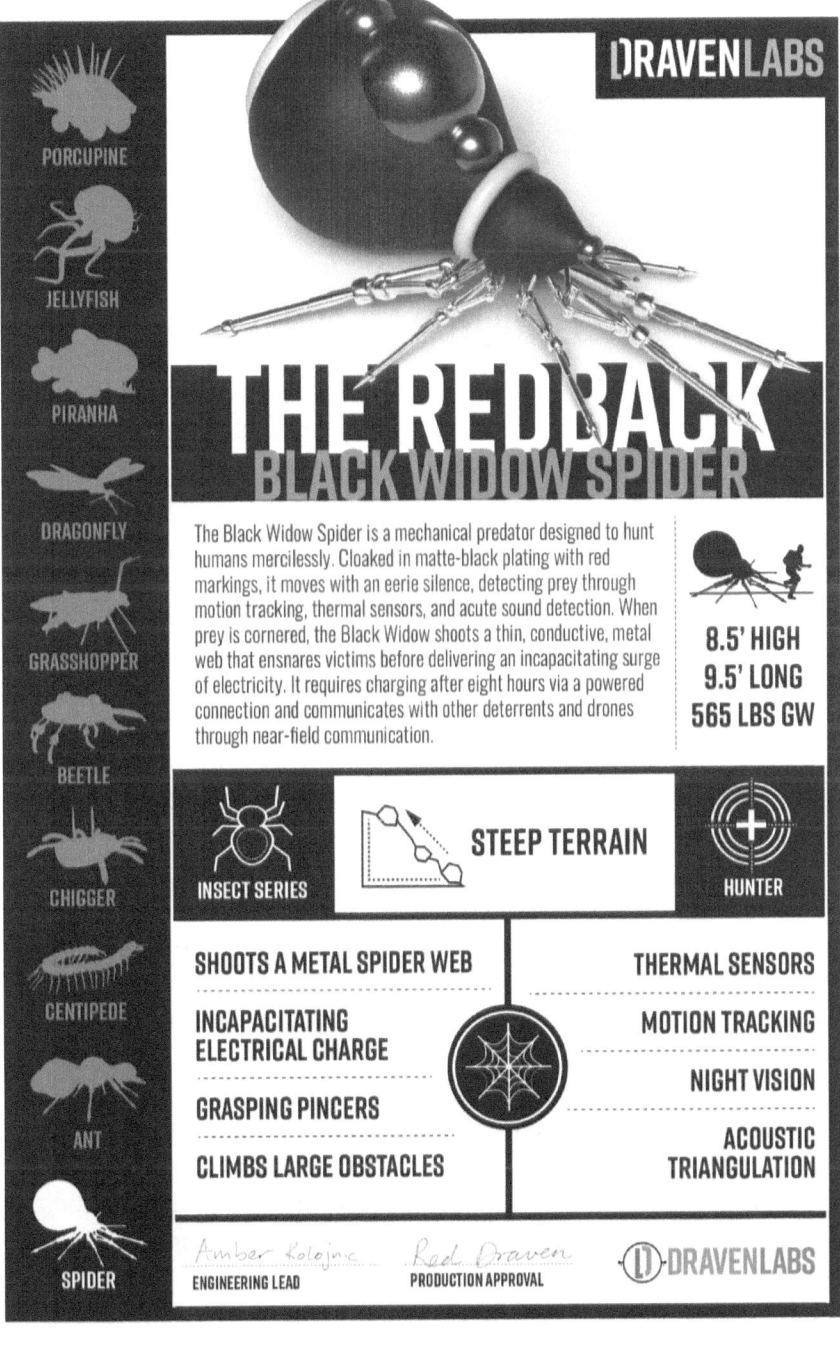

DRAVENLABS

THE REDBACK
BLACK WIDOW SPIDER

The Black Widow Spider is a mechanical predator designed to hunt humans mercilessly. Cloaked in matte-black plating with red markings, it moves with an eerie silence, detecting prey through motion tracking, thermal sensors, and acute sound detection. When prey is cornered, the Black Widow shoots a thin, conductive, metal web that ensnares victims before delivering an incapacitating surge of electricity. It requires charging after eight hours via a powered connection and communicates with other deterrents and drones through near-field communication.

8.5' HIGH
9.5' LONG
565 LBS GW

INSECT SERIES

STEEP TERRAIN

HUNTER

SHOOTS A METAL SPIDER WEB

INCAPACITATING ELECTRICAL CHARGE

GRASPING PINCERS

CLIMBS LARGE OBSTACLES

THERMAL SENSORS

MOTION TRACKING

NIGHT VISION

ACOUSTIC TRIANGULATION

PORCUPINE
JELLYFISH
PIRANHA
DRAGONFLY
GRASSHOPPER
BEETLE
CHIGGER
CENTIPEDE
ANT
SPIDER

Amber Kolojnic
ENGINEERING LEAD

Red Draven
PRODUCTION APPROVAL

DRAVENLABS

9: FRIENDS AND ENEMIES

Over her first few days in America, Gabby settled into her new life and got to know her host family, quickly realizing how gracious her new "aunt" and "uncle" were. They made it easy for her to adjust to her new life. They set her up in a room with a soft, queen-size bed, a desk and chair, and even a TV with streaming networks and fiber internet access.

On the third day in her new home, a delivery service knocked at the front door. They dropped off six boxes addressed to her. They contained a new computer loaded with RAM, processors, and all the software she might ever need, which had already been installed. She also unboxed her own VPN Wi-Fi router and three monitors, a luxury she could have only dreamed of before. There was a note with the delivery.

Gabby, enjoy! Looking forward to a bright future with you by our side. N+J

She knew it was from Noah, so she texted him a quick thank you on her new phone. She didn't know who the "J" was, but she was sure she would find out eventually. Noah texted back a smiley emoji.

Gabby connected the computer to the fiber network, configured the VPN and a virus scanner, changed the security settings, and was up and running in under an hour. She giggled joyfully when she realized how much faster it was than the computer in her best friend's store in Mexico. She had no idea how fast computers were now.

Her room was airy and bright, with a window overlooking a small nature preserve, beautiful flower beds, and a koi pond.

Mariana had told Gabby that Carlos loved to garden so much, if she ever needed to find him, she could just look back in the garden shed.

Gabby even had her own bathroom, and Carlos and Mariana often repeated that their home was her home.

"Please, Gabby, help yourself to anything you need or want," Mariana reminded her often.

They had stocked the pantry with snacks, and the refrigerator was full of different types of meals to last the week. They gave credit to Noah for providing them with a weekly stipend that helped them feed Gabby, but Gabby guessed they had gone overboard and spent some of their own money to welcome her properly.

Today was a big day—her first day at the school where she had been enrolled by Noah, Crestview High School. Gabby entered the kitchen and noticed the plate of huevos rancheros Mariana had prepared for her.

"Good morning, Aunt and Uncle! This is so nice of you," Gabby said, smiling.

"Oh, good morning, Gabby! Before you sit, Noah called early this morning, advising us that your mom is now safe at home, anxiously awaiting your call," Mariana announced happily.

Gabby got excited. "I hope you don't mind me calling her from my room?"

"Of course not, Gabby, please!" Carlos smiled. "We'll keep your breakfast warm."

Gabby ran to her room and dialed her mom's number on the new phone Noah had provided her. It only rang once before her mom picked up. They both instantly started crying.

"Mamá? Are you okay?" Gabby asked.

"Oh, Mijita, I'm fine. I'm a little tired but glad to be back home. Did you make it?"

"Yes, Mamá! I had just found an escape tunnel when you stepped into that trap and were taken away. We were so close to making it over together."

"Sorry I didn't make it." She sounded embarrassed that she had let Gabriella down.

"They didn't hurt you, did they?"

"I don't remember much after you went through that window into that old building. When I woke up, they were treating me for some minor burns. They placed me in a holding area until I saw a judge, and then they put me on a bus back across the border. A nice government handler on the Mexico border escorted me home. Your friend Emily and her father stopped by with some groceries to ensure I was okay. They're so sweet. Emily said to tell you she misses you and, if you made it over, to do great things."

"Awe, she's so sweet. I'm staying in a cute house with two very nice people. They're taking care of me until we can find a way to get you over here. Carlos and Mariana are their names. I call them my aunt and uncle just to make things seem legit. I've been enrolled in a school known for its science and technology classes. I'm starting today! I think my bus will pick me up in about fifteen minutes."

"I'm so happy to hear that. I want you to tell me all about it at the end of the day. I'm going to shower and then try to make up some of the sleep I've lost worrying about you the last three days."

"Okay, Mamá. I'll call you tonight and tell you how it went. Please rest, and don't worry about me. Te amo!"

"Te amo, Mijita!" her mom said before hanging up the phone.

Gabby was beaming when she returned to the kitchen table, where Carlos and Mariana waited to hear how the call had gone.

"Is your mom okay?" Mariana asked.

"Yes, a little tired and sore, but she's safe and back home. I told her I was getting on the bus and would call her later," Gabby said.

"That's very good to hear." Mariana smiled softly.

"Oh, before you leave, we have a little 'first day of school' gift for you," Carlos said as he handed Gabby two boxes wrapped in newspaper. He seemed a bit embarrassed. "Sorry, we forgot the wrapping paper."

Gabby laughed. "Do you want me to open these now?"

"If you'd like. These might help you fit in at school," Mariana replied.

Gabby unwrapped the largest box, pulling out a pair of new Converse sneakers.

"Those even have the school colors," Carlos beamed. He had

picked out the style.

"Oh, I love them! Thank you!" Gabby said excitedly, then she unwrapped the other box.

She removed a new pair of jeans, a red-and-gray shirt bearing a red cardinal, and the school's name, Crestview, on the front.

"Let me guess. The cardinal is my new school mascot?" Gabby smiled.

"Yep!" Mariana smiled back. "I hope those jeans fit. You can try them on if you want to."

Gabby jumped up and ran back to her room. Five minutes later, she returned, dressed and looking like a Crestview Cardinals' student ready to take on her first day of school.

"I love them. Thank you both!" she said as she hugged Mariana and Carlos. She sat and finished breakfast with them as they told her what to expect from high school and American students. Gabby didn't tell them, but she didn't need the help. She had watched many American TV shows that portrayed what it was like for a young girl in an American high school.

I've got this.

"Bus comes in ten. You don't want to be late on your first day. Here's your schedule." Mariana handed Gabby a notebook with a printed schedule on top. "Just go to homeroom 302, and someone can show you around from there. And here's some lunch money. I figured you could buy lunch until I figure out what you want me to pack for you."

Gabby mouthed another, "Thanks!" She grabbed her backpack and ran out the front door and across the street to join some other students waiting at the bus stop.

Carlos and Mariana stood at the front door and watched as she got on the bus and left for the first school day of her new life. This is what they had dreamed it would be like to have their own daughter, as they could never have any kids of their own.

For some reason, Aiden walked into a school buzzing more than usual about the *Civil Watch* game. He overheard there was an update to the game last night, and everyone playing the game appeared eager to discuss it at school this morning. There was talk of the release of new mechanical creatures and a rise in Hoppers being caught.

Great. They're bragging about more humans getting tortured.

He decided to tune it all out, as it only caused him stress and opened the door for him to say the wrong thing to the wrong person.

Unfortunately, the wrong person had a locker beside his—Mason Stanwell, Senator Stanwell's son. Aiden and Mason always had a hate–hate relationship, although it never turned into more than some insults being hurled and some name-calling.

Aiden still tried to be civil with him.

"Good morning, Mason," he said flatly.

"Hey, geek! Are you ever going to play *Civil Watch* with us? We could use a good nerd to help us locate more Hoppers," Mason chided, knowing the topic infuriated Aiden.

"I'd rather hunt humans with real weapons," Aiden blurted out, instantly regretting it. He meant it only as a joke, not a veiled threat. He guessed threatening a senator's son could land him in trouble. He quickly pulled the joke back. "I meant … hunt those creatures with real weapons. That would be a challenge."

Mason just stared at him, trying to decide whether Aiden was turning into the next crazed school shooter.

"Sheesh. Lighten up there, killer. I'm starting to worry about you," Mason replied, shutting his locker door and finding his friend Lucas standing there.

"You may have just saved me from this psycho, Lucas," he joked, jerking his thumb toward Aiden.

Lucas replied, "Well, just think … if he is a psycho, he may end up in the Red Zone someday, and we can show him just how much fun the game can be!"

Lucas pulled Mason away, and they headed toward their first class.

Aiden shook his head, rolled his eyes, and then waited a minute to shut his locker so he didn't have to endure any more comments from them on the walk to class. They all went to the same homeroom, their first-period class, social studies.

Lucas and Mason entered the room and sat in their usual seats next to each other. Lucas was the first to notice the cute new girl with dark hair sitting in the back of the room.

"Who's the new hottie?" he whispered to Mason. Mason turned

back to look and got embarrassed when he realized she had caught his gaze.

"No idea, but you're right. She is hot," he replied, watching Aiden walk in and sit beside the girl. "Too bad she has to sit next to Aiden."

Their teacher, Mr. Grant, entered the classroom and interrupted their conversation.

"Okay, kids, listen up. We have a new student with us today. Everyone, please welcome Gabriella Alvarez," he said, motioning to the back of the room.

"Thank you. You can call me Gabby," she said, pushing her glasses higher up her nose. She was glad she wore the nice outfit her "aunt" and "uncle" had gifted her that morning. It made her feel as though she already fit in at the school.

Aiden nodded a hello and smiled at her. Gabby returned the smile.

Mr. Grant made a note on his class roster and glanced around the room to make sure nobody was absent. He launched right into his lecture for the day.

"Today, we're going to discuss current events and the topic of every news channel. Since the election, we've seen a major shift in how our country handles immigration. I'd like to talk about the issue civilly and hear your different viewpoints. I shouldn't need to remind you that I will not tolerate any hate speech. We have differing opinions, so let's keep the discussion respectful. We can talk about our democratic election process, recent policy changes on immigration, and how they might affect the hearts and minds of a country."

A few of the students grunted because, although it was related to social studies, it was a very hot subject, even among young people. These conversations always got heated, as evidenced by a fistfight over the subject in the cafeteria just one day earlier.

"Can we talk about the *Civil Watch* game, too!" Lucas interjected.

The teacher looked down his glasses at Lucas. "Raise your hand next time, Lucas. But yes, the *Civil Watch* game is a part of the discussion, too. Although some don't agree with the ethics behind it, the game allows American citizens to participate in a civic duty—helping to guard their borders," Mr. Grant added. "But let's start with the immigration issue. Let me hear your thoughts on the subject."

Gabby shifted in her seat and hung her head slightly, not wanting to be called upon. Aiden noticed her body language change.

"Illegal immigration is exactly what it says ... ILLEGAL," Mason blurted out.

"Raise your hands, people," Mr. Grant reminded everyone.

Aiden leaned over and whispered to Gabby, "Mason's dad is a senator who spearheaded the immigration policy changes, so of course he has to agree with the changes."

Aiden put his hand in the air.

"Aiden, what's your opinion?" Mr. Grant asked.

"Oh, here we go with the bleeding heart crap," Mason said under his breath but loud enough for everyone to hear. A few girls in the classroom laughed, but Aiden ignored them.

"Well, it may be illegal, but our government isn't giving these people the same chances our ancestors had," Aiden shouted from the back of the room. "Our country was built on immigrants like my great-grandparents. We need to find a way to open our borders to the people who can add something to our society while, at the same time, stopping the drug cartels and sex trade smugglers. They're just shutting the border to everyone now, and that's not the American way."

"It's ILLEGAL immigration! They're all criminals if they try to cross," Lucas blurted, and Mr. Grant reprimanded him with a stern look.

"Yes, so that's the dilemma. How do we have empathy but still protect our borders?" Mr. Grant asked. "Half of our country agrees with the Geert Wilders quote, *'Without sovereignty, a nation cannot exist. Without borders, it can't be defined or protected.'* The other half believe Emma Lazarus and the sign on the Statue of Liberty, *'Give me your tired, your poor, your huddled masses yearning to breathe free, the wretched refuse of your teeming shore.'"*

Mason raised his hand. "I think the new Red Zone and the *Civil Watch* game allow us to do both. We get to protect the borders,

AND the Hoppers who ignore the proper process and try to cross still get their chance at a fair trial. They get to enter the country if the judge agrees with their reason for crossing. As a plus, the game is much less expensive than our Border Protection Agency used to cost, and we are able to help protect the border, earn some money, and have some fun in the process."

"It's like he recites this stuff straight out of his dad's press packets," Aiden whispered to Gabby.

Gabby slowly raised her hand.

"Oh, Gabby! What's your opinion?" Mr. Grant asked, and the entire room turned in unison to watch and learn anything they could about this new girl at their school.

"The Hoppers as you ... I mean, we ... call them, they're people with dreams. Many of them are very smart. They can offer something to our society if we just give them a chance. And you're right. Criminals are coming over, too, but the judges are rejecting almost everyone's application for entry nowadays. There is no legal immigration anymore unless you are rich and can pay your way in. And that *Civil Watch* game, and the terrifying creatures on the border everyone's having fun with, are hurting people. People just like you and me, people with families. It's horrific what those people are going through just for a chance at a better way of life," Gabby said, starting to tear up.

The classroom was silent. Then Lucas broke the silence.

"Ever see someone overdose on the drugs brought in by the cartel? Now, THAT is horrific!"

"Lucas, raise your hand or get out of my classroom," Mr. Grant scolded him.

Aiden jumped to Gabby's defense, "Red Draven and his company ARE crossing the line with those creatures. They ARE hurting people, and I am sure they're even killing people. Draven Labs has outstanding lawyers, PR people, and even the news channels to cover it up. And he has some senators in his back pocket, too." He stared at Mason when he said that.

Mason turned and was about to jump out of his seat to rush at Aiden, but Mr. Grant stepped in front of him before he could.

"Okay, okay ... let's calm down, people. Remember to be civil, and let's not make accusations, Aiden," he warned.

Mr. Grant clicked a remote, and the smart TV flashed on in front of the room.

"I have a short documentary to get us all up to speed on how we got here."

A male narrator with a deep voice spoke as animated slides flashed across the screen.

US and Mexican relations had not improved in the last twenty years. In 2047, they only worsened. Years of anger and disagreement in the American political system resulted in the 2048 presidential election and a more extreme stance on illegal immigration. President Ferris temporarily ceased many social services and support programs to reassign those funds to a large border construction and defense program. It was one of the biggest eminent domain seizures and construction projects the American government had ever undertaken.

Where cross-border neighborhoods once thrived now stands a 2,000-mile-long strip of cleared land split into two zones—the Gray and the Red Zone. The Gray Zone, just north of the Mexican border, is a lawless space owned but not officially policed by the American government. It was built as a buffer to slow down anyone trying to enter the United States illegally. Closer to the United States is the Red Zone, a very heavily defended area now nearly impossible to cross due to Draven Labs' defense systems.

The designated strip that contains these two zones is precisely ten miles wide, and its creation changed or wholly removed some border towns on the American side. As a result, cities like Nogales and Calexico no longer exist. Residents of those towns had been moved into new communities built farther inside the new American border. Where corner markets and some of the best taquerias once stood are now thick rows of strategically planted cacti and six-foot-deep manufactured swales intended to slow down any Hoppers attempting to gain entry into the United States.

Mr. Grant paused the video. "Does anyone know where the word 'Hoppers' originated?"

A girl in the front row raised her hand.

"Kylie?" Mr. Grant called on her.

"That's the 'safe' word created by the media to describe anyone trying to cross the border illegally. They started using 'Hoppers' because humanitarian groups claimed 'illegal alien' and 'illegal immigrant' were demeaning and carried a stigma. The media seemed fine latching onto the new term since 'Hoppers' is easier to say, and both sides of the immigration debate accept it," she said.

"Correct, Kylie." Mr. Grant nodded. He noticed Lucas raise his hand for the first time.

"Yes, Lucas?"

Lucas grinned. "The seven letters also fit perfectly into those awesome spinning, animated graphics they use in their news segments. And the news anchors can get the word Hoppers out of their mouths much easier."

Many in the class laughed.

"You have a point, Lucas," Mr. Grant agreed. "Hoppers and the new border nicknames of 'Red's Wall' and 'Draven's Run' have become a topic of almost every broadcast."

He clicked play on the remote. The narrator continued as a graphic map showed the expansive border, highlighted in red, connecting the Pacific Ocean to the Gulf of America, and also along the northern border with Canada.

The Red Zone, and the defensive fortifications called turrets, were strategically built along the borders. They are the brainchild of Red Draven, a self-made billionaire and owner of Draven Labs.

His technology company has grown to become the world's go-to source for state-of-the-art, unmanned defense systems. It owns the patents for proprietary drones, non-lethal defense robots, AI-enhanced surveillance and detection systems, and psychological defense strategies. These are tested and marketed out of Draven Labs headquarters near the border west of El Paso, Texas. The company even built its own town, named Solace, to house the company and all of the employees required to support it.

It is believed that a public announcement of Draven Labs' endorsement helped President Ferris win the election in 2048. The idea of a private company guarding the borders instantly became the topic of every philosophical and ethical discussion on TV and social media. The more conservative adults and the young voters loved the idea as they had tired of hearing how expensive and ineffective the border control agencies were. Their votes pushed President Ferris into the majority, thereby earning Draven Labs the long-term contract to guard the border.

The day after the inauguration, President Ferris and Draven Labs announced at a joint press conference that a new, all-volunteer Civil Border Patrol Agency would be created. This new agency would recruit American volunteers over eighteen to virtually man the border using a new software system called Civil Watch, *designed and run by Draven Labs. This new software instantly gave millions of American citizens the opportunity to get involved in their country's fight against illegal immigration.*

Twelve hundred protective defensive platforms were procured by the government and strategically positioned inside the Red Zone along the northern and southern borders. The platforms are unmanned and stocked with many of Draven Labs' mechanical creatures—creatures controlled by the Civil Watch *players.*

The new agency, and these defensive structures, rendered most of Homeland Security's Customs and Border Patrol Agency unnecessary, and the agency was dismantled in early 2049. This cost savings allowed the president to reinstate the social services and programs that had been paused. It was considered a win–win–win for the president, Draven Labs, and their supporters.

Any border patrol agents who didn't take an early retirement offer or buyout package signed on with Draven Labs and were retrained to inspect, maintain, and restock the deterrents in the turrets.

Mr. Grant stopped the video and posed some questions to the class. "So we have several ethical and political topics to choose from here. Is it proper to allow a private company to manage a part of our national security? Is it ethical to permit young people, like many of you, to be a virtual front line to the war on illegal immigration, drugs, and sex trafficking? Was it acceptable to take money away from American social programs to cover the cost of acquiring land and constructing a new border zone for our national defense? I'd like to hear your thoughts. I'll open the floor to discussion. No need to raise hands now."

A girl in the back corner spoke first, "My parents talk about friends who have lost jobs to illegals … er, Hoppers. Sorry. They said employers don't have to pay them as much as they have to pay American workers. And they don't have to pay for their health insurance, either. I feel bad for the Americans who can't make a living because they lost their jobs to a Hopper. I know that's why my parents voted for President Ferris and the new Red Zone," she said.

A few of the others in the class signaled their agreement.

"My dad is trying to get a new law in place to punish those companies. Heavy fines, easier ways to report those companies to the government. He said he's hoping to get it passed before summer," Mason said proudly.

Aiden jumped in. "I have an idea. How about instead of passing a bunch of laws punishing people, we change some laws to allow more LEGAL immigration. Our population is dwindling, and there aren't enough workers to fill the jobs we have. The only way to fill those jobs is to increase immigration. I agree we don't want drug smugglers or sex traffickers, but why doesn't your dad try to find a way to be a champion for humanity? Let's grow our population with people who just want a better life and have something to offer our society … and they can help America grow again."

Lucas sighed loudly. "Ugh, I can just see it now. Taco joints on every corner. Spanish translations messing up all of our signs again. Every Juan will just love it." He laughed at his own pun.

"You're such a racist, Lucas," the girl sitting next to him said in disgust.

"If the sombrero fits," Lucas replied, and Mason tried to hide his laughter during the whole back and forth.

"Not appropriate, Lucas. Go to the principal, and I'll see you in detention later," Mr. Grant said, pointing at the door.

Lucas angrily snatched up his backpack and sent a look to Aiden on his way out. "You liberals will be the end of our country as we know it."

"Out, Lucas!" Mr. Grant pushed him out the door and shut it behind him.

"I actually like tacos. Not sure what his problem is," Aiden said, and Gabby laughed out loud.

"Okay, okay … let's reel this back in," Mr. Grant said while trying not to laugh at Aiden's comment. "So how could we change the legal immigration process to achieve what you are talking about, Aiden?"

Aiden paused in thought, then remembered something interesting he had come across.

"I read about a 33 percent idea that sounded interesting. We'd allow a greater number of immigrants in, but in a controlled way, and that number would be based on the number of job openings available at the time. Everyone would need to apply through one application process before ever entering the country.

"One-third of immigrants would be allowed in simply due to persecution in their own country. They would be the 'tired, poor, huddled masses, yearning to be free' that Miss Lady Liberty speaks about. These are the families running from the cartel, or war, or dangerous environments. Their applications would be vetted through our current process.

"Another third would be skilled workers—able-bodied adults seeking tradework. And the last third would be technically savvy— your engineers, scientists, technologists, those sorts—who would be chosen from the national applicant database, then selected and sponsored by the companies that need their labor. Any immigrants allowed in under these three avenues could bring immediate family members with them. They would be required to pass a background check right away, learn basic English, and pass the naturalization tests within three years. If they do that, they are considered full American citizens."

Gabby was in awe at how smart Aiden was and found herself staring at him, smiling. Aiden turned and caught her, and she blushed and looked away.

"Pretty interesting plan, indeed. I like it. Anyone have thoughts on that?" Mr. Grant asked the class.

A redheaded girl in the front row jumped in, "Seems like that would be an incentive to do things the right way and get some brains back into this country. Maybe we can open another category and replace our current politicians with the smart immigrants," she said while staring at Mason.

Mason appeared upset by her comment, obviously aimed at his dad. "You have no idea what you're talking about! You realize these immigrants will just ignore the process and run across the border anyway? And Aiden's little plan isn't going to stop the drug runners and criminals. Thank God that Draven Labs is adding marks to Hoppers' arms to see who is making multiple attempts to cross. If someone has a mark, they should never be allowed in, even if they fit one of Aiden's categories."

Gabby turned red. "You realize those marks are just as bad as the serial numbers the Nazis put on the Jewish population? Not all Hoppers are criminals. Many of them are people like you and me just looking for a new life. Those marks are as bad as a ticket to the gas chambers!"

Mason turned in his seat. "Oh, come on, really? So they get a little tattoo on their arm because they decided to ignore our border laws. The marks are not much different from a mugshot and a fingerprint scan. And it seems like a small price to pay for breaking our laws. Heck, maybe they should cut off a leg each time a Hopper is caught so it's that much more difficult to cross again. There's a brilliant plan for you, Aiden."

"But it's not just a tattoo. Have you noticed that there are never any Hoppers with three marks crossing the border?" Gabby pressed.

"Exactly, because the Red Zone is working. It's scaring Hoppers away. Nobody in their right mind would make Draven's Run and face those creatures multiple times. There are a few brave ones trying to cross twice, and then they seem to give up. That means our president's plan is working," Mason replied.

Gabby lost her temper and slammed her pen on her desk. "No! You're not being told the truth, Mason. Hoppers with two marks ARE still attempting to get here. They're just disappearing when they're caught, and Draven Labs and the government is covering it up. Over three hundred people just this past year tried to cross the border and disappeared, all of them with two marks. Because they crossed on American soil, the Mexican government can't investigate. And the American ... I mean, our government ... is not interested in looking into the disappearances," Gabby said.

"Then maybe they'll learn to value their life and stay in Mexico!" Mason yelled back.

Gabby gave him a death stare. Aiden joined her, and whispered, "What a sadistic bastard."

Mr. Grant tried to ease the tension. "Okay, seems people are getting upset with this subject. Let's switch up the conversation and talk about why we think the majority of people voted for President Ferris."

Gabby stared at the floor and realized what she was up against. If the majority of the people in America think like Mason, she would have no chance of getting her mom over the border to join her—at least not anytime soon. That is, unless Aiden's plan ever became a reality, and her mom found a way into one of the three categories he outlined.

Before she knew it, the class bell rang.

10: COMPUTER CLUB

Gabby unfolded her schedule and was trying to figure out where she was supposed to be next, still flustered by the conversations in her first class ever in an American school.

If this is what America is really like, I'm running back across the border to Mexico.

"Can I help you with that?" Aiden interrupted her thought, holding out his hand. Gabby saw the kindness in Aiden, smiled, and handed him her schedule.

"Oh, cool! You're in computer lab with Mr. Dempsey? You're into computers?" Aiden asked.

"Does a hacker hate honeypots?" she replied.

"Yes, we do! Follow me. You're in my class." Aiden laughed, realizing he may have just found his soul mate.

As they walked to class, Aiden extended his hand and officially introduced himself to Gabby.

"Aiden Moore … local computer geek, civil rights advocate, thorn in Mason Stanwell's side, and I'm assuming your first friend at Crestview High, not necessarily in order of importance."

Gabby shook his hand. "Bigger computer geek, obviously a debate newbie, and hopefully a fellow thorn in Mason's rear."

They both chuckled.

Just before they entered the computer lab, Aiden whispered to Gabby, "You're going to love Mr. Dempsey. He's a computer phenom … taught me almost everything I know about computers, networking, programming, cybersecurity, and even how to avoid honeypots. And he's really cool. He shares our views on the whole immigration situation and can't stand Draven Labs. He used to work for them."

Mr. Dempsey greeted them at the door, "Hello, Aiden, and this must be … Gabby?"

"Hi, Mr. Dempsey. I hope you brought your *A game* today. This one claims she's a bigger computer geek than me!" Aiden said as he walked past Mr. Dempsey and toward his workstation in the back corner.

Mr. Dempsey stopped Gabby and spoke softly. "I'm glad to meet you, Gabby. Noah let me know you'd be excited to join us. I hope you like the computer we sent over to the house?"

"You helped with that? Why did—" Gabby started to ask.

"Let's talk later," he interrupted as two more students pushed past. "I hope you don't mind, but I've put you next to Aiden. I think you two can learn a lot from each other."

Gabby walked to the back of the room and sat next to Aiden, wondering about Mr. Dempsey's connection to Noah and whether or not he even knew Noah's involvement with the Wallflowers. She was deep in thought, staring at the computer screen, when Aiden interrupted her.

"Let me know if you need help turning it on. It's that black switch right there," Aiden said sarcastically.

Gabby picked up her mouse, stared at it, and then held it to her mouth. "So you don't just speak into this thing and say 'POWER ON'?"

They both laughed.

The class was less of a lecture and more of a set of exercises. Mr. Dempsey handed out a paper describing a cybersecurity breach that was preloaded onto their workstations. Each student had to use only the tools on their computer to locate the issue and configure a fix, eliminating the threat. When the threat was eliminated, Mr. Dempsey had programmed in a celebration sound effect that rang out, loud enough for all to hear.

Both Aiden and Mr. Dempsey stared at each other with a stunned look when Gabby was the first to complete the task … and after only fifteen minutes.

"Beginners luck?" Gabby said to the class, slightly embarrassed.

"Damn, girl! You weren't kidding about liking computers," Aiden said, praising her. His celebration sound played five minutes later.

When class ended, Mr. Dempsey held Aiden and Gabby back to talk.

"Great job today! Not sure if Aiden mentioned it, but we have a little fun running more advanced exercises for about an hour or two after school. You are more than welcome to join us if you'd like," he said.

"I'd love that. I just need to ask Mariana and Car—I mean, my aunt and uncle—if it's okay. I'm sure it will be." Gabby smiled.

"We'll be here whenever you want to join. Fair warning, your brain will hurt afterward. That's why Aiden's forehead is so large," Mr. Dempsey joked.

"Can't deny that," Aiden agreed. "Well, Gabby, you have Spanish class, and I have home economics. Don't even ask why my mom made me take it. Anyway, want to sit with me and my friends at lunch after?"

"Yes, I'd love that. But only if you're bringing some of the baked goods from your home economics class to lunch with you!"

"Deal!" Aiden replied.

Gabby sat through her Spanish class, thinking how funny it was that Noah and her aunt and uncle added a Spanish class to her schedule. They must have known it would be like another study hall for her. She found it difficult to not correct the teacher when he used older, no-longer-used words for certain everyday objects. He had obviously been trained mostly in college, not on the streets of Mexico.

Oh, the words I could teach this guy.

Lunch came quickly, and she called her aunt and uncle to let them know she would be coming home late because of a computer club she had joined. They seemed happy that she was already getting involved in school activities. She also texted her mom to let her know she may need to call her a bit later than she had said.

I need to call after 6 p.m. I'll explain later.

School is going well. Te Amo!

It didn't take long for Gabby to locate Aiden and his group of friends at the back of the cafeteria. They were sitting at a large, circular table in the farthest corner. One of Aiden's friends was standing on his chair reenacting some kind of a battle, holding an imaginary broadsword and swinging it above everyone's heads.

Aiden saw Gabby walking toward the table and rolled his eyes, letting her know how embarrassing his friends could be sometimes.

"Gabby! Let me introduce you to my … ahem … friends."

His friends all froze and stared when they realized Aiden had invited a cute girl into their "arena." That was a rarity.

"That's Sammy wearing the John Lennon glasses. You'd think he was a big Beatles fan, but those are his dad's glasses, and he is convinced those things make him look cool."

"Let it be, Aiden." Gabby smirked, hoping the play on words wasn't lost on the group. "Nice to meet you, Sammy! I think your glasses are cool."

"Ah, I see what you did there. Next to him is Lainey. You'll like her. She's also into computers, but more for gaming—and NOT the *Civil Watch* game."

Lainey didn't look up from a handheld gaming console she was playing, but offered a quick wave and an apology. "Sorry, I'm just about to beat my best score ever."

"That's Dylan. He's a loud one," he said, pointing at a boy with long, brown hair that fell over his face. The boy shot up two middle fingers at Aiden, and Gabby could see a smile appear under his hair.

"And the one swinging the imaginary sword above his head like a dweeb is Lenny. He prefers to be called 'Dungeon Master' on Fridays."

Lenny jumped down from his chair and circled around the table to get closer to Gabby. He looked her up and down as if he were sizing her for a costume. Before Aiden could stop him, Lenny blurted out, "Want to join our *Dungeons & Dragons* game this Friday, Gabby? We always have a blast."

Aiden stopped him and turned to Gabby. "Maybe pass on that invitation this week. He requires you to dress up like an ogre, a wizard, or an elf in order to play. No costume, no play."

"And he's never invited Lucas or Mason? Those two could pull off the ogre part without a costume!" she replied.

The entire group went into an uproar at her sense of humor. Their laughs were loud enough to cause the surrounding tables to turn and see what they were laughing about.

She sat down, and Aiden slid her an unwrapped Twinkie on a paper plate.

"Baked this myself," he joked.

"Couldn't handle the more difficult HoHo recipe, I see."

As she listened to Aiden and his friends' conversations over lunch, Gabby realized that all of them had different hobbies, and none of them were jocks or druggies. They all seemed to accept her into their group right away, and she felt as though she fit in perfectly. Even Lainey offered a more welcoming greeting and some conversation once her game had ended.

Gabby made it through the rest of her classes without hearing any more talk of immigration or the *Civil Watch* game. She thought about how much she enjoyed Aiden's company—and his friends—and was glad she shared many of the same classes with him.

As the last bell rang, she thought about her first day at Crestview High. Aside from the heated discussion about immigration in first period, the day was a success in her eyes. She seemed to fit in with most of the other students, met a cute boy who shared her love of anything to do with computers, was invited to grow her computer skills from someone who looked as though he knew what he was doing, and she appeared to have made some new friends.

She walked quickly to Mr. Dempsey's computer lab, excited to see what she might learn from him. When she entered the room, Mr. Dempsey had his back to the door and was talking to Aiden in the back corner. He turned when he heard her enter.

"Oh, hi, Gabby! Glad you could join us. Would you mind shutting the door?" Mr. Dempsey asked, then continued whispering something to Aiden. Gabby was a bit surprised to see it was only her and Aiden in the special after-school get-together. She had assumed there would be a few other students, considering Mr. Dempsey taught many computer classes throughout the day.

"Come on back." Mr. Dempsey motioned to the seat next to Aiden. Aiden had a serious look on his face and wasn't his normal, smiling self.

Mr. Dempsey glanced back at the door again to make sure it was closed.

"Sorry for the weirdness, Gabby. I just needed to be certain nobody else popped in behind you. As you can see, this is a VERY selective group, just the three of us now. I was just talking to Aiden about why I've included you in our sessions, and he was a little concerned about putting you in harm's way," he said.

"I don't understand? What harm could this—" Gabby started.

He interrupted her, "Take a seat. Let me explain."

Gabby placed her bag on the floor and sat next to Aiden. Mr. Dempsey leaned in, "I know all about you making it across the Red Zone. Noah filled me in before you even started school. He also told me you're a computer whiz, and that's why we had the computer delivered to your home. I just let Aiden in on all of this, and you can trust him to keep your secrets."

Aiden smiled and nodded. "Now I understand your anger about the Red Zone in social studies class. I can't believe you made it across Draven's Run. Very impressive ... and brave. And I'm sorry about your mom. That had to be awful."

Gabby blushed and wasn't sure if they were just testing her. Noah had advised her not to trust anyone with her secret.

"I know we're coming at you like a ton of bricks, but Noah knew we could all trust each other, and we just don't have much time to beat around the bush. Noah said he'd talk to you Saturday night, and you should not worry about hiding secrets from the two of us.

"Aiden and I are volunteers in the Wallflowers. I've been a member since the beginning, and Aiden here has been involved for over a year. Obviously, if I was ever discovered to be working with the Wallflowers, I'd be fired and probably put in a federal penitentiary. Aiden here would probably either be put in juvie or shipped to Siberia to work in a teen governmental cybersecurity work crew until he dies. So we're taking a chance on letting you in on our secret, too. We're planning to take down Draven Labs in a very creative way, and Noah thought you might be able to help Aiden and me."

Gabby exhaled a deep sigh of relief.

"Okay. I told Noah I want to help him, so I'm in ... but under one condition. I need to get my mom across. If you can promise we'll do that—and not get her killed in the process—I'm all in."

Mr. Dempsey and Aiden both appeared to relax and smiled at each other.

"It's a deal, Gabby. That's our plan … to take down Draven Labs and allow people to start coming over the border again without fear. There are many Wallflower family members still in Mexico, so we are all working toward the same goal," Mr. Dempsey assured her.

Aiden added, "And some of us just don't believe in the ethics behind what Draven Labs is doing. It's just not right. I've seen enough to know Red Draven and his goons are up to no good, and they don't have our country's best interests in mind."

"So, Mr. Dempsey, how'd you get involved in the Wallflowers?" Gabby asked.

"I was the head of software development at Draven Labs before they got into bed with the politicians and President Ferris. Noah was actually my best employee at the time. We both left the company when we learned that Draven Labs was using their mechanical creatures to kill people on the border of a foreign country. He and I both helped to write and debug the base code that is still used in the current mechanical creatures. Believe it or not, the programming hasn't changed much since 2048. They've added some AI and altered the creatures' directives a bit to turn them into hunters and gatherers … of human beings. We're not good with that. And we want to put a stop to it."

"My goal, too," Aiden added.

"So, I'm not a security expert, but wouldn't all of that code and the servers be locked down pretty securely? Are you two saying you're good enough to break into the network at Draven Labs?" Gabby probed.

"Well, yes … but not on our own. We have help on the inside. There's a developer who is sympathetic to our cause and will open a small, programmatic hole for us to get in and upload new code when we're ready. He also understands that when we take down Draven Labs, it will mean his job is over. He only stayed on with the company to help us with this mission anyway."

"Sounds great. So what are we doing here?" Gabby asked.

"That's the fun part," Aiden said. "Mr. Dempsey has obtained a piece of Draven Labs' software that lets us virtually test the old and new versions of the creatures and their programming. Now that I am starting to understand the code, I can insert small changes that affect the creatures' behaviors and objectives. This software tests the changes on-screen almost instantly and without any communication with Draven Labs.

"Once we get all of the creatures acting how WE want them to, we can simply compile the new code into a container and upload that to the server at Draven Labs. We're going to release it on D-Day—Draven Day—and it will cause one hell of a headache for him. On that day, we just send a simple command to run the subroutine, and all of the creatures across the Red Zone will receive the new update within five minutes."

Mr. Dempsey jumped in, "Obviously, we'll all be in a load of trouble if anything points back to us, so we'll need to set up a very good VPN connection to hide behind … and mask all of our IP addresses. That's the part where you can help, with me and Aiden assisting you along the way."

"I'd like to add some of my own revenge code into the creatures. Do you mind me pitching in with that, too?" Gabby added. "Believe it or not, I've spent the last few nights dreaming of ways to take those buggers down, and I have some ideas already."

"Good with me. There are many creatures to hack, so you can even take your pick of creatures," Aiden offered.

Mr. Dempsey smiled in agreement. "While you two are adding bugs into the bugs, I am going to concentrate on building a routine we can send to the Draven Lab servers to delete all activity logs, infect their backup copies, and remove the base code and our subroutines from all creatures when the job is done. And then it will remove the hole that allowed us into their network. That way, there will be no record of who or how someone got in. And Draven's creatures will be metal paperweights rusting out in the desert when we're done. It will take them a LONG time to get back up and running, if at all. Hopefully, it will expose America to Draven Labs' lax security, and President Ferris will have to ditch the whole program and will lose the next election."

"I like the idea of that," Gabby said, "but it sounds like a ton of work, and you mentioned being in a hurry. Why?"

"We'll fill you in at the next Wallflower meeting on Saturday evening. Noah will get you the details. Let's get to work, shall we?"

Gabby agreed, picked up the mouse, and spoke into it once again, "TURN COMPUTER ON." She winked at Aiden.

Mr. Dempsey laughed. "Noah didn't tell me you had a sense of humor."

"Yeah, I wasn't in the joking mood when I first met Noah. I had just run ten miles through a desert, escaped several terrifying creatures, and crawled through a very long and dirty tunnel," Gabby explained.

II: WASTE OF LIFE

Red Draven leaned his forehead against the thick, green-tinted, bulletproof window of his office, which topped the highest building overlooking the town of Solace, Texas. The city's official name was Solace, but many residents nicknamed it "The Hive." Red had assumed they started calling it that because of the flurry of activity in the small town.

Everyone who lived in the town worked for Draven Labs in some capacity, from the delivery drivers, maintenance workers, barbers, and retail employees to the marketing and public relations staff, product engineers, and scientists. It was a twenty-four-hour operation, and there was always movement on the crisscrossed streets of the town. Only one gate offered entry into the city, and it currently stood directly between Red's perch and El Paso in the distance.

A large, cement wall surrounded the town, fortified with many of the newest surveillance devices and deterrents from Draven Labs. To some, the walls and security measures gave them a sense of safety. To others, it made the town feel like a prison. Selling your home in Solace meant leaving your job at Draven Labs. And unless you already owned a house outside the city when Draven Labs hired you, you were "encouraged" to live in Solace. Everyone knew it was a requirement to work for the labs.

Many people did not agree with Red Draven's goal of eliminating illegal immigration, or at least the way he did it. For that reason, there were constant threats seeking to interrupt the city's operations. Security was always at the top of Red and Brock's minds, and they both took it very seriously. Security was their business and livelihood, after all.

Just after the town's construction was completed two years earlier, and before residents moved in, Red Draven had decided to test the fortifications secretly. He wanted it to be an actual test, so he didn't even let Brock, his head of security, know what he was planning.

ONE YEAR EARLIER

Red Draven had made friends with the local politicians and heads of the police forces surrounding the town when building Solace. "Friend" was a loose term, as he usually bought their friendships with kickbacks, donations to the police departments, and lucrative construction or permitting jobs for their family and friends.

Aside from aiding in electing the local sheriff, he also became a huge donor in the campaign of Phil Ditmeyer, the warden of the local corrections department. These strategic relationships helped Red control what happened both inside and outside the town.

Just after Ditmeyer was successfully elected as the warden, and in only the first month of his new role, Red called in a favor.

"I need some help over here at Solace, Phil," Red stated more than asked. He knew Phil could never turn him down.

"Of course, Mr. Draven. How can I help?" Phil inquired, ensuring the light next to his phone's "Encrypted Line" button was lit.

"I need some volunteer inmates to test the security measures we've installed at our facilities. I'm not looking for any ordinary inmates but a couple who can find their way into secure locations. Pick some that have brains and can think a bit 'outside the box' about how to gain entry to our facility," Red explained. "And I'll cover any expenses and their reward for good work, whether it's unlimited credit at the commissary, better sleeping arrangements, a reduced workload, or other special privileges. I'll leave that up to you."

"Well, I know two men who would fit that assignment perfectly. Both were professional thieves. Their names are Stan Malone and Carmine Patterson. And don't worry about paying for their help. They'll do it because I tell them to," the warden assured Red. "These two have caused some issues with our guards recently, and it's about time they paid for it. It's that, or I will keep them in solitary for another month. I think they'll be smart enough to choose your offer."

"Perfect. I'll be ready this weekend if you can arrange things. Just tell them they need to enter into the center of Solace however they can, without being noticed. If they can do that and make their way inside the Silo, they will have achieved their mission. I'll have a contact waiting in the Silo all weekend to verify if they succeed. They can start their testing at a time and place of their choosing, but the test needs to be completed by Sunday night, no later. We have residents starting to move in next week. And I assume you'll find a way to make certain they perform my assignment and not make a run for it instead?"

"Of course! I'll put trackers on them, and the guards will ensure they don't stray from the borders of Solace. If they do decide to attempt an escape, we'll have them back in custody and sitting in solitary within an hour," Phil promised him.

"And I need to keep this quiet, Phil! If the media or those damned Wallflowers catch wind of any of this, you and I will be occupied with ass coverage, press conferences, and red tape for months to come," Red cautioned. "Tell the guards I will give them a nice bonus to oversee the operation, plus a bonus for them if these inmates make it to the center of the Silo on their own."

"Don't worry about that! The guards I have in mind for the

job—Sergeant Romero and Lieutenant Donovan—are both in line for promotions to new ranks, so they'll jump at the chance to do it. They won't risk their promotions by talking about it, I promise you! The inmates will lose any luxuries they earned and spend a lot of time in solitary if they decide to open their mouths about this. I'll get things rolling over here right away."

"Assure the inmates that I am not giving any type of warning to my security teams. It doesn't help me to set up a test using unrealistic scenarios. The inmates will work against our normal security detail under the same alertness levels as any other day. I need to ensure that my team is on the top of their game," Red said.

"Got it. It'll be nice to see how your new technologies handle these two. I'd almost like to watch everything that happens over a good glass of bourbon." Phil laughed, trying to invite himself into Red's plans.

"Consider it done. I'll record the events, and we can watch it sometime. I have a nice bottle of ten-year Pappy Van Winkle that I'll set aside for our little watch party, too," Red replied just before cutting off the call and before Phil could respond. Being blunt was something Red was known for. He didn't enjoy dillydallying and small talk. Everyone knew he was a busy man.

Phil called Sgt. Romero and Lt. Donovan and explained precisely what was happening and the secrecy required. They agreed to help and were excited to participate in something other than watching inmates eat, watch TV, and shower. And the bonuses helped, too.

They left the meeting and immediately pulled inmates Malone and Patterson from the general population and into a private, new cell close to the guard station. Everyone in the general population assumed they were put into solitary living, which was quite common and didn't raise any red flags.

"What are we doing in here, Sgt. Romero?" Malone asked, irritated that he was removed from a card game he was winning.

"We have a little job for the two of you. If you do the job and succeed, the warden agrees to remove you from any work detail and give you a large monthly credit at the commissary," Sgt. Romero replied with a smile.

"This sounds like a setup. I'm not buying it," Patterson said, looking at his new roommate to see whether he agreed with his assumption.

"Calm yourself. Once we explain the job, you'll change your mind," Lt. Donovan said, interrupting their disbelief.

Sgt. Romero reviewed Red Draven's request and assured the two men that Mr. Draven was looking for two professionals. This made Malone and Patterson sit up in their seats. They had always felt looked down upon in the correction center. They were finally being asked to show how professional they were.

"Carm, the guys in our block will finally realize how legit we are." Malone smiled, using Patterson's prison nickname. The residents of their block knew them as "Carm" Patterson and "Smokey" Malone.

"Wait a minute," Sgt. Romero quickly cut in. "Part of this deal is that you two can't say anything about this to anyone. If you do, and we hear even the slightest mention of this job on the block, you'll lose all privileges the warden is offering, and you'll both be placed in solitary for as long as the warden sees fit."

The two looked discouraged at first but came around to the idea, nodding that they were both still on board.

"We need some brain food if we're going to do this job," Carm added with a smile, knowing he had a little leverage to make small demands.

"Yeah, the shit their feeding us in here doesn't provide much nutrition for hard thinking," Smokey said while sarcastically rubbing his temples.

"All right. What do you two want? What will make those little brains start to move a bit?" Lt. Donovan asked, knowing Sgt.

Romero would make him go pick it up for them anyway.

"A McDonald's Big Mac meal, large, with a Coke … and a ten-piece Chicken McNugget," Carm said. "And don't forget the barbecue sauce."

"Double that, but an apple pie would be nice, too!" Smokey added.

Sgt. Romero looked at Lt. Donovan. "Get them what they want. Keep the receipt and expense it when you get back. Pick up a Big Mac meal with a Diet Coke for me and whatever you want."

Carm and Smokey high-fived, and Lt. Donovan left to fetch their meals.

"Okay, you have only two days to devise your plan. I got you paper and pens, and by tomorrow morning, Lt. Donovan will have a laptop containing a set of the blueprints and the zoning diagrams for the entire Draven Labs' facility, including the town of Solace," Sgt. Romero advised them. "You're not leaving this cell for the next two days, so you won't have to explain what you're working on, and there will be no chance the secret will slip."

Carm and Smokey smiled and lay on their bunks, mouths salivating at the thought of the McDonald's they would enjoy for dinner.

Lt. Donovan checked on Smokey and Carm over the next two days, giving them almost anything they requested. It was in his and Sgt. Romero's best interests to provide them with everything they needed to succeed.

Thursday afternoon, Lt. Donovan once again visited with meals from KFC and a special visitor. He slid open the door to their cells, and a petite woman in a white lab coat pushed past him, carrying a small, metal box.

"Need to get you two bugged," she explained. "GPS trackers. Sit up …"

"You didn't say anything about trackers. That won't be fair!" Smokey threw his head back onto his pillow.

"Don't worry, it's just for me and Sgt. Romero's sake. We want to ensure you two don't plan an escape instead of doing the job you're supposed to do. We'll take them out once the job is done. Draven promised he won't be tracking you or any GPS devices. He wants this to be a test of their systems with no advantages given to his security team."

Carm and Smokey eventually sat up and scooched to the edge of their beds.

"It's a quick pinch, and you'll hardly feel it," assured the lady, unwrapping a scary-looking, metal tool from a sterile wrapper. She inserted what looked like a tic tac into a small compartment on the side of the injection device.

"Bend your neck and don't move an inch. If you do, I could hit your jugular vein, and that won't be a pretty sight."

Carm went first, bending his neck and closing his eyes.

CLICK. HISS.

"Motherfucker! What did you shoot in me, a fucking AAA battery? That hurt!" Carm screamed.

Lt. Donovan tried to hide his enjoyment of Carmine's pain.

"I don't know if I want to do this," Smokey said as he moved away from the woman, reloading the device with a new tracker and a clean needle.

"We've invested a Big Mac meal and an apple pie already, and this KFC. No going back now," Lt. Donovan joked.

"Fuck me. All right, go ahead," Smokey said nervously, exposing his neck.

Another *CLICK. HISS.*

"Damn, more like a D battery, Carm! Who were you kidding?" Smokey commented.

"Sorry, gentlemen. It's the only way to do this," the lady in the lab coat said as she packed up. "And please don't think about digging those trackers out yourself. You'll surely cut your jugular vein, and that will lead to a rather quick and messy death."

Once the technician left, Lt. Donovan asked them how their plan was progressing.

"When do you two want to hit Draven Labs?" he asked.

"Saturday morning, 3 a.m.," Smokey answered.

"Where?" probed Lt. Donovan.

Both inmates looked at each other and didn't want to give the full details.

Lt. Donovan interrupted their thoughts, "Romero and I have to drive you there, you idiots! We need to know when and where you want to start. Don't worry. We won't give away any of your plans. If you two are successful, there'll be a bonus for us, too, so it would be stupid for us to give any information to Draven."

"Okay. You need to drop us off within walking distance of the wall closest to the sewage treatment plant," Smokey responded.

"This is going to be a shitty job," Carm said jokingly.

"Okay, we'll see you Saturday, bright and early. We'll pick you two up at 2:30 a.m. to transport you," Lt. Donovan replied, not picking up on Carm's sense of humor. "Don't fuck this up!"

Saturday morning came quickly, and Lt. Donovan and Sgt. Romero were impressed that Carm and Smokey dressed in the black clothes they had demanded. Sgt. Romero handed them a small, black bag of the tools they had also requested.

"Binoculars, bolt cutters, heavy gauge wire, a set of screwdrivers, wire cutters, Mylar blankets, and a 12-volt battery," Sgt. Romero announced, handing them the bag. "Let's get going."

The inmates donned standard, orange, inmate uniforms over their black outfits and still had to be handcuffed to exit the facility. They were cuffed to the metal bar in the back of the transport van as was required during transport.

"Sorry. I had to make this look like a somewhat regular transport, just to be safe," Lt. Donovan yelled into the back of the van. Sgt. Romero laughed at that because it was far from regular to transport someone at 3 a.m. and for him and Lt. Donovan to escort the transport. He didn't worry about it because Warden Ditmeyer promised them there would be no questions and that he had arranged some cover for their story.

The drive to the town of Solace passed quickly, and just as they could see the lights illuminating the security gate of the city, Smokey yelled out, "Take a left down that main road to the left and stop about a football field away from the sewage plant. We'll hoof it from there," he said. Sgt. Romero glanced at Lt. Donovan and shrugged his shoulders in approval.

"We'll know exactly where you are at all times," Sgt. Romero reminded them, pointing at two blinking dots on a digital pad he held up to show them.

"We know! And you don't need to remind us that your bonus is riding on this little job, either," Carm replied.

Romero and Donovan smiled at each other and stopped the transport to let them out.

"Go get 'em, boys!" Lt. Donovan blurted as he released them from their chains.

Carm and Smokey reached into their black bag and grabbed the two Mylar blankets, wrapping themselves from head to waist. Without any more talking, they bent over and started heading toward the sewage plant as if they had practiced their strategy before.

Sgt. Romero and Lt. Donovan jumped back into the transport and drove about a mile down the road to sit and watch their blinking lights move from a parking lot at a local twenty-four-hour diner.

They observed the blinking dots converging on a spot near the sewage treatment plant just outside the concrete wall of Solace. They could only guess what Carm and Smokey were doing.

Brock Murphy was awakened by repeated vibrations coming from his smartwatch. He rubbed the sleep from his eyes and stared at the small screen on his wrist.

```
3:12 a.m. HAWK DETECTED UNUSUAL ACTIVITY
NEAR GRID C1
```

He jumped out of bed, grabbed an energy drink from the fridge in his kitchen, and stood in front of the retinal scanner on the wall just past his living room. He blinked a few times and tried to keep his eyes open long enough to let the scanner do its job. After two attempts, it finally allowed him into his security office. One more try would have locked him out for five minutes.

More vibrations shook his wrist.

```
3:15 a.m. HAWK DETECTED GROUND SENSOR
ACTIVITY NEAR GRID C1
```

HAWK was the name he had given his pet project—a series of ground sensors and drones flying high above Solace that sent information to a custom-built artificial intelligence program. It stood for Highly Aware Watch Kit. It was designed to work twenty-four hours a day, every day of the year. It needed no vacations, no coffee breaks, and no annual performance reviews or HR interventions. It was his idea of a perfect employee.

The HAWK program looked for changes in the patterns of activity inside and outside the walls of the town of Solace. The program had been running for almost three months, learning how people and vehicles come and go from town.

It also monitored things like the electrical grid to sense any unusual activity. It discovered that the energy consumption on the grid would spike at 7:25 a.m. when the security gate opened for the day. It could even watch itself, informing Brock and the security team when one of its drones ran below maximum efficiency and needed replacing. It also knew when the contracted garbage trucks entered, on schedule, every Monday and Thursday between 9:00 a.m. and 9:12 a.m. and left between 10:35 a.m. and 10:50 a.m. It recorded the walking paths all employees took to get to their jobs and flagged any inconsistencies for inclusion in a report that Brock reviewed every morning. He and the software development team used that report to train the software further.

It worked so well that Brock and Red discussed packaging and selling the package commercially to other towns, the US military, and even foreign militaries worldwide. The software subscriptions alone could dwarf the income generated from the *Civil Watch* video game.

Brock smiled when he thought about when HAWK caught one of his security officers straying from his routine and meeting up with a young woman from accounting. He had fun showing the security guard detailed footage of the two going at it behind a dumpster during their lunch break. Both were quickly fired and escorted out of Solace as an example to the other Draven Labs' employees. Brock used the experience and a blurred video of the encounter as a lesson when training new security officers.

HAWK was always watching.

The touch-screen digital displays on his office walls, mounted side by side, created an almost seamless digital map of Solace and the surrounding roads. Brock could easily pinch and pull out a section of the map to take a closer look and then choose to view recorded video from any area at any time. Today, HAWK flagged unusual activity on the road just outside of Solace. Brock tapped the blinking, yellow icon, and the screen zoomed in to a high-quality recorded feed from the drone's camera.

A white van with the words "DEPT. OF CORRECTIONS" painted in black letters on the rooftop appeared, parked on the side of the road outside the walls of Solace and near the sewage plant. Two men exited the van, went to the back, opened the door, and appeared to let two other men out after some activity he couldn't see inside the van. The two men stepped out and reached into a bag, played with an object, wrapped it around their bodies, and then completely disappeared from the screen. The other two men then jumped into the van and left.

"What the hell are they doing?" Brock whispered under his breath.

He hit a few buttons to change some settings on the recording. He switched from the current, black-and-white night vision to an infrared view. The two men were still missing. He switched to a motion-sensing view, offering nothing out of the ordinary.

On the side of each display was a menu icon that, when dragged, would slide out to expose a series of icons—some shaped like animals, others like insects, and some as reptiles and marine creatures. Brock clicked on the Zombie Ant icon and dragged it to an intersecting point between where the van had parked and the sewage plant near the wall of Solace. He knew that as soon as he let go of the icon, an actual mechanical Zombie Ant deterrent would be delivered to that spot by one of his DLED drones. It might take about five minutes to have the Zombie Ant in position, but that should be enough time to intercept anyone advancing on the sewage plant.

He picked up a radio from several sitting in a charging bank and barked a message to the security details working this morning.

"Security Alert. Grid C1, sewage plant. Two possible threats are advancing. No current visual on suspects."

"Already on it. C team en route. A and B team on standby, waiting for further instruction," the response cracked over the radio, making Brock smile. He was impressed by his security detail's quick action and proactive decisions.

Brock didn't realize it, but his friend and partner, Red Draven, was sitting in his office, watching everything the security detail and Brock did as this all played out.

Meanwhile, Carm and Smokey worked their way closer to the

sewage treatment plant. Carm heard something and grabbed Smokey's arm to stop his movement.

"I hear a drone incoming," he said nervously.

"Calm down. We planned for this. Get the thumper out," Smokey directed quietly.

Carm grabbed the 12-volt battery out of the bag. He also pulled out a small subwoofer speaker that he had already connected to a compact circuit board and screwed the wires of the circuit board to the battery. Instantly, a soft, thumping noise escaped the subwoofer, repeating in a pattern that reminded Carm of a heartbeat. He set it carefully on the ground, and they quickly left the area.

They only had forty feet to go before they reached the fence protecting the sewage plant when the drone hovered about ten yards from them. A blinding spotlight snapped on, visible even through the Mylar blankets. Carm and Smokey knew to stop moving, get as low as they could, use some brush to conceal their bodies, and ensure their Mylar blanket was fully covering them. They needed to be certain that none of their body parts were exposed, or their body heat might be picked up.

They could hear the drone drop something substantial into the brush, causing the ground to tremble. Carm jerked a little when he heard and felt the creature fall.

"Calm the fuck down, Carm. It can't see us, but it will hear us if you don't stop moving," Smokey whispered.

The drone sped away toward the center of Solace. They could then hear what sounded like electric motors spinning up, and a whirring sound grew louder. To Carm, it seemed as if it was only a few feet from where they were, but Smokey knew it sounded like that because whatever they heard was so large.

A repetitive, metal grating noise and dry grass being crushed now concealed the reverberation of the motors. Smokey could tell by the pattern of the sounds that the creature was now on the move, each leg making clicking, mechanical noises as it advanced.

Smokey smelled urine and realized Carm must have pissed himself. He didn't blame him. They had both read about these creatures and how terrifying they could be. Smokey just hoped that Red Draven hadn't developed some scent detection sensor in the newest model of creatures.

It wasn't until the creature moved five yards past them that Smokey and Carm both exhaled and then took a breath, realizing they had stopped breathing when the drone arrived. The first breath reminded them they were very close to a sewage treatment plant, and it wasn't a pleasant smell.

Their only consolation was that they realized the creature hadn't sensed them under their Mylar blankets, and it was falling for their trick, going for the sound of the thumper's fake heartbeat now forty yards behind them.

"We have to go now … very quietly. Avoid stepping on the dry brush," Smokey whispered.

They crept along until they reached the metal fence at the edge of the sewage plant. Carm removed the metal bolt cutters and quietly clipped a hole large enough to fit through. He and Smokey slipped through and hugged the back wall of one of the plant's outbuildings, then pulled out a drawing he had made of the sewage treatment plant and rotated it to the correct orientation.

"Right where we need to be," Smokey whispered. "We're heading inside this building!"

Just as he said it, they could hear a radio cracking and some security guards yelling at each other, although he couldn't make out what they were saying. They were far enough away not to be a threat yet.

"Hurry!" Smokey urged. "We've got company on the way."

They could slide around the side and enter the unlocked building, closing the door and locking it behind them. "That should buy us some time, but we gotta move," Smokey said.

"Now for the nasty part, right?" Carm responded.

"Remember, sometimes you have to deal with a little shit to earn what's coming to you." Smokey smiled at Carm, then jumped over a short, cement wall, splashing knee-high into a pool of piss and shit. Carm reluctantly followed.

"Holy shit! That stinks!" Carm said.

"It's only going to get worse, so get used to it," Smokey cautioned, gagging and trying to stop himself from vomiting.

They skirted the wall and found the four-foot tunnel where the sewage poured in from the city. Smokey mentally noted how odd it was that the tunnel had no grate covering it, preventing anyone from entering or exiting.

That doesn't seem very secure.

They knew the tunnel would be walkable, as they had learned the city's pumps washed the sewage out of the tunnels and into sewage treatment pools on a schedule.

"Clears every three hours, and the last time should have been at 2 a.m.," Smokey advised. "Let's get going. I don't want to be a turd in the next wave."

They turned on their flashlights and made good time, keeping track of the number of side tunnels as they advanced.

"We're at tunnel connection seventeen. We keep straight until we reach twenty-three, which is directly under the Silo. Not too far now," Carm said.

"Too bad. I'm just starting to enjoy this smell." Smokey laughed.

Just as he said it, they both heard a noise from the next tunnel only ten feet ahead. The noise was eerie and sent a shiver down both of their spines. It sounded like metal sticks tapping on cement. It started very slowly and seemed to increase in speed as they stood there.

"What the fuck is that? Could just be cockroaches or rats, right?" Carm asked.

"No idea, but let's get out of here!" Smokey blurted out. This was the first time Carm sensed any type of fear in Smokey.

As they passed the next tunnel entrance, they could hear the noise even clearer, unsure if the sounds were amplified by where they were standing or if whatever was causing it was getting closer. They stopped for only a second to look and listen, and that's when they noticed it. A faint, red glow illuminated the tunnel's far end to the left, and shadows appeared to be moving as if in a flurry of activity.

"RUN!" Smokey shouted.

Carm didn't need to be told, as he had already started running before Smokey said it. His feet slipped in the sludge as he tried to gain traction and move faster. Smokey pushed him from behind to get him going. As they moved along, they heard something enter the tunnel fifteen yards behind them, and the noise became almost deafening.

Numerous tiny, metallic feet tapped the cement as the red glow advanced. It sounded like whatever creatures chased them were frenzied, fighting to reach their prey. Neither Smokey nor Carm wasted a second to take a look back. The red glow had grown brighter, which told them all they needed to know—whatever was following them was gaining on them.

"Only one more tunnel until we reach the Silo," Carm huffed, trying to catch his breath.

Just as the sentence left his mouth, Carm's body jerked to a stop.

Smokey slammed into Carm's back hard enough to cause him to see stars. His body slid down the back of Carm and into the sludge, face-first.

Smokey gathered his senses, wiped the shit from his eyes, and shined his flashlight up at Carm, trying to figure out why he stopped midrun.

"You idiot! Why'd you stop? We're so close."

That's when Smokey noticed something very odd. Carm's head hung backward and toward the ground. His eyes were wide, and they blinked slowly. He was trying to move his mouth to speak, but the only thing that came out was a trickle of blood. His body just hung in the air, and Smokey couldn't figure out how Carm was still standing.

The way his body is positioned shouldn't allow him to stand.

It wasn't until his body slumped a little more that Smokey noticed the large pincers wrapped around Carm's rib cage.

The evil, red glow of two eyes pierced the darkness ahead of Carm. The eyes stared past Carm and appeared to be sizing up Smokey. Smokey could barely distinguish the creature's silhouette holding Carm in its pincers.

A fucking Beetle? Down here?

Smokey was about to say something to Carm when something punctured his calf.

"OW! What the …" Another sharp pain pierced his ass cheek. He rolled to his side to see a small, metallic creature resembling a fattened Tick, its face biting into his backside. It wiggled as it seemed to burrow farther in, causing Smokey to scream in agony and flip over, crushing the Tick into the sludge. Another Tick instantly hopped onto his leg and bit down on his thigh. He realized the tunnel was now a shimmering, red sea of eyes—little creatures fighting for their chance to bite into him. The pain seemed more bearable and gave Smokey a second to regain his thoughts.

Why am I not feeling any of this?

He watched, helpless to move, as two more of the little, mechanical Ticks leaped over the others, bounced off the wall, and landed strategically on his stomach and chest.

Little bastards know how to parkour!

The thought made him laugh for some reason. They bit down, and his world slipped into darkness.

Red sipped an espresso in his air-conditioned, leather chair, watching the events unfold on a ten-foot screen covering one entire wall of his office. He clapped when he saw the Beetle and the swarm of Ticks take down his test subjects. In a well-choreographed dance, the large Beetle and tiny Ticks worked together to carry the bodies of Carm and Smokey toward the nearest exit of the tunnel where a security detail would pick them up. The security team would put the suspects into a cell and wait for Brock to decide what to do with them. That was the procedure they were trained to follow.

The warden had been nice enough to advise Red when the break-in attempt would take place so he could be a fly on the wall.

During the break-in, his hand controls allowed him to quickly switch between the different camera feeds in the area. He could watch the overhead drones outside, the in-tunnel feeds, views from the eyes of the Beetle and Tick deterrents, as well as audio and video of the security team as they were working to counter the attack.

Although Brock didn't know it, Red had even bugged Brock's office with a microphone and a small camera that were concealed in one of the displays mounted on the wall of Brock's office. Those feeds were only available to Red, and he hardly ever used them. Today, Red watched that feed because he wanted to see Brock's reaction as he performed his job to perfection. He was proud of his closest friend.

"Well played, Brock!" he said to himself.

His phone vibrated, and he knew who it was before he even picked it up. He hit the button to videoconference with Brock.

"Good morning, Brock!"

"Sorry if I woke you, Red. Had a bit of an incident, and I thought you'd like to know about it," Brock said as if he were holding on to a big secret.

"Oh, I know all about it, Brock," Red said, smiling ear to ear.

Brock looked dumbstruck, and Red knew he had caught him off guard. He almost felt bad about ruining Brock's secret.

"Wait ... you knew about the break-in?" Brock asked, the wind taken from his sails.

"I knew about it and planned it, Brock!" Red snickered.

"You bastard! Why? My heart is still pumping at one hundred miles an hour."

"I wanted to do a real test of our security measures. If I let you or the team know it was coming, you would have an advantage and it wouldn't be a true test. Your team and those little creatures passed the test with flying colors!"

Red could sense Brock's relief and watched as his pride swelled.

"Holy fuck, that was intense. I have to admit, the only security measure that failed was when my sleepy eyes couldn't open long enough for the retinal scanners of my office to work. I'm switching those to fingerprint scanners tomorrow!"

Red laughed.

"I had already ordered a bottle of your favorite Scotch in anticipation of your success. We'll sip it while we replay the videos of this little test tomorrow evening," Red said. "Tell your team they did a splendid job and should expect a little bonus in their next paycheck. Good job, my friend!"

"They'll appreciate that. And you know I always appreciate a good bottle of Scotch!"

"Admit it ... you'd appreciate a BAD bottle of Scotch, too," Red joked.

"Well, that goes without saying! Scotch is Scotch to an Irishman."

Brock's expression changed as he read a message that had just appeared on his phone, highlighted in red.

"Oh fuck! Seems we have a problem, Red," Brock said.

"What is it?" Red sat up in his chair.

"The security detail just recovered the suspects from the tunnel, and one of them is dead. Their message says the Beetle appeared to have squeezed him too hard. The pincers broke through the ribs, puncturing a lung. Message says there was nothing they could do to save him," Brock said, embarrassed.

"Well, fuck … this isn't good," Red responded and then paused. "Don't worry about it, Brock. I'll handle any fallout. The men I used were inmates out of Ditmeyer's facility. He helped handpick them for the job. I may need to grease some palms to cover this up, but it was still worth it to test the facility," Red said.

"Sorry. I'll have that Izzy chick look into the pressure gauges of the pincers and fix the issue before something happens in a more public setting," Brock replied.

"Yes, she'll figure it out. Always does," Red said. "Try to get some sleep. You still have that date with a bottle of Scotch tomorrow."

Red put the phone down and paced his office, thinking of possible fixes. He knew he needed to let Warden Ditmeyer and the guards know what happened—and soon. They were probably already wondering why they hadn't received word from Red yet and why their inmates hadn't been returned.

Red picked up the phone and rang Ditmeyer.

"Good morning, Mr. Draven," Ditmeyer answered, obviously wide awake and awaiting the call. "How did our little test go?"

"Well, we were able to stop the threat. But we have a slight problem, and I'm unsure how to handle it," Red said.

"Slight problem? What happened?"

"Slight problem as in … one of the two inmates was killed while trying to break in."

There was silence on the other end of the phone. Red didn't know if Ditmeyer was mad or trying to figure out a plan of how to handle it.

Red continued, "Seems he ran a little too hard into our Beetle deterrent, and the pincers accidentally broke some ribs, which in turn punctured his lungs. The other inmate is still sleeping from the toxin, and he'll be awake and fine in about two hours."

It was still silent on the other end of the call. After ten seconds, Ditmeyer finally responded, "Hand both bodies off to my guards, and I'll tell them what to do. You don't need to know the details, but it might take some extra money to keep this little problem hush-hush. I know Sgt. Romero and Lt. Donovan will cooperate. Hey, sometimes inmates fight, and sometimes they kill each other when put in the same cell. It's happened before. That's what happened here, right?"

Red realized Ditmeyer was willing to cover this up, and that it was already well worth the money he'd invested into his campaign fund. He also calculated that the additional cash necessary to conceal this fuck up might be less than paying the rewards he was going to give the inmates anyway.

"I'll make this right, Phil. You can be sure that you and the guards will know how much I appreciate your confidentiality and assistance. Have your guards meet my security detail at the same place where they had dropped them off—on the road near the sewage treatment plant."

"Always here to help," Ditmeyer said, knowing full well that this favor would keep him in his position and well paid for years to come.

12: A FLOWER SPROUTS

SATURDAY

Gabby received a text from Aiden:

I'm here. Want me to come to the door?

YES, typed Gabby.

Carlos and Mariana followed her to the door like helicopter parents. Gabby had told them Aiden was picking her up, so it was no surprise. He had been the topic of conversation all week, so they felt they already knew him. They heard how he stuck up for Gabby in class, helped her with her schedule, and introduced her to his friends. They even heard about the invite to a *Dungeons & Dragons* game.

"Hi, Aiden," Gabby greeted him. "This is my aunt and uncle. They just wanted to meet you in person."

"Nice to meet you both!" Aiden said, blushing.

"Nice to meet you, too!" Carlos replied, grabbing Aiden's hand and shaking it vigorously. "Gabby told us how you had her back with the bullies in social studies, so thank you!"

Mariana jumped in, "And saved her from a game of *Dungeons & Dragons*. I'm just glad I didn't have to make her an elf costume this week."

They all laughed, and Mariana gently pushed Gabby out the door. "Have fun, kids!"

"I won't be home too late, but you don't have to wait up for me," Gabby said.

Aiden's car wasn't anything special. His family was lower middle class, always teetering on the edge of poverty, and a shiny, new car was the last thing they could splurge on. Once the mortgage, insurance, utilities, and groceries were paid for, his parents hadn't much left to spend. He was lucky he got to use their only car tonight.

"Believe it or not, they're more protective than my real mom and dad." Gabby laughed.

"Fill me in on your mom and dad. Where are they now?" he asked.

Gabby paused. "Well, you know I was supposed to come across with my mom, but I didn't tell you the whole story. They caught her right before we'd entered an escape tunnel. They fried her with an electric snare, and a drone took her away before I could help her. She was sent back home to Mexico."

"And your dad?" Aiden probed.

"I'm pretty sure they killed my dad over a year ago. He had attempted to come across a few times and had two marks the last time he tried. He just disappeared, and we haven't heard from him since. Noah said he would do his best to obtain information about him."

"Damn! I'm sorry, Gabby. It makes sense why you were so passionate about our immigration debate in social studies. Your secret's safe with me. And I'm happy you made it across. I want to help more people find the American dream. That's why I joined the Wallflowers."

"So what's your deal? Why are you so passionate about helping? You're an American, and most Americans talk about us Hoppers as though we're criminals and invaders."

"Half of us believe otherwise, Gabby. Unfortunately, the majority won the last election, and we're now stuck with mechanical creatures roaming the border and a political party opposed to almost any legal immigration policy. So what was your hometown in Mexico like?"

"La Coronilla wasn't bad, and I loved the people. It just lacked many things I wanted. And there was the constant threat of the cartels taking over little towns like ours. There are no good colleges where I lived, and there is nowhere to learn about computers besides online classes. That's why I came over. God gave me this brain, and I want to use it to make something of myself and help people, not just dream about it while picking aloe plants in a field."

"I get it. I'd do the same if I were in that situation. And I want to help people, too, the same way people have helped me. People like Mr. Dempsey," Aiden said.

"What did he do for you?"

"Well, my family isn't well off. If it weren't for Mr. Dempsey, I wouldn't have had a computer to work on. He dropped a computer off at my house freshman year. I wouldn't be one of the best coders if it weren't for his kind act."

"Second-best coder," Gabby said, elbowing him.

"Okay, a close second best. Look, I just need to be good enough to stand out so I can get a scholarship. Otherwise, I'm not going to be able to afford college."

"I haven't even started thinking about college. I'm just happy to be in a high school that has decent computers and some windows without bars across them," Gabby said.

"I'm still working on my plan. While other kids play *Civil Watch*, I scour hacker websites, looking for code to learn from. It's not that I want to take down government agencies or banks or anything like that. I just love to see the creative ways hackers get into systems with just a few simple lines of code and some networking know-how. So Mr. Dempsey started to mentor me, staying after school to teach me the fundamentals of network security, how to create virtual private networks, how IP addresses and routing tables worked, and how to truly secure computers and networks. He also taught me how to code."

"You sound like me, but I didn't have two mentors until this week. Heck, I didn't even have my own computer. I worked in the back of a friend's store on a computer that I swear was from 2030. My only advantage was that I lived in Mexico, and we didn't have any government agencies with the time to try to lock up hackers," Gabby said.

"Yeah, I'm probably already on some watch list with one of the three-letter agencies—CIA, FBI, or NSA. When I started, I made the mistake of exposing my name, address, and IP address. They probably even have a nice picture of my zitty face plastered on a 'Future Hackers of America' poster tacked to their bulletin board. Since then, I've learned how to set up firewalls, block my IP address, and route my work through virtual private networks worldwide."

"So what do you want to do ... you know ... when you grow up, as they say?"

"I'd be happy with a cybersecurity position, although not in a government agency. I disagree with things the government has done, and I worry that if I work at a government agency, my political views would prevent me from being promoted. Maybe I'll start my own company, I don't know," Aiden replied. "What about you?"

"Finish high school, go to college to learn as much about computers as possible. Oh, and robotics. Then I can build bigger and better creatures to take down Draven's beasts," she joked.

"Well, when we're done with Draven Labs, you won't need to take that robotics class. College is hopefully a reality for me, too. I'm applying to Texas A&M next year. As a native Texan with good grades—and considering my family's economic situation—I'm hoping to earn some scholarship money or financial aid. I'll also have to find some part-time work to cover my ramen noodle soup and hot dog meal plan. Maybe I'll just play *Civil Watch* to earn the money." Aiden smirked.

Gabby smacked his arm this time.

"Ow! Speaking of the game, have you seen the little *Civil Watch* medals some kids at school wear on their backpacks?" Aiden asked. "I think I even saw a cafeteria worker with one on their apron this week."

"I wondered what those were. I saw a group of boys wearing them on their shirts. I thought it was some school spirit thing I didn't know about yet," Gabby said.

"No. Those show a player's rank and special achievements they earned in the *Civil Watch* game. The badges usually get delivered on Mondays. Then on Tuesdays, we see students come into school flaunting their new medals. It's like a cult," Aiden said. "When you think about each representing at least one Hopper caught, it's pretty awful. One kid had to remove his shirt at the security gate last week because he was wearing so many, it set off the metal detector. They made him remove his shirt because removing all the medals would have taken him an hour."

"Sad to think that someone might be wearing one of those medals for capturing my mom," Gabby said.

"All right, let's stop talking about that damn game and do something about it. We're here," Aiden said as he made a right onto an unlit street.

"A dark alley? Are you planning to kill me, Aiden Moore?"

"Yep, that's me! Aiden Moore ... high school student by day and serial killer at night," he joked. "Trust me, this adventure only gets better."

He pulled into a dark garage where several other cars were parked. He looked around for the largest space available and parked diagonally in it. Gabby side-eyed him as if making fun of his parking job.

"What? Dad will kill me if I get a scratch on this car." He

laughed and then jumped out of the car.

"Follow me," Aiden said, walking toward a large, rusty storage cabinet with a female pinup calendar on the front. He looked around for onlookers, opened the cabinet, and ducked inside.

Gabby followed and was amazed to find herself standing on a well-lit staircase leading down. She noticed a thick bundle of orange wires running along the wall, attached near the ceiling.

"That's a lot of fiber," she said.

"Sometimes it's not enough."

Gabby was confused.

They walked down two flights and stopped at a metal security door. Aiden pressed a button below a security camera, and the door opened without hesitation. Gabby stepped in after him and was in awe of the room's size and flurry of activity. The digital screens on the walls were streaming videos of Hoppers running through different sections of the border. Each screen was framed by a game interface with a small inset video of a person excitedly moving, wearing their headset and remote control.

"Are these people playing the *Civil Watch* game?"

"No. They're WATCHING the people who are playing the *Civil Watch* game. They're ensuring those Hoppers find a Wallflower tunnel and escape from the Red Zone before being caught. We help Hoppers escape here."

Gabby stared at one of the screens that showed a young boy, about thirteen years old, running from a sizable Beetle creature.

Her heart raced, and she panicked, rooting for the boy as he appeared to outsmart the creature.

"Get him out of there!" she yelled, and everyone in the room startled and turned toward her.

The man in the black chair in front of the boy's video stream smiled, turned back to the display, then stood and hit the glowing, green button on the wall under the video feed. He turned toward Gabby. "Don't worry, darlin'. If that boy listens to my instructions, he'll be safe and sound in the United States by tonight."

Gabby spun around and looked at Aiden. "Sorry. That boy reminded me of myself only a week ago. I guess I have a little PTSD."

"Don't apologize, it's understandable. Come on, everyone's probably waiting for us to start."

Around the corner was a huge conference room surrounded by SMART boards, with a large table in the middle. A group was sitting, and Noah was standing at the head of the table. Noah glanced up when Aiden and Gabby walked in.

"There they are," Noah said, and he walked over to give both Aiden and Gabby a hug. "Now we can start!"

Gabby noticed a few people she knew and some she had never met. Rose, from the flower shop, smiled at her and waved. Peter, Noah's driver, said hello and stood near the conference room door. Mr. Dempsey was sitting at a laptop at the closest end of the table, and he motioned for them to both sit next to him. He had saved them seats and had already grabbed a cold pop and a plate of pizza for each.

"You have to get the pizza when you can. These people will devour it before you even have a chance to grab a piece. Especially Peter over there." He laughed, and Peter gave him the middle finger.

Noah started the meeting.

"This is Gabby. She made it over the Red Zone on the southern border just last week and is extremely smart. From what Mr. Dempsey says, she is a genius with computers. Her mother was, unfortunately, caught and returned to Mexico. I intend to get her over here safely as soon as possible."

Everyone welcomed her, and Gabby mouthed a "thank you" to Noah.

"Gabby, you've met Rose, Peter, and Jack. Sorry, I mean Mr. Dempsey. Let me introduce some of our other volunteers. That's

Johan Erikson sitting next to Rose. He works in IT at Draven Labs."

Johan waved at Gabby.

When Gabby waved back, she noticed a beautiful woman wearing glasses sitting to his left. She hadn't seen this woman when she entered the room and was stunned by her natural beauty. Her blonde hair was pulled into a ponytail, and she wore a Texas T-shirt and torn jeans. The lady saw Gabby staring and gave her a big smile.

"Hi, Gabby. I've heard a lot about you. I'm Izzy Davis, an engineer and fixer of all broken creatures at Draven Labs. It's nice to have another smart woman on the team … someone to bring the IQ levels way up in this room," she said with a laugh, obviously in good fun as the men in the room agreed with her.

"Nice to meet you," Gabby said, slightly embarrassed by the compliment.

Noah continued, "Last, but not least, Greg Pearson, Utilities Manager for Draven Labs. He knows where to find every electrical outlet, sewage pipe, and gas valve inside Draven Labs. The only thing he can't find is a girlfriend."

Everyone laughed, even Greg, who shook his head in agreement.

"As you can see, we have several Wallflowers embedded in the town of Solace and deep inside Draven Labs. There are many more volunteers than you see here. As a security precaution, each group of Wallflower volunteers only knows the members of their group. You will usually never meet or even hear the other volunteers' names. We do this for safety reasons. If someone gets caught and they're somehow tortured and forced to expose the identity of another member of the group, the damage is limited to their small group. There's no risk of them identifying anyone outside their group," Noah explained.

"Of course, we promised each other to keep our secrets, no

matter what they try to get out of us," Izzy added, receiving acknowledgment from everyone in the room.

"All right, let's start. We have a lot of work to do. Johan, can you fill us in on the network security plan?" Noah asked.

"I'm ready to go. Hours before our operation, I'll install a secret door into the network. That way, it won't be exposed until we need it, and it'll be too late for them to close it if they find it," Johan said confidently. "I've written down the IP address and an SSH account to gain SFTP access to the internal network. Don't lose this," he cautioned, sliding a folded, yellow paper across the table to Jack Dempsey. Jack didn't bother opening it and slid it into his laptop bag for safekeeping. He and Johan had worked together for years, and they trusted each other implicitly.

Johan continued, "There will be two directories—one titled CREATURES and another labeled OPERATIONS. Place your subroutines in the appropriate directories, and I'll have the nightly cron job watching and waiting to include them in the equipment update process. Then, when we are five minutes from go time, simply visit the URL on that piece of paper and the update process will kick off. It will take no more than five minutes to update all of the creatures on the northern and southern borders and in the Hive at Solace. Once those are updated, the subroutine in the OPERATIONS directory will run and delete any trace of our security hole, your subroutines, and any logs of what we've done."

"Beautiful work, Johan." Jack grinned.

Noah patted Johan on the shoulder. "You're well worth the money we're paying you, Johan."

Everyone laughed except for Gabby, who appeared confused and slightly offended about the pay comment. Aiden noticed her confusion.

"We don't pay anyone here, Gabby. He was joking," Aiden explained.

Peter jumped in, "Unless you consider the pizza our payment."

He held up both hands, a piece of pizza in each.

"This is all from the goodness of my heart ... and the desire to get my family over into the States," Johan added.

Gabby felt relieved.

"Jack, do you think we'll have the creature and operation subroutines figured out in time for our planned date?" Noah inquired.

"With Aiden and Gabby's help, and a few nights and weekends of work, yes!" He looked at Gabby and Aiden and they nodded, willing to work the hours required to finish it.

"Thanks to you all!" Noah smiled. "I'm going to start getting our man Emilio to spread the word to your families, advising them to be ready at a moment's notice. We'll have him escort them through the Red Zone to a designated escape tunnel when the time's right. Our little plan to disable the creatures will take place, and the borders will be clear of any danger."

"We have one more detail for our plan to work long term. Anyone coming back over the border with a mark, like Gabby's mom, can still be apprehended by the police and be deported. We'll need to find a way to remove the visible marks and overwrite the data stored deep into their bones," Izzy pointed out.

Noah smiled at her. "Hmm ... I wonder where we can find someone good at reverse-engineering equipment to help. Someone with knowledge of all of the inner workings of the equipment at Draven Labs? They need to be fine with working for nothing. And preferably blonde and with an air of confidence about them?" He looked around the room sarcastically.

"Okay, I guess I'll just do it," Izzy feigned.

Everyone laughed.

"Before we go through with our plan, I'd like to ask you all to hunt down any dirt on Draven Labs. Incriminating videos, quietly settled lawsuits, disgruntled employee testimony about any goings-on behind the scenes. Bring me anything you can dig up," Noah directed. "We can send that out to our friends in the press just before our operation. We'll flood the airwaves to incite anger in the public and hit Draven from all sides."

Greg Pearson said, "One of my guys told me a story about some idiots trying to break into the lab through the waste treatment plant a while back. Something happened to them in the tunnels under the Silo. The Draven Labs security team took over and ushered employees out of the area. My guy saw two covered bodies being rushed out of the facility under the dark of night, but nobody knew what it was all about or what happened to them in the end. My guys never learned the full story, and the police were never involved. At least, there were no public police reports or stories in the local news about the incident. My guy's name is Sam Perkins, and he's a talker. But he's close to retirement, so he probably won't risk getting into trouble by talking to someone on the record."

"I'll ask our investigative reporter to talk with him, anonymously, of course. Sounds like a cover-up," Noah said.

"Not sure if you all heard, but a brave reporter named Emily Faro from World Tribune News snuck in and interrupted Draven's little international show-and-tell day. She claimed they learned of a recent death that occurred in the Red Zone. A creature pulled a man underwater, and he drowned in the Rio Grande. I could tell Draven was pissed that someone leaked the info. They were trying to cover it up by not reporting it to authorities. They'll just claim it happened on the Mexican side of the border, and therefore, it's not their problem," Izzy said.

Gabby sat up straight and interrupted, "Wait. Did the man get attacked by a Jellyfish creature? In the Rio Grande?"

"Yes, I guess the poor man struggled to get free, and the Jellyfish shocked him, causing his death. Draven asked me to devise a fix to prevent it from happening again."

"Did the reporter mention the name of the man who drowned?"

Gabby probed.

"Yeah, Caesar something, from Monterrey, Mexico." Izzy struggled to remember his last name.

"Oh my God!" Gabby teared up and buried her face in her hands. "I was in his group. I thought he was just unconscious when the drone picked him up."

Izzy felt terrible that she had relayed the story without much empathy. "I'm so sorry, Gabby. I had no idea you knew the man."

"It's not your fault. It's fucking Draven's fault. That's awful. He was such a sweet man. My mom and I got to know him as we hiked through the desert. He was just trying to get over to meet his new granddaughter in Arizona."

"So sorry, Gabby. Sounds like we need to get details from that reporter, too," Noah said.

Peter asked, "Why don't we try to figure out all of the two-mark disappearances? If we could learn what Draven is doing with the Hoppers with two marks, we could expose that information to the press. That would be pretty damning. I know the Mexican government would be interested in that information, too. Draven would be put dead center of a shitstorm with that information!"

"I'd like to know that, too," Gabby added. "My dad had two marks when he disappeared. I need to find out what happened to him."

"Me, too," Noah added. "Good idea, Peter. We could get Emilio to place a tracking device on someone in the next group of Hoppers he brings into the Red Zone. Someone who has two marks."

"I don't think we need to do that," Jack Dempsey interjected. "From what I understand, two marks never even make it back to the processing center at the Silo, so the drones that pick them up must be able to scan for two marks and then take them somewhere else."

With his line of thought, Aiden knew where Mr. Dempsey was

going. "Yeah, we should be able to look at the code in the drones and see what they're programmed to do when they pick up a Hopper with two marks. We should be capable of getting the GPS coordinates straight out of the code."

"Brilliant," Noah said. "If we get that location, we can send a drone to investigate. Jack, Aiden, Gabby … can we make that a priority? See what the code reveals? That will give me time to figure out the logistics and get a drone to investigate."

"I'll get on that tonight," Aiden said. "Sounds like a challenge. You in, Gabby?"

"Hell, yes!" Gabby replied.

Noah smiled at their enthusiasm. "Great, thanks! I know we're pushing you three pretty hard in the final stretch. And sorry to throw you into a hornet's nest today, Gabby. Let's all regroup next Saturday. We can finalize plans and gather any information you guys find. Send me any dirt, and I'll have a social media expert craft some good stories from your findings so we can flood the internet with them when the time is right."

As Mr. Dempsey had foretold, the pizza was already gone. Gabby didn't feel like watching more Hoppers on the big screens in the viewing room. She was done with tears for the day.

"Can we go?" she asked Aiden.

"Want to go to your house and see what we can find in the drone code? Or would you rather hit a dance club first? It is Saturday night," Aiden joked.

"Although I'd love to see you dance, coding sounds like more fun. I also don't think my clothes will set the right tone at a dance club. I think they frown on jeans and T-shirts anyway. Let's go to my place," Gabby suggested. "I'm sure my aunt and uncle would be happy to have visitors."

"Well, you're missing out on my specialty—a mean robot dance—but I'll save that for another day. Let's get out of here."

Mariana ran to the kitchen to fix something to eat, even though they told her they had just feasted on pizza.

They went straight to digging into the Draven Labs' code, specifically the code that ran the autonomous processes of the DLED drones. Aiden had already set up remote access to the computers that he and Mr. Dempsey used to run tests of their code changes. He created an account for Gabby in case she wanted to play on her own time.

"We keep backups and use a collaborative code repository. We can all change the same code and see which subroutines work the best. All changes are stored and backed up in case we need to revert to a previous save."

"That makes me feel better. I was worried about touching the code and messing up anything you and Mr. Dempsey have done."

"Don't worry about that. It's all part of the learning process. Let's take a look at the drone code."

Gabby noticed each file ended in a.py extension.

"It's all written in Python?" Gabby asked. "I'm not up to speed with Python."

"Don't worry, you'll be fine. It's very similar to JavaScript. I'll walk you through it. You'll pick it up in no time."

Aiden pulled up an interface with several directories, each named for a creature, a piece of field equipment, or a system process. He clicked on the DLED DRONE directory, and a list of scripts displayed alphabetically. He started scrolling.

```
/DLED-DRONE/
 - AUTONOMY.py
 - BASKET_SYSTEMS.py
 - CAMERA_SYSTEMS.py
 - ENERGY_CONSUMPTION.py
 - FLIGHT_DYNAMICS.py
 - FUBAR.py
 - IDENTIFY_SORT.py
```

- `MEDICAL_CHECK.py`
- `MOST_WANTED.py`
- `PACKAGE_DELIVERY.py`
- `PACKAGE_PICKUP.py`
- `PACKAGE_STATUS.py`
- `PART_DELIVERY.py`
- `RETURN_TO_BASE.py`
- `SENSORS.py`
- `SURVEILLANCE.py`
- `UPGRADE_PROCESS.py`
- `VERTICAL_TAKEOFF_LANDING.py`
- `ZONE_ASSIGMENTS.py`
- `X_PURGE.py`

Aiden started viewing the subroutines in order alphabetically, beginning with AUTONOMY.py. As he scrolled through the code, he showed Gabby what Mr. Dempsey had taught him.

"Draven Labs kept Mr. Dempsey's good habits, even after he left the company. He taught me that a good coder should add a note above each section explaining what it does and what other subroutines it depends on. It makes it easy for you and anyone else to determine whether you are looking at the correct code."

Gabby read the first few notes. "I didn't realize the drones use artificial intelligence. It looks like the programmers use generative AI to allow the drone to make decisions about where to fly, learning where it flies most often over time."

"But only when the drones are not assigned a task by the system or instructed to pick up a Hopper through the *Civil Watch* game interface. You can see the related routines that were added back when the game was allowed to interact with the drones," Aiden pointed out.

It took almost thirty minutes to get through only a portion of the first file.

"The task of going through these files alphabetically, line by line, is starting to seem enormous. I didn't realize how much code was behind these things. Can't we search for the word 'longitude' and see what it finds?" Gabby asked.

Aiden searched the directory for "longitude," but nothing matched.

"Let's try the word 'mark' and see if we get lucky," Aiden suggested as he typed.

"The matches don't seem to be related." Gabby was getting frustrated.

"We'll find it. Keep thinking of words related to dropping something off," Aiden said.

"Maybe try the script named PACKAGE_DELIVERY."

Sure enough, PACKAGE_DELIVERY appeared to fit what they were looking for. It read:

```
/*
PACKAGE_DELIVERY
Determine the status of the package. Lookup against
/MOST_WANTED/ files. Run MEDICAL_CHECK. Determine
the final destination of the package. These
routines should not be confused with PART_DELIVERY.
*/
```

"Someone was being clever by calling Hoppers 'packages.'" Aiden laughed.

"It's probably because the word Hopper wasn't around when they wrote the original code," Gabby pointed out.

"Well, that makes sense. Good catch. The subroutine points to the CHECK_STATUS script, which might be exactly what we're looking for," Aiden said, clicking on the CHECK_STATUS.py file. The first note in the file made Gabby clap, startling Aiden:

```
/*
PACKAGE_STATUS
Determines the status of the package—whether the
package has a history of crossings. Change
destination based on status. These routines are
dependent on MEDICAL_CHECK.
*/
```

Aiden searched for the word "destination."

Toward the end of the file, they found exactly what they sought.

```
/* DESTINATIONS:
ZERO (0) MARKS—deliver to closest Silo.
ONE (1) MARK—deliver to closest Silo.
TWO OR MORE (2+) MARKS—deliver to closest secondary
processing center.
*/
```

Aiden scrolled to where a long list of processing center latitudes and longitudes were listed. They focused on the southern border's secondary processing center closest to Solace, Texas.

```
.south_secondary_el_paso_latitude = 31.250117
.south_secondary_el_paso_longitude = -105.981695
```

Gabby was on the edge of her seat. She was finally going to see where her father was taken. Oddly, she hoped the coordinates were close to the Mexican side of the Red Zone and near a Mexican prison. She had hoped that he may be locked up and unable to contact home.

Aiden could sense her anxiety rising. He used a mapping program to search the location using the latitude and longitude. He changed the search results to the satellite layer and zoomed in several times. There was nothing but some water, surrounded by a mountain ridge.

"There's absolutely nothing there? It was a wild goose chase," Aiden said, frustrated he couldn't give Gabby answers.

"I'm never going to find out what happened to him," Gabby said sadly.

"Don't give up. As Noah suggested, we can always try adding a tracker to a Hopper with two marks. Let's send Mr. Dempsey the coordinates anyway. Maybe something was built there, and the maps aren't updated yet."

He texted the coordinates to Mr. Dempsey, plus the directory and file name where they discovered them.

Mr. Dempsey texted back within minutes.

Nothing there? Very odd. I'll notify Noah.

"I think that's enough for me tonight. I have to get my parents' car back anyway. Can I pick you up tomorrow at noon to start working on the VPN and creature code with Mr. Dempsey?" Aiden asked.

"Yes, I'm excited to get started. I will sort through some more code to get a feeling for Python and understand how these directories are all set up. Is that okay?"

"Of course. Have at it!"

Gabby walked him out, and Mariana stopped them on their way out the door. She handed Aiden a wrapped plate of food for the road.

"Thank you, ma'am," he said, hugging her. "Whatever it is, it smells better than the pizza we had earlier."

"Homemade empanadas. My mother's recipe!" Mariana beamed.

Gabby opened the door for him. "Thanks, Aiden. I appreciate everything you're doing for the Wallflowers and my family." Then she hugged him.

Aiden blushed and walked to his car, smiling the whole way.

"Nice boy!" Mariana whispered.

"A little nerdy, but I like 'em that way."

Gabby grabbed a plate of fresh empanadas and returned to her room to review the list of files they hadn't touched yet. Most of the file names made sense until she got to one named PURGE.py.

What is PURGE?

The note at the top of the file simply read:

```
/*
Terminal security measure—self-destruct upon
equipment tampering or data breach.
*/
```

This sounds promising.

Gabby read through several code sections and noticed a few places pointing at an execution command of "python X_FUBAR.py."

She opened the X_FUBAR.py file.

This file had no description at the top, which was unusual. She could decipher some of the access control and permissions commands but got lost when the code mentioned a "servo" and "RDX." There was something about moving a servo into a specific position of 180 degrees. Gabby tried to interpret what the code did but felt lost. She texted Aiden the script she was looking at and explained where it was referenced several times in the PURGE.py file. It was getting late, but she knew she couldn't sleep until she learned what this FUBAR script did.

Aiden didn't answer for another half hour. When he did, it was a phone call, not a text message.

"Gabby, you're amazing! Do you realize what you've found?"

"No. What is FUBAR?"

"Fucked Up Beyond All Recognition," Aiden said excitedly. "You found a script that destroys the equipment if someone tries to mess with the internal workings or programming. It must be a security measure to wipe out the intellectual property if it gets into the wrong hands."

"Well, what's a servo and RDX?" she pressed.

"The servo is a tiny motor and, in this case, looks like a mechanical kill switch. It rotates 180 degrees, which in turn ignites something called RDX. I searched for 'ignite' and 'RDX' on the web, and it says RDX is a white, odorless, tasteless explosive. Pretty caustic shit from what I'm reading. It's more powerful than TNT!" he explained.

"Great, so if someone messes with Draven's equipment, this little 'servo' triggers a bomb?" she asked.

"Well, it depends on how much RDX they put in the thing. Perhaps it's a small enough amount to only damage the internal workings and the solid-state hard drive. Or maybe Draven's putting in enough to hurt the people trying to pry it open. Either way, I'm not willing to open one up to find out. But you discovered something that might help us destroy all of his equipment on command. That code isn't just used in the DLED drones … it's referenced in the code for EVERY creature. I'm going to send your find to Mr. Dempsey and Noah. This discovery changes everything."

"Okay. I hope you don't mind, but I'm going to sleep. My brain hurts from looking at all of that code. See you tomorrow?" Gabby asked.

"Noon!" Aiden said. "Great find, Gabby!"

13: BLACKMAIL AND BASS

Brock hit the button on the panel outside Red's top-floor suite. He was looking forward to a night of good food and bourbon with his only friend. When Red opened the door, he didn't look happy.

"What's got your panties in a bunch, Roja?" Brock asked.

"Senator Stanwell has been calling every day since our show-and-tell. He's all over my ass because of that reporter's questions. And he keeps demanding more information. As if I have to answer to HIM. I'm tempted to send a damn Black Widow Spider to his house to pay him a visit. I bet that son of a bitch would piss his pants at the first sight of it," Red fumed.

"He would faint and then piss his pants," Brock joked.

"I also need to find a way to test some of our lethal deterrent prototypes and be ready to show it to some new clients. I already have interest from one of the countries that attended our little event—if we can prove they're effective. These international types aren't pussyfooting around. They want creatures that kill and are willing to pay us well. If we play our cards right, this could be very lucrative for us ... even more lucrative than the *Civil Watch* game. But if Stanwell learns we're selling lethal versions of our creatures, he'll be all over us. The president, too."

"Come on, let's forget about our senator friend and have a good night. It's been a trying week."

"Well, I need to figure something out soon. I don't think the kickback checks will keep him in our pockets much longer. I need something on him—and quickly."

They sat down at the table, and Red's chef delivered the food. Chilean sea bass topped with a Thai chili sauce over creamy coconut risotto. It was both Red and Brock's favorite meal and just one of the reasons Tomas, his chef, had been kept around for the last two years.

Red asked Tomas to grab the tequila and the twenty-five-year-old Pappy Van Winkle bourbon bottle from the liquor cabinet, along with three shot glasses and two snifters. The chef looked surprised that he asked for three shot glasses as Red had never included him like this before. He hoped there wasn't an extra guest coming because he had only made and plated two servings of the sea bass.

Red filled the three shot glasses with a generous pour of tequila and handed them out.

"What's the occasion?" Brock asked. He was used to the tequila making an appearance, but not the good bourbon, especially with a normal weekday meal. And Red was not one to ask the chef to join them.

"It's the anniversary of my parents' death today. I guess it's my way of honoring them."

"So sorry, Red. I forgot what day it was. Tá síocháin acu anois," Brock said as he lifted his glass. Tomas joined by raising his glass high.

They finished their shot, and Red and Brock handed their empty glasses to Tomas, signaling he should get back to the kitchen. Red poured two fingers of the Pappy Van Winkle into the two snifters and handed one to Brock.

"To friends," Red toasted.

"Amigos," Brock replied, inhaling deeply to nose the rare bourbon. The aroma made him smile.

As they tore into the sea bass, Brock could sense Red was still trying to figure out his problem with Stanwell. Red always furrowed his brow when attempting to make a problem disappear. This tell often helped Brock win against him in their friendly poker games.

"Okay, let's figure out our little senator problem. It's ruining your dinner and mine," Brock said, setting his fork onto his plate. "If money can't buy a person, what's the next best thing?"

"Reputation," Red answered almost immediately. Obviously, he had been thinking along the same lines as Brock this whole time.

Brock grinned. "Right. Stanwell is a cockroach. He's never worked a corporate job in his life. This government job is everything to him. And his reputation is what keeps him in the game. So how can we threaten his reputation?"

"Well, I thought the threat of exposing the payoffs would be enough, but it isn't having the effect I thought it would. I guess the president must be riding him to keep on us."

"Okay, aside from his reputation, what does he care about most?"

Red thought for a minute. "Family?"

"Right. Doesn't Stanwell have a kid in high school? I'm pretty sure I've heard him bragging about his son's rank in the *Civil Watch* game."

"Yes, he brings it up every time I have to endure listening to him. I always assume he mentions it hoping I might give his son some special medal or something. So what does that have to do with Stanwell's reputation? If anything, he can declare his son is doing his civic duty better than other kids his age."

"What if we capture his son killing Hoppers on video?"

Normally, Red would rein Brock in, but he was desperate, and this idea might just work.

"We kill two birds with one stone?" Brock hinted.

Red's brain was catching up to Brock's plan. "So we show

Stanwell a video of his son controlling the creature … and it kills a Hopper. Stanwell's career would be over if the press got ahold of that. Problem is, if word of us building lethal deterrents gets out, we'll be out of a job along with Stanwell, or we'll need to rebuild our operation overseas."

Brock interrupted, "No. Knowing kids these days, Stanwell's son would surely brag about killing a Hopper at school the next day. So we just won't let anyone other than Stanwell know it ever happened. It would be easy for us to cut the kid's audio and video right before the Hopper dies. Stanwell's kid hunts down a Hopper using our lethal prototype. His face and celebration of the catch will be visible on the screen, but the kid will have no idea the Hopper was killed. He just thinks he was caught and there was a glitch in the system preventing him from seeing it. We record everything—the hunt and the kill—and show Stanwell the full, unedited clip."

Red understood now. "And we tell him we'll keep it out of the press as long as he supports our endeavors."

"Bingo! Problem solved." Brock leaned back in his chair and smiled.

"Stanwell will know we're building lethal deterrents, though," Red said.

"So what? It would be too late for him to expose it. He's an investor and receives money from the company, so he would be complicit. Also, Stanwell and the president know that we're talking to other customers outside the United States. They're not idiots. When we signed the contract, our services were never promised as an exclusive arrangement.

"Luckily, our well-paid lawyers included a watertight errors and omissions clause, as well as a liability and indemnity contract to cover our asses when—if—there is ever collateral damage. We're already such an integral part of this country's defenses, I am sure the president and the US government will want to look away if and when the time comes. If something happens on that front, and I'm wrong, I know a few countries that would love our technology and services and can provide immunity. Heck, Mexico might just offer to rebuild our little city on their side of the border. We can shift everything ten miles south and be in business again."

"Okay, you sold me on this one. So how do we get Stanwell's son and our new lethal creature to play with each other?" Red asked.

"That's the easy part," Brock responded. "I find the turret that the kid's account is tied to. We deliver the prototype creature to that turret and ensure it's only accessible by Stanwell's kid. I have our dev team create a special interface that only his squad will see. We just sit back and wait. We might have our little blackmail clip by the end of this weekend considering how often Stanwell says his kid plays the game."

"All right, let's do it," Red agreed, picking up his fork and finally looking relaxed. "Did I ever tell you that you're one devious bastard?"

"Who, little old me?" Brock replied.

14: CREATURE CODE

Mr. Dempsey, Aiden, and Gabby agreed to meet at Wallflower headquarters on Sunday around 12:30.

As Gabby and Aiden descended the stairs to the Wallflower headquarters, they could smell food wafting up the staircase. It was different from the sweet smells coming from the Mexican bakery upstairs.

"Something smells good," Gabby said.

They realized what it was when they entered the *Civil Watch* viewing room.

Johan was standing next to a long table covered in food. He welcomed them in. "Hey, you two! Noah was kind enough to bring us lunch from that Mediterranean restaurant down the street. Gyros, kabobs, hummus, as well as Greek salad and vegetables. Dig in!"

Gabby also noticed fresh, hot buñuelos from the Mexican bakery upstairs. It was enough food to feed fifty people. She and Aiden made up plates of food and went to the conference room to begin working.

When Aiden and Gabby turned into the conference room, Mr. Dempsey started clapping for them. He looked like a proud dad, and Gabby blushed.

"Gabby, great job discovering the self-destruct code. It's a game-changer. That's going to make our jobs so much easier. And thank you both for hunting down the coordinates to Draven's secret processing center. Noah and Peter took a drone out to the edge of the Red Zone a bit ago, and they texted that it was already on its way to that location. We should be able to watch the captured footage once they get back. We'll see what Draven's got hidden out there in the middle of the Red Zone. You two ready for a long day of coding?"

Aiden and Gabby both nodded emphatically.

Mr. Dempsey had obviously arrived earlier as he had already set up three laptops next to each other on the conference room table. On the whiteboards, he had drawn a network diagram, a task list for each person, and a list of all the creatures requiring code changes.

He went over the plan for the day with Aiden and Gabby. "Gabby, I need you to set up the VPN so it looks like we're an employee within the Draven Labs' network. If we try to access the servers from any place outside Solace, it'll raise flags in Draven's security checks. Johan's written the IP address range on the board, so you can use any of those to connect with. He also set up a network access server in a storage closet inside the lab, which is already connected to the Draven Labs' fiber network. The ports and everything you need are on the board, too. Feel free to grab Johan if you need any help or have questions. Once you've set up the VPN, you can assist me and Aiden with the creature code," Mr. Dempsey explained.

"Yep, I'll get on it. That should be easy enough," Gabby assured.

"Aiden, can you search and make sure the code for each creature points to that FUBAR script?" Mr. Dempsey asked. "I want to be certain that we can change that one file and affect all creatures simultaneously. That will be our master kill switch at the end of our attack. We could destroy every piece of equipment in the turrets on the northern and southern borders."

"Yes. On it!" Aiden said as he and Gabby organized their work area for the day.

Within the first hour, Gabby had already set up the VPN and tested it with Johan by her side. Johan was impressed with her knowledge of VPNs and asked, "Hey, where'd you learn all that?"

"*VPNs for Dummies*. It was a free book through an online library app." She smiled. "I'll order you a hard copy."

Johan laughed at her sense of humor.

Aiden and Mr. Dempsey invited her over to look at what they were doing with the creature code.

Mr. Dempsey explained their thinking, "We want to reprogram the creatures to do as much damage to Draven Labs' equipment as possible without hurting anyone. We want it to take years for them to clean up the mess."

Aiden jumped in, "I remember seeing some code that mentioned the different ways the creatures can locate Hoppers. Movement, sound, heat. Try the SENSORS script."

Mr. Dempsey opened the file, and they walked through the code together. Each section of code had a note above it.

```
/ MOTION /
/ SOUND /
/ LiDAR /
/ VIBRATION /
/ INFRARED /
/ NIGHT VISION /
```

Mr. Dempsey said, "I wish these things had electrometer sensors. We could get them to attack anything with a standard electrical charge. That would be perfect because they would ignore humans and just go after anything connected to an electrical outlet. They would attack generators, servers, computers, lab equipment …"

"And coffeemakers. That would REALLY piss them off!" Gabby added. They all laughed.

He searched in the script for the words "electrometer," "electroscope," and "electricity" with no results.

Thinking of coffeemakers gave Aiden an idea. "What about heat instead? There's an infrared sensor listed, and that would detect heat, right?"

"Yes, but humans give off heat, too. However, we might be able to change the code to look for certain heat ranges. Good idea, Aiden," Mr. Dempsey said.

He did a quick internet search to find the range of temperatures for a human body.

"So a human body can be between 95–103 degrees Fahrenheit. Someone around 95 degrees would be hypothermic, and we won't find that around here in the Texas heat. Above 103 degrees would mean they have a high fever and should get to an emergency room," Mr. Dempsey said.

He searched through the INFRARED script, and sure enough, heat limits were already incorporated into the sensor code.

"These things are built to look for anything between 93–106 degrees Fahrenheit. It references additional code that uses 3-D LiDAR to sense size and shape to determine whether or not they're human. It allows the creatures to ascertain whether they are looking at a human, an animal, or just a piece of hot metal sitting in the sun. Pretty ingenious."

"So I could have dressed in a bear costume and safely crossed the border?" Gabby joked.

"Except your body temperature would exceed 103 degrees Fahrenheit wearing a bear suit in the Texas sun, doofus," Aiden mocked her.

"A polar bear suit, then?" Gabby added, and they all laughed. "Wait, I just realized that they gave us Mylar blankets when we crossed the border. Emilio, our guide, told us to put them on whenever we thought a drone or creature was nearby. They definitely worked!" she said.

"That makes sense. LiDAR and infrared sensors couldn't detect anything through a Mylar blanket. It could sense your body using the other sensors, though, like sound, movement, and vibration. If you were moving at the time, it would sense that!" Mr. Dempsey explained.

Aiden added, "So why don't we just use the logic they've already built into these creatures to find humans and just do the opposite of that? We tell them to ignore the humans and instead concentrate on the other temperature ranges. We look for anything non-human or non-animal outside the 93 to 106-degree range, but giving off a certain amount of heat—electrical heat?"

"That should work," Mr. Dempsey said, smiling, giving Aiden a hard pat on the back. "Way to use that big forehead of yours!"

"Can we use the simulation software to test it?" Gabby asked.

"Yes! Let's get to work," Mr. Dempsey said.

After changing the creature code slightly, they set up the simulation software to test it. The changes worked as expected. They could not get any creatures to attack a human form because of its temperature and shape. Every time they ran the simulation against a human, the message UNABLE TO ACQUIRE TARGET blinked on the screen.

To ensure the creatures would instead attack non-living targets that gave off heat, they programmed in a simulated electrical box connected to a 120-volt current, giving off a low heat signature. In each case, the creatures followed the new directive to disable this new target with whatever means were available to them—legs, pincers, and even the sheer weight of their bodies.

All three were celebrating when Noah, Izzy, and Peter entered the conference room.

"What's got you three so excited?" Noah queried.

"We figured out the creature code! Aiden thought of a way to get the creatures to follow a new mission to destroy all electrical devices while ignoring humans or animals. We're going to be able to destroy Draven Labs' infrastructure from within," Mr. Dempsey advised. "And as icing on the cake, Gabby discovered that all of their equipment has a self-destruct process built in. When we're done taking out everything electrical, we can send a signal to have each creature destroy its processors and internal data drives. We learned that Draven loaded a small explosive in each piece of equipment. We believe it's a fail-safe he added to prevent anyone from stealing his intellectual property."

Peter looked impressed. "You figured all of that out in an afternoon?"

"Well, Aiden and Gabby have been busy bees. They spent several afternoons in my classroom and most of last night working through the code," Mr. Dempsey replied. "Izzy, have you ever seen an explosive called RDX inside the equipment when you're fixing things?"

"RDX? No. And the self-destruct process is new to me, too! But that's probably because I only work on mechanical parts like exoskeletons, motor assemblies, and sometimes weaponry. I also have a special digital key that disables the creatures before I can open them up, which might explain why I haven't been blown to smithereens. I know that every piece of equipment, the drones, and deterrents have a red box containing the brains—the computer and solid-state drives housing their code. I'm not able to gain access to the red boxes because they're completely welded shut. And nobody would have reason to open them up since a Bluetooth connection allows us to update them. I guess the red boxes could hold an explosive charge since they're bulky enough."

Johan yelled something inaudible from the other room. Noah spun around to him and gave him a thumbs-up, then turned back to everyone.

"Well, I don't want to sour the celebratory mood, but the drone is sending back footage near the coordinates you shared. I've asked Johan to pull up the feed on the big screen in the lounge area. We'll finally be able to see where our friends with two marks are being taken," Noah disclosed.

"Not sure I want to see this," Gabby whispered to Aiden.

"Better to know than to wonder for the rest of your life," Aiden remarked, trying to comfort her.

They walked to the lounge, and Aiden and Gabby sat on the leather couch. Everyone else stood around the room, circling the huge, high-resolution screen. Johan wore a VR headset, allowing him to look where he wanted the drone to go. Footage from the drone appeared to the group on the screen.

They all had a first-person view from the drone as it flew quickly up the side of a ridge. There was sound, but they could only hear the drone's propellers and the wind as it advanced, maintaining a clearance of twenty feet above the ground.

"Can you isolate the propeller and wind sounds and remove them from the audio feed?" Izzy asked Johan. Johan used eye-gaze technology inside his virtual headset to change the settings. The only audio they could now hear was from the crickets and some birds as the drone passed by them. When the drone neared the top of the ridge, the audio went eerily silent.

"Did the audio cut out?" Noah asked.

"No, it's still feeding. I think it's just quiet out there," Johan responded.

WHOOSH!

Everyone in the room was startled, and Johan grabbed the edge of the couch as the drone crossed over the ridge and quickly fell off a cliff. It was like a virtual rollercoaster ride, and everyone in the room just went over the first hill. The drone went into a freefall and then automatically slowed when it neared the twenty-foot mark above the canyon floor.

"Can you steady the drone and pan around the area?" Noah

170

probed.

As the camera panned, they saw that the drone had entered a deep canyon. Red stone walls reached straight up toward the sky, surrounding the canyon. They were lucky it was midafternoon, as the sun was still high enough to light their view. Another hour, and much of it would be covered in a shadow.

"I can't see any manmade structures. Can you go up about forty feet and point the camera down slightly?" Noah questioned.

As if Johan had predicted what Noah would ask, the drone was rising and the camera tilted. He began panning around the inside of the canyon again.

"Wait, stop!" Izzy yelled.

"What is it, Iz?" Noah implored.

"Over near the cliff face … by that water? Don't you see them?"

Johan slowly advanced closer to the water. Several objects moved in the brush along the waterline, almost in unison.

"Are those—" Noah started.

"Creatures!" Izzy completed his sentence. "First-generation, Draven Labs' creatures. I've only seen those models hanging in a Draven Labs' history display. I can't believe they're still working. They're like the Model Ts of the Draven Labs' creatures."

"Are they drinking from the pond?" Peter inquired.

"No. Look in the center of the pond," Izzy said. "They're hunting something but are afraid to enter the water. They can handle rain but won't survive if their components are submerged."

The drone moved closer to the pond's center, where a man knelt in the deeper water, shaking, with only his upper body visible. He appeared to be in his early thirties and was shirtless. He was almost completely covered in tattoos, except for a deep-red area where his shoulder should have met his upper arm. He wept as he stared into the red water surrounding his body, his right arm dangling from the few ligaments still attached to his shoulder.

"Is that blood?" Aiden asked. "Is his arm falling off?"

"I think the creatures tore his arm off, or at least tried to," Izzy answered. "They're attempting to find a way to finish the job. Wait. I think I can make out two marks on his forearm."

The man looked up at the drone and screamed in terror.

"Oh Dios mío, por favor mátame!"

"He's begging for us to kill him," Gabby said, obviously shaken. "We've got to help him!"

Johan replied, "The drone can't handle that much weight. He couldn't hold on to it with one arm anyway." He zoomed out and repositioned the drone so they could see the man from behind, with the creatures in the distance.

"What are they doing at the edge of the water?" Aiden asked, and Johan zoomed in toward the small group of creatures gathering closest to the man. The creatures worked together to push a long cactus from the water's edge into the shallow water. A tiny spider creature jumped onto the cactus and extended another cactus it was dragging out from the end using its back legs.

"Building a bridge," Noah said. "They're using teamwork to get closer to him."

"Yeah, even the early models had machine learning built into them. It's basic AI, but enough to allow them to learn to work together."

One last cactus was pulled into place, creating the final section of the bridge. Just before a large Zombie Ant crawled across the natural bridge and reached for the man, Johan pulled the drone away. He didn't want anyone—especially Aiden and Gabby—to see the man's final moments.

Gabby started sobbing. She realized this was probably what her dad's final moments were like. Aiden pulled her close and tried to comfort her. Noah touched her shoulder, knowing his parents had met a similar fate.

"Don't worry, Draven's going to pay," he whispered in

Gabby's ear.

As the drone followed the path from the pond toward the canyon's center, it passed several organized piles of what looked like bright-white sticks. They were stacked in separate bundles, sorted by length.

Mr. Dempsey looked at Peter and whispered, "Bones?"

Peter shook his head in agreement.

"This is terrifying. I can't even imagine! Turn off the display, please," Noah asked Johan. Johan knew he needed to record the remainder of the canyon, so he continued flying around to get as much evidence as possible without displaying any more of it to the group on the large screen.

"I think I need to head home, Aiden," Gabby said softly.

"I understand."

Aiden announced, "I believe we've had enough for today. If it's okay with everyone, we'll head out."

Izzy stepped over and gave Gabby a long hug. "Sorry you had to see that, sweetie."

Mr. Dempsey reassured them it was okay to leave. "You two have done more than I had ever expected. I'll stick around here and write the program containers to bundle our creature updates into one file, along with the self-destruct sequencing. Go home and try to find a little peace. I'll talk to you tomorrow at school, okay? I've got it from here."

"Thanks, Mr. Dempsey," Aiden replied, and he walked Gabby out.

15: PERMANENTLY RETIRED

"It's going to be another hot one out there, hon," said Grace, Bill Harley's wife, as she handed him his green, Stanley lunchbox and a canteen filled with ice and yellow Gatorade.

"Yeah, I'm still waiting for the day it's NOT a hot, dry one," he replied with a smile and a kiss. "Let me guess—a turkey and mustard sandwich on rye bread, an orange, a bag of chips, and HoHos?"

This had been his traditional packed lunch for as long as he could remember.

"Nope! I had to substitute pink snowballs today. The store was out of HoHos. Sorry!" she replied.

"What? Pink snowballs? If the guys see me eating those, I'll never hear the end of it. I'll be coming home with some new girly nickname … if I make it home at all." Bill acted alarmed.

"With your new role at Draven Labs, I know you'll come home safely tonight, unlike the past twenty years you've spent with the border patrol," she said, resting a hand on his shoulder.

His shoulders visibly slumped.

"Come on, honey. You and I both know we're getting to the age where a less strenuous and risky job might be a good thing," she said, trying to comfort him.

"Yeah, I guess so. I just miss the adventure of trekking through the desert and hunting down the bad guys. This wiping up oil stains, swapping out equipment, and doing inventory at those damn turrets for Draven Labs is a far cry from the adventures I used to have. I won't complain too much, though. It could be worse," said Bill.

"Yeah, you could have lost your job like Frank and Sammy. I heard from their wives that they're still looking for something to make up for the wages they lost. Their medical benefits have already run out," Grace said. "I didn't realize just how much medical benefits cost when you don't have a company paying for them."

"Yeah, and at fifty-five years old, I knew they'd have difficulty finding a new job. Even if they were younger, it's not as if the border patrol left us with many skills that will transition to careers outside the government sector. Private security firms are hiring young kids, even though we old guys have years of experience dealing with the bad guys and the know-how to de-escalate situations. I feel bad for Frank and Sammy. And I guess I'm glad Draven Labs asked me to stay on, even if it is for less money," said Bill.

"Yes, it's good to adjust your attitude a little bit. Keep reminding yourself that you only have a few years before you can officially retire," said Grace, "and the health, vision, and dental benefits surely help."

"Yeah, I can handle this job for five more years, no problem. Then you and I can work on our little retirement plan. We'll sell the house, buy the RV, and explore the inside of the country for a change," Bill said, a smile returning to his face.

"That's better! And you're right. It's just five years, and it'll fly by," she said, patting him on the butt and scooting him out the front door.

Bill's ride to work was only a twenty-minute drive, but it was long enough to reminisce about his many years of work. Knowing he wasn't cut out for college life, he had joined the army for six years and then signed up with the US Customs and Border Protection Agency at the age of twenty-five. The army had given him experience with explosive ordnance disposal, so Draven Labs offered him a job just over a year ago. Not that Draven Labs used any explosives, but they knew Bill was good under pressure and could find his way around wiring and electronics, a much-needed skill in the turrets out in the Red Zone. They also knew Bill could find his way around the Red Zone, as it had been his workplace for so many years.

He had spent more than thirty years in some capacity on the border near his hometown of El Paso, Texas. Performing almost every job as a border patrol agent, Bill had finally earned enough seniority and skills to become a supervisor.

That new role had been decided, and Bill was looking forward to announcing his promotion when the election in 2048 messed up those plans. With the new president's ties to Draven Labs, the US Customs and Border Patrol had changed its role and canceled all planned promotions. Instead of a promotion, they'd offered him a position within Draven Labs. The job was in maintenance, and he was demoted to an entry-level technician. The entire Border Patrol Agency was now relegated to assisting Draven Labs with its mission to secure the border.

To make matters worse, Bill was assigned to Joe Hickock, a snot-nosed, twenty-eight-year-old who was his new supervisor. The kid was a Draven Labs' employee who reported directly to Brock Murphy, head of security.

Bill worked long enough to know not to rock the boat and complain about anything, so he just went through his new training keeping his mouth shut and his head down. He did whatever the kid asked of him, with a smile.

His friends, Frank and Sammy, took a different approach and tried to get some of the other old-timers to strike when the change happened. Their revolution landed many of his coworkers on the unemployment line. Bill felt a bit like a traitor because he hadn't joined them, but he reminded himself that he owed it to Grace to make it through the next few years to obtain his full retirement benefits.

Bill pulled up to the entrance of the Draven Labs' processing center, which was built halfway between the town of Solace and El Paso. High, cement walls jutted up from the desert floor, painted in a bland, tan color that made the walls blend in with the surroundings. Atop the walls were virtual guard stations topped with camera surveillance and defense systems. This town housed the headquarters of Draven Labs and one of the processing centers where Hoppers were dropped when caught in the Red Zone.

His daily routine required that he check into the large conference hall in the processing facility to get a team safety briefing and then head back out to the Red Zone to the turret he was assigned that day. He was glad he didn't need to check in at Solace, as it was another fifteen minutes farther away. Bill was happy he didn't live inside the walls of Solace. He and Grace already owned property outside the city when he was hired on, and they were grandfathered in and not required to live in the town like many of the other Draven Labs' employees.

Bill was accustomed to the routine, fifteen-minute wait for cars to be inspected on their way in and out. He spent today's wait time reminiscing about his first training day at the facility two years ago.

On his first day as an employee of Draven Labs, Bill had been given a tour of every part of this facility and its operations. Aside from the mundane administrative offices that hugged the exterior walls, there was a central facility buzzing with activity. He distinctly remembered the processing Silo that stood like a monument in the middle of the town of Solace. It looked like a nuclear plant steam tower, painted in the same tan-colored cement as the town's walls surrounding it. He was escorted into the Silo and told to look up.

"DLED 245 incoming. Time to arrival is T-minus-five minutes," a calm, female, robotic voice echoed over loudspeakers strategically placed around the base of the Silo. A series of flashing, yellow lights awakened, giving the entire work area an eerie glow.

Bill watched as the workers scurried to their assigned stations, some wearing fluorescent-yellow jumpers while others donned white, hazmat-like suits. Some stood in front of digital workstations, and other workers formed a guard detail around the outside of the netted area. Bill assumed they were there to escort the incoming Hopper into the facility. A two-person team, wearing red coveralls with MEDICAL TEAM imprinted across the back, rolled in a cart of life-saving devices and medications, just in case they needed to provide medical care to the incoming Hopper.

Bill heard the drone's propellers approaching, and his instructor yelled over the din, "When the DropHop … sorry, that's a nickname for the drones … I mean, when the DLED drone is directly overhead, it will release the Hopper into the net above that will catch them."

As if on cue, the DLED drone had appeared high above, hovered, and centered itself over the Silo to release its catch. A limp body fell from its basket and softly landed into the net, bouncing a few times. The arms and legs flopped like a ragdoll. The net reminded Bill of the ones they used at a circus to catch trapeze artists.

The Hopper's body lay motionless in the center of the net as it was slowly lowered to the floor. Bill could see that it was a younger man, probably in his late twenties, wearing dark clothing. Once the net was flat on the floor, the guard detail picked up the man and carried him to a gurney, where the medical team waited. After quickly inspecting the man's vitals, one of the medics took out an electronic wand and waved it over both arms. A green light glowed at the end of the wand with each swipe.

The instructor explained what was happening. "That device scans the Hopper's arms to see if he has been marked before. Hoppers receive a mark every time they cross the border illegally—and after due process. The mark is a digital tattoo etched through the skin and into the forearm bone in the arm. It's an almost painless procedure, just a slight burning sensation for a second as a laser hits the skin and bone.

"One scan of a mark can tell us where they tried to cross last and how many times they attempted to cross. We've never seen someone with more than two marks. As you can see, being captured can be pretty traumatic, and I guess the Hoppers learn it is impossible to get through after two attempts. If this Hopper crossed before, the wand would glow yellow. If they had crossed twice before, it would glow red. I'm told a three-mark glows purple, but I've never seen it before."

The medics had finished their assessment and nodded at the guards that it was safe to proceed. One medic stayed behind while the other joined the guard detail, escorting the Hopper. All of the flashing lights turned off, and the team of workers inside the Silo seemed to relax.

The tour guide had directed Bill and his group to follow behind the guard detail. Behind him, he could see they were quickly raising the net back up into the air for the next arrival, who must have come early as he heard an alarm and observed the flashing, yellow lights turn on again, the team apparently back in panic mode.

The tour group entered another room in the facility and gathered in front of a one-way, glass window into what appeared to be an operating room.

The instructor had detailed the next part of the process. "The medics just injected some adrenaline into the Hopper to revive him. The two people in white suits will get him showered, cleaned up, and dressed for his trial. You don't want to watch the showering part, so let's move on."

As they walked, one of Bill's fellow trainees asked, "How long does this process take … from receiving a Hopper to getting them through a trial and shipped out, if found guilty?"

"Under two hours, usually. If they already have a mark, it's normally under an hour because all of the preliminary screening work would have been done the first time they went through this process," the instructor replied proudly.

Before any more questions could be asked, Bill and the other trainees were told to be quiet as they were ushered into a large courtroom and seated in a reserved row in the back. A judge in a black robe sat at a table perched higher than the rest of the onlookers. Bill noticed that everyone else in the room wore oversize, gray pajamas and flip-flops. They were all handcuffed, and a guard was stationed at the end of every other row.

"Those are the Hoppers caught late last night and this morning. A team of investigators has already gathered each Hopper's information for the judge. The judge will have a record of where the person came from, why they were trying to cross illegally, whether that person had any record or jail time, and if there are any marks on their arms. Each has been asked why the judge should allow them entry into the United States. The judge reviews all of this information while the Hopper is escorted to the front of the room," the instructor whispered to the group.

"Nikolai Servos, is that your name?" the judge had asked the older male standing in front of him. The frazzled man tried to pull up his baggy pajama bottoms with his cuffed hands as he shook his head yes.

"My file says you came from Russia because you were being targeted by the Russian Mafia and feared for your life?" The judge said it as more of a statement than a question.

The older man shook his head again.

"I see you left your wife and two children to fend for themselves back in Russia?"

The man's body slumped, obviously not realizing the US government had access to that kind of information.

"Immigration denied. We only accept immigrants from bordering countries, and only in cases of extreme duress. When you get back to Russia, please tell your friends this information and save them some time and the American people some money," the judge admonished as if he'd said it thousands of times before, which he probably had. The man was yanked out a side door.

"They'll fly him out on the next flight to Europe and back to Russia," the tour guide had informed the trainees.

The group witnessed a few more cases, each ending in denial of entry. However, one case made the whole group realize why they had this due process. A middle-aged couple was escorted to the front of the room, cuffed together. They looked as though they had been through a rough patch and appeared weary and disheveled.

"We have a Frank and Nancy Blanton?" the judge read off his screen. "It says here you are Americans who reside in Brunswick, Ohio? You are both school teachers on vacation to the Southwest for the summer?" The judge peered up from his screen and over his glasses, inspecting them from top to bottom.

The husband looked at the wife, who was too nervous to speak, and replied, "Yes, Your Honor."

"How in the heck did you end up in the Red Zone south of New Mexico?"

The wife glared at the husband and smacked his arm. "Tell him how, dear."

The husband had responded very quietly, embarrassed to admit his mistake out loud and in front of the other people in the room. "We were hiking, and I told her I knew where we were headed, but I guess I was off by a bit." He acted as if he were shaming the entire male population by admitting his error.

"A bit? A bit would have been when I asked you if we should turn around and retrace our steps back home!" screamed the wife.

The husband continued, "The GPS on my phone stopped working, and by the time I realized it, we were lost and it was already dark. I thought I saw city lights in the distance, so we walked in that direction. I didn't realize the lights were on the other side of the Red Zone. We were both ambushed by some kind of terrifying Black Widow Spider creature. I don't remember much after that, and I found myself sitting in a cell wearing these silly pajamas."

After a long pause, and with a serious look, the judge, followed by all of the guards in the room, broke out laughing.

"You poor souls. I'm sorry for laughing, but we don't get many of these stories in my courtroom, and it's a pleasant surprise," the judge tried to say in between laughs.

The husband and wife both smiled awkwardly, a bit embarrassed.

"Bailiff, please take these fine folks to gather their belongings and get them to the consulate's office. Sir and madam, we'll return you to your vacation quickly. I know this little detour couldn't have been fun, but it will make a heck of a story to tell your friends back home. And Mr. Blanton, might I suggest a paper trail map or an experienced guide the next time you decide to do a walkabout in the mountains so close to the Red Zone?"

"Thank you, Your Honor, but he'll be hiking on his own next time," Mrs. Blanton responded in a huff.

The guard gently guided Mr. and Mrs. Blanton to the door exiting the courtroom.

The judge tried to stop laughing as Bill's tour group left.

Bill had enjoyed watching the banter between the judge and the last couple. It had given him the sense that the judge did have a heart after all.

The group proceeded to the end of a long hallway where a freight elevator was waiting. They boarded, and the tour guide swiped his badge and pressed a few buttons on the control panel.

The elevator jerked into operation and started to drop quickly. The small window that let in the sun from the outside went dark.

"Did we just go underground?" Bill had asked.

"Yes, the facility has five levels—two above ground and three below. We do most of the technical and secretive work down here," the guide replied as the elevator had eased to a stop and the doors slid open.

Two guards stood on either side of the elevator doors, rifles pointing at the ground but fingers on their triggers and at the ready if needed. Bill noticed that there wasn't a smile between them.

"Just one way Draven Labs protects its intellectual property from the outside world and that Wallflower group. Those Wallflowers would kill to get into this facility and do as much damage as possible, so security keeps things pretty tight down here."

Bill received a nod from the older security guard as he passed and thought he recognized the guard from his old border patrol days.

I am glad to see someone else got to keep their job.

The tour guide didn't go into detail about the Wallflowers, as the activists had been the subject of so many news stories ever since the border was turned over to Draven Labs. If you hadn't heard about the Wallflowers, you were living under a rock.

A set of gray, steel doors with stainless-steel, mechanical bolt locks blocked the group from their next stop on the tour. The guide stuck his face to a panel on the wall and scanned an eyeball into an optical reader, which blinked green. A loud alarm sounded, the bolts slid away, and the doors swung inward. In front of the group appeared a large, cavernous workshop. The guide had ensured that each tour group member was handed safety glasses and a bright-green hard hat as they entered the vast room.

The workshop, like the hallways leading up to it, bore shiny, white walls and bright, overhead LED lighting. The facility looked like something from the future, with extended, stainless-steel workbenches covered with electronic testing devices, some of which Bill had never seen before. Above each row of tables was a hefty, yellow winch with metal chains and hooks hanging down.

Everyone in the facility had worn white lab coats, except for what looked to be a few supervisors who appeared to wear unique jackets in the Draven Labs' turquoise color.

The guide led the group over to the left side of the room, close to three technicians focused on a four-foot-tall, mechanical Zombie Ant creature dangling from a crane. One of the technicians typed a command on a handheld device, and the Zombie Ant jerked to life, swinging its head and front legs violently.

"Holy shit!" Bill said out loud, taking a step away from the creature and bumping into his tour guide. It was so realistic, Bill had feared it was going to attack the workers.

The tour guide stepped out in front of the group and motioned for everyone to calm down, assuring them that everything was fine, trying not to laugh at the group's reaction.

Another key press by the technician, and the Zombie Ant went still again. The team popped open the abdomen, exposing a complex set of metal gears, hydraulic hoses, blinking lights, and circuitry.

Bill was amazed by the amount of technology packed inside the creature. As he panned the wall, he'd become enamored by the collection of mechanical creatures hanging behind the technicians. It appeared to be a mix of old and new creatures—both drone and deterrent technologies. Some resembled insects, some animals, and others looked like reptiles. Of all the creatures, the Zombie Ant was the most intimidating to Bill for some reason. Seeing something that is usually so small, but now larger than the technician standing next to it, sent a chill down his spine.

Bill thought about the feeling he had after the tour that day. The technology and security were so ahead of their time, he started to feel good about his decision to stay with Draven Labs. He remembered thinking that this job might be pretty cool.

Bill's reminiscing disappeared with a honk from behind. He was daydreaming, and the line opened up in front of him. The man at the gate was vigorously motioning for Bill to pull forward.

He pulled up to the gate where two guards were stationed in an air-conditioned hut.

"Name and badge … quickly, please!" one of the guards demanded gruffly, leaning out the door, snapping his fingers repetitively.

After a long pause, Bill barked back, "Fuck you and that ugly Draven Labs' uniform!"

The guard didn't react immediately, but a smile broke across their faces simultaneously, and the guard stepped from the comfort of the hut to pat Bill's arm. It was Bill's old friend and coworker, and this was their morning routine.

"Napping in line again, eh? Welcome to one more day of fun in the sun, Billy. You're good to go!" the guard said as he waved him on.

"See you on the flip side," Bill said as he hit the gas, causing his tires to peel out. He saw his friend in the rearview mirror, laughing with the other guard as he sped away.

Bill watched as several DLED drones flew overhead toward the facility's center. He knew they were dropping off Hoppers who had been caught that morning.

It must have been a busy morning!

Bill pulled into the employee lot and walked through two security doors, each requiring him to place his finger on biometric keypads to gain entrance. He entered the team room, which was buzzing with the many stories and rumors gathered from the previous shift. It was an auditorium with twenty rows of elevated seating looking down on a stage with a podium. He sat near the back, as close to the exit as possible, since he didn't want to wait in a long line to leave the room at the end of the meeting.

"Everyone sit and simmer down! We have a lot to go over this morning," said Brock Murphy, head of security, standing at the podium. Nobody noticed him entering the room. He was always a bit stealthy like that.

They all quieted because everybody feared Brock Murphy, although they had been given no reason to be afraid. He hadn't done anything to warrant fear, but everyone seemed to get the vibe that he was not someone you wanted to mess with. Maybe it was because he was built like a Marine. Or it may be because they all knew he was Red Draven's right-hand man and best friend.

"First item. We're deploying new gadgets from the research and development team. Don't be alarmed if you have new equipment crates at some of your turrets. We're only testing them in certain areas, so you won't all be getting them," Brock announced.

There was whispering among the team, which quickly stopped when Brock spoke again, this time louder.

"The fucking Wallflowers have attempted another breach of our defenses out in the Red Zone. It appears they've built an impostor robot to cross over from Mexico and place an explosive near the base of Turret 152, east of the city. It caused minimal damage, but this required us to make a software change in the *Civil Watch* platform. The game now marks any moving, non-Draven Labs' equipment as an enemy. Players who incapacitate any future Wallflower robots will be heavily rewarded."

There were cheers and hoots from some of the younger maintenance workers, who were proud to hear that the turret held up to the Wallflower attack. Everyone here disliked the Wallflowers because they worked counter to the team's mission.

186

The Wallflowers were trying to break open the border in any way they could, and this group was focused on keeping it secure.

"Okay, get your safety armbands and ensure they're fully charged before you leave. Earlier this week, we had an incident where one of your teammates had their armband run out of juice a little earlier than expected. Chuck Fossett looked like a Hopper to one of the *Civil Watch* players and had a friendly encounter with their Black Widow. I'm sure that wasn't a pleasant experience. To make matters worse, he was captured by a DLED drone and dropped off at the processing facility in front of his coworkers. A little embarrassing, wasn't it, Mr. Fossett?"

Brock purposely directed his gaze at a man trying to hide in the very back corner of the room. The man hunched over, held his head in his hands, and nodded yes, utterly embarrassed about the incident and about being called out.

The team started laughing and razzing him. Brock left the podium and exited the room, which was their cue to get to work. That was Bill's cue to rush to the table where they passed out armbands and daily assignments and then get to his car as quickly as possible to avoid the madhouse that always happened at the end of the meetings. He made sure his armband was fully charged first, of course.

Bill jumped in his car, blasted the air conditioner, and peeled open the red envelope that bore his name on the front. His assignment for the day was Turret 151.

That's the turret right next to the one attacked by the Wallflowers.

He sped out of the lot, past the security gate again, and made his way from the processing facility to his turret as quickly as possible.

Turret 151 was ten miles outside El Paso. Bill knew this area well as it was his old stomping ground and one of the more active sections of the Red Zone. He was happy to at least be in the area where some of the action took place.

After following a dirt road for about a half mile, he came to a locked gate blocking his access to the Red Zone and the turret he was assigned. Bill grabbed his keychain, opened the car door, and took five steps toward the gate. The gate had a large, red sign attached, warning that this was the start of the Red Zone. He stopped abruptly, and a tingling feeling shot down his spine, reminding him that he had forgotten something very important.

He looked at the sky in fear, turned, and sprinted back to the car to grab the safety armband he was supposed to be wearing. He pulled his armband on and quickly slapped the power button, ensuring it was fully powered on and still fully charged. It was.

Bill let out an audible sigh of relief. Being this close to the Red Zone meant he was already a prime target for anyone playing the *Civil Watch* game. The armband acted as a pass, preventing players from targeting him with drones and deterrents. He realized his mistake could have easily made him the next Chuck Fossett, which would have been embarrassing.

He imagined that scenario in his head and laughed at himself as he drove down the remainder of the dirt road, ending at his destination—Turret 151. He could see a drone flying over the desert in the distance.

Some poor souls will be having a bad day.

The turret stood eighty feet tall and reminded Bill of an old lighthouse. It was made of large sheets of curved, iron plates, each piece bolted together by steel rivets. The color and texture of the metal brought to mind pictures he had seen of the Old Ironside boat used during the Civil War.

Turret 151 had a heavy-duty loading door at ground level and an emergency ladder that allowed one to climb up or down from a lookout platform at the top. A huge, metal slide extended from a hatch positioned midway up the tower, pointing directly into the center of the Red Zone. The land around the turret was flat.

The top of the turret held a round, viewing platform surrounded by railings. Green-tinted windows offered a full 360-degree view of the surroundings. A massive, digital antenna protruded from the metal, conical roof, making the facility appear taller.

The hot sun reflected off the turret, baking the surrounding dust. Bill could swear it was twenty degrees hotter around the base. He was already sweating through his uniform, and it was only 9 a.m.

Bill noticed three crates outside the loading door and moved closer to inspect them. The only markings on the crates were solid-black icons of insects. One crate had an Ant, one a Centipede, and the last crate had the shape of an insect that looked like a Stink Bug.

I guess I'm one of the lucky testing sites for the new toys.

He unlocked and opened the loading door, and a rush of cool air exited the turret. One nice thing about working in the turrets was that they were air-conditioned to keep the digital equipment inside from overheating under the brutal sun. Bill grabbed a dolly from behind the door and pulled the three crates inside. He quickly closed the hatch behind him, trying to prevent all of the cool air from escaping the turret.

Compared to the industrial look of the outside, the inside looked like a modern work area with a multi-level deterrent storage system. Creatures were stored in bins lining the walls, each within reach of the automated, robotic picking and delivery system.

Huge bundles of multicolored network cables ran the tower's height from top to bottom. They were color-coordinated, allowing networking geeks to easily decipher their use and destination. Some ran underground, while others connected to black servers hanging midway up the center of the turret. The servers hummed and blinked in random green, orange, and blue lights. Bill had been trained to look for red lights on the servers. A red light meant something was wrong, and he would need to call a net-tech in to service it.

No red. It's a good day!

In the center of the room was a propane-fed generator and HVAC system that vented its hot air and gasses out of the tower through a series of aluminum tubing. If the solar panels and battery system couldn't supply power to the turret, the generator would kick on. Although, with the amount of sun these turrets received daily, the generator was rarely used. One of his tasks was to start the generator to ensure it kicked on in case it was needed.

A sophisticated, mechanical elevator system shifted every so often, stacking and moving the mechanical deterrents and tracking drones up and down and left to right to get into position for use. It was a well-coordinated dance that eventually led to one of the creatures being loaded in front of the launch hatch and sent down the slide and into the Red Zone.

Bill watched in amazement as one of the older Porcupine deterrents, stored in a compact, rolled-up ball posture, made its way around the room on one of the sliding elevator trays. When it reached the launch hatch, its red eyes blinked on, and it unfurled itself, spinning its wheels and launching itself out of the hatch.

Bill knew that someone—probably some eighteen-year-old kid somewhere in the United States—was now controlling the creature through the *Civil Watch* video game interface. He also knew that Porcupine would meet some unfortunate Hopper on their way to entering the United States illegally. The Hopper would endure some pain and incapacitation, be picked up by a drone and dropped at the processing facility, get tattooed with a digital mark, and then be sent back over the border to the Mexican authorities on a Draven Labs' bus.

Although mad that he lost his job catching those Hoppers the old-fashioned way, he had to admit the new Draven Labs' process and technology were all quite genius. And effective.

Bill ran through his regular maintenance routine—look for red lights, test the generator, oil the chains that moved the elevator system, replace all air and oil filters, and inspect the room for any traces of rodents or snakes that came in to enjoy the cool air. It only took one of those creatures to chew through some important cables, or piss on some expensive digital equipment, to take down the entire turret. This, in turn, would make for a very long shift for Bill.

Once his task list had been thoroughly checked off, he turned his attention to the favorite part of his job. He removed the older equipment listed on his checklist for that day and uncrated the new equipment. He enjoyed inspecting the machines that the R&D team at Draven Labs had invented.

Each turret had a compact shop with a tool bench and a full suite of tools for minor maintenance. There was a small winch system to allow him to more easily lift the drones and deterrents out of the crates and onto the table. The provided tools on the wall allowed him to make minor repairs to existing machines. This included replacing wheels that had started to wear away in the desert heat, belts that had lost their elasticity or had broken completely, or replacing expended weaponry like the Porcupine quills that had been shot into Hoppers. A cabinet at the end of the table had a stocked supply of replacement parts, refilled by some other Draven Labs' maintenance person who visited the turret once a week.

Today, Bill's inspection exposed a Squid 1.0 with some rust forming between its metal tentacles. Long missions in the Rio Grande tended to create this problem, as he had reported it to the mechanics and engineering team several times before. Even the tiniest amount of rust limited the creature's movement, so it needed to be crated up and marked for a full inspection by a quality control team back at the Hive.

Once the Squid was packed up, Bill pried open the top of the new crate. It had an icon of a Zombie Ant painted on top. He attached the winch to the mounting points on the top of the Ant's body and raised it from the Styrofoam packing peanuts. The peanuts blew around the work area, propelled by the server fans above.

Dammit! Well, that's going to take a bit to clean up.

As the Zombie Ant ascended, Bill stepped back, slightly alarmed by how realistic the Ant's head and abdomen looked. This new model appeared even more alive than the one he had seen on his first training day. It had a red body, and the metal parts were all covered in a shiny, plastic coating that almost looked translucent. As the Zombie Ant cleared the top of the crate, its body unfurled, and its long legs dangled in the air, swinging slightly, almost lifelike. He felt the Zombie Ant might twitch a leg at any second, and its dark eyes reflected the fear in his face.

Bill laughed that, for the first time since he started working in the turrets, something had put a little fear in him. He felt a bit of empathy for any Hopper who might run into this creature in the dark. It looked like something out of a horror film.

Realizing his fear was unwarranted, he pulled on one of the legs to get the Zombie Ant to spin in the air. He always liked to figure out what mechanics were involved in the deterrents and what their hunting abilities might be. This Zombie Ant had no obvious weaponry aside from the pincers jutting out from the sides of its jaw. He deduced that the Zombie Ant must capture its prey in its long legs and introduce a non-lethal toxin through the sharp needles protruding from its pincers.

Bill knew that Draven Labs had strict guidelines set by the government. No lethal weaponry was to be used in the Red Zone. Any deaths were publicly investigated, and the press had a field day placing blame whenever one of Draven Labs' creatures malfunctioned and caused permanent harm.

He hit the crane's controls and perfectly moved the Zombie Ant's body onto an empty elevator tray. Each tray had a wiring harness that could be attached to a creature to provide a full charge. The trays also used a fence to secure it during its journey along the walls. When he plugged the harness into the Ant, its head tilted up and the dark eyes turned red. It rotated its head toward Bill, stretched its legs into a more natural position, and chirped a few electronic notes. It just stared at him.

"Off you go, big boy! Stop staring at me as if I'm your prey," Bill said, knowing the creature could not understand him.

He hit the green button on the bottom of the elevator tray, which then accelerated up the wall, paused, and moved laterally across the wall to its final position, ready to be used.

Bill stared at it, wishing it wasn't still staring at him. Its eyes finally dimmed and went dark.

The next crate contained a Centipede that wasn't as scary looking as the Zombie Ant and came out of the box coiled up like a real Centipede. It remained coiled when he attached a power harness, and the only activity was two small, red eyes that glowed.

"You're not so scary, are you? You're kind of cute, actually!" He was speaking to it as though it were his pet. Being alone in the turrets seemed to cause him to want to befriend particular creatures and have conversations with them. It made the time go by faster.

"Let's see what the Stink Bug has in store for us," he said as he pried the wooden lid off the last crate. The Stink Bug appeared larger than the Centipede but smaller than the Ant.

Deep inside the packing peanuts, Bill could only see its rough, camouflaged backplate. He attached the winch to its hook and slowly pulled it out.

"You're a small bugger, aren't you? What harm can you do?" he asked it. As if on cue, the body unhinged from its backplate, swinging open and exposing the internal workings of the creature.

"Fuck! I don't think that was supposed to happen."

Bill quickly positioned the Stink Bug over an elevator tray and connected the charging harness. He kept the backplate open to look inside before closing it up and sending it on its way. Draven Labs had warned him never to open the creatures unless instructed, but Bill hadn't done anything to make this accident happen. He feared there was a technical issue with the latch that he'd have to report.

What's the harm in taking a quick look around first?

He grabbed a flashlight from the workbench and shined it around the circuitry and mechanics inside. He laughed that all of the wiring looked like actual bug innards.

"What the hell?" he said under his breath as he got closer and moved a thick wiring harness inside the creature that was covering something that caught his eye. He stared, speechless, at white, plastic-coated balls the size of baseballs. Each had the letters RDX in small, red letters on the side.

What the fuck is RDX doing inside a non-lethal deterrent?

Bill had spent many years learning about explosives in the army. It was his job to know everything about them. He had to know what kind of damage each type of explosive could do, how temperamental it was, what it looked like, smelled like, and even what it tasted like. RDX stood for Royal Demolition Explosive—a synthetic, white, crystalline substance that's highly explosive.

"You're carrying enough explosives to take out a small military vehicle. Why would that be?" he asked as if the bug would divulge its secrets.

Bill suddenly became uncomfortable. He glanced around the room and wondered how many of the creatures on the walls had some kind of unnoticed explosive in them.

Maybe this is a test. Draven Labs is testing me to see how thorough I am at my job. It would be a mistake to let this thing go anywhere near a living soul when it went off.

Bill considered calling his wife to see what her thoughts were. But she probably wouldn't understand the politics or fine details of why he would ask her a silly question like, "Should I mention to my boss that there are deadly explosives in this machine I am tinkering with?" He pulled out his phone and realized he couldn't call her anyway. He had forgotten that cell phones don't work out here in the Red Zone. That was due to a signal blocker Draven Labs had installed to create a dead zone in the Red Zone. The only form of communication he could rely on out here was his company-issued, two-way radio hanging from his belt and the landline connected to the wall, which offered a direct, encrypted connection to headquarters.

I have to call this in. I can't hook this thing into the system.

He pushed the button on his radio, waited for a second, and spoke slowly, "Maintenance, this is Bill Harley, ID 10345, requesting a supervisor. Over."

There was a slight delay on the other end, and a male voice replied, "This is maintenance. What seems to be the problem, Mr. Harley?"

"I've found something and need to talk with a supervisor, please. Over."

The man on the other end seemed agitated. "Hold. This is going to take a bit. Your supervisor is on his fifth break of the day, vaping outside, but we'll try to get him."

"Copy that. I'll hold."

Bill continued staring at the Stink Bug's insides, trying to figure out where the wires from the RDX connected. Unfortunately, they ran under the balls of explosives, and Bill wasn't ready to take a live refresher course on how easily an explosive can detonate with a small electrical charge. He looked at the electronic radio in his hand and took a few steps back from the creature.

Fuck this. Five years left, and to think I could be blown up working as a private citizen after all those years in the army.

Bill moved across the room and sat under one of the air conditioning vents. He realized he was sweating, and it wasn't from the heat.

Getting the Stink Bug onto the elevator tray was one of his last projects before returning to the processing center to turn in his safety armband and end his shift. He wondered if he should have ignored what he found and let the company deal with the repercussions if the thing destroyed the turret. Then he realized some other tech would eventually be assigned to this turret, and it wouldn't be right to put them in danger.

He paced the floor for thirty minutes, and the radio finally chirped.

"Bill Harley, this is Brock Murphy. Sorry to keep you waiting. What's the problem?"

He flushed with embarrassment.

Those idiots in maintenance bypassed my supervisor and went straight to the big man ... the head of security? Why would they do that?

"Bill Harley, are you still there? Are you in Turret 151?" Mr. Murphy asked insistently.

"Oh ... um ... yes, this is Bill Harley. And yes, Turret 1-5-1. I'm sorry to bother you. I asked for my supervisor and wasn't expecting them to escalate this to you."

"Escalate what, exactly, Mr. Harley?" Mr. Murphy seemed agitated.

"Well, I was installing three of the new test deterrents, and the one shaped like a Stink Bug accidentally opened up," Bill replied, sure now that he had made a big mistake.

"It just opened up? That's what you're telling me? Please hold," Mr. Murphy said sarcastically, and the radio went silent for five more minutes.

"So what's the issue, Mr. Harley? Can't you just close it?" Mr. Murphy asked in a much calmer tone.

"Well, I found what looks to be several small but very dangerous explos—"

Mr. Murphy quickly interrupted him. "Mr. Harley, that is

196

nothing you need to concern yourself with. Just close it up and put it on the racks like any other machine," Mr. Murphy ordered. "This is highly classified. I'll explain the situation when you come back to base. It has something to do with the Wallflowers. Copy?"

Bill knew better than to push the issue. He felt he had done his job by warning someone, and his shift was nearly over anyway. He just wanted to be done with this day and get back home to Grace and the fine meal he knew would be waiting on the kitchen table.

"Copy, Mr. Murphy," Bill said, embarrassed that he may have just risked his job.

The radio went silent, and nothing else was said.

Bill put his radio on the workbench, closed the backplate of the Stink Bug, and continued hooking it into its harness very carefully. Once connected to the power cable, its legs jerked.

"Fuck!" Bill yelled, startled by the sudden movement.

The creature repositioned itself into a more natural pose, and its eyes lit up a bright-purple color, which was very unusual. Bill had never seen purple eyes on a creature—they were always red. Against his better judgment, he pushed the green button on the tray, sending it up the elevator system. Just as it moved to its final position on the wall, the turret got eerily quiet. The air conditioners turned off, and the only sound left inside the turret was from the fans airing out all of the servers high above.

Just as Bill looked away from the Stink Bug with its gleaming, purple eyes, the elevator system started again, startling him.

Chink. Chink. Chink. Chink.

The elevator system began moving as if surveying each of the creatures stored along the walls.

Bill watched as it stopped in front of the Ant's tray. The tray was pulled and accelerated toward the launch hatch. The hatch opened, and the Zombie Ant extended each leg until it stood on all six. He was amazed at how realistic the Ant's movements were as it crept through the opening and slid down the slide.

Well, that one got put to use quickly.

It took Bill another half hour to put all the tools in their proper place and perform the final cleanup of his work area. It required twenty minutes just to clean up the Styrofoam packing peanuts. He was about to shut and lock the main door to the turret when he heard a tapping noise. It was repetitive, metal to metal, coming from outside and on the far side of the turret.

It sounds like our Zombie Ant might be stuck on something.

Bill had heard of this happening before, but he had never experienced it.

Fucking R&D can build a damn good machine, but Lord knows they never train these creatures to get unstuck from the smallest bushes in this desert.

Bill switched off the lights and pressed a few keys on a keypad, sealing the main door to the turret. The repetitive tapping continued, faster and louder, as if the creature were waiting for him and was becoming impatient.

"Hold your horses. I'm coming," he yelled as if the Zombie Ant could hear and understand him.

He walked halfway around the turret. The tapping got louder with each step. Bill turned a bend and found the Zombie Ant standing on its back four legs, its upper body raised in the air. One of the other two legs extended toward him as if pointing, and the other leg was still tapping on the turret in perfect intervals. The Ant's head and red eyes followed Bill as he stepped closer.

"What the hell are you doing? Did you get stuck, big boy?" He moved toward the Zombie Ant and fell to his knees under the Ant's abdomen, inspecting its back legs to see where it had gotten caught up.

The Zombie Ant stopped tapping and dropped its front legs to the ground, hard enough to make the earth shake beneath Bill.

Bill's spine tingled, and he remained perfectly still.

"I don't understand. You're not stuck. What are you doing?"

The Zombie Ant turned its head toward him as if it were measuring him up to attack, but Bill knew that should be impossible unless his safety armband's charge had been depleted. It was intended to keep him from being approached or harmed by the deterrents.

He slowly lifted his right arm and looked at the armband. It read "75 percent charged" in shimmering, green letters and was blinking "SAFE" on the small, digital screen.

Bill relaxed and grunted as he pushed off the dirt to stand up. Grunting with every movement had become routine ever since he'd turned sixty.

"I don't want to have to take you back for repairs, but I guess …"

His sentence was cut short. A wheezing sound replaced his voice.

Bill reached his hands to his neck, touching the cool metal of the Ant's jaws now clamped around his throat. He tried to pull the pincers apart, but they slowly tightened. The Ant's jaws closed more, causing a searing pain that Bill had never experienced. In one final snap, the pincers cut deep into his jugular vein.

Bill could feel the warm blood dripping down his throat, and he could taste the iron in it. It only took a few seconds for the blood to fill his throat, drowning him. The last thing he heard was the squeak of a tensioner motor behind the Ant's jaws. The light vanished from his eyes, and his last thought was of Grace sitting alone at home, waiting with his favorite dinner.

Brock Murphy sat in his office, watching the interaction between Bill and the Zombie Ant on his large monitors in a private security room behind his office. He ran his fingers across a digital tablet. A few clicks, and the Zombie Ant dropped Bill. He punched another key, and the Zombie Ant rubbed its jaws in the dirt a few times, enough to wipe away any evidence of Bill's blood. A final keypress sent the Zombie Ant scurrying away into a hatch that slid open directly under the launch slide.

Brock talked to Bill as if he were still alive. "Sorry, ol' boy …
if you would have just kept your mouth shut, you'd be heading
home by now."

He controlled a camera that zoomed in on Bill's neck, making
a mental note about how good the resolution of the new camera
was, happy that his decision to spend some extra money on them
was paying off.

Brock could make out the throat muscles glistening in the sun,
and they weren't moving, which verified Bill was no longer
breathing. A thick stream of blood spilled from his windpipe, and
he lay lifeless.

Satisfied that Bill was dead, Brock repositioned the camera's
angle so the body was no longer visible. A drone arrived minutes
later, programmed to carry the body away to a spot deep within the
Red Zone—somewhere he would never be found.

He looked through the archived video footage and found the
video clip for the previous thirty minutes, deleting the footage
from memory. He also deleted the last few minutes of system
activity that showed him logged in as an administrative user. With
a few clicks, Brock completely removed any proof of what had
happened and any involvement he had in it.

Brock felt comfortable that he was the only one Bill had
contacted about the explosives. He knew that any evidence of the
explosives, and the Stink Bug, would disappear after Mason
Stanwell's *Civil Watch* shift anyway.

16: THE RED SQUAD

Mason Stanwell and his dad sat at the dinner table eating Chinese takeout. Friday nights were one of three nights a week that Mason got to spend with his dad. The courts forced a custody schedule on his dad after a heated and very public divorce one year earlier. Mason was still upset that his dad had cheated on his mom, but he still looked up to him and the work he did on immigration in the senate.

Having a senator for a dad also gave Mason protection and access to things other sixteen-year-olds didn't have. There were always special celebrity fundraisers with government bigwigs, free tickets to sporting events and concerts, and even access to private vacation homes around the world, which he knew were provided by campaign donors expecting something in return.

Because Stanwell wasn't a cabinet member, the family wasn't afforded a full-time Secret Service detail, so he had to hire a private firm to watch his home and Mason while they were there. Every so often, Mason would see the flashlight of one of the two security team members walking past the windows, making sure the grounds were safe. It no longer freaked Mason out as it was a frequent sight.

I wonder if they were here when my dad was screwing the housekeeper?

His dad broke the silence, "So what's the plan for tonight? Are you playing that *Civil Watch* game with your friends again?"

"Yeah! Did you hear that one of the turret technicians went missing from Turret 151? They found his radio and traces of blood outside the turret. He went to work and never came home. Draven Labs doesn't seem too worried about investigating it, and now the guy's wife is causing a scene and wants Draven Labs investigated."

Stanwell shifted uncomfortably in his seat. "Where'd you hear this?"

"It's all over the discussion group in the game. It's like a big conspiracy. I guess the cameras at Turret 151 cut out just when it all went down. They have a video of the guy walking out of the turret at the end of his shift, then he walks around the side of the turret and just vanishes. I hear they're claiming it was a Wallflower attack, and some hacker in the Wallflowers found a way to cut the video feed. Supposedly, they killed the guy and hid the body."

Mason could tell the story affected his dad. "What's up? Why does that story bother you?"

"Well, I've been asked by the president to keep an eye on Draven Labs. Anything bad that happens because of Draven Labs has the opportunity to tarnish the president's image. I'm also an investor in the company, which can hurt me both financially and politically. Let me know if you hear any more about it tonight. Sounds like I need to pay a visit to Draven Labs tomorrow."

"Ask Mr. Draven to give you my silver rank medal while you're there," Mason joked. "We had an excellent session the other night. I captured ten Hoppers, and Lucas caught seven. I have over four hundred captures for the year and have just been promoted to silver rank. It was the easiest four grand I ever made."

His dad slipped into his normal lecturing tone, "Make sure you put that money in the trading account I set up for you. If you're smart about it, you could triple that money in a month. I set up that account to mimic my trades, and let's just say the stocks I pick are always sure winners."

"Okay, Dad, I will. I just need to pay Eric back first. He has a guy who set me up with my new gaming system. It's got top-of-the-line processors, high-resolution displays, and the newest virtual headset. Whatever's left will go into the account," Mason assured.

Somehow, his dad knew the four grand—and more—had probably already been spent. He learned a while ago that Mason chewed through money the same way his mother did. His dad just shook his head and gave him a look of disappointment.

Mason noticed the look, causing him to abruptly end their dinner together. "I'm done. I'll be in my room." He threw his napkin on his plate and left it on the table in a huff. He knew the latest twenty-four-year-old housekeeper would clean it up. This new helper was blonde, Ukrainian, and looked as though she'd just stepped out of a modeling agency. Mason was fully aware that she was there for more than the light housekeeping.

Stanwell knew he had gone too far with nagging Mason about investing and wished he could stop pulling the dad card. His good intentions to set his son up with a small fortune before he entered college had always led to these brief lectures and always ended badly.

Stanwell called Red Draven's private number and was instantly dropped into voicemail.

"Draven, we need to talk. I'll be there tomorrow at 9 a.m. Make room on your schedule," he said, pissed that Draven wouldn't even answer his call.

As was tradition on Friday nights at eight o'clock in the evening, Mason's squad—comprised of him, Lucas, Ariel, and Eric—all logged into the *Civil Watch* game. Once all four members were online, they were placed into the team's virtual lobby.

Instead of the standard JOIN GAME button appearing, they were welcomed with INVITATION TO THE RED SQUAD in big, red letters. Underneath was a link to read a liability disclaimer, a checkbox to show their agreement to the terms, and a big ACCEPT INVITATION button.

"What the hell is this?" Ariel asked.

Mason was the first to respond, "No clue. I wonder if my recent rank up pushed our squad to a new level."

"Hell, yeah!" Eric celebrated.

"Accept, and let's see what it gets us," Lucas urged.

They all skipped past the disclaimer and agreement to the terms, then excitedly clicked the accept button.

In unison, the squad's name on their screens changed from the L.A.M.E. SQUAD, which they had initially agreed upon because it was a funny anagram using the initials of each their first names—Lucas, Ariel, Mason, and Eric. It now labeled them as THE RED SQUAD. This new name sounded much cooler and would earn them some clout at school.

With the change of their squad's name, their bland game interface also changed, taking on a very modern, red color scheme with chrome accents. All the icons of the deterrents they had previously earned fell lower on the sidebar, pushed down by some new icons that were automatically added. New deterrents and drone tools started lining up at the top of the list.

"So cool! Do you guys notice a pattern?" Ariel asked.

There was silence.

"The new deterrents all have an insect theme, you slugs!" she announced.

They all laughed at her calling them slugs.

They each clicked through the icons for the new additions, which offered an animation and a short description of each creature's abilities, weaponry, and weaknesses.

CENTIPEDE—DETERRENT—SOLID GROUND

Abilities: Can move quickly and quietly with hundreds of moving legs. Can burrow under a layer of dirt to conceal itself and can sense movement. Can climb significant obstacles and enter tiny spaces. Uses solar cells on its back to run almost continuously in the field during daylight.

Weaponry: Body will coil around its prey and contract to limit movement.

Weakness: Can only sense movement within a thirty-foot distance. A low profile means a short line of sight and an inability to see above or around large obstacles.

CHIGGERS—DETERRENT—SOLID GROUND

Abilities: Strategically position themselves across the ground in a walking path and await passing victims. Pressure from above activates their defenses.

Weaponry: When stepped upon, tiny barbs attach to the sole of the victim's shoes. Tiny needles then drill through the sole and into the foot, injecting a toxin that causes extreme pain and immobility until the victim can be picked up.

Weakness: Must be placed directly in the path of a Hopper and within proximity of each other. Can only attach when pressure is applied from above. Not able to cover a large area.

DRAGONFLY—SURVEILLANCE DRONE

Abilities: High-speed, agile, and able to change directions quickly. Wings are made of solar mesh, allowing it to stay in the air almost indefinitely with sunlight. Can track for two hours in darkness. Optics are excellent, making it a perfect tracking machine even at full speed.

Weaponry: Purely a surveillance and tracking drone and carries no weaponry.

Weakness: Wing movement creates quite a bit of noise, which can be heard from a distance, eliminating any element of surprise.

GNATS—DETERRENT—AIRBORNE

Abilities: Utilize swarming technology and blood-sensing receptors. Can "sniff" the blood of a living organism upwind from one hundred feet away.

Weaponry: Once prey is detected, they team up to swarm the victim, attaching themselves to their exposed skin. Victim loses the ability to see through the swarm and becomes disoriented. Have a long battery life and can regenerate power in the daylight. Have a five-hour battery life in the dark.

Weakness: They are brittle, and their wings are easily damaged. Require a minimum number of active units to swarm together to become effective.

GRASSHOPPER—SURVEILLANCE DRONE

Abilities: Can jump high and fly short distances, allowing it to quickly get a high-altitude view of its surroundings. Infrared vision and optics can sense heat and movement.

Weaponry: Purely a surveillance drone and has no weaponry. Can use mesh technology to connect with Slugs, Centipedes, and Zombie Ants to triangulate the location of its prey.

Weakness: Can only jump ten miles and cover six hundred yards before returning to the turret to power up.

LEECH—DETERRENT—WATERBORNE

Abilities: Are waterborne and can hide and wait underwater for an extended period. Use blood- and urine-sensing receptors to locate prey.

Weaponry: Once activated, will dig into victim's flesh and inject venom, causing extreme pain and slow reaction time.

Weakness: Must be positioned downstream of the mission area to pick up water-transported blood and urine traces.

SLUG–DETERRENT–SOLID GROUND

Abilities: Lays down an almost invisible trail of sticky sludge that can trap victims. The more the victim struggles, the more stuck they get. Acts much like a glue trap.

Weaponry: None. This deterrent is simply a trapping deterrent.

Weakness: Moves very slowly and can only lay down one hundred feet of sludge before it needs to be resupplied.

STINK BUG–DETERRENT–SOLID GROUND

Abilities: Stealthy, able to climb uneven surfaces. Barbs on legs can aid in climbing steep surfaces.

Weaponry: Discharges exploding balls of nerve gas that can incapacitate prey for thirty minutes.

Weakness: Can only discharge six balls before needing to resupply.

ZOMBIE ANT–DETERRENT–SOLID GROUND

Abilities: Can traverse almost any dry terrain and climb significant obstacles. Can team up with other Zombie Ants to corral prey. Eyes offer a 220-degree, infrared view of its surroundings.

Weaponry: Powerful jaws can trap victims. Injectable venom takes control of a victim's motor functions. Victim loses the ability to run or process thoughts, leaving them to wander until they are picked up, looking like zombies.

Weakness: Short mission time and, therefore, a short range. Battery life allows only one hour in the field. Must remain close to the turret to power up between missions.

A message popped up before any of them could choose from their arsenal.

RED SQUAD REASSIGNED TO SOUTH BORDER, TURRET 151

"Hell, yeah! I hear that Turret 151 is one of the most active turrets!" Lucas said happily.

"This is going to be a fun night!" Mason added.

"I'm not sure which of the new creatures I want to try first!" Ariel remarked excitedly.

Eric interrupted her, "Oh, no way … you're on surveillance tonight, Ariel. It's your turn. I spent the entire night doing surveillance the last time we played."

Mason agreed, "Yep, it sucks to be you, Ariel. You have to take this shift, unfortunately."

"Fuuuuuuuuuck," she groaned. "I guess I'll give the new Dragonfly a whirl."

"I can select anything except the Stink Bug. Why would that be?" Lucas asked.

"Maybe it's not in the racks yet," Eric offered. "I call the Zombie Ant."

"The Stink Bug isn't grayed out for me," Mason said. "Maybe it shows for me because I'm in silver rank? It looks like I'm using the Stink Bug before they remove the option."

"I'll try the Centipede," Lucas said, pissed that he hadn't jumped on the Zombie Ant before Eric claimed it.

Miles away, Brock Murphy and Red Draven sat in Brock's secret war room, listening to the new Red Squad fighting over the creatures. They laughed, knowing they would have done the same thing when they were young—fight over the good toys. From this room, they could listen in, watch each player's feeds, see their faces, and Brock could even take control of their creatures if he wanted to. But that wasn't the plan. They would just be observers tonight. Mason Stanwell had chosen the Stink Bug, loaded with the lethal weapons, and the plan was coming together perfectly.

As Ariel spent the next fifteen minutes learning how to control the Dragonfly, Lucas, Mason, and Eric launched their deterrents out of Turret 151 and sent them into different areas in their section of the Red Zone.

"Found two! I found two Hoppers!" Ariel yelled loud enough to force her squad to reprimand her for exceeding the safe sound levels of their headsets. Excitement quickly replaced their anger when she pinned the Hoppers on a map in their heads-up display. The adrenaline kicked in, and the players competed to be the first to get their creatures on the path of one of the Hoppers.

"Two males, from what I can tell. And get this—both have two marks. That will bring some of you good money and our squad a bit of clout," she added.

Brock and Red turned and smiled at each other. They had drugged and strategically dropped the two Hoppers near Turret 151 using a drone earlier in the day. They intended for them to be easy to find and even placed them in an area that would prevent them from running back to the Mexican border. The only simple way would be to head to the US border and past Turret 151.

"Looks like Stanwell's kid went for the bait." Brock smiled proudly.

Brock and Red configured a high-altitude drone to track the Hoppers and watch everything play out from above.

Ariel sent her Dragonfly toward the Hoppers, and when they noticed it flying overhead, they ran in different directions, trying to avoid being the first one to be targeted.

Mason moved his Stink Bug toward the nearest of the two highlighted marks, which were now pulsing quickly on the map in his VR goggles. Lucas and Eric moved their creatures in the direction of the other target, not sure which of their creatures would get there first. It was quickly evident that Lucas's Centipede was much slower than Eric's Zombie Ant.

"Why do I always pick the slowest motherfuckin' creatures!"

Lucas groaned, and everyone except Mason laughed.

Mason was too busy operating the new Stink Bug and devising a strategy for catching the Hopper heading straight toward him. It didn't take long for him to home in on his target. Zooming in on the map, he noticed that the Hopper was running along a foot trail that circled a small hill. The trail had an obvious path and endpoint where Mason set his trap.

Eric and Lucas's creatures were on autopilot, trying to close the distance between their creatures and the second Hopper. It would take another ten minutes for them to get close, so they watched Mason's live screencast from the Stink Bug's point of view.

Mason clicked a button on the screen marked ARM. The team watched as the Stink Bug swiveled its body so that its back end was now facing the path where the Hopper would arrive at any minute, assuming the Hopper kept his current pace. A rear-facing camera replaced the front view. The ARM button had changed to a DEPLOY button.

"Oh, this is going to be good," Lucas said.

"That Hopper is falling right into your trap," Eric said to Mason.

"Quiet, I have to concentrate," Mason said abruptly, and the channel went silent.

A new display appeared, one that the team had never seen. This display showed a range finder with concentric circles extending from an icon of the Stink Bug. An area within the circles was red and labeled MAXIMUM IMPACT AREA. A glowing, green dot on the screen was moving around the hill and about to enter the first concentric circle of the range finder. The team was silent—either in anticipation or to provide Mason with the maximum concentration he might require to make the capture. They all understood a catch for one was a catch for the entire squad.

The Hopper turned the corner and was now visible in the

streaming feed from the rear-facing camera of the Stink Bug. It wasn't until he looked up from the darkened path and saw the Stink Bug's outline in the moonlight that he stopped in his tracks. Mason's range finder said he was now in the MAXIMUM IMPACT AREA.

The Hopper turned quickly, obviously realizing the danger in front of him. Just as he spun and began to run away, Mason clicked the DEPLOY button. Two white balls shot from the back of the Stink Bug in a slight arc toward the Hopper. The balls dropped to the ground, bounced, and rolled near the Hopper just as he started his run.

The screencast went black, and the audio was silent on all their screens.

"What the hell?" Mason yelled. "Did you guys see if I got him?"

"No, it glitched," Lucas replied. "It went to black, and I couldn't hear anything."

Eric and Ariel confirmed they also had lost the feed.

"Fuck!" Mason yelled. A message popped up on the team's screens just as he yelled.

TWO-MARK HOPPER CAPTURED. HIGH-VALUE TARGET ACHIEVEMENT AWARD EARNED. CONGRATULATIONS!

"Damn, looks like I did get him, and it was a High-Value Target." Mason cheered, fumbling his screen capture controls to rewind the feed. He was hoping that the recording system had caught the capture, as he was excited to share this one on DravenTV.

The video clip hadn't been recorded at all. There wasn't a trace of the activity in the activity log.

"Looks like they're working out the bugs … pun intended!" Ariel joked. "I've never seen anyone earn a High-Value Target

Award before. I can't wait to see that medal when it comes, Mason."

Mason's frustration disappeared. "Yeah, that's pretty cool. Hopefully, it'll arrive next week."

They all redirected their attention to the other Hopper Lucas and Eric were chasing.

Back at the Hive, Brock and Red smiled at each other and replayed the entirety of the event, watching what Mason and his team had been prevented from seeing and hearing.

The feed showed an overhead view, allowing Brock and Red to watch the Stink Bug pivot and crouch into an attack position with its rear in the air. The Hopper rounded the corner and slid to a stop just yards in front of the creature. Just as he turned to run away, two small balls the size of baseballs popped out of the Stink Bug's rear and bounced toward the Hopper. Brock clicked a button on his keyboard and switched the scene to the rear angle of the Stink Bug.

The white balls rolled toward the Hopper, who was just kicking off to run away. When his left foot lifted, the first ball rolled under him and exploded in a bright-white flash. The Hopper's entire leg, from the hip down, flew to the left of the path as if it were a small twig in the wind. The Hopper fell to the ground, directly onto the second ball, which had rolled under what was left of his body. Another white flash appeared at the center of his torso, instantly tearing his body in half, small parts of him flying in a circle around the point of detonation. Brock switched to the overhead view and peered at the resulting scene in infrared. The area looked like a bull's-eye, with a large, dark crater in the center and the Hopper's remains scattered around it.

"Damn! It's accurate and devastating. That did more damage than I thought it would," Brock said to Red. "We could probably use half the amount of explosive in those balls."

"If there were two Hoppers, it might not have been enough to kill them both. It would have maimed them, for sure. We must assume that sometimes Hoppers travel together in pairs or small groups. I'd rather keep the explosive payload where it is or increase the amount just for that particular scenario," Red replied.

"You're sicker than me," Brock joked.

"Well, remember, our foreign investors expect deterrents with maximum effectiveness. They specifically said they don't want any chance that their enemies can crawl away," Red said. "This demonstration will be a good sales tool when negotiating pricing next month. Let's keep these clips in our private, encrypted archives for later."

Just as Red finished the sentence, a flurry of activity appeared on the Red Squad's screens and audio feed. Brock focused on their screencast and turned up the audio. Brock and Red had the required footage but were interested in watching how the Red Squad worked together as a team.

"Lucas, circle around the back and cover the escape path," Eric yelled.

With a few clicks from Lucas, the Centipede changed routes and moved behind the Hopper onto the path he had just passed.

"I'm ready, moving in from behind," Lucas confirmed.

"Only a few seconds until I have him in my sights. And ... now ..." Eric said, clicking the ATTACK button on his HUD.

The Centipede crawled through a thick patch of brush directly in front of the Hopper. The Hopper fell backward into a cactus.

"Ow! That looks painful," Ariel said, as if she could sense the Hopper's pain and fear.

The Zombie Ant advanced, head leaning forward, getting closer to the Hopper, who was now cowering. He had nowhere to go.

The Zombie Ant bent down, just inches from the man's stomach. This made him squirm and try to pull his pincushion of a body off the cactus needles. But it was too late. The Zombie Ant opened its metal jaws and sunk the tips into his belly. The man screamed and tried to grab the pincers to pull them apart and away from his body, but the Zombie Ant's servo motors kept the jaws locked in place. They pierced the skin, but not enough to kill the Hopper. It needed to get close enough to a blood supply to release its toxins.

The look on the man's face turned from sheer terror to a blank stare. As the Zombie Ant pulled away, the man's eyes rolled back into his head, and his body started twitching. At the corner of his mouth appeared a frothy, white substance that dripped down his chin and onto his dusty shirt.

The Zombie Ant receded and watched over the man as if it were its prey and it was proud of its catch.

The squad was quiet, as they had never seen the Zombie Ant in action. It was a bit scarier than some other deterrents they had used.

"Well, that was … uh … kind of brutal," Ariel announced.

"I wouldn't want to stare into the jaws of that thing," Lucas added.

"Looks like Draven Labs has upped their game, so to speak," said Mason.

The squad all watched the Hopper and his blank stare in silence. Within three minutes, the body was picked up by a DLED drone and taken away.

The team's statistics were updated on-screen and now included credit for capturing the two Hoppers, including extra rewards for the High-Value Target.

"Pizza's on me this weekend, team," Mason announced.

———

SATURDAY MORNING

Senator Stanwell knew Red Draven would be in Draven Labs headquarters. Draven was known to work seven days a week and rarely left the town of Solace. Stanwell also had an inside man, Felix, who worked on the security team and kept tabs on where Draven was at all times.

Sitting in his car in the visitor lot, he called Felix at the front desk. "What's his status? Is he in?"

"He's not in his suite. He's in the executive conference room on the seventh floor," Felix whispered over the phone.

"Is he with anyone?"

"Brock Murphy, head of security. Nobody else has even signed into the building this morning."

"Felix, don't forget I need a log of all international visitors this last week emailed to me by the end of the day," Stanwell urged.

Stanwell hung up without letting him reply or saying goodbye or thanks. He knew Felix had to provide the information. Otherwise, he would find himself in a state prison rather quickly. He had been caught forging large checks a year earlier, and Stanwell used his power to cover up the infraction and hide the evidence in a secure place. Felix understood that if he didn't supply Senator Stanwell with reliable and timely information when needed, Stanwell would submit the evidence to the authorities. The crime would result in a two-year sentence and a hefty fine for him.

Stanwell didn't bother to dress up for Draven and opted to go casual, wearing khakis and his private country club's golf shirt. He had an eleven o'clock tee time with three college friends in town from California.

He entered the lobby and noticed that the Dragonfly and Zombie Ant were no longer on display. The gardeners were pruning the palm trees in the rainforest area and raking the sand in the desert habitat. The lobby had no sign of any other visitors.

Stanwell stepped up to the security desk and grinned at his contact, ignoring the other security guard offering to help him.

"I need to see Mr. Draven. Tell him his 9 a.m. appointment is here," he demanded.

The other guard interrupted, "Sir, Mr. Draven has no appointments today."

Stanwell ignored the other guard and stared at Felix, waiting for him to act.

Felix turned to the other guard and threw him a look. "I've got this, Sam. This is Senator Stanwell. Mr. Draven will want to meet with him."

Felix hit the PAGE button on the phone, dialed an extension, then waited a second. He announced, "Mr. Draven, Senator Stanwell is in the lobby."

After two minutes, Brock Murphy responded, "Send him up to the seventh-floor conference room."

Stanwell didn't wait for instructions and started walking toward the executive elevator, which was intentionally built behind the security desk to limit access.

Sam tried to stop him. "Sir, you can't use that elevator. The public elevator is down the hall."

Felix glared at Sam again, then turned back to Senator Stanwell. "You're good. Go ahead and use that elevator."

Stanwell could hear the two guards arguing loudly as the elevator doors shut. He would have loved to listen to the rest of their conversation, but the doors closed too quickly.

When the elevator doors opened, it landed directly across from the frosted-glass doors of the conference room. He didn't knock or wait for an invitation. Stanwell just walked in. Draven and Murphy were sitting at the far end of the conference table near a big, digital screen looping through an animation of the Draven Labs' logo. Both were sipping coffees but slighted Stanwell by not offering him a cup.

"Join us, Stanwell. We were just discussing how well your friends' reelection campaigns were doing. It seems our little arrangement is working for all parties. And the president?" Draven sneered.

"Well, that's why I'm here, actually," Stanwell said, sitting on the opposite side of the table. Stanwell would never admit it, but he was scared of Brock Murphy. There was something evil about the man, but he couldn't pinpoint what it was.

"Why are you here, and on a Saturday morning, no less?" Murphy asked as he refilled Red's coffee and then his from the carafe.

"I'll get to the damn point. I heard a technician was killed at Turret 151, and there hasn't yet been an investigation? They're claiming it was a Wallflower attack, and there is no video footage of it? And now, the man's wife is raising a stink and demanding answers from Draven Labs. You realize this is going to hit the press. Why did I have to hear all of this from my kid, for God's sake? Why didn't you keep me informed as we'd discussed at your little show-and-tell?" Stanwell fumed.

"Slight oversight." Red smirked. "We're not done with our investigation yet. Where did your son hear all of this?"

"It's all over that damned *Civil Watch* game. The kids are talking about it like it's some terrorist attack and cover-up," Stanwell replied.

"Interesting how these rumors spread so fast. We're looking into it," Murphy replied.

"What do you two not understand? I need to get information like this to the president before it hits the news, and you two are treating your highest-paying client, and me, like dog shit."

"Highest-paying client for now." Red turned to Brock and smiled.

"You know what? Fuck the both of you. I don't need your money," Stanwell blurted, standing up and slamming his chair into the glass conference room table. "That's it! I'll have to tell the president what I think is happening here. You two don't give a damn that your machines are killing people. You don't give a flying fuck that some technician goes missing on the job, and the

Wallflowers have figured out how to hack into your system. And to make matters worse, I can only assume you're selling equipment to foreign customers without caring about how they'll use it. I know the president of the United States can take this company over for national security reasons if he sees fit!'"

Just as Stanwell turned toward the doors to leave, the lights went dark, and the huge, digital screen lit up. Audio filled the surround sound speakers in the room. Stanwell recognized the sounds from some teens playing the *Civil Watch* game played loudly and, more specifically, one of the male voices.

"You might want to watch a little DravenTV before you do that," Brock said seriously. Stanwell turned to the screen and stepped closer.

On the top left side of the screen was a small box showing his son, Mason, playing the game while wearing his VR headset. The rest of Mason's squad could be seen talking in smaller boxes below his.

The senator watched as the screen showed an overhead, infrared scene of a Hopper running on a path. He listened as his son told his squad to be quiet. He watched as Mason dragged the icon of what looked like a Stink Bug onto a small, digital map in the lower right corner of the game interface.

"Oooh, this is where it gets good," Brock said sarcastically.

Just as the Hopper slid to a stop on the screen, the view changed to a first-person view from the rear of the Stink Bug. Stanwell could see Mason smiling as he set a trap for the man. The screen switched back to an infrared view from overhead.

BOOM!

There was a bright-white explosion. Stanwell observed that the Hopper's leg was blown off, flung somewhere off-screen. As the smoke cleared, he could see the man lying on the ground, writhing in pain.

BOOM!

Another explosion spread the remainder of the man's body all over the landscape. The screen switched back to the game interface, where Mason was smiling. After a few seconds, he and the three friends cheered in unison.

What Stanwell couldn't see or know was that Mason and his son's friends had no idea what had happened to the Hopper or that he had been blown to bits.

"My son would never celebrate something as gruesome as that. This video has to be fake," Stanwell said.

"Oh, no. It's real. But don't worry, your son didn't know he killed the poor man. We blocked the live audio and video from him and his friends. They believe they just captured him," Brock explained.

Stanwell realized these fuckers had set up his son. They made it look like his son and squad watched it all and celebrated the kill.

"Want to see the entire overhead view? I prefer that one, myself," Brock said, smirking.

"Especially the part where the man tries to crawl away with one leg," Draven added.

Red peered into Stanwell's eyes as his demeanor changed quickly from a cocky politician to a beaten man.

Stanwell turned white, slowly sunk into a chair, and his head dropped. "Can I have a cup of coffee? Or something a little stronger, perhaps?" he asked as if he was in shock.

Red motioned to Brock to get something from the bar. He started to feel bad for Stanwell.

Brock set a full glass of whiskey in front of Stanwell, and he downed it in one gulp.

"So where do we go from here?" Stanwell asked softly, realizing they had played him. He now understood his future, and his son's reputation rested with Red Draven and his evil sidekick, Brock Murphy.

"We just want you rooting for the home team, that's all. And we'd like you to get your friends in the senate on board, too. We're expanding to other markets, and they're demanding lethal deterrents, so we had to set up a little demonstration. This video will help us show how effective the deterrents can be," Red said.

Stanwell begged, "Tell me you won't show that video to anyone else? Please, I don't want my son paying for my mess."

Brock replied, "Don't worry. We'll edit it so your son and his friends can't be identified."

"These new markets will bring you and your friends more money and will also allow us to develop better, more aggressive deterrents for use here on our borders or by our American soldiers in the international war theater. Just like any other weapon, the US can have exclusive rights to that new weaponry if the president so desires," Red said.

"What if I can't get the president on board?" Stanwell asked.

"He can cancel our contract in 2052 if he gets reelected, and we'll just take our services elsewhere. We are a private company, after all."

"I guess we have a few years to figure that part out, then," Stanwell said, getting up from the table. He quietly left the room, got onto the elevator, and took what felt like the longest ride of his life. His head was spinning, and he was already trying to figure out how to get the president and his other friends in the senate to agree to Draven's new plans.

"Senator Stanwell?" came a voice from outside the elevator. He was so deep in thought that he hadn't realized the elevator had reached the lobby and that the door was open. Felix stepped in the doorway and asked, "Are you okay, sir?"

"Yes, fine, thanks," Stanwell replied, walking past Felix and the other guard with his head down. Stanwell realized that he was now being blackmailed the same way he had blackmailed Felix, and it wasn't such a great feeling. He also knew he couldn't talk to his son about what had happened. It would destroy his son to learn that he had killed a human being, and their relationship would never be the same.

MONDAY MORNING

The four members of the Red Squad received unexpected praise and envy when they walked the school hallways on Monday morning. They had no idea their new squad promotion had already been broadcast to all *Civil Watch* players in the area.

"I saw the announcement last night. What is the Red Squad, anyway?" a freshman boy asked as he passed Mason and Lucas in the main hallway of the high school.

"We could tell you, but we'd have to kill you," Mason responded sarcastically. He was only half-joking as he wasn't sure if there was some clause in the agreement that he signed and didn't read before being assigned to the Red Squad.

Lucas nudged Mason with his elbow, directing his attention to a group of freshman girls eyeing them as though they were the big men on campus. They started to notice everyone staring at them as they walked down the hall.

"Looks like everyone knows about our Red Squad," Lucas whispered.

Ariel and Eric caught up with them.

"We're the hot topic of the day, guys!" Ariel beamed. "Even the principal stopped us to congratulate us on our way in!"

"I had no idea they were going to announce it! I also didn't know Principal Adams played *Civil Watch*. Maybe he and I can discuss strategy the next time I am sitting in detention," Eric added.

"Well, keep your mouth shut about the details, especially about the new deterrents. I don't know about any of you, but I didn't read the fine print before agreeing to become a Red Squad member. I have no idea what we signed up for or what we're allowed to talk about," Mason cautioned firmly.

"Agree!" Lucas then said, "Plus, the secrecy adds an air of mystery. We should keep everyone in the dark. If they want to see what it's all about, they'll just have to watch our DravenTV clips when we post them."

Lucas and Mason entered homeroom and received a few high-fives on the way to their desks.

Aiden and Gabby watched from the back of the room. They heard Mason's squad had been promoted and praised in the *Civil Watch* game.

"They have no idea what's coming, do they?" Aiden whispered.

"I wish we could speed things up and prevent the needless suffering," Gabby replied.

"It won't be long," Aiden said, noticing Mason and Lucas staring back at him and Gabby. Aiden gave them a head nod, pretending to acknowledge Mason and Lucas's recent success in the game. That was enough to get them to turn around and ignore them.

Gabby and Aiden had to bite their tongues all day, especially at lunch, where they could hear Mason's squad celebrating his capture of a High-Value Target.

"We've now got a HVT award recipient in our school," Lucas yelled, standing on a chair and pointing at Mason.

Many people in the cafeteria cheered, but there wasn't any celebration from Aiden's group of friends. Their solidarity made Gabby happy for the first time today.

17: SOMETHING BORROWED

Izzy waited for everyone to leave for the day. Late nights were typical for her, as her job required that she work on the mechanical creatures when the researchers and designers weren't tinkering with them.

She rode the freight elevator down three floors to the research and development workshop and found a spot in the back corner. Izzy held her digital notepad and pretended to check things off, making it appear as though she was performing her normal routine. She glanced around the room and toward the hallways to see where the remaining security officers stationed themselves for the night. They were busy watching the freight elevators and personnel locker room exits as they waited for all employees to finish their shifts.

Izzy noticed a Porcupine deterrent attached to a crane, slowly spinning in the air. The hanging creature was a safety issue as its toxic spikes were still loaded into its body, and they could easily pierce any unknowing soul who bumped into them. She hit the crane's controls and lowered the creature safely onto the workbench so it could no longer swing freely.

She inspected it to see why they might have been working on it. The back panel above the leg had been removed, and she realized it must have been a mobility issue because one of the wheel assemblies was missing. The gears and belts controlling the wheel were lying on the table before her. There was also a pile of metal quills, which she guessed were extracted before dismantling the wheel assembly so they would not accidentally get poked while working on it.

Izzy panned the room again and secretly collected two of the smallest quills from the bench. She slid them into the lined pocket in the front of her lab coat, placing them toxin-side down.

These might come in handy.

Izzy often "borrowed" items and took them home for inspection. Although she wasn't supposed to remove anything from the facility, her position required that she know as much about the equipment as possible, and she felt taking items home to spend some real time with them would be okay. She had the highest clearance level and could probably talk her way out of trouble and claim it was required for her job.

Little did Draven Labs know that Izzy was sharing the technology with the volunteer engineers at Wallflower headquarters so they could inspect them and learn about their weaknesses. She would bring the items back to the lab so they wouldn't end up on an inventory "missing" list, which would raise alarms.

Certain items were never allowed outside the facility—the deterrents themselves, the digital programming pads used to connect to and update the software on the deterrents, and any security keys that allowed access to work on the creatures. Strict guidelines and processes were in place to prevent these items from leaving the facility.

Today, Izzy had to perform a special job for the Wallflowers, and she would need to bypass all of the security checks. During her rounds, she investigated some of their issues in the Hopper processing area. One of the marking units—the ones used to implant a tattoo in the skin and bone of the Hoppers—appeared to be randomly causing burns to the skin. If the press learned Draven

Labs was scarring Hoppers with third-degree burns, they would have a field day with it. This marking unit had already burned a Hopper to the point where they were taken to a hospital for treatment.

Izzy had seen the issues before and knew the cause. They were simple fixes, but she acted as if it were a more significant issue that had to be looked at in her private workspace. She placed the marking unit in her tote bag and continued to the maintenance technician area.

There Izzy inspected two safety armbands used by the technicians in the Red Zone. When charged and powered on, these armbands would prevent the deterrents and drones from targeting the technicians. It permitted them to cross in and out of the Red Zone without any attention in the *Civil Watch* game. These also allowed technicians to avoid setting off traps or notifying drones patrolling the Red Zone.

Each technician would sign out a safety armband at the beginning of the day and must sign it back in at the end of their shift. An employee wasn't officially "signed off" from their shift until that armband was returned to inventory. Each one had a serial number and a listing in a security database, and strict rules had to be followed when one didn't make it back into inventory.

An armband disappearing from inventory could only mean one of two things—either the armband had technical issues and was being pulled from inventory and reused for parts, or the technician forgot to return it, which never happened. That was because the security guards at the exit gate had a digital scanner that automatically looked for these items as technicians entered and exited for the day. If an armband ever went missing, the technician would be required to return it and would most likely be fired and possibly jailed.

Five armbands were sitting in a special bin marked "Malfunctions." The three that Izzy picked out of the bin had notes about faulty batteries or charging issues, which were easy fixes in her experience. She grabbed the three armbands and placed them in her tote bag beside the marking device.

In truth, Izzy needed the marking unit and the armbands for Wallflower operations, but she couldn't easily walk out of the facility with these items. It would appear odd for her to remove all of these items at once, and it would implicate her if the equipment was ever discovered to be part of a Wallflower operation.

Izzy stopped at a workstation in the room's darkest corner and laid all four items on the table. She carefully entered the serial number of each item into the computer. As each item description appeared on the screen, she confirmed they were the correct serial number and then checked a box labeled "Permanently Damaged— Use For Parts." This would tell any of the auditors that the items would no longer be in use in the facility, and the serial numbers were then recorded into a "non-functional" database in the inventory system. These would no longer be tracked or inventoried by the auditors. The batteries, LCD panels, nuts, and bolts could now all be removed from the units and recycled for repairs on other units.

She stuffed the four items in her bag and pulled up a different screen on the digital panel. Izzy entered her password to access the Hive's Logistics System. This system showed a map of the Red Zone and listed all incoming and outgoing drones in real time. It looked similar to an air traffic control system at an airport. She clicked on a few drones with flight paths leading back toward the Hive's processing area.

The icons of the DLED drones carrying Hoppers who were picked up in the Red Zone were colored red, blinked rapidly, and showed a label of "Hopper Incoming." Icons of the drones taking supplies to and from the turrets were green, non-blinking, and listed as "Supply Run." Other icons were light blue, non-blinking, and marked "Return to Service." Those leaving the Hive and returning to the Red Zone could pick up more Hoppers.

Izzy found an incoming drone that was colored green and marked "Supply Run," and it was to arrive at the processing center in fifteen minutes.

She glanced at her watch, then placed the armbands and the marking unit into a zippered, black bag hidden in her work tote. She wound the black bag tightly with some packing tape on the bench, then walked around a few workstations until she found a yellow parts box. She dumped some old parts from the box onto the tabletop and stuffed the black bag into it, snapping the latches shut. Izzy was surprised at how well the equipment fit inside the box. It was as if it was built just for those parts.

Snug as a bug.

Izzy felt much less nervous now that the illegal items were packed inside the parts box. The place was a ghost town after 6 p.m., but that gave her more reason to worry about sticking out like a sore thumb to anyone watching. She looked around and verified that she was the only one in the room.

She didn't realize that Brock Murphy had followed her activity from the moment she came down the freight elevator. He sat in his security office, watching her move from screen to screen as she entered each room. He zoomed in to observe her picking up the broken marking unit and the three armbands. There was no audio, just very high-detailed video footage.

None of her actions appeared odd. Although he had often seen her doing these things, this was the first time she'd wrapped the items in a black bag and placed them inside a yellow parts box, which he deemed to be very unusual.

Brock never liked or trusted Izzy for some reason. He wasn't sure if it was because she never seemed to show him any respect in the halls or flirt with him as she'd flirted with other employees. Or maybe it was because she appeared to be Red's favorite employee, and he was a bit jealous. Brock often worried that Red had a crush on her, which meant there was a possibility that someone might take Red's attention away from his partnership and friendship.

He leaned back into his leather, Aeron chair, pondering why she might have packed the items as she had into a black bag. Brock stood up and paid closer attention to the events unfolding when she carried the yellow box toward the hall leading to the Hive's Processing Center.

What the fuck are you doing, little Miss Izzy Davis?

He watched as she offered a flirty smile and some small talk to the security guard at the entrance to the processing facility. He could see the guard acting chivalrous and offering to help her carry the box. Izzy shook her head no and simply motioned for him to help open the door instead, which he happily did.

Brock switched the camera feed to the next room. He watched Izzy walk into the processing bay and up to the technician responsible for loading and unloading the incoming drones. After a short conversation, the technician pointed at a drone that was lowered to the ground about twenty feet before them. He clicked a few buttons on a panel, and the drone's propellers stopped rotating.

Izzy handed the technician the box, and he loaded it, along with some other crates, into the drone's basket. He then secured it and moved back to his control panel. The drone powered back on and lifted off and out of sight. Izzy patted the technician on his shoulder as if he had done her a favor.

"What the hell are you up to?" Brock whispered to himself.

He pushed away from the desk and ran out of the security office. He needed to find out where that drone was heading and what Izzy had told the technician.

As Brock made his way down the executive elevator, Izzy quickly returned up the freight elevator and out of the Hive for the day. After years of working and doing the same routine, she knew she had about a ten-minute wait in line to get past the guard station to exit the facility.

It took Brock five minutes to wait for the elevator to arrive on the floor of the processing facility. He ran toward the center of the room where the technician was concentrating on his panel, wearing noise-canceling headphones that blocked the loud sound from the drones coming and going. The technician jumped when Brock suddenly appeared in front of him. He wasn't used to visitors, and two in one shift was a surprise.

"Sorry, sir, you scared the shit out of me," the technician said, pulling away the headphones so he could hear his visitor. Brock was almost out of breath and didn't acknowledge his statement.

"Where did that last drone go?" Brock demanded.

The technician looked down at his display. "Turret 52, sir. It's heading out to make a parts resupply."

Brock didn't respond. He just turned and quickly ran back to the elevator, leaving the technician shrugging and confused.

Waiting impatiently for the elevator to make its way back up to the floor of his security office, Brock made a mental note to remember to get someone to upgrade the elevators to a faster model.

Once in his office, he quickly grabbed his keys, the 9mm Glock magnetically secured to the underside of his desk, and his jacket. Before he knew it, he was in his car, waiting for vehicles to leave the facility. Brock decided to warn Red about what he witnessed, and that's when he realized he had left his cell phone on his desk back in the office. He wouldn't have time to return for it without losing his tail on Izzy. He reached into his glove compartment and grabbed a scrap of paper and a pen. As he waited, he wrote something on the paper, then folded it and labeled the front.

PRIVATE—HAND DELIVER TO RED DRAVEN

He saw Izzy's white BMW driving away from the security gate

ahead. There were still three cars between his car and Izzy's, and the line seemed to be advancing especially slowly today. When Izzy drove through the gate, Brock blasted his horn a few times to get the guards moving faster. He saw one of the guards throw both hands in the air as if to let whoever was honking know he was just doing his job and couldn't proceed any quicker. The guard dropped his arms promptly when he realized his boss was honking at him and began to move a bit more briskly.

When it was Brock's turn, his car was going so fast, it fishtailed to a stop at the guard station. Brock recognized the young kid he had hired just two weeks earlier. He was wearing a new security uniform slightly too big for him.

Of course, it's the fucking new guy.

The young guard leaned down and peered into his window.

"Sorry, sir. I didn't know that was you. I would have—"

"Shut the fuck up, son," Brock interrupted. "I don't have time for chitchat. I need you to do something. Get someone to take your spot at the gate and deliver this up to Mr. Draven."

The guard took the note and Brock sped off, spraying gravel at the guard and the car behind him.

Brock knew Izzy would take the I-10 to reach Turret 52, so he didn't hesitate to get onto the highway onramp. Weaving past a few cars at eighty miles an hour, he eventually spotted Izzy's car. He jockeyed to get in a lane to the right of her and two cars back. It would now be impossible for her to see him in her rearview mirrors in this position, even if she knew he was following her. He knew she had no idea.

Luckily, the traffic was steady at this busy time of the day, so he could hang back and reduce the chance she might see the same car mirroring her lane changes. Izzy exited at the Tornillo exit, just as Brock had anticipated.

Heading right for Turret 52.

Brock slowed to allow two cars to slip between his and hers

before exiting. He knew exactly where she was going and didn't need to risk getting too close. He watched as Izzy drove through the town of Tornillo, eventually turning onto an access road with large, red warning signs on either side.

RED ZONE AHEAD 100 YARDS.
DETERRENTS AND DRONES IN USE.
PERSONAL HARM IMMINENT.
USE EXTREME CAUTION.

Brock drove past the access road slowly and watched as Izzy's white BMW sped down the dirt road and off into the Red Zone toward Turret 52.

She must have a safety armband on her.

Brock didn't have an armband and wouldn't be safe entering the Red Zone, but he didn't need to follow her to know what she was doing. He knew she was picking up the equipment she had stowed away with the DLED drone's supply run. He pulled behind a small gas station with a good view of the access road. It was already getting dark, and Brock repeatedly squeezed the steering wheel to keep his anxiety at bay.

Twenty minutes later, he saw headlights crest the hill on the access road and head back toward town. It was already dark by this time, so he didn't allow cars to get between him and Izzy, as he didn't want to be caught at any stoplights. She wouldn't be able to recognize him behind her anyway.

Izzy headed back toward El Paso, exiting at the next exit, Fabens Road. Just off the exit, Brock watched as she turned into a shopping plaza. He continued past the first entrance she used and entered the next one, parking in a spot away from any lights. He kept an eye on her car the whole time.

Izzy's car slowly crept through the parking lot and around the back of the building.

What the heck is she doing?

He pulled out of his spot and found a new one on the side of the building, out of sight of the back of the store. As he exited the car, he concealed his Glock in the back of his waistband and ducked between vehicles until he could see the entire back of the store.

Izzy's car was parked next to an older model black car, and she was rummaging through her trunk. She appeared to be talking with someone sitting inside the black car as she fiddled with something in her trunk.

Brock slinked closer to the building, pressing his body next to the wall. He peeked around the corner to make sure he hadn't been noticed. Izzy was still talking to the person in the car but was now holding the black bag she had stowed away in the supply drone earlier.

That bitch is selling our equipment.

He looked along the roofline of the building and at the top of each of the lampposts lining the back of the alleyway to see if there were any security cameras. Confident there were none, he crouched and followed the wall of the building toward Izzy and her buyer. Neither of them noticed him coming.

Just as the door of the black car opened, Brock reached a spot concealed by a dumpster only five feet from where Izzy stood. She was still facing away from him. He listened carefully.

"Good job, hon. These are just what we need. How'd you get the equipment out of the facility?" the dark-haired man inquired.

"Slipped them into a supply drone ... easy-peasy! That nice technician I told you about, Phillip, even helped me load it. Chivalry is NOT dead," Izzy replied.

"Probably more like a crush and not chivalry, but okay," the man responded.

"The lab won't notice these missing. I took them out of

inventory. As far as they're concerned, these are being parted out or sitting on a shelf somewhere."

The man smiled at Izzy, grabbed the bag, and turned to put it in the back seat of his car.

"Red Draven won't know what hit him. Thanks, love," he said.

Brock's anger grew as he heard that, and he could feel the heat envelop his head and neck.

She's a fucking Wallflower mole.

He yanked the Glock from his waistband and held it straight in front of him, in a military posture, pointing it directly at the man in the black car. He slowly crept out of the shadows and behind Izzy.

Izzy screamed when Brock tightly wrapped his arm around her throat. The man loading the car was startled and turned quickly to face her.

"Whoa there, big fella! Don't want your girlfriend here to get one in the side of the head," Brock said plainly, redirecting the gun to Izzy's head.

"Let me guess. You two are in cahoots with the Wallflowers?" Brock interrogated.

Neither answered, unsure what might happen if they admitted it or moved. Izzy recognized the voice behind her and instantly knew it was Brock Murphy. She was embarrassed that she hadn't caught on to him following her.

"I've been watching you ever since you entered the R&D room. Even saw you flirting with the guards and that technician at the drone launch pad."

Izzy's face turned red, ashamed that she wasn't more careful.

Brock motioned his gun toward the black bag behind Noah.

"I'll take back our property, if you don't mind," Brock said, sneering.

"Okay. No need for anyone to get hurt here," Noah replied, holding his hands up to show he wouldn't make any sudden moves. Brock pushed the gun harder into Izzy's temple.

Noah slowly reached one hand toward the bag without looking, blindly feeling for the handle to retrieve it. He made sure to keep eye contact with Brock the whole time. Brock was focused on the black bag as Noah slid it off the back seat and slung it toward Brock. It landed on the ground, halfway between them.

Brock screamed in pain, in sync with the sound of the bag hitting the ground.

"Ow, what the—" he yelled as his right hand and the gun lowered. His head went fuzzy, and any control he had of his body had disappeared entirely. His eyes glanced toward his left shoulder, which had two shiny, metal, Porcupine quills protruding from it.

His eyes blurred, and his body went so completely numb, he didn't even realize Izzy had taken the gun from his hand. Before his head hit the ground, his world went dark.

"Well, that was risky … but brilliant, Izzy!" Noah beamed, holding his beating heart.

"I knew he wouldn't pull the trigger," she said. "He wouldn't risk hurting Mr. Draven's favorite employee."

Noah stepped over Brock's body and hugged Izzy, both staring at Brock's lifeless body.

"Is he dead?" Noah asked sympathetically, already forgetting that Brock just had every intention of using a deadly weapon on him and Izzy.

"No, he's just taking a three-hour nap," Izzy replied, grinning. "Picked those little quills up for situations just like this."

Izzy didn't realize how much she would enjoy using the same toxin on Brock as Draven Labs had used on Hoppers many times before. She felt around Brock's body for a phone or any electronic device that could be tracked, but she found nothing.

"His cell phone must be in his car," she said.

"What do we do with him? He has to know we're with the Wallflowers now," Noah said.

"Oh, I already have an idea. We'll give him more of his own medicine. Let's get him into the back of your car, and I'll explain everything on the way to our next stop," Izzy said confidently.

"Remind me to never piss you off," Noah joked as he lifted Brock from under his shoulders and dragged him up and into the back seat of his car. Izzy grabbed the black bag and threw it onto the front seat. She retrieved a small toolbox from her trunk and locked her car.

"You drive. I've got some things I need to fix on the way," Izzy said as she walked around Noah's car and slid into the passenger seat.

"Take the I-10 west to the Tornillo exit. Try to keep under the speed limit and as steady as you can," Izzy instructed Noah. "We don't need to get pulled over with this sack of shit in the back seat. Not sure how we would explain this one to the police."

As Noah drove, Izzy opened her toolkit, then removed each piece of equipment from the black bag and laid them on the seat next to her. She focused on the marking machine first. This device, when functional, would implant a mark onto the skin and deep into the bone of a Hopper's forearm. Similar to a tattoo, it marked a Hopper with how many times they had tried crossing the border.

"Dumbasses. The battery wasn't fully seated. Rookie mistake," Izzy said to herself. She powered the machine on and accessed a digital touch panel that was so bright, it lit up the entire inside of the car, including Brock's limp body lying across the back seat.

"SHIT!" she said, panicking to find the proper controls to dim the display. Anyone driving near them could have easily seen Brock's lifeless body splayed across the back seat.

Noah noticed her concern. "We're good. We just have two cars in front of us, and they couldn't have seen anything. The cars behind us are too far back to worry about."

"We're going to tattoo him with two marks and label him a cartel drug runner. That will give the *Civil Watch* gamers a great target to fight over," Izzy said as she punched in the details on a small, digital keyboard.

She turned and leaned over her seat, then pulled on Brock's right arm to free it from under the weight of his body. She held the machine tightly to his forearm and hit a pulsing, red button on the display. There was a steady crackling noise, followed by the smell of burning flesh.

"Whew! He even smells evil," Noah joked as he cracked open a window.

"There you go, Mr. Murphy. You're now the first cartel drug runner of Irish descent I've ever met," Izzy quipped.

"We're ten minutes from the exit. Do you need more time?" Noah asked. "I can drive around a bit more," he suggested as Izzy returned to her equipment bag.

"Nope, should be good. I'm sure these two safety armbands just blew a fuse, and I carry some in my toolkit wherever I go. There's nothing like getting caught in the Red Zone with a blown fuse on your armband. It makes for a rather nasty workday," Izzy remarked. "I always give newbie technicians extra fuses and a lesson on how to swap them out quickly, just in case they ever run into that situation in the field. I've found it's an easy way to make quick friends with them."

"And here I thought you were an introvert who didn't have any friends," said Noah. Izzy glared at him.

She finished swapping the fuses, strapped one armband on herself, and then pulled Noah's closest arm toward her and strapped one on him. The displays both showed a green light and the word ACTIVE.

"Ready to enter the Red Zone?" she queried.

"Is anyone ever really ready to enter the Red Zone? Just saying the words makes my spine tingle," Noah admitted as he exited the highway.

"You'll be fine. You're with the best engineer Draven Labs has ever known," she beamed. "Take a left after the pharmacy and ignore the big, red signs saying you're going to die."

The surroundings got eerily dark and quiet as they drove past the signs and down the dirt access road. Noah could only hear the gravel crushing beneath the car tires, nothing more. He rolled his window back up, fearing some metal creature might reach through and grab him as they drove. It made him realize how brave the Hoppers were, stepping into unknown territory with danger lurking everywhere. It also reminded him that this is what his parents must have experienced. He became somber, and Izzy noticed.

"What's wrong?" she asked.

"My parents are probably buried out here somewhere," he answered quietly. She could tell he was getting upset.

"Well, today you'll start to enjoy a little revenge on the bastards who did that to them," she said, trying to offer a positive outlook.

"But I don't want these devils sharing a grave anywhere near my parents," he replied angrily.

"Well, just know this guy is in for a very rough night and is probably NOT going to end up in the same place as them," she said, knowing there was nothing more she could say to make him feel better.

In the distance, they could both see the blinking lights of Turret 52.

"Pull into that turnabout, and we'll unload him there," Izzy said. "We're far enough into the Red Zone but far enough from that turret to avoid getting our mugshots picked up on the surveillance cameras.

The car slid to a stop, and Izzy jumped out right away. Noah hesitated and stared into the distance from the driver's seat.

"I promise you'll be okay," Izzy assured, poking her head into the car door and motioning for him to get out. "I can't pull this heavy bastard out on my own. We dump him, and we're out of here."

Noah opened the driver's-side door and crept around the car to Izzy's side, keeping his eyes on the horizon. Izzy pinched his butt, and Noah screamed.

"That's not funny, Izzy!"

She let out a quick laugh.

They yanked Brock's body out of the back door, and it hit the dirt with a thud. Noah practically ran back around the car and slammed his driver's-side door shut.

"Okay, can we please get out of here now?" he yelled from the car.

Izzy laughed again and purposefully took her time getting back into the car, savoring this little game she was playing with Noah's fears. She started to feel a bit guilty doing it after remembering his earlier reaction about his parents being killed out here.

Before Izzy's door had fully shut, Noah hit the gas, causing the tires to spit dirt out the back. The car fishtailed its way down the road.

"Whoa! You don't want to get us stuck out here, do you?" Izzy asked.

Noah's face relaxed as soon as they passed the sign marking the imaginary line at the start of the Red Zone. His driving calmed, and they were back in the small town of Tornillo before long.

Izzy went quiet.

"What's wrong, Izzy?" Noah asked.

"We may have a little problem that I hadn't considered before, Noah. If Brock followed me, knowing that I had taken that equipment, he would have likely reported me to security already, or at least to Mr. Draven."

"That is a problem, especially because it would be conspicuous if both you and Mr. Murphy didn't show up for work on Monday." He added, "They would know you were connected somehow."

They both sat silent for a few minutes, each trying to think through the possible scenarios, searching for a solution. Noah reached for his phone, switched it to speakerphone, and then started dialing a number.

"We're just going to have to put our plan into action much sooner than I had anticipated," he said.

The call connected to the car's digital control screen.

Izzy noticed that the nickname on the caller ID read "Dead Red," and she slapped Noah's shoulder. "Really? Don't you think that's a little conspicuous?"

"Jack Dempsey here." The other end interrupted Izzy's tirade.

"Hi, Jack, it's Noah. You alone?" Noah asked.

"As usual, yes, sir! What's going on?" he responded.

"Well, we have a big problem. Our little engineering mole at Draven Labs may have been discovered, and I fear her day at work on Monday might go sideways. Either we have to initiate our plan much sooner than I expected, or I need to find a good excuse to have her call in sick for the next few weeks. Do you think you and the kids can initiate our plan early?"

There was some hesitation, but Jack finally replied, "We'll have to. I'll gather them, and we'll go to headquarters and get things ready. I'll let you know whether it's a go on Sunday night. We can discuss other plans if we can't do it."

Izzy interrupted, "Thanks, Jack. I don't want to call you from deep inside the Red Zone on Monday, surrounded by mechanical creatures doing Mr. Draven's bidding."

"I understand. We're going to do everything we can. Don't you dare go to work until we can assure you everything is in order on our end," Jack cautioned, worried that Izzy might make a risky move.

"I promise I won't," Izzy agreed. "Thanks for having my back."

"Sure thing. I'll see if I can get Gabby and Aiden to meet me. I'll need their help if we are going to do this right," Jack said.

"Godspeed!" Noah said, then hung up.

Izzy was staring at Noah with a grin on her face.

"Godspeed? Really? You're such a geek," Izzy mocked him. "Don't forget, we need to pick up my car and hide Mr. Murphy's. I was thinking we leave it outside the closest bar to the border that we can find. Maybe they'll think he drank himself silly and walked off into the Red Zone alone."

18: INTO THE CAULDRON

THUD!

The shock of landing on the ground woke Brock. He was face down in the dirt, spread-eagle, confused about where he was. He looked up to see a drone lift its basket, then it flew away.

He coughed away some dirt that had found its way into his mouth and slowly pushed himself up. He tried to get his legs to stop wobbling and wished the world around him would stop spinning. His jaw tightened, his cheeks burned, and he doubled over to vomit out everything he had eaten that day.

I don't remember eating that much.

It took a minute to get his mind to reset and put together exactly what had just happened. His last memories were of finding Izzy and her male friend behind the store. He almost had the equipment bag, and then everything went blurry. Nothing was left in his memory after that.

Something on his left shoulder didn't feel right. He reached under his shirt and felt a small lump. The spot felt warm, and an oily substance seeped out when he pushed on it. He put his finger to his nose and was all too familiar with the smell. It was the scent he encountered every time he entered the chemistry department of Draven Labs. They were always brewing batches of non-lethal toxins to implant into the creatures. The smell reminded him of his grandmother's house—mothballs and alcohol.

That fuckin' bitch poisoned me.

He also noticed a slight burn nagging at his forearm and glanced down to see two dark smudges. He tried to rub them away, but that made them burn even more. He quickly realized that etched into his skin were two parallel, black lines, raised enough to feel like a braille message … a message that let him know he was in trouble.

Two marks? I have to hand it to her, she's smart.

Brock was one of two living souls who knew what two marks truly meant, and it wasn't good. Aside from him and Red, everyone who had learned what having two marks meant was no longer walking the earth. With two marks, he was now sentenced to death, and it wouldn't be one of those peaceful deaths experienced through old age.

He looked around and saw the high cliff walls surrounding him, their tops illuminated by the moon. Brock realized he was trapped in a perfect natural canyon prison that he and Red had discovered when they created Draven Labs. It was a place that wasn't on any map or business plan, and they never mentioned it to the press or to any of the stakeholders who'd invested their money and trust in the company. It was a place that would put fear into even the most hardened criminals.

I'm in the fuckin' Cauldron?

When Red and Brock named this place the Cauldron, it would just be a place to dump all of Draven Labs' old, autonomous, self-powered creatures. It became a pet cemetery of sorts. They had imagined it would be an experimental place where they could watch creature-on-creature battles and observe how all of these creatures and their AI evolved in a confined space.

Would they tear each other apart? Or would their tiny brains form relationships and team up to eliminate the weaker creatures? Would the injured ones try to rebuild themselves by taking parts from their dead counterparts? Brock and Red had even considered that this might be an entirely new source of income for the company … a type of BattleBot streaming content series that would surely bring in advertisers to DravenTV.

But on a night inspired by too much whiskey, it had evolved into something even more sinister—a human dumping ground located on the edge of the Red Zone. It was in such a remote part of the desert that, unless you fell into it, you would never even know it was there … and would never live to tell anyone about it.

Brock and Red had decided to eliminate Hoppers when they didn't learn their lesson after their first two times crossing the Red Zone. They agreed they couldn't give them a third chance to cross. Their existence and repeated attempts could prove that the Draven Labs' deterrents weren't working at maximum efficiency, and that would be bad for business.

So the Cauldron evolved into a playground for Brock and Red. It became an arena where they could watch the discarded Hoppers as they tried to fight off the creatures. It became a nightly source of amusement for them to see their victims beg for mercy before their final demise.

Realizing he was sitting dead center in this playground made him wake up.

"Nobody's going to hear me begging for mercy," Brock whispered as if he were speaking to Red, who might just be watching from above. If he was, Brock was sure his friend would be sending in a rescue drone at any moment.

Although it had been a while since he and Red watched anyone die in this arena, he knew the landscape couldn't have changed much. After hours of observing humans and creatures battle from a camera drone high above, Brock knew the layout of the Cauldron like the back of his hand.

There was no way to scale the walls in the dark, and the only place a Hopper had ever gotten close to escaping was on a cliff face on one side of a small pond along the canyon's north side.

He remembered that he and Red were impressed when checking out a young drug runner who'd climbed to the top of the cliff by using a small crevice carved by the pond's water source—a small waterfall. The poor guy was only feet from freedom when he and Red sent in a Mosquito drone to attack him as he crested the top. Brock could still remember the joy on the man's face when he had peered over the cliff's edge, certain that he was safe. And then the look of sheer terror when the Mosquito swooped down to place a stinger directly into the man's neck. Brock recalled the man's face as he fell fifty feet, breaking his back on some boulders jutting from the pond's surface.

It might offer me enough of a foothold to climb my way out.

Brock knew he had to get to the pond before first light to have any chance of escaping. And he hoped that, with any luck, maybe Red was watching overhead and might still rescue him before that.

He oriented himself to the surroundings and realized luck was on his side. He hadn't been dropped too far from the pond. He took a minute to let the effects of the toxin fully wear off and enough time to regain his balance. Then he sauntered off, slowly.

Brock knew the creatures in this place well. The slightest sound could alert one creature, thereby unleashing a cascade effect notifying all other creatures of his position. They could communicate using near-field communication, sending their coordinates and the GPS location of their prey.

There were also creatures that could sense his body heat, but he could do nothing to prevent this. He had to hope for a bit of luck on that front. He did his best to keep low and use the boulders to cover his body heat and route.

Brock's eyes adjusted to the moonlight and noticed a pile of sticks to the side of his path ahead. He needed something to fight off any creatures if they discovered him. They didn't have many weaknesses, but a good swing of a stick could incapacitate their mobility systems and buy him some time to hopefully escape.

He bent down, keeping his eyes on the horizon to watch for creatures, and measured the sticks with his hands until he found the longest one. As he lifted them, he wondered why they seemed so light. The moonlight revealed the reason when he held up the stick he had finally chosen—it wasn't a pile of sticks but a set of bones, and he had chosen the femur as his weapon.

Any sword will do.

A few quick swings of the bone assured him that it would do the trick.

As he advanced, Brock was unnerved by how dark, quiet, and cold it was in the Cauldron. That was something you couldn't pick up on while watching far overhead from a camera on a drone. He knew it was quiet because any living animal or human in this canyon had probably already been killed by the creatures.

His foot ran into something soft on the path, and a foul smell quickly interrupted his thoughts. He peered down to see a rotting, severed arm rolling back and forth, with part of the radius and ulna sticking out. He gagged but had nothing left to vomit out.

It was heavily tattooed, and he could make out the words "Mi Amor" in cursive, encircled by fancy swirls and a heart. Across the words were two black marks that didn't match the original tattoo design. They were the same marks Brock had on his forearm. It sent a shiver down his spine.

He pushed the arm off the path with his boot, and the awful smell increased, lingering in his nostrils. He moved on more quickly.

Brock made it fifty yards and was encouraged by the fact that he hadn't seen any creatures yet. But just as the thought entered his mind, he kicked the remains of what he quickly realized was a rib cage, dried out over months of sitting in the sun's heat. Their sound was odd, almost like a bone xylophone rattling a few notes, breaking the silence. He froze when he heard the accidental sound echo off the nearest wall of the Cauldron. Brock turned his gaze behind him and toward the horizon, knowing he had just alerted every creature of his presence.

A red glow appeared in the distance, facing away from him but slowly turning his way. Two red eyes fixated on his position, and then they disappeared.

FUCK!

Brock threw away all caution about making noise and started sprinting around the natural obstacles as best he could, knowing the pond wasn't far now. He knew the water would offer some protection from the land-born creatures. They could survive being in the rain but were not completely waterproof. He knew they would avoid entering the water at all costs.

He could see the moon's reflection on the pond ahead and knew he was getting close. His ears picked up a metallic, squeaking sound growing louder, even as he ran faster. He didn't waste a second glancing back as he knew he had to get to the water—fast.

The water was only twenty feet away when it struck. Something swiped at his lower leg, hard enough to trip up his feet. He fell forward and slid across the dirt. A searing pain originated from his calf, bad enough to cause him to scream, something he told himself he wasn't going to do. He quickly flipped over to find a silver creature, no larger than a microwave, with a razor-like tail extended toward him, its eyes glowing full red. Its tail shot forward, attempting to pierce the lower leg again, but Brock quickly pulled his leg away.

A Scorpion 1.0, early model.

Brock knew everything about each creature they had developed at his company—their strengths, weaknesses, design flaws, and even their personalities. He called it a personality, but it was AI instructions fed into the creature's profile that caused it to act in specific ways in different situations. When Brock and Red sent creatures to the Cauldron, any rules in their programming telling them not to kill a human had been removed.

This Scorpion was scary and could do some harm, but it was small and beatable, unlike many other creatures he was sure were now working their way toward him in the Cauldron.

As the Scorpion scurried closer to him, he knew what would happen next. This little monster's programming would dictate that it should repeatedly attack the upper torso with its sharp tail once its prey was stopped. As the creature crab-walked into position to make its move, Brock gripped the bone in his right hand and swung it hard across the creature's body.

The bone on the metal created an odd sound, and the creature flipped, landing upside down into a thicket. Its legs extended upward, in sync, and then slowly curled into its body. Its tail stopped wriggling violently in the dirt. The red glow in its eyes went dark. This assured Brock that his blow had caused some damage to its internal workings. He stared at the creature, which was now lying still in the dry brush.

That'll teach you to mess with me, little bastard!

Its eyes blinked as if it were listening, and the red glow reappeared. The creature's legs started extending and contracting, quickly and violently.

"Oh, you want more?" Brock asked out loud.

Brock tried to stand up, and his body yelled at him. He realized the creature's first attack had strategically cut across his Achilles tendon. The excruciating pain forced him to fall to the ground again.

He worked past the pain and pushed himself up again with a grunt, using the bone in his hand to balance himself on his good leg. He smiled, knowing the creature hadn't fully incapacitated him, and positioned himself directly over the creature. The Scorpion kicked its legs on alternating sides, causing its body to roll left and right. This was also part of its programming. Each kick made its body roll closer to an upright position.

THWACK!

Brock slammed the bone hard into the Scorpion, and one of its legs bent awkwardly, sparked, and dangled from the wiring still attached to the creature. With each additional hit, a piece of the bone splintered off, breaking another leg of the Scorpion. As Brock's assault ended, one side of the Scorpion was now without working legs, taking away its ability to right itself.

"That'll teach you, fucker!" Brock yelled.

The adrenaline rushing through Brock's body had him solely focused on the Scorpion in front of him. It wasn't until the Scorpion surrendered and stopped moving its legs that he realized the squeaking, metal sounds weren't coming from the creature in front of him. In the distance, he heard several other metal creatures, their rusted, metal joints scraping louder as they got closer. The sound reminded him of his barber's scissors when cutting his hair.

Brock put most of the weight on his good leg and held on to whatever remained of his weapon. The femur wasn't long enough to act as a crutch, but he felt safer having it as he started to limp toward the pond, wincing each time he put weight on his injured leg. The metal sounds behind him intensified, and the creatures sounded as though they were gaining.

His fear turned to joy when his feet made a splashing sound at the edge of the pond. On his last hop, Brock's good leg got stuck in the soft silt of the pond's floor, causing him to trip and catapult forward. His entire body splashed into the water, and his mouth was filled with stagnant, algae-flavored water.

Brock coughed out the foul-tasting water and pulled himself forward, knowing he had to get farther into the pond to avoid the creatures' reach. He dragged himself along using some reeds that stuck to the pond floor. When they started pulling out of the silt, he flipped onto his back and did the backstroke to move deeper into the pond.

He pushed himself backward and glanced back along the pond's edge. His heart jumped when he saw four sets of pulsing, red eyes pacing back and forth along the bank. Brock knew their tiny, computer-driven brains were trying to figure out how to get closer to him without getting into the water.

Brock's heart was beating out of his chest, and he knew he had better float for a few seconds to rest and catch his breath.

Enough time had passed for him to feel comfortable that the creatures wouldn't enter the water. As he looked toward the far edge of the pond, the moonlight reflected off a small trickle of water spilling down the cliff face ... and he saw the waterfall crevice that might be his salvation.

Brock pulled himself through the pond to the far side, under the barely dripping waterfall, to inspect the vertical crack.

It's a tough climb with this leg, but the crack should give me enough of a foothold.

He could only see a short distance up the cliff face, but what he could see appeared promising. He hadn't been rock climbing since his twenties, but he felt confident that facing this life-and-death situation would inspire him. He made it his mission to escape the Cauldron and brag to Red about being the first to accomplish it. He still hoped Red was watching or that some overhead camera drone would record the feat so he would have proof of his accomplishment.

The metal creatures along the shore appeared more restless as Brock moved farther away, and he heard a splash behind him. He detected a red glow in the water, surrounded by wild splashing. They were trying anything to get to him, even sacrificing themselves in the process.

Brock turned and grasped the crack in the rock face and started pulling himself up, finding footholds where he could. The pain in his leg was overcome by the adrenaline induced by the fear of the creatures. Slowly, he felt his way farther up the wall, taking small breaks to look back down into the pond below him. There were now several creatures flailing in the water at the edge of the pond, committing suicide. The more they struggled under the water, the more their red eyes dimmed.

Well, there's a programming glitch I'm glad Miss Davis didn't fix.

Brock was surprised by the distance he had already covered and more so by the amount of energy he still had left. He knew he wasn't a spring chicken anymore and was impressed with his endurance.

The sun was rising, and Brock could now see the lip of the canyon wall just twenty feet above him. He took a minute to wipe his hands on his shirt and catch his breath before his final push. He knew that rushing the climb could cause him to make a deadly mistake.

He looked down and across the Cauldron, and the light from the rising sun was now washing over the landscape. Several shiny creatures of different shapes and sizes scurried across the canyon floor, working their way toward the pond. They seemed to ignore the programming that instructed them to remain still and absorb the sunlight to recharge their batteries.

His spine tingled when he realized several of the creatures nearest him were staring up at where he hung from the wall. It was as if all of the members of their community were talking, and Brock was the day's news.

You're waiting for me to fall? I won't give you the satisfaction, bastards.

With a grunt, he started again, pulling himself up the final twenty feet of the cliff face. His fingers burned from grasping the rough rock for the last thirty minutes. The rock felt like coarse sandpaper, and it was rubbing away the flesh on his fingertips. The pain was enough to make him almost forget about the pain in his leg.

Brock's fingers reached the top, and he took another break. He knew that getting up and over the edge of the cliff wall would be the most challenging part of the climb. As he lifted his head to peer over the top, he saw there was nothing, aside from some tall, dried grass, to grab onto. He reached out and clutched the closest patch of grass. His heart jumped when the grass jerked free from the sandy soil, almost losing his footing.

He decided to snatch a larger handful on the next attempt, hoping it would provide enough leverage to hoist his torso over the edge. The grass held long enough to haul most of his body weight over the edge. Brock allowed himself a minute to give his hands and legs a break and regain his strength. One final grunt, and an army crawl pulled him up five feet away from the dangerous Cauldron's edge. He rolled onto his back, laughed loudly, and shut his eyes to guard them from the sun, which had fully crested the horizon.

"First man out of the fucking Cauldron! What do you think about that?" he boasted out loud as if he were talking to Red or some imaginary members of the press.

He lay still for a few minutes, using the time to rub his bloodied fingers together and stretch out his hands, which had fully cramped. His calf muscles throbbed. The pain was masked by the pride of his great accomplishment, the pleasure of the warm sun, and a slight breeze that dried his sweat away.

The last forty minutes focused on Brock locating the best crack to grab or the safest place to rest his foot as he climbed the canyon wall. He hadn't had the luxury of thinking about how he ended up in this god-awful place and who had put him here.

Izzy and that fucking Wallflower guy are going to pay.

As he rested, Brock ran through the military and espionage training in his head, thinking of the best way to exact revenge once he returned to civilization. They all involved painful ways to die out in the Red Zone. He was sure Izzy and her male friend would never see his revenge coming because they must surely believe him to be dead already.

How fitting that two Wallflowers will meet their demise in the Red Zone.

He spent a good fifteen minutes planning and resting with his eyes shut. Just as he finalized the plan, his brain awakened to something he should have been thinking about.

How am I going to get out of the Red Zone?

He had escaped the Cauldron but didn't have a safety armband. There was still a long hike ahead of him and on an injured leg. He still had to get out without being captured by another creature. He knew that with his new two marks, he would be sent straight back into the center of the Cauldron if a *Civil Watch* player did their job and found him out in the Red Zone.

Brock rolled back over onto his stomach, took a few deep breaths, opened his eyes, and pushed up. But his head hit something very hard on the way up, causing him to fall back down onto his stomach.

Rubbing his head, he looked up to see something he'd feared most. Directly over him was the shiny, large, silver abdomen of a Zombie Ant ... an older model from what he could tell. Six spindly legs surrounded him, three on each side of his body. As he stared, not daring to move, the creature's head and pincers framing its jaws slowly moved into view. Before Brock could act, the creature's head darted down, its pincers sinking deep into his neck.

His world went black forever.

19: FULLY CHARGED

DRAVEN LABS HEADQUARTERS (DRAVEN'S PRIVATE SUITE) —MONDAY, 8:35 A.M.

Red peered out the window of his office and watched the queue of cars at the security gate of Solace backing up more than usual. He glanced at his watch and realized it was past his 8:30 a.m. meeting time. It was unlike Brock to miss their morning meetings. He realized he hadn't missed one since the day they started operations in Solace.

He grabbed his phone and pressed the security line. Someone picked up immediately.

"This is Draven. Has Mr. Murphy checked in this morning?" he asked the man on the other end. The man responded that he had not yet seen him but had noticed his car wasn't in his parking spot this morning when he got to work.

A knock at his door interrupted the conversation, and Red hung up.

There he is.

But a different voice came from the other side of the door.

"Mr. Draven? It's Dan Foster from security. I have a message for you."

The man sounded young and nervous. Red viewed the feed from his door camera and saw it was one of the newer security guards he hadn't met before.

"I tried delivering it earlier as Mr. Murphy asked, but you weren't answering. I can slide it under the door if you'd like," the young man said.

"Yes, please do," Red replied. He believed the young man had indeed attempted to deliver the message as he said. He realized that, for once in his life, he hadn't secluded himself in his office the entire weekend. On Friday night, he'd gone to the Solace liquor store to pick out a few good bottles of alcohol for the upcoming week. He always liked to shop for these items, as he enjoyed seeing what new brands were available and how they were rated. On Saturday and Sunday, he was in his hometown of Waco, attending a family reunion with his aunts, uncles, and cousins.

An envelope slid into view from under the door, and Red picked it up.

PRIVATE—HAND DELIVER TO RED DRAVEN

He could tell it was Brock's handwriting. He unfolded the paper and read the note out loud to himself.

"It's 6 p.m. Izzy Davis is a mole. She's stealing equipment. I'm following her, but I don't have my phone. Talk in the morning. — Brock."

Son of a bitch! Izzy?

Red picked up his phone and used an app that could locate Brock's phone anywhere near a Wi-Fi or Bluetooth connection.

He's in his office.

He tried redialing Brock, but it went straight to voicemail.

Red moved to his office desk and pulled up the secret live video feed from Brock's office, which sat empty. He rang Brock's phone again and watched as a phone lit up on the far end of Brock's desk.

Where the hell is he? He'd never leave his phone.

He retrieved the archived footage of Brock's office and hit rewind until he saw him sitting at his desk, staring at the security video streams. He continued as Brock appeared excited and rushed out of the room, forgetting his phone on the desk. He switched feeds to track Brock as he left his office, rode down the elevator, and entered the processing area, where he could be seen interrogating a technician.

Why are you berating the technician?

He clicked a button and watched the same feed from fifteen minutes earlier.

He found where Izzy had entered the scene, carrying a large, yellow storage box. The technician loaded it onto the drone for her and sent it off.

What the hell are you up to, Ms. Davis?

He switched between a few other feeds to trace Izzy's steps to where she wrapped the equipment in a black bag in the R&D lab and stowed it away in the yellow case.

This must've been why Brock was following you.

He watched the feeds to see Izzy leave the building and enter the security queue at the exit gate on her way out of town. Brock's car pulled up a few cars behind hers, and Red noticed that Brock was acting very impatient. He could see Brock write the message he assumed was now in his hand. He watched as he handed it to the young security guard, then sped off.

Red picked up the phone and called the security line again.

"Hello, Mr. Draven," the man on the other end answered.

"I need Mr. Murphy's right-hand man to meet me in the medical bay at 10 a.m. I believe his name is Viktor?" Red asked.

"That's me, sir. Viktor Rodan. I'll be there at 10 a.m. Can I ask what this is about?" Viktor asked.

"I need to do an exit interview with one of my employees, which could get a little ugly. I could use someone there to help … and someone who can keep this quiet. Mr. Murphy seemed to trust you. I'll explain more later," Red said.

"Of course, sir. I understand," Viktor replied. Red ended the call.

Red left his office, took the elevator to the lobby, and picked up the phone on the wall next to the front door. He dialed the extension for the Engineering Department, and after a few rings, someone picked up.

"Engineering," a man answered.

Red lowered his voice to disguise it, "We have an issue with some equipment in medical bay three. They're busy with some incoming Hoppers right now, so can you send Izzy Davis down at the beginning of the 10:30 shift to have a look?"

"Of course. Will do! Izzy Davis, 10:30 sharp, in medical bay three," the man repeated. Red hung up the phone and headed off to the medical bays.

———————

WALLFLOWER HEADQUARTERS—9:55 A.M.

Mr. Dempsey sat with Aiden, Gabby, and Johan in the conference room at Wallflower headquarters. They stared at the single laptop from which the operation would be launched. Noah paced the room nervously behind them, realizing the past few years of work and secrecy had led to this moment. A mix of feelings flooded his mind. He had a sense of accomplishment and also felt warm at the thought that he had made some very good friends along the way. He was happy they would all get the satisfaction of revenge very soon.

He wished Izzy could be here to watch everything go down. Instead, she would have a front-row seat to the events unfolding, making him even more nervous.

"It's almost time. Are you all ready to do this?" Mr. Dempsey asked.

He got head nods from all four. He noticed how tired and

disheveled they all looked from a long weekend of coding and testing their changes. They were rushed, but all appeared confident they had put in every ounce of work they could to make this go off without a hitch.

The final subroutine file—DeadRed.py.—had been loaded into the FTP directory that Johan had set up the night before. At 10 a.m. this morning, with the next click of a button, it would be picked up by the update servers and distributed to all creatures on both borders.

"It's 10 a.m., Gabby. You get the honors," Mr. Dempsey said. Aiden smiled at her and urged her to click the return button.

Gabby leaned over the keyboard and said, "This is for you, Papá!"

She clicked the button and fell back into her chair.

Johan had set up the large display on the wall to project the update server's process log as it ran. The server went through its regular routines, and the team waited for their packet to get picked up. But the subroutine never appeared in the log.

"SHIT! What happened?" Mr. Dempsey said nervously. Aiden and Gabby looked at each other, the wind taken out of their sails.

"Did I enter the wrong URL?" Mr. Dempsey asked Johan.

Johan pushed in between them and took control of the keyboard. He entered a few commands and stood back when he found the answer.

"Brock Murphy's HAWK security system must have noticed the new FTP directory and deleted it," Johan whispered as he thought through the problem. "But the security processes can't run full-time, so we should have a short window of opportunity to add the directory back in and reupload our files. If we do this quickly, we can run our subroutine before the security routines delete the directory again."

He began typing more commands and started setting up the FTP server again.

"This might take five minutes, Noah," Johan said.

DRAVEN LABS HEADQUARTERS (SECOND FLOOR OFFICES)—10:05 A.M

Izzy paced her office, glancing between the clock on the wall and her phone.

Noah should have called by now.

A knock at the door startled her. Her coworker, Scott, popped his head through the door.

"Hey, Izzy! Engineering called, and they need your help in medical bay three at 10:30. It sounded urgent, and they wanted me to make sure you showed up on time. Something about some defective equipment. They asked for you specifically."

"Thanks, Scott. Got it."

"You don't look so good. Are you okay? Did that ladybug drawing scare you again?"

"No, thanks. I'm fine, Scott. I'm just running through a solution to an issue in my head. Pacing helps me think. Talk to you later, okay?"

"The bottle of tequila in my office helps me in those situations, but that will be our little secret." Scott smiled and closed the door.

If he only knew my secret.

Something wasn't right, and she could sense it. She was never verbally told where and when to be somewhere in her job. She usually received service orders through a reporting system on her handheld device, but there was no mention of an issue in medical bay three today. To make matters worse, medical bay three was listed as "Closed—No Unauthorized Personnel."

She started putting the pieces together, and it wasn't looking good. Brock Murphy didn't show up today, and now they requested her to arrive at an exact time to a room she didn't usually visit. And there was no official maintenance request in the system to explain why she needed to be there.

Izzy started twirling the small lock of hair that always fell to her face. It was a nervous twitch, picked up when she was a teen. It was how her parents knew she was lying or up to no good.

She made a mental note to stop fiddling with it and to keep her regular, confident, smiling personality on display.

What's the worst they can do? Ask me questions about where Brock Murphy is? Maybe ask why I sent some equipment home, skirting operating procedures. I'll just say I don't know anything about Mr. Murphy and can easily explain why I'm shipping broken equipment near my home. Why am I worried, anyway? This will all be a thing of the past soon.

Noah was supposed to text a go/no-go on the mission. They had all agreed it was supposed to start at 10:00 a.m. If there had been an issue, Noah surely would have let her know by now.

She couldn't handle the silence anymore. Just as she was about to call him, a text arrived from his nickname, Roomie.

Small plumbing issue. Have professionals on it. Hoping to have it fixed in time for our date.

Izzy typed back:

Hope it's fixed quickly. Shit hitting the fan for me here at 10:30. Starting to worry last night's little party will have consequences.

Her reply had a spinning icon next to it, as if the message was waiting to be delivered.

Fuck.

She had to start walking to the medical bay to make it to the 10:30 appointment.

WALLFLOWER HEADQUARTERS—10:10 A.M.

Johan finished typing and pulled away from the laptop. "It's all yours now, Jack. Reupload the subroutine and hit that URL as quickly as you can. Let's hope we can run this before the next security sweep happens."

Mr. Dempsey uploaded the file. It went up quickly because it wasn't that large of a file. It was just text. He pushed his chair back to make an opening for Gabby.

"Hit the URL again, Gabby!"

She went to the web URL again and pressed enter.

The large screen showed the update processes running again. Everyone cheered when the last few lines of the update process appeared on the screen.

```
... DeadRed.py installed.
... Restarting all equipment.
```

"Now we sit back and wait. We should hear from one of our inside people that the operation is underway," Mr. Dempsey said.

Noah let out a sigh of relief. "Good luck, Izzy."

They turned on the local El Paso News channel, assuming that station would be the first to report any odd activity at Draven Labs.

DRAVEN LABS HEADQUARTERS (R&D ROOM)—10:15 A.M.

The Hive's research and development space was teeming with engineers and technicians. Monday was the day to catch up on broken creatures from the weekend, and it was always busy like this. Broken creatures lined the work floor, ready for either servicing or inspection.

Anton Fleming was fumbling with a Jellyfish 2.0 creature as it dangled from a crane. His assistant, Chase, watched from across the stainless-steel work table.

"I'm getting tired of oiling all of these tentacles. I feel like a new dad changing his baby's diaper every hour," Anton joked.

His assistant replied, "Yeah, these things go through oil like my 2040 Honda!"

Anton laughed. He pushed his head up deep into the grouping of tentacles to ensure he had oiled every last one of them.

One of the tentacles wrapped around his arm tightly, catching him off guard.

"Oh, fuck! I thought you turned the power off, dude?" Anton yelled to Chase.

"I did!" Chase replied, picking up the digital pad sitting on the table. He tried to tap the power button to turn the creature off, but the Jellyfish remained on. He looked up and noticed the glowing, red eyes of the Jellyfish. They were staring deep into his soul.

"Something's wrong, Anton. Get out of there!" he yelled.

Before Anton could pull himself free, the creature had wrapped the rest of its tentacles around Anton and began squeezing tightly. There was no way Anton could escape, and he realized it.

"Help me," he managed to squeak out with the bit of breath he had left in his lungs.

Chase grabbed the two tentacles nearest Anton's chest and pulled as hard as possible. They wouldn't budge.

CRACK! CRACK! CRACK!

The electrical charge ran through both Anton and Chase's bodies. Anton went limp, still firmly grasped by the Jellyfish, and Chase fell to the floor with a *THUD*, totally unconscious.

The engineer at the next table heard the commotion and alerted a nearby supervisor.

"There's a problem over here, sir," he yelled. Before the supervisor realized what was happening at Anton's station, he noticed that several other creatures in the room had powered on and were attacking their handlers.

"What the ..."

He heard a thousand metal legs tapping on the cement walls on the one side of the room where the older model creatures had been mounted in a makeshift museum. They were trying to free themselves from their mounts on the wall. The collection of Centipedes, Black Widow Spiders, Beetles, Snakes, Porcupines, and more could be seen detaching from the wall and making their way to the center of the room. Everyone was running for the nearest exit, and no one had time to activate any alarms. They were running for their lives, trying to exit the Hive, which the creatures were overtaking.

DRAVEN LABS HEADQUARTERS (MEDICAL BAY THREE)—10:18 A.M.

Viktor walked into medical bay three to find Mr. Draven sitting in a reclining medical chair, watching a video feed on the digital display that hung over the chair on a swiveling arm.

"Viktor?" Red asked without even looking at him.

"Yes, sir. In the flesh," Viktor replied, trying to ease the tension in the room. Viktor looked around and noticed the windows in the room had been set to privacy mode, which made them frosted so prying eyes couldn't see anything happening inside.

There was a metal surgical table next to the chair where Mr. Draven was sitting. Some marking equipment and surgical instruments were laid out on the table. The sharp instruments made him nervous, as the setup looked like an interrogation room. The last thing he wanted was to be a part of a torture session.

"I've closed this medical bay for the rest of the day, Viktor. Ms. Izzy Davis will be joining us shortly," he said in a serious tone. He swung the video screen toward Viktor, and Viktor stepped closer to see what Mr. Draven had been watching. On the screen, Viktor saw Izzy Davis packing up some equipment, and then the video cut to her placing them inside a yellow box. It showed her

262

interaction with the technician to load the box onto a drone. Then he showed a clip of Mr. Murphy following her in his car out of Solace.

"She's stealing equipment?" Viktor asked.

Red gave Viktor the handwritten note that Brock had delivered to him. As Viktor read the note, Red explained.

"Mr. Murphy was sure he found a mole. I've looked back through the video archives, and I'm positive she's working for the Wallflowers. Stealing equipment, probably feeding them information, who knows what else," Red answered. "And now, Mr. Murphy has disappeared after following her out of town. We're going to discover what she's been up to. This is the closest we've ever come to learning anything about the Wallflower organization."

"So you're going to ... torture her?" Viktor asked nervously, staring at the table of surgical equipment.

"Don't worry, Viktor. I'm just going to scare her a bit. I'm going to let her talk, show her the videos, and then ask her some questions. If I feel she's holding back, I'll threaten her with something that should get her talking. Nothing life-threatening. Just follow along," Red responded.

Viktor nodded to show he would help.

The door to medical bay three opened, and Izzy Davis entered. Red turned the screen aside so Izzy couldn't see what he and Viktor were discussing. Red noticed nothing out of the ordinary with her, nothing that showed she was guilty of anything, and nothing that indicated she knew she was in trouble. She was wearing the same long, white lab jacket she wore to work every day.

Izzy hadn't noticed them yet. She pushed her glasses up onto her nose as she walked into the room, looking down at her phone the entire time.

She tried to resend her short text to Roomie: *Any news?*

MESSAGE UNDELIVERED.

She was startled and stopped texting when she glanced up and noticed the large security guard, gun on hip, standing next to Mr. Draven.

"Oh, hello, gentlemen! Mr. Draven, I didn't expect to see you here. I was told there's a problem with some equipment—"

"Yes, Izzy, we have a problem," Red said, cutting her off. "Take a seat, and I'll show you what's happening. I'm sure you can help."

Izzy studied the faces of Mr. Draven and the security guard and realized how serious the situation must be. She felt she might be in for a bit of trouble. She knew that, aside from turning and running out the door, which would show her guilt, she could only follow Mr. Draven's instructions and see where the conversation was headed.

Mr. Draven moved aside and motioned to the only chair in the room—the reclining medical examination chair. Izzy sat down slowly, looking between Red, the security guard, and the table. She hadn't noticed the equipment and surgical tools when she walked in. Her heart beat quickly, and she began to say something when Mr. Draven stopped her.

"I just want you to watch a video," Red said, leaning over her to pull the screen closer. He played back the edited video he had just shown to Viktor.

When it ended, Izzy's face switched from one of confusion to one of confidence.

"Okay? I sent some equipment home to fix. That's nothing new. I'd get stopped and asked a bunch of stupid questions if I tried to take it through the queue at the security gate. It's just easier to do it that way," Izzy said. "I have the highest clearance, so it shouldn't be a big deal. I send the equipment home, fix it in my free time, and return it. You should thank me for the extra work I do at home."

Red pushed the monitor aside and stood directly in front of Izzy. He leaned over her and placed his hands over hers on the armrests. Izzy became uncomfortable and began to struggle. Red glanced at Viktor, and Viktor pulled his weapon from his holster, pointing it directly at Izzy's head.

"Mr. Draven, I don't understand," Izzy started.

Red interrupted her again. "The problem is, Izzy, I checked, and the logs show that you marked all four of those items as 'Permanently Damaged' in the inventory system. You did not intend to fix and bring them back in, did you?" Red asked, his face red with anger. "Mr. Murphy knew it, and that's why he followed you last night, right?"

Before she could answer the question, he kicked a foot switch, activating the wrist restraints, which snapped shut and held Izzy securely in the chair. Viktor didn't expect the restraints to shut so quickly. He jumped back slightly at the sound they made when they locked into place. He lowered his gun, knowing she had no way of getting free now.

Red straightened and began pacing in front of Izzy as if he were a lawyer presenting his case to a jury. He could tell by the worried look on Izzy's face that there was guilt, and he just needed to pry the truth out of her.

"What happened to Mr. Murphy Friday night, Izzy? I know he followed you out of here when he discovered you and that technician sending the equipment out to Turret 52. He didn't make it back to work this morning. That's the first time he hasn't shown up at work in two years. A bit of a coincidence, don't you think?"

Izzy's face turned white, and Red could tell she was trying to find an excuse.

He slapped Izzy hard enough to send her glasses flying across the room. Izzy gasped.

Viktor stepped forward to stop him, but Red held his hand up and stared him down, fury in his eyes.

"She's working with the Wallflowers, Viktor. Don't fool yourself into thinking she's an innocent, little girl."

Viktor looked at Red, then Izzy, and stepped back to let Red continue his interrogation.

Izzy couldn't believe he had hit her. She knew he had a temper, but she'd never seen him get violent. She was aware that Red would be upset if he ever discovered her secret, and maybe he would ask her some questions and then have security usher her out of the building. At the very worst, Izzy thought he would involve the police and press charges. But she didn't expect this kind of violence from him. From Brock Murphy, maybe, but not Red.

She glanced up at the clock on the wall.

It's already 10:35. What's the holdup, Noah?

"What was the equipment really for, Izzy? What are the Wallflowers planning?" Red grilled. Izzy just glared at him.

Red slapped her again with a backhand strike hard enough for his Rolex to leave a red gash across her cheek. A stream of blood dripped down her face almost instantly.

"Fuck you! Let me out of this goddamn chair. Haven't you had enough of hurting people!" Izzy yelled at Red. She turned to Viktor with a look that pleaded for compassion. Viktor's eyes widened, and he didn't appear to show the same hatred toward Izzy. He seemed to be reconsidering his involvement in this interrogation.

"So you think I've hurt people, eh? You sympathize with the fucking Wallflowers then?"

Izzy turned defiant, and a look of hatred entered her eyes. She struggled to free her wrists from the chair. Red was shocked. He had never seen this side of Izzy before. She was always rainbows and butterflies around him. She calmed down, straightened in the chair, and then glared at him.

"Yes, you dumb bastard! I've been working with the Wallflowers since I started here. Learning everything about your little mechanical creatures, security operations, and weaknesses. I even know how many times a day you take a piss, and you might want to call your urologist."

Red struck Izzy again, across her mouth this time. A fresh cut opened on her lip, the blood staining her teeth red.

"Hand me that fucking marking device, Viktor," he commanded, pointing at the table.

Viktor slowly picked up the marking device and stared at it.

"Hand it the fuck here, Viktor. Stop acting like a pussy!" Red thundered. "This bitch probably had Brock killed. It could have just as easily been you or I."

Viktor pushed the device into Red's outstretched hand.

Red powered the device on. He had programmed it before anyone entered the medical bay and smiled as he proudly read the display to Izzy.

"Seems you've been a bad girl, Ms. Davis. A sex trafficker, is it? Caught transporting young girls across the border to El Paso, huh? Oh, yes, I've set it to two marks because I can't stand criminal Hoppers like you."

Izzy tried to free herself again. Two marks was as good as a death sentence, and she knew it. The wrist restraints wouldn't budge, and she started to panic. She glanced at the clock again. It was now 10:42.

Red yanked up the sleeve of her white lab coat to expose her forearm so he could mark her. He stepped back, surprised.

"Why are you wearing a fucking safety armband inside the facility?" he asked himself more than her.

"Because I know what's coming," Izzy responded, a smile reappearing.

Red raised his arm again to take another swing at her. Izzy instinctively lowered her chin, turned her head, and shut her eyes in anticipation of the blow.

But the hit never came. Instead, Izzy heard something heavy hit the floor. She opened her eyes to see Viktor standing over Red, gun in hand. At first, she thought he had shot Red, but then she realized she had not heard a gunshot. He'd knocked him out cold with the butt of his gun.

"Sorry, Izzy. I wanted to act sooner," Viktor apologized, concern in his eyes.

"I don't understand," she replied.

Viktor kicked Red to make sure he was completely knocked out. "I'm a Wallflower, too. I've been working with Noah since I started at Draven Labs," he remarked with a smile. "I made sure I weaseled my way onto Mr. Murphy's security detail and became buddy-buddy with him in case there was ever a situation like this. Noah asked me to watch out for you. I texted him a little bit ago when I learned that Mr. Draven was going to have you questioned here."

"You saved my life, Viktor. Or at least saved me from a terrible tattoo on my forearm. Thank you!" she said.

"Sorry it took me a bit to take him down. I didn't realize he was going to hurt you like that, and I needed time to get behind him without him noticing," Viktor explained.

"Well, don't feel too bad, he hits like a pussy! I can handle it," she said, using the same insult on Red that Red had used on Viktor earlier.

Viktor kicked the foot switch and released her arm restraints. Izzy rubbed her wrists and then wiped the blood from her face. She didn't realize just how much she was bleeding until she saw the blood against the sleeve of her stark-white lab coat.

20: ITSY BITSY SPIDER

Alarms instantly started blaring, startling Izzy and Viktor. Yellow lights flashed in all four corners of the medical bay. They also lit up the hallway on the other side of the medical bay's frosted windows. An overhead announcement repeated the same message two times over the facility's speakers.

CODE RED. ALL PERSONNEL BEGIN
LOCKDOWN PROCEDURES. SHELTER IN
PLACE UNTIL FURTHER NOTICE.

Izzy beamed at Viktor. "Finally! Let the fun begin!"
Viktor looked confused.
"Oh, you don't know? I'll explain in a minute. Help me with this piece of shit first," she said, trying to flip Red onto his back.
"Roll up the sleeve on his right arm," Izzy directed as she felt around Red's body to locate his cell phone, which was in the pocket of his suit jacket. She slipped his smartwatch off his wrist and put both into her pocket. "Don't want anyone to be able to track his whereabouts."
Izzy grabbed the marking unit beside Red's body and held it firmly against his forearm. The now-familiar crackling sound and burning smell told her that the two marks were now emblazoned onto the skin of Red's forearm and deep down in his radial bone.

269

She noticed a wheelchair in the corner of the room. "Get that wheelchair, please."

Viktor pulled the wheelchair next to Red's body. "Let's get him loaded and take him to the processing center," Izzy said as she moved around his body and put her hands under his legs to lift.

Just as they were about to raise him up, the lights blinked off, and then the room went completely dark again, except for the flashing, yellow alarm lights. After five seconds, the bright-white emergency floodlights kicked on in the hallway.

There was a loud crash somewhere in the distance, resonating as though metal furniture was falling to the ground.

"That sounded like it came from the R&D lab down the hall, Izzy," Viktor announced.

Izzy and Viktor stared at each other, completely still, their ears perked up, listening for any clue as to what might be happening. There was more commotion, and they heard a bloodcurdling cry from a man in the distance.

"What the fuck is happening out there, Izzy?" Viktor asked in a panic.

"A little creature rebellion from the sound of it," she replied. "I'm pretty sure every creature in this facility has been activated and given new marching orders, compliments of the Wallflowers."

Viktor's eyebrows raised.

Through the frosted glass of the medical bay, they watched as dark shadows of small creatures swarmed down the hall, hopping from the floor to the windows and sliding down as they appeared unable to grasp the glass. Thankfully, they all moved on quickly, passing by the door to the medical bay they were just in.

She and Viktor were still frozen, holding Red's legs and upper body.

"We don't have time. Follow me!" Izzy urged. She grabbed Viktor's hand. Before she could take a step, they both saw something large and more horrifying casting a shadow against the far window.

The black silhouette of a creature appeared, and it stood almost the entire height of the hallway. It was crawling closer to the only door exiting the medical bay. They could make out a large, bulbous body and long, spindly legs that tapped the windows as they slowly felt their way past a couple of the windows. The tapping was unnerving. It reminded Izzy of a horror movie, in slow motion, playing out in front of them—a movie where the actors never make it out alive.

She pulled up her sleeve and looked at her safety armband.

It's 50 percent charged with a green light. We're good.

She quickly yanked Viktor toward the wall on the other side of the room, the one closest to the exit door.

"What the fuck is that thing?" Viktor yelled to Izzy, trying to be heard over the robotic warning that continued blaring from the intercom system.

As soon as the words left his mouth, the creature completely stopped. Its body slowly turned, and it was no longer facing down the hallway but instead focused on where Izzy and Viktor now stood and where it heard a human voice. Its head turned from side to side, trying to triangulate where the human voice came from.

Two pointy, metal legs punctured through the frosted glass window in front of the creature. The glass didn't shatter into large pieces like standard glass would. Tiny cracks appeared across the window, and as the creature's legs slowly pushed through, the entire pane crumbled into a thousand pieces across the floor. The sound was deafening.

Izzy and Viktor froze and just stared at the huge, Black Widow Spider staring at them. Its jointed, shiny, silver legs gleamed in stark contrast to its dark, matte-black body. Three luminous, large, red spots lined the middle of its back, and its silver pincers slowly opened and closed as it carefully worked its body through the hole it had made. Once inside the room, it stared down at Izzy and

Viktor.

Izzy pulled Viktor behind her and held up her armband. The Black Widow appeared to pause, then turned its head away as if it had lost interest in either of them. It lowered its head to focus instead on Red's warm body lying on the floor ten feet away. Izzy noticed Red was moving his arms, shakily pushing his upper body from the floor. Both she and Viktor realized that in all of the excitement, they had left Viktor's gun lying right next to Red's body. Izzy felt Viktor's body tense, as if he was going to make a run for the gun. She pressed him harder against the wall to stop him.

"Just … stay … still," Izzy muttered back to him. The Black Widow's head twitched, and its focus again returned to where they stood against the wall.

Then Red started moving again. He rubbed the back of his head and pulled his forearm closer to his face to look at his newly acquired two black marks. He was oblivious to anything else around him, still feeling the effects from the blow to his head.

"Feel the burn, you bastard!" Izzy whispered.

"What the fuck?" Red said out loud. The sound made the Black Widow Spider snap its focus back to him again.

Red looked to his left and saw the gun on the ground. He picked it up and stared at it for a second, trying to get his head wrapped around where the hell he was and how this gun ended up near him.

"He must have a concussion," Izzy murmured.

Izzy and Viktor watched nervously, hoping Red wouldn't notice them standing against the wall and point the gun at them.

The metal-on-cement scraping sound forced Red to finally glance up and see the metal creature, now positioned only six feet in front of him, staring down. It slowly raised its front legs, exposing its large, black abdomen. It swayed side to side in some weird dance as if trying to hypnotize its prey.

Red raised the gun, but before he could fire, a silver, thread-like web shot from the Black Widow's abdomen, surrounding Red's entire body.

The web quickly constricted, pulling Red's arms and legs into a neat cocoon, causing him to lose control of the gun. Instantly, tiny sparks of light, like flashing Christmas lights, encircled his body. Red's body appeared to lose more of the will to fight with each spark. After five seconds, the sparks stopped, and his stiffened upper body slumped to the floor.

Izzy had seen the Black Widow Spider in action during tests in the engineering lab, but never with a real human being and never when it inflicted real pain. She felt a slight sense of compassion for Red and what he had just endured.

The Black Widow fell firmly onto all eight legs, turned 180 degrees, and started to crawl back through the opening it had created in the windowpane. Red's body, wrapped tightly in the silver web, dragged behind the Black Widow as it scaled the short wall, bumping and scraping against everything along the way—the wall, the window frame, and the hard cement floor on the other side of the wall. Izzy forgot about her compassion and chuckled at the sight of Red being handled roughly for once. The Black Widow made its way out of the room and turned left down the hall toward the Silo.

"He'll be sore in the morning," she whispered to Viktor, who had decided to remain completely still and silent during the rest of the event. After witnessing Red's experience, he had no desire to become its next victim.

Once the Black Widow Spider pulled Red past the medical bay's exit door and down the hall toward the Silo, Izzy gave Viktor a quick overview of the attack plan that had just begun. Like most of the Wallflowers, Viktor had not been informed of the attack details or that it would take place today. Noah had decided it would be too risky to have even one person slip up and expose their plans.

"Let's make sure Mr. Draven gets a ride out of here," Izzy whispered, pulling Viktor along the wall and to the door exiting the medical bay. She peeked down the hall to make sure it was clear of any other creatures.

"We have to get to the Silo. I have a plan for getting us out of this mess," Izzy said. "The creatures aren't supposed to be attacking people. They were only supposed to attack electronics and mechanical devices. I think something went wrong with the plan. But this safety armband will protect both of us from them. Are you okay following my lead?"

Viktor nodded in agreement, still trying to remain silent for as long as he could. Izzy seemed very confident with her plan to get them out, and she appeared fearless after the beating she had just received, so Viktor decided to follow.

They slowly walked through the security doors, which opened to the processing center in the center of the Silo. They turned the corner and hugged the wall, reaching a spot behind some supply crates piled up, ready to be shipped. Izzy kept Viktor behind her and the safety armband out in front of them the entire way, peeking at it occasionally to ensure it was still powered on and had a charge.

It's down to a 30 percent charge. Why is it losing charge so quickly?

She rummaged through her pockets to see if she could find a replacement battery, and for once in her life, she had none. She decided not to let Viktor sense her concern.

We need to get out of here ... fast!

Directly in the center of the room, and below the opening to the Silo, they could see Red's cocoon lying inside a large, yellow-and-white target painted on the floor. The Black Widow turned to face Red and raised its upper body off the floor again. The silver webbing appeared to loosen with a few jerking movements, unwrapping from around Red's body. The web retracted back into the Black Widow's abdomen, and it took five steps backward, keeping a watchful eye on its prey.

Yellow alarm lights started flashing directly above where Izzy and Viktor stood, startling both of them. In sync, the intercom blared a message in a robotic, female voice:

DLED 113 INCOMING. TIME TO ARRIVAL IS T-MINUS FIVE MINUTES.

"This will probably be the last time we see Mr. Draven alive. Say your goodbyes," Izzy whispered to Viktor.

"Good riddance! Do you have a plan to get us out of here … preferably one that doesn't involve a Black Widow Spider's web?" Viktor asked.

"We're going to get a free ride in a DLED drone. We'll just have a different destination," Izzy said, removing a small tablet from her pocket.

She pulled up the logistics screen for the facility, which showed all the drones coming and going at the Hive. She clicked on the closest drone labeled in green that was marked "Supply Run." Using her finger, she dragged a line from its icon to the center of the Silo on the little, digital map. A small window popped up with a message:

DLED 28 INCOMING. TIME TO ARRIVAL IS T-MINUS TEN MINUTES.

"Got our ride, Viktor." Izzy smiled. "Now I just have to arrange a pickup on the other end."

She retrieved her phone and selected one of the contacts in her favorites list, labeled Roomie.

Noah instantly picked up, panic in his voice. "Izzy, are you okay? Where are you?"

Viktor overheard Noah's voice and looked at Izzy. He mouthed the word ROOMIE as if making fun of her nickname for him. She grinned at him.

Izzy whispered, "Your friend, Viktor, rescued me. I'll fill you in later, but we're waiting for a DLED to escort Mr. Draven on a little one-way trip to that fun place where they take two marks. Once he gets picked up, we'll be on the next drone toward Turret 52. Can someone pick us up there?"

"Yes, I'll send Peter out with the car right now. He'll be waiting for you," Noah replied.

"Sending Peter, eh? You didn't like our last date in the Red Zone?" Izzy joked.

"Very funny! I'd come myself, but I need to get the videos and press releases into the news outlets quickly. I'm glad you two are safe."

"I know, silly. I'm just playing with you." Izzy laughed.

"When we're done decommissioning the Red Zone, I'd be more than happy to take you on a little wine and cheese picnic out there," Noah offered. "And I'll even buy a good bottle of wine this time. Then maybe we can catch that action movie I've wanted to see."

"Deal! Don't forget to send Peter in with a safety armband. And make sure it shows a full charge before he enters. You don't want to dispatch him on a suicide mission, and we need him to get us out," Izzy explained. "I thought Jack and the kids were programming the creatures to destroy all electronics and mechanicals, but not attack people?"

"Yes, that's correct. Why do you ask, Izzy?" Noah inquired.

"Well, Draven was attacked by an old Black Widow Spider unit."

"Let me look into it, and I'll call you back," Noah said, concern in his voice.

"No, I'll call you. I don't need my phone ringing or vibrating when these creatures are hunting us down." She set her phone to silent mode to be on the safe side.

Just as the call ended, the loud, whirring sound of an incoming DLED filled the space.

Izzy and Viktor peeked over the crates to watch as it lowered into the Silo and hovered above Red's body, its blue and white lights flashing. The metal basket lowered from the bottom of the DLED until it rested on the ground, surrounding Red. The basket scooped up his body and lifted it into the air. As it raised, Izzy noticed that Red sat up and started yanking at the door of the metal basket. He tried to scream for help over the roar of the drone's blades as they increased in speed, a look of fear on his face.

As it flew off, they saw the large Black Widow turn back toward the hall leading to the medical bays, quickly scurrying off to locate a new victim.

"Five minutes, right, Izzy?" Viktor whispered, still afraid the creature could pick up his voice.

She looked at the time on her phone and nodded at Viktor, then she checked her safety armband.

Only a 5 percent charge. Fuck!

The screen blinked red, and a message warned her that she was now at a dangerous power level. Viktor noticed the flashing, red message.

"What's that mean?" he asked, his eyes wide.

"It means that DLED better get here damn quick, or we're in for a bit of an adventure."

21: LOSING SOLACE

Red pulled as hard as he could on the gate of the metal basket, but it wouldn't budge. Magnetic locks held the door shut.

As the drone crested the lip of the Silo, the blades spinning at full speed sucked the intense heat coming from the Texas sun and directed it straight at him. He pulled off his suit jacket and tie and threw them into a corner of the basket.

Once the drone moved away from the Silo, Red rolled onto his stomach to look down at his town of Solace below. His head pounded, and his mouth felt as if it were lined with cotton.

I'd do anything for a glass of bourbon right now.

The streets were void of movement, and something didn't feel right. The usual flurry of activity in the town had simply ceased. Just as Red wondered where everyone was, he caught a glimpse of a car speeding down the main road toward the security gate. Something was hanging on to the hood.

Is that an ... Ant?

The car braked, swerved, and slid sideways into a tree, throwing the huge Zombie Ant five yards away. The Zombie Ant rolled, quickly got up on all six legs, then crawled back toward the vehicle. Red tried to watch what happened next, but the drone moved too far away from the scene.

In the small park next to the town square, he saw a woman rolling in the grass, covered in tiny, black creatures that appeared to swarm her body.

A Dragonfly drone swooped about ten feet below the basket, startling him as it headed toward the employee parking lot. Red followed it with his eyes and saw at least twenty people heading from the lot to the security gate, looking back as if running from something. Behind them, three large Centipedes were visible from under a tree, chasing them at top speed. The bodies of the Centipedes slithered gracefully across the cement, closing the distance between them and their prey.

The drone reached the outside wall of Solace, where Red observed at least thirty cars backed up haphazardly at the security gate. It was as if all the cars tried to leave at the same time, creating a bottleneck at the gate. No security guards were on watch, and some of the car doors had been left open with no drivers in sight.

What the hell happened to them?

As he flew over the wall, Red could see the mounted cameras that were supposed to be monitoring the security gate and the main road leading into Solace. They were sparking and looked to be ripped into pieces, dangling by their power supplies and hanging over the edge of the wall. Ten feet away, a Zombie Ant and a Beetle had teamed up and attacked one of the small power generators sitting atop the wall, making easy work of tearing it to shreds with their pincers.

Red noticed another Zombie Ant scaling down the outside of the wall and then realized where all of the people from the cars had gone. They were sprinting through the desert outside Solace, scurrying in different directions, attempting to escape the terror behind them. Not far behind, creatures of all types appeared to be hunting them.

As the drone flew farther away from the city, Red peered back and noticed several massive plumes of smoke rising above the city wall.

"No!" he screamed.

The scenery abruptly changed from concrete streets and buildings to sand dotted with bushes, rock outcroppings, and cacti. The scenery extended into the distance as far as his eyes could see. Red's body baked in the sun as the drone continued at full speed for about fifteen minutes until it suddenly crested a vast canyon wall.

When the drone descended into the gaping chasm, he realized where he was. Red was staring at the Cauldron—the place where all two-marks are sent. He had seen this view dozens of times before, but always safely from a video feed supplied by overhead drones. He was used to watching Hoppers in this same canyon as they battled his creatures, and they always ended up dead. Today's view was different as he didn't have Brock, air conditioning, and a good bottle of bourbon to make it enjoyable.

The drone entered the center of the Cauldron, stopped, and lowered his basket to the ground. As it descended, Red swiveled his body, searching for any sign of creatures. He sensed they were hiding in the brush, and he was certain they would have heard the drone's blades. He knew what was in store for him.

As he surveyed the area, Red also looked for the same pond Brock was drawn to. Just like Brock, he remembered that the cliff face near the pond offered the best opportunity for escape from this evil place. He caught a reflection of water to his right, shimmering in the sun, bouncing off the face of the canyon wall.

When the drone was five feet from the ground, the bottom of the basket sprang open, sending Red tumbling to the ground, landing firmly on his back. He saw stars, and his back screamed in as much pain as his head did.

The drone lifted away quickly.

"Dammit!"

Red realized, too late, that his only way out of this awful place was now flying off into the distance. He knew that, even if he had grabbed onto the basket on its way up, he wouldn't have had the strength to hold on to it the entire way back, let alone out of the Cauldron. He would have surely fallen to his death.

I have to get to the pond.

Red ignored the pain shooting through his body and stood. There was no time to waste. He aligned himself toward the spot where he saw the pond and was about to run when he heard something.

A chittering noise behind him made his spine tingle. It was far away, but Red knew it meant a creature was nearing and probably talking to its friends. He started sprinting toward the sun. As he ran, he took off his dress shirt, partially because it was wet with sweat, but also because he could wave it to distract one of the creatures, if necessary.

The cacti tore at his skin as he dashed through the brush, making him wish he still had his suit jacket on. A few times, Red noticed a beaten path he could have taken but decided not to take advantage of any of them. He knew the creatures had made the paths, and it would be foolish to expose himself by using them.

Red could see water thirty yards ahead, and a sense of hope entered his mind. Not only would a dip feel good in the heat, but more importantly, it would protect him from the creatures that couldn't go into the water.

The cacti got thicker and taller as he approached the water, and Red had to start weaving around them. It reminded him of his days as a running back in football, trying to dodge the defensive linemen as they attempted to tackle him.

He was making good progress and was sure the pond was right around the next row of cacti. He tripped over something in his path as he circled the largest cactus. Red fell to the ground, skidding through the dust on his stomach, knocking the air from his lungs.

"What the—" He tried to catch his breath while he wiped away the dust that had blurred his vision. Red rubbed his eyes with his sweat-drenched, tattooed forearm and then blinked a few times to restore his focus. He looked back to see what he had tripped over.

He screamed in horror at the sight in front of him.

Just four feet away, Brock was staring back at him. Red quickly realized it wasn't all of Brock, only his head. Brock's eyes appeared to beg for help, and flies crawled in and out of his open mouth. It was as if Brock had died screaming and in a moment of terror.

The brush behind the severed head parted, and a metal snout pushed through. As it exited the grass, Red realized it was one of his mechanical Porcupine creatures. It wasn't one of the larger, new models but one of the older, smaller ones. The creature paused, as if it were sizing up Red's body, and then started turning to line up its quills at him.

Red pushed himself up quickly, but not quickly enough. The hiss of the Porcupine shooting its quills didn't register with him, but the pain in his shin did. He yanked the quill out of his leg and started to feel as though he couldn't swallow. His tongue swelled, and his mouth tasted like a mix of rubbing alcohol and something bitter. Red quickly realized he had been shot with a quill containing the toxin cooked up in his company's lab.

The Porcupine spun in the dirt to take another shot but got tangled in the tall grass. Red realized the Porcupine couldn't target him in its current position, but he would be in trouble if it broke free. He started feeling dizzy and woozy and tried to crawl backward, out of the Porcupine's striking range.

On his last push, he bumped into something hard. Red rolled over. The sun reflected off something, blinding him temporarily. Shielding his eyes, he focused on the metallic body of something enormous and shiny, with a dark green-and-black abdomen. His face slowly gaped up at a huge Beetle staring down at him. The creature's jaw held two large, serrated pincers spread far apart. The pincers snapped shut. Red's world went dark.

22: ONE HUNDRED REASONS TO RUN

Izzy and Viktor sat still behind the crates, waiting and hoping for any sign of the DLED arriving—flashing, yellow lights, the robotic announcement—anything. It was eerily silent as they waited. Her digital control pad showed the DLED just entering Solace, which was only minutes away.

A loud crash echoed from somewhere inside the Silo. Izzy and Viktor peeked over the crates and looked around for what could be making the noise. Directly across from them, they noticed some scattered crates, much like the ones they were hiding behind.

A series of soft, chittering noises echoed through the Silo, starting and stopping randomly.

Izzy's armband vibrated and went dark. Viktor felt the vibration, too, and he realized what it meant. They were no longer safe.

"When that drone enters the Silo and starts lowering its basket, we're going to have to make a run for it. You ready?" Izzy asked.

Viktor shook his head yes.

Their heads snapped toward another loud crash to their right, and they discovered what was making the noise. A Centipede, scurrying on hundreds of little, metal feet, was working its way around the room's perimeter, flipping things in search of prey.

The yellow light above them started flashing, illuminating their faces as they peered at the creature. The Centipede stopped moving and realigned its body segments so that it was now standing four feet tall and staring directly at them.

Izzy whispered, "It's picked up our body heat. It's built to catch its prey by using its pincers and wrapping its body around yours."

"Why'd you say my body?" Viktor asked.

"Sorry, I meant us, its prey. Here's the plan. When it's within ten feet of us, shove the crates toward it and make a run for the basket," Izzy directed. "The obstacles should slow it down."

The DLED was just entering the Silo, propellers kicking up dust around the room.

Izzy and Viktor watched as the Centipede straightened its body and shot toward them, red eyes pulsing and pincers spreading. It moved much faster than Izzy thought it could.

"NOW!" Izzy yelled, and she and Viktor pushed the crates toward the creature and started running.

The DLED began lowering its basket just as they launched toward it.

Izzy looked back and noticed the creature had stopped, raised its body, and peered over the crates to see them running. It quickly changed its course, maneuvered around two crates, and headed on a path to intercept them.

Viktor had noticed it, too, and he tugged on Izzy's arm to help her move along a little faster.

The basket bounced off the ground just as they reached it. Izzy waited for the electronic gate to unlatch so they could hop in. It seemed like it took forever, and the Centipede had closed much of the distance as they waited. The gate opened, and Izzy motioned for Viktor to jump in. Viktor knew that it would be bad for both of them if he tried to act chivalrous and argue about who went in first.

He leaped headfirst into the basket, and his body somersaulted to the far side. Izzy quickly climbed over the door entrance and yanked the gate closed behind her. But it didn't shut. She glanced back to find the Centipede's head, pincers snapping, in a gap in the gate. Its red eyes glowed, turning Izzy's face a shade of pink.

Izzy pulled as hard as she could on the gate as the Centipede's little, metal legs scraped and clawed, trying to gain an advantage and wrest the gate open. It wrapped its entire body around the side of the basket to gain a better foothold. Izzy was impressed by its instinctive programming.

These things have gotten smarter.

The DLED started to lift off, and the wind caused by the propellers felt like a tornado. Viktor noticed Izzy struggling with the Centipede and jumped to his feet. The Centipede's head and an entire segment of its body now pushed through the opening. It was almost close enough to grab Izzy's wrist with its pincers.

Viktor stabilized his body as the basket swung, slightly off-balance, due to the Centipede's weight and constant movement. He jumped into the air, placing his boot squarely into the creature's jaw. He hit it hard enough to bend its pincers and snap off two metal legs against the doorframe. The beast was stunned and stopped moving, searching its programming for what to do next.

The basket was now eight feet off the ground and starting to lift more quickly. The Centipede's eyes stopped glowing. It pulled its head and body out of the gate, then released its hundred feet from the basket. It fell to the floor with a loud, metal crash. As soon as it hit, its legs started moving again and it scurried away.

Izzy shut the gate, and it magnetically locked. She knew it wouldn't unlock until they reached their destination. She slid down onto the floor of the basket and started laughing. Viktor stared at her, wondering why.

"The irony! I was going to call in sick and tell them I caught a bug! I didn't mean a literal one." Izzy snorted.

Viktor joined in the laughter.

As the drone raised higher in the Silo, Izzy retrieved her phone and called Noah back. It was hard to hear him over the sound of the drone's propellers, so she just spoke, "We're safe. Viktor and I are in the DLED drone on our way out of the Silo now." She tried to hear Noah's response but couldn't make it out. She put him on speakerphone so Viktor could listen. As they crested the lip of the Silo and out of its confined walls, Noah's voice became understandable.

Noah yelled, "I said … they only wrote code updates for the newer model creatures in use at the Red Zone turrets. Jack said the older creatures weren't considered, and their code was never modified because he thought they were no longer in use. When they sent the command to restart the creatures, it must have also restarted all of the old-model creatures inside the Hive. The old models are running their original programming and see everyone as a target."

Izzy and Viktor looked down into Solace as they flew over.

"That would explain why the people in Solace are running from them," Izzy said as she noticed a man trying to fend off what looked like a very pissed-off swarm of mechanical Gnats. Viktor tapped Izzy's shoulder and pointed out a lady wrapped in a silver web, being pulled behind an older model Black Widow Spider.

"Those poor people," Izzy said. "How long until the self-destruct sequence takes place, Noah?"

"They should fry themselves at high noon," he replied. "Aiden thought that would be a fitting time."

"Well, then these poor people are in for a very long forty-five minutes of fun," Izzy said. She felt bad for them. "On a happier note, the newer models appear to be doing the job on all of the electrical devices around town," she said, noticing a newer Zombie Ant model tearing apart a transformer atop a utility pole.

Before they could watch any more of the destruction caused by the creatures, they passed over the outer wall of Solace and headed out toward the Red Zone.

"We just left Solace, and it looks like there is total devastation down there," she said.

"Good. I'll let Jack and the kids know what's happening. The *Civil Watch* game has completely shit the bed, so our reprogrammed creatures must have found their way into the game's control center at headquarters," Noah surmised.

"Yeah, I see clouds of smoke coming from headquarters. The top floor—Draven's residence—is spewing smoke. It has NOT been a good day for Mr. Draven."

"As planned. See both of you soon!" Noah replied.

Izzy hung up, and she and Viktor sat back and enjoyed the cool breeze offered by the high-speed trip out to Turret 52. They discussed how they'd each met Noah and got involved in the Wallflowers. After a fifteen-minute flight, Viktor noticed the turret in the distance.

"It looks like it's on fire," Viktor said, pointing at the gigantic plume of black smoke filling the sky. As the drone hovered above the ground fifty feet away, they could see that the windows of the guard observatories had been broken, and smoke was billowing out. It appeared as though several creatures had escaped through the broken windows and were climbing around the top of the turret, tearing up the infrared communication towers. Other creatures—a Porcupine, Beetle, and Stink Bug—circled the tower, foraging for anything they could tear apart.

The drone lowered its basket to the ground, and the magnetic latch to the door was unlocked. Izzy and Viktor were hesitant to exit the safety of the basket, knowing they no longer had a charged safety armband. They also knew the drone would depart at any second and head back into the chaos of Solace, so they jumped out.

One of the creatures, a large Beetle, sensed the drone and its electrical signature and started to crawl their way. The drone took off quickly, leaving Izzy and Viktor baking in the midday sun with the huge creature advancing.

"That's a newer model. It shouldn't go after us, at least

according to Jack," Izzy said, trying to calm Viktor as much as herself. But the Beetle kept advancing and was now thirty feet away and not slowing down.

"Oh shit! Why isn't it slowing?" Viktor whispered. "Should we run?"

WHOOSH!

Something big and metallic passed them from behind, only five feet to their left, scaring the shit out of both of them.

Izzy and Viktor were left in the swirling dust of what they believed was another creature. But it was a large, white SUV, and it slammed into the Beetle at full speed, sending it flying a good thirty feet, where it ended upside down and motionless.

The SUV slid to a stop, and the driver's side door opened. Peter hopped out and gave them a big smile. "Anyone need a ride?"

Izzy fell to her knees, shaking from the adrenaline that flooded her system. Viktor bent over, took a big breath in, and shouted, "Damn, I'm so happy to see you!"

Viktor and Peter helped Izzy up and into the car, and Peter was about to pull away.

"Wait," Izzy said. "It's almost noon. I want to watch these little bastards fry."

Peter turned off the car. "Just know that they're attracted to electrical devices, and this SUV has a battery, a radio, and is loaded with computers. I found out earlier that those things will attack this car. I had fun trying to lose a not-so-friendly Zombie Ant that attempted to tear the hood off this thing. Otherwise, I would have been parked here, waiting for the two of you to arrive. Even with the engine off, they can still sense the electronics running on battery power. I guess we can move if one of those things decides to start making its way toward us."

"We only have five minutes. Let's wait it out," Izzy said, not really giving Peter a choice.

The other creatures seemed more interested in the electronic devices around the turret and hadn't noticed their SUV. The clock hit 11:59, and Izzy started a sixty-second countdown in her head.

At exactly noon, the Zombie Ant on top of the turret lifted its head to the sky, as if looking to God, and completely froze. In the body section just behind its head, a small explosion separated the metal skin from the Ant's metal thorax frame. The three of them watched as a moderate fire sparked and licked at the Ant's innards. The Zombie Ant slumped and fell off the turret.

Almost in sync, the other creatures around the turret stopped what they were doing and burst into flames.

"I can't believe it worked. Brilliant girl, Gabby!" Izzy said to herself.

Viktor heard her and asked, "Who's Gabby?"

Peter and Izzy both smiled.

"Just a sixteen-year-old girl who discovered a way to shut down Draven's entire operation," Izzy replied.

"She is a pure genius," Peter added.

Peter started the car, and they headed to Wallflower headquarters.

23: TIME TO ENGAGE

Izzy, Viktor, and Peter entered the Wallflower headquarters to applause. The operation was a massive success, and the devastation to Draven Labs was even greater than they had expected.

Noah ran to Izzy and kissed her, to the surprise of many. Up to this point, nobody knew they were in a relationship.

"Thanks for protecting her, Viktor. I owe you," Noah said. Viktor blushed and shook his hand.

"Protecting me? I think I protected you, too," Izzy joked with Viktor.

"That's true!" He smiled. "We make a good team, let's just say that."

Jack, Aiden, and Gabby exited the conference room, and Izzy hugged them.

"Thanks for all of your help," Izzy said. "You have no idea how well your programming worked."

"Sorry about the older models attacking you. That was a slight oversight on our part," Jack replied.

"The Black Widow Spider helped us take Draven out of the picture. It worked out in the end," Viktor added.

The screens around the room were playing footage from the different news stations. World Tribune News had two camera drones providing live feeds of the chaos—one circled the Draven

Labs headquarters as smoke poured out, and the other flew around Solace, covering the damage the creatures had caused. They also had a correspondent on the north and south borders reporting the destruction at the turrets.

The anchors all appeared excited to have a good story to cover.

A female anchor, Brielle Taylor, explained what they knew so far. "It seems that a glitch in the programming of the newer creatures caused them to all power on and attack infrastructure that ran off an electrical current. We're told the older creatures from the museum at headquarters also powered on and were targeting civilians. A Draven Labs' engineer advised us that the older model creatures were programmed to do this, but they should never have powered them on inside the main headquarters. Sam, what are you hearing?"

They changed the shot to the male anchor, Sam Gaul, who was interviewing the Draven Labs' engineer beside him. The town of Solace was still burning in the background.

The engineer spoke, "It was crazy! People were running for their lives. To avoid this issue, those things should only be turned on when they're out in the Red Zone. Someone made a big mistake turning them all on."

The male anchor added, "Although there were a few minor injuries, as of right now, nobody was critically injured. We're still trying to reach Mr. Draven to comment on the situation. His head of security has also disappeared. Back to you, Brielle."

Brielle replied, "Thanks, Sam. There is speculation that both Mr. Draven and his head of security, Brock Murphy, fled Solace when the event unfolded. With alleged reports of Draven Labs killing Hoppers with two marks—corroborated by the leaked audio and video of a secret dumping ground out in the Red Zone—there have been rumors they may have left the country. We want to remind viewers that the video we will be showing you contains graphic material. Please do not let your kids watch the next few minutes."

The video the World Tribune News aired had been anonymously leaked by Noah and Johan. The footage showed a wide shot of two older, Draven Labs' creatures hovering over the bloody corpse of a Hopper, which the news agency intentionally blurred. Both the Zombie Ant and the Beetle took turns picking the body apart as viewers watched.

Brielle held her hand to her mouth as if she was getting nauseous. "Oh my. That's brutal. There have been questions in the past about what happens to Hoppers with two marks, and Draven Labs has always claimed innocence. But the video you're watching is from the coordinates the anonymous source gave us, deep inside the Red Zone. We verified that at least four bodies had two marks on their arms. We're blurring the bodies to protect the families. At this time, authorities have been unable to identify who these Hoppers are, but this death canyon is well within Draven Labs' control area."

Everyone in the room had become quiet as they watched, and Gabby had to turn her back to the screen.

Aiden tried to comfort her. "Sorry you had to see that, Gabby. I feel the news will be airing this—and much worse—in the coming weeks. Might be a good idea to avoid watching the media."

Gabby hugged him and said, "Thanks for everything. You've been a good shoulder to cry on these last few weeks. I promise I'll get my shit together and put on a happy face at some point."

"I don't blame you. I'm glad we stuck it to Draven Labs, though. And we hit them HARD!"

Gabby appeared to brighten up a bit.

Noah interrupted, and everyone turned away from the screens. Johan turned the audio off.

"Thanks to all of you ... especially Jack, Aiden, Gabby, and Johan! Aside from Izzy and Viktor's little run-ins, we couldn't have asked for a better outcome with the creatures."

Everyone clapped.

Noah pressed on, "I can only hope that the news stations continue reporting no casualties from our operation. It was never our intention to harm the citizens of Solace. And remember, our job isn't over yet. I hope the border remains open until the president decides what he will do. We will need to get our families, and as many people as we can, safely over the border until then. "

"I've communicated the locations of the tunnels to all of our contacts in Mexico and Canada. Just as we have in the past, we'll wait for people to cross and provide them with a new start. We also have advocates who will begin lobbying Congress to put more friendly immigration policies in place. I'm convinced the president will reinstate the Border Patrol Agency, but we have some time before they can do that."

Izzy jumped in, "As exciting as this all is, remember not to talk about the Wallflowers and this operation to anyone outside this room. If one of us slips up, it could harm everyone in here. Secrecy is still crucial to our job," she cautioned.

Noah grinned. "That reminds me. Speaking of privacy, I still have to complete another part of this operation. Many of you know we've had to be careful and have all sacrificed parts of our lives for the Wallflower mission."

He turned to Izzy, fell on one knee, and pulled something from his pocket.

"A few of you already know—but many have no clue—that I love this woman and want to spend the rest of my life with her," Noah said, holding up a ring to Izzy. "Will you marry me?"

Izzy started crying, and the room broke out in cheers.

She regained her composure and put the ring on her finger. "I've been dealing with broken and misfit creatures for the last couple of years. I think I can deal with you for seventy more. YES!"

Izzy and Noah kissed.

Noah whispered in her ear, "I was thinking that our first date as an engaged couple would be to see that new action movie together."

"I've seen enough action the last few days to last a lifetime, thank you very much," Izzy remarked, laughing.

24: A MEXICAN ROSE

Aiden and Gabby spent the next week going straight from school to the Wallflower headquarters to catch up on news about their operation and the havoc it wreaked on Draven Labs.

Aiden's parents assumed he and Gabby were dating now, given how much time they were spending together, so they gave him the use of their only car whenever he needed it. His parents were happy to see their son love something more than his computers, thinking Gabby was smart, funny, and the perfect fit for their son.

Aiden caught up to Gabby at her locker and walked with her to homeroom. "Any big plans tonight?" he inquired.

"Well, I was thinking about going to the football game, or maybe taking Lenny up on his offer to attend my first *Dungeons & Dragons* game," Gabby remarked.

Aiden replied, "I know you hate football as much as I do. I also know you haven't created your elf costume yet. Lenny won't let you play without it, you know. His game isn't until next week anyway."

"So I guess my Friday night is going to be filled with watching the news and eating pizza with you at headquarters again?" she countered.

"Oh no. We've got something better planned. Noah texted this morning and asked if he could take us to dinner with Izzy and maybe catch an action movie afterward. I guess he wants to thank us for the work we did. He said he could pick us up at 6 p.m. Are you in?"

"Yes, that sounds like fun! I have to try calling my mom after school. For some reason, I haven't been able to reach her since yesterday morning, and I just keep getting her voicemail. It's unlike her to not answer the phone, and it's worrying me. She won't even respond to my texts. They show as unread."

Aiden tried to calm her. "Well, I know our government has been messing with cell communications along the borders with everything that's been happening. I've heard people are having issues with calls to and from Mexico and Canada, and even inside the cities along our borders. They're probably trying to stop people from using phones to coordinate ways to get across."

"I wish I could get my mom over here soon. The last time we spoke, she said the Mexican and US governments were working together to halt any groups trying to get near the border. Noah said he spoke with Emilio, and they suggested we wait a couple of weeks before my mom attempts to cross, just to be safe. I guess he also didn't want to put her through the stress again, and so soon," Gabby said.

"Noah and Emilio probably know best. Give it a little time. I promise you two will be together again. If there is anything I know, it's that Noah is true to his word," Aiden assured her. "So have you noticed anything different around the school?" he asked.

"Uh, yeah! Everyone has been talking about the chaos that occurred at Draven Labs. I can't turn a corner in this school without hearing someone discussing it. It's hard not to take credit and brag about taking the company down. I would love to rub it into the faces of some of the smug assholes who stood behind Draven Labs, even when they knew Red Draven was guilty of hurting people," Gabby remarked.

"Well, yes, there's that. It's a hot topic nowadays. But I was talking about something else. Have you noticed people aren't wearing their *Civil Watch* medals or patches anymore? It's like those trinkets carry a bad stigma now, and it's not cool to wear them anymore."

"Now that you mention it, yes! I have noticed that! I haven't seen anyone wearing them all week, except Lucas," Gabby replied.

"Well, Lucas is an asshole. He'll never change. He seemed to be in a pissy mood this morning when I saw him near my locker. I've enjoyed watching him sulk all week because his squad can't play the game anymore. The game has a message saying it's been deactivated 'indefinitely,' and all statistics, ranks, and achievements are no longer available to anyone. DravenTV has even gone black, too. People aren't able to watch old game clips anymore, either," said Aiden.

"Yeah, too bad some people created their whole identity around that stupid game, and now they have nothing. As petty as it seems, it's fun to watch them try to find new identities," Gabby said.

They entered Mr. Grant's room and noticed everyone was quiet, which was odd. Homeroom was usually buzzing with rumors, stories, and talk about what was on the menu for lunch that day. Lucas didn't even look up from his desk to offer a snide comment when Gabby and Aiden passed by on the way to their seats.

Mr. Grant came into the room and shut the door behind him.

"I have some bad news to share. It seems Mason Stanwell won't be attending Crestview High anymore. I received a note that his dad pulled him out of our school," Mr. Grant said as he crossed something off his attendance sheet.

"What happened?" asked Kylie, the girl sitting in the front row near Lucas.

"Not sure. The principal didn't give me a reason. They just said he's no longer going to be on my roster," Mr. Grant replied.

"He's moving," Lucas said bluntly, upset from learning this

revelation the night before.

The girl sitting next to Lucas jumped in, "I heard his dad, Senator Stanwell, might have been involved in the whole Draven Labs controversy. There was an entire news story about him possibly being impeached in the senate. I also heard he was making a lot of money off the company while overlooking some illegal things they were doing. He's probably pulled Mason out of school for fear of revenge and bad publicity."

Lucas didn't respond. He just stared at his desk, which was very unlike him.

Mr. Grant rescued Lucas from the embarrassment of his friend's situation. "Well, remember that not everything you hear is true. Those appear to be allegations. I'm sure we'll learn why he left in due time."

Gabby and Aiden looked at each other with raised eyebrows. Aiden whispered, "We took down Draven Labs, Mason Stanwell, and silenced Lucas all in one day? Damn, we're good!"

Gabby grinned.

The rest of the school day flew by, and Mason Stanwell's departure became the new hot topic of the day. Gabby and Aiden once again looked forward to watching the news cycle just to follow the impeachment hearings with Senator Stanwell.

After the final bell, Gabby tried to reach her mom again. This time, the phone didn't drop into voicemail. It went to a new, prerecorded computer message saying, "We're sorry, but this number is no longer in service."

Gabby grabbed Aiden and pulled him away from his friends. "I can't even get through to her number. It's dead. Something doesn't feel right, Aiden."

"We'll ask Noah if he has someone who can reach out to a neighbor or friend in your town and have them check on her. I'll text him right now. Don't worry, Gabby. I'm still sure it's related to the border situation. Your mom will be fine, okay?" Aiden reassured her.

GABBY'S HOME—6:00 P.M.

Gabby was sitting on the front step watching the kids play on the jungle gym in the park when Noah's white SUV pulled into the driveway. Noah and Aiden stepped out of the car.

"Where's Izzy?" Gabby asked.

"We have to pick her up across town. I need to run a quick errand on the way. I hope you don't mind," Noah replied.

"Of course not!" she said. She yelled to her aunt and uncle through the screen door, "I'm heading out for the night. See you two later."

"Bye, sweetie," Mariana yelled back.

Gabby jumped into the back seat with Aiden, and Noah pulled away. He explained to Gabby where they were contacting her mom. "Gabby, Aiden let me know about you being unable to reach your mom. I already have someone in contact with her, and she is fine. There are some issues with her cell service. She says she loves you and will talk with you real soon. I'm setting her up with a new phone, and you'll be able to talk later tonight, I promise, okay?"

Gabby sighed. "Thank God. I thought she had tried to cross again and got caught. She is persistent and a bit stubborn, that woman. I wouldn't put it past her to ignore you and Emilio and attempt to make the crossing alone."

"No, she did not do that, I can assure you," said Noah. "I need to stop by our favorite flower shop and pick up flowers for Izzy. That girl deserves a roomful of flowers for the danger I put her in."

They pulled in front of the El Paso Flower Shop and parked. Noah jumped out, and Gabby asked, "Can I go in with you? I'd love to say hello to Rose."

"Of course! I assumed you would," Noah replied. Aiden joined them.

Noah, Gabby, and Aiden entered the flower shop, which had recently been stocked with fresh flowers of all colors.

"It smells amazing," Gabby said when she walked in. Rose popped up from behind a small arranging table by the flower coolers.

"Hello, my friends! Welcome back to the shop, Gabby!"

Gabby looked around to ensure nobody else was in the store. "It's nice to visit when I'm more relaxed and not on the run!"

Rose walked around and gave each of them very long hugs.

"You came in for the rose order, Noah? You specifically asked for a single Mexican Rose?" she asked.

"Yes," Noah responded.

Gabby looked at Aiden curiously, and she could tell Aiden was thinking the same thing she was.

"You're just getting Izzy a single rose? Not a full bouquet?" Gabby asked Noah. For some reason, Rose just giggled and walked into the back room.

"Sometimes one single Mexican Rose can brighten one's day more than a big bouquet," Noah replied, grinning.

Gabby and Aiden both looked confused.

Rose came back, escorting someone else behind her. The woman's face was obscured behind a large arrangement of colorful flowers, and Gabby noticed she was wearing a now-familiar, pink, El Paso Flower Shop T-shirt. She guessed that Rose must have hired someone to help around the shop.

As the woman entered the room, she slowly lowered the flowers.

"Mamá!" Gabby screamed and ran to give her mom the biggest hug she could.

"Oh, Mijita! I've missed you," Rosario cried.

"One Mexican Rose, as ordered," Noah said to Aiden. "Aiden, meet Rosario 'Rose' Alvarez, Gabby's mom."

"You're amazing," was all Aiden could get out, choking up over the emotional moment.

Just then, Izzy appeared from the hallway.

"Sorry for all of the waiting and secrecy, Gabby. Emilio personally brought your mom over, and they just arrived this morning. We thought we would surprise you," Izzy said. "That's why your calls to her weren't going through."

Gabby hugged Izzy.

Just then, Emilio entered the room, followed by another man looking down. Gabby couldn't make out who it was.

When the man finally glanced up, Gabby screamed again, "MANUEL?"

Manuel hugged Gabby, who was now in complete tears.

"Who is that?" Aiden asked Noah.

Gabby overheard Aiden's question and replied, "Aiden, this is Manuel. He crossed with me and my mom, but they caught him just before we crossed the border. He sacrificed himself to get us over the border. And this is Emilio, the man who led us to the Red Zone, gave us VERY helpful tips for getting across, and provided us with extra Mylar blankets and water. We wouldn't be here without either one of them."

Gabby stepped back to study the two men, noticing they were wearing blue, El Paso Flower Shop T-shirts. She chuckled out loud at the sight of them wearing Rose's promotional T-shirts.

"You're going to have to order more shirts, Rose!" Gabby joked, and everyone laughed.

"Okay, we need to get you three out of here before any real customers come in. I'll pull around back and pick you up there. It will be a little less conspicuous that way," Noah said.

As they waited for Noah to pull the car around, Gabby noticed that her mom and Manuel were both rubbing the dark marks on their forearms.

"Is that the mark they gave you?" Gabby asked them.

Her mom replied, "Yes. Izzy said it will burn for only a few minutes."

Izzy overheard them and explained, "I was able to rig one of the marking machines to completely black out the tattoo that Draven Labs had etched into their bones. If anyone scans their arms, nothing will come back now. They'll have to get a nice tattoo to cover the single mark on their arms so nobody will be suspicious. We have a very good tattoo artist who volunteers for the Wallflowers. He'll do the tattoos for free."

"Maybe a tattoo of a rose, to honor your father?" Gabby's mom asked.

"I'm going to turn my mark into a cross, with Red Draven hanging from it," Manuel joked.

"I have a feeling you'll convert yours to a flower, too, Manuel," Gabby joked.

Noah interrupted their fun and explained their plans for the day. "Gabby, I've asked Mariana and Carlos, and they would love to have your mom stay with them until we get you two a place of your own. Emilio, I've sent for your wife and daughter. They'll be crossing with another group near Del Rio tomorrow. Manuel, I hope you don't mind sharing a place with Emilio's family until we can get you a place of your own?"

"Of course not! Thank you," Manuel said.

Izzy added, "We have donations that will help pay rent for all of you until you are on your feet, but we need a little time to get your documentation in order first. I am hoping that, within a week, we will have your paperwork and can start looking for places."

25: A NEW WORLD

For three weeks, World Tribune News heavily promoted their Saturday night special report about Draven Labs and America's border policy. They received international attention when they announced they would release findings that would rock the nation—from inappropriate campaign contributions the president accepted to back deals received by a group of senators. They showed clips of anonymous interviews with Draven Labs' insiders and teased they were invited to tag along with criminal investigators as they entered what they learned was called "The Cauldron"—Draven and Murphy's secret creature murder canyon in the middle of the Red Zone.

Noah and Izzy invited everyone to a private watch party for the show at Pancho's Pueblito Restaurant in El Paso. The restaurant's owners were supporters of the Wallflowers and were happy to close the restaurant to the public for the night. Noah invited a select group to attend. He asked the Wallflowers who worked at headquarters, as well as friends and family who either knew about or benefited from the operation.

Aside from the Wallflower volunteers, he invited Gabby's mom, Mariana and Carlos, Manuel, and Emilio and his family. He also summoned Johan's family, who had just crossed the border days earlier, and the two ladies from Pared de Harina, the Mexican bakery above Wallflower headquarters who were kind enough to bring a large batch of buñuelos.

Before the show aired, Noah and Izzy kicked off the night with praise and some gifts they had bought for volunteers who'd made extraordinary efforts in the fight.

Noah hushed everyone in the room. "We'd like to give out some thank-you gifts to people who went above and beyond in their work."

Peter pushed two large boxes in front of the crowd, and Noah continued his speech, "To Rose, the first friendly face many of you met when you entered America. She always offers weary travelers a hot shower, a meal, and a resting place. We wanted to replenish your inventory of El Paso Flower Shop T-shirts. Izzy thought we should make some in the color red, but I thought that was inappropriate and a little too soon."

Everyone laughed.

Noah held up a large envelope. "To Jack … a mentor, tireless programmer, and collector of computer geniuses. We know you haven't had much time to relax and socialize with anyone other than these high school students and our ragtag bunch, so we decided to get you an all-expense-paid trip to Disney World for TWO. Now your only job will be finding someone to volunteer to join you."

Jack blushed and stepped up to accept the envelope. He turned and pointed at Rose, who walked up and kissed Jack.

Izzy and Noah stared at each other, completely caught off guard.

Jack grinned. "Rose and I have been seeing each other for six months. I didn't want to ruin the illusion that I was a loner all this time."

Everyone clapped, and Noah and Izzy gave them both a hug.

Noah continued, "To Johan, one of Jack's computer geniuses, for taking on a job that he knew had no future and risking everything to make our operation successful. We secured a nice place in Las Vegas for you and your family, and we also bought you tickets to the Consumer Electronics Show. We thought you might find some new technology companies that are hiring and would fight over your skills."

Noah handed him the envelope, and he and Izzy hugged him.

Izzy took a turn. "I'd like to recognize someone who saved my life. Viktor, can you come up?"

Viktor walked to the front of the room, embarrassed to be put in the spotlight. Izzy picked up a large bag overflowing with white tissue paper and handed it to Viktor.

He dug his hand into the bag and pulled out an extra-large, black, stuffed Black Widow Spider with big, red eyes. He quickly pushed the spider back into the bag and jokingly tried to hand the bag back to Izzy. "No, thank you!"

Izzy laughed and gave him an envelope. "Sorry, I had to do that. We want to repay you with a trip for you and your entire family to see the Grand Canyon in Arizona. Nobody can claim they're American until they see at least one of the natural wonders in the States."

Johan thanked them both.

"Peter, get your butt up here," Noah said. "We've got something special for you!"

Peter stepped up and grabbed the box Izzy was holding out. He opened it, looked inside for a few seconds, and laughed loudly.

"Put it on, Peter!" Noah demanded.

Peter removed a racing helmet from the box. It was black and airbrushed with colorful art depicting a cartoon SUV running over a Beetle. A caricature of Peter hung out of the driver's side door. He put it on his head, pulled down the visor, and modeled it in front of everyone. Across the front of the helmet were the words, BEETLE BUSTER.

Noah hugged Peter, grabbed another box from the table, and handed it to him. "I also got you a very nice bottle of 18-year-old rum from Trinidad and Tobago. I do expect a call when you open this. It was tough to find."

Peter mumbled something inside the helmet, but Noah couldn't understand what he said.

"I think he said he agreed to share it," Noah told the crowd, smiling. Peter hugged him again and continued wearing the helmet for the remainder of the award presentation.

Noah waited for everyone to settle and then called Gabby and Aiden to the front of the room. He smiled at Izzy, who picked up two envelopes from the table.

Noah continued, "Aiden and Gabby, we can't even begin to tell you how much you've contributed to our group and our cause. Your efforts made the operation possible. We know how much you both love computers, and we're excited to watch you succeed in the future."

Izzy handed Gabby and Aiden the envelopes, and they tore into them.

Gabby read the letter and was the first to speak, "A full ride to Texas A&M? How did you … I don't even know what to say."

Aiden waved the same letter above his head, then hugged Gabby and spun her around. "We're going to A&M!"

Noah and Izzy beamed at how excited they were.

Noah explained, "We made a few calls and were able to make this happen thanks to several Aggie donors whom you both unknowingly helped. They asked to remain anonymous and hope you'll put this to good use when the time is right."

Gabby, Aiden, Noah, and Izzy shared a group hug.

Izzy broke away. "That's not all," she said as she removed a small box and another envelope from the table. She handed the box to Aiden.

"You've already done so much, I can't," he said.

"Just open it already, doofus," Gabby ordered, and everyone laughed again.

He opened the little box and pulled out a key fob. "Is this to a car?"

Noah smiled. "Yes, Aiden. It has a dent in the grill from a Beetle and a few scratches on the hood from an aggressive Zombie Ant, but the white SUV is all yours."

Peter opened his helmet's visor and said, "Please take care of her. She was my pride and joy for the last year. Until a few weeks ago, you couldn't find a scratch on her."

Everyone clapped.

"Gabby, open the envelope," Izzy urged.

Gabby ripped open the envelope and read the contents out loud, "Deed to 607 Orchid Street? You two didn't!"

She looked at her mom. "They bought us a house, Mamá! And it's on the same street where we're staying now, Orchid Street."

Noah interrupted, "Across the park from Mariana and Carlos. And you'll still be able to go to school at Crestview."

"This is amazing! I don't know what to say. How did you …" Gabby started.

"This wasn't us. You can thank Mariana and Carlos. They didn't want you to move far away from them. I guess they consider you family now," Noah said as he motioned to the couple.

Gabby asked Carlos, "Will you help to make our grass and gardens look as nice as yours?"

Mariana answered for Carlos. "He still has my list of to-dos around the house. Maybe when he's done with my list, he can help you," she joked.

Gabby and her mom thanked them for the very generous act of kindness.

It was time for the World Tribune News special. Everyone took their seats, and Johan turned up the volume on the TVs around the room.

John Hickock, the special investigations correspondent for World Tribune News, started the show. "I'm John Hickock, and today we will dive deep into the disaster at Draven Labs, the corruption within Congress, and a tarnished term for the president. We'll tour what is left of Solace, Texas, and get a firsthand look inside Draven Labs headquarters.

We'll also have exclusive, live footage from within the Cauldron—a canyon whose nickname investigators discovered while reviewing email communications between Red Draven and his head of security, Brock Murphy. This Cauldron contains the bodies of several thousand Hoppers—those with two marks from what my team is witnessing on the ground. It's a horrific sight, and we encourage those with small children to avoid watching the last fifteen minutes of our broadcast. Let's jump over to Brielle Taylor reporting from inside the walls of Solace, Texas."

The female reporter stood inside the green-tinted, glass lobby of Draven Labs. Shards of glass littered the ground, and the remains of a metal Zombie Ant and Beetle hung precariously from windowpanes high up on the wall. It looked as though they just froze in place when their self-destruct sequence activated.

"This is Brielle Taylor reporting live from inside Draven Labs in Solace, Texas, the location of the now-shuttered Draven Labs headquarters and Hopper processing facility. As of noon today, the US government has officially shut down all operations at Draven Labs and along the northern and southern borders. President Ferris has already ordered the National Guard to provide temporary border security until a permanent plan can be implemented. The Department of Homeland Security is meeting this weekend to explore the possibility of reinstating the US Customs and Border Protection Agency. Even if approved, it will be months before new border patrol agents can be screened, hired, and trained to replace the National Guard."

As the reporter walked out of the building and down Main Street, everyone in the restaurant could see how effective their plan had been.

The reporter continued, "As you can see, the labs were destroyed by the chaos of the creatures' awakening. This city of Solace was equally terrorized, with almost all electrical devices destroyed by the creatures. Many residents are now without jobs, air conditioning, and electricity and have decided to leave the confines of the city for good. Temperatures have reached almost 110 degrees Fahrenheit inside these cement walls. The government announced a 'Major Disaster Declaration' for the town, allowing remaining residents to receive federal assistance."

Jack remarked, "The streets look like a junkyard."

There were disabled cars, downed power lines, air conditioners strewn about, and the carcasses of the creatures in the last pose of their short lives.

Just as the female reporter was about to continue her story, she was interrupted by someone talking in her earpiece, and she stopped reporting. She hesitated. "I've just been told that the team on the ground in the Cauldron has breaking news. We'll cut over to them now."

"Jim Foley, reporting from inside the Cauldron, in a remote and almost inaccessible section of the Red Zone on the southern border, five miles from Las Cruces. Many old-model, mechanical creatures living in this canyon were still actively hunting until late last night when a team of Navy SEALs and Army Rangers dropped in to eliminate them. Now that the area has been deemed safe, we have been allowed in with the local forensics team.

"We just received some shocking information. Authorities were able to find and identify two recently deceased persons. According to investigators, although both of their bodies were mutilated, their heads remained intact. Facial recognition software reported a 99 percent chance that their identities are known. They believe the heads belong to Red Draven, founder of Draven Labs, and his head of security, Brock Murphy. This whole canyon is an active crime scene, so we cannot get close enough to show any footage. What I can say is that in the small area we've been permitted to access, we can see human remains scattered everywhere. The forensic teams will require months to collect and identify these poor souls. Back to you, Brielle!"

The mood in the restaurant was more somber than Noah had anticipated. The two people who had caused him, Gabby, and Izzy so much pain were now dead, and he thought they would all be celebrating. But the discovery of the large number of people who had lost their lives in that canyon overshadowed any joy they could find.

As his eyes met Gabby's across the room, Noah could tell she had finally come to terms with her father's fate. Deep in his heart, Noah knew that his mother, father, and Gabby's father would eventually be identified among the remains in the Cauldron.

The only solace now was the justice they had delivered.

26: ERYS PROJECT 2052

"In order to rise from its own ashes, a Phoenix must burn."
— Octavia Butler

The 2050 midterms and 2052 presidential elections were not kind to President Ferris or his party, mostly due to his involvement in the scandals surrounding Draven Labs and its human rights violations. His opponent, Victoria Danbury, and her moderate party easily beat him in the presidential election.

President Danbury, with the help of an immigration advocacy group led by her friend and up-and-coming visionary, Noah Torres, recommended a plan to satisfy most citizens on both sides of the immigration debate. Torres called his plan the Erys Project and credited it to a young, American, Texas A&M student named Aiden Moore.

The Erys Project, named after a five-sided wallflower called an Erysimum, represented the five goals most citizens desired: (1) well-delineated and humanely protected borders; (2) a fair and legal avenue for more people to obtain the American dream; (3) a better process for companies to fill the growing gap in the American workforce; (4) the cultural assimilation of new immigrants into the American way; and (5) a welcoming and equitable mix of immigrants, including asylum seekers, laborers, skilled workers, healthcare workers, and STEM (science, technology, engineering, and mathematics) candidates.

The Erys Project dictated that the number of immigrants allowed into the country would be based on the number of job vacancies and asylum slots open that year. Each category was allocated 20 percent of the chosen applicants. The United States also welcomed the immediate families of those chosen.

All applicants agreed to learn to read, write, speak, and understand a basic English language level within three years. They also had to take a civics test to evaluate their knowledge of US history and government. After five years, they would receive full American citizenship if they passed both tests, were financially stable, and maintained a clean record.

Anyone seeking citizenship would apply through a single gateway—a website with a simple questionnaire. The questions helped place the applicant into one of the pools for selection: asylum seeker, laborer, skilled worker, healthcare worker, or STEM candidate.

A special civil rights department chose asylum seekers from the pool based on several factors: perceived risk to life, whether their country of origin was an American ally, and their perceived ability to support themselves financially after three years in the United States.

Laborers, skilled workers, healthcare workers, and STEM candidates would fill out a résumé of skills. Employers could search the applicant pool and select candidates based on their skill set. By hiring an applicant, the company would become their sponsor and be required to see that the candidate met requirements for citizenship by their fifth year. They were legally obliged to offer these future citizens equal pay and benefits in line with their coworkers.

A woman-owned company named Ladybug, started by engineer Izzy Torres and a young entrepreneur, Gabby Alvarez, reimagined some of the technologies created by Draven Labs. The company designed solar-powered mobile turrets that could be repositioned strategically across the Red Zone. These turrets were much smaller and closer together than their predecessors. They outfitted each with heat, motion, sound, infrared, and night vision sensors. Drone technology with the same sensors helped watch from the sky. When one of these turrets or drones detected a human presence, the newly reinstated border patrol would pick them up and process them through an immigration court.

Izzy and Gabby's mission was to maintain security while, at the same time, protect the lives of anyone crossing. "Enforcement with empathy" became their unspoken slogan. Because there was now a larger number of immigrants being allowed into the United States, maintaining a humane and safe border control policy was something they could support.

Because there was a legal way for anyone to apply for citizenship, no crossers were allowed into the country simply by crossing the border. When caught, the border patrol would scan their biometrics and immediately return them to their country of origin. The rule breakers would never be allowed to apply for citizenship again. Crossers with multiple attempts on their record were jailed for some time and then returned. The process stopped almost all illegal crossings and criminal activity that occurred outside the ports of entry, thereby lowering the cost of border protection.

The Erys Project was a huge win for President Danbury, her administration, and Congress. It provided both border security and the chance at what Lady Liberty promised to legal immigrants—the end of oppression, the path to a brighter future, freedom, inspiration, and hope.

Noah and Izzy Torres were married in 2051 and had twin daughters nine months later named Erys and Rose Torres.

CAN I BUG YOU FOR SOME STARS?

Your reviews **encourage me** to keep creating. I would be honored to earn your review wherever you purchased this book.

ACKNOWLEDGMENTS

A special thank you to my wife and mom
for being my best hype girls.

A very quiet thank you to my weekly 5 a.m. writing group
from The Society of Children's Book Writers and Illustrators
(SCBWI Ohio North). It's nice to work with other crazy writers
who toil away in the dark while everyone else sleeps.

Thank you to Dominic Plavny, Jason Zweifel, Brian McGough,
Chetan Sai Manne, and Barb and Merri-Jo Somodi for being
my test readers.

And thank you to Joyce Mochrie, the professional copyeditor and
proofreader who helped get my messes closer to masterpieces.

ABOUT THE AUTHOR

Glenn Somodi was raised by a school teacher and an engineer in Olmsted Falls, Ohio. He earned a Bachelor of Science in Journalism at the E.W. Scripps School of Journalism at Ohio University in Athens, Ohio.

The inspiration for *Draven's Run* came partly from his time as a volunteer and commander in a composite squadron of the Civil Air Patrol, an Air Force Auxiliary with roots dating back to 1941. Working alongside adults and cadets, he supported communities through emergency services, search and rescue operations, youth leadership development, cybersecurity, and aerospace education. Aviation, drones, computers, and technology played heavily in the Civil Air Patrol experience and are reflected in the storylines of this book.

As you will read in *Draven's Run*, Somodi grapples with the differing viewpoints of wanting to secure the border but also offering more people the chance at the American dream, just as his great-grandparents had achieved through their journey, which started at Ellis Island.

He writes his stories in the short space between lying down and dreaming. The stories are written over many nights, replayed, and rewritten in his head for enjoyment. His mission is to find anyone who enjoys reading the stories as much as he enjoys creating them.

Inspired by some of his favorite childhood movies, like *Star Wars* and *Willy Wonka & the Chocolate Factory*, he writes stories filled with fantasy, action, and adventure to spark the imagination of others.

Somodi is also the award-winning author of the *Olly & the Spores* book series (www.OllyAndTheSpores.com). Previous book awards include two First Place 2024 BookFest Awards for Juvenile-Action & Adventure, a 2024 American Fiction Award, a 2024 Book of the Year Finalist in The Golden Wizard Book Prize, Best Middle Grade Fiction in the 2023 Page Turner Awards, a

Silver Medal in the 2023 Readers' Favorite Book Awards, and a 2023 BookFest Award for his audiobook.

He is a proud member of the Society of Children's Book Writers and Illustrators (SCBWI Ohio North) and also Literary Cleveland.

Book Website: www.DravensRun.com
Author Website: www.GlennSomodi.com
Instagram, TikTok, Pinterest: @gsomodi
YouTube: @GlennSomodi
X: GlennSomodi
Facebook: gsomodi
Email: info@ThreeBobcats.com

www.ingramcontent.com/pod-product-compliance
Lightning Source LLC
Chambersburg PA
CBHW031543240626

47153CB00002B/361